BEAR FACTS

SHIFTERS UNBOUND
BOOK 15

JENNIFER ASHLEY

JA / AG PUBLISHING

CHAPTER ONE

Goddess help him, but life with bears could be a serious pain in the ... fur.

Take, for instance, one fine January morning when Shane strolled out to the kitchen for breakfast to find Cormac, his mother's mate, already up and pouring himself a bowl of cereal. A giant bowl—the whole box streamed into it.

Shane groaned and slapped his hand over his eyes. "Gods, I do *not* want to see that first thing in the morning."

The flow of cereal halted as Cormac upended the box. "Sorry, did you want some? It's Honey Bits."

"No, I mean I don't want to see *that*."

Shane snatched his hand from his eyes and pointed at the vivid pink robe that barely encased Cormac's big body. It was Shane's mom's robe, with embroidered red roses down the placket.

Cormac glanced down at himself. "It was the first thing I found to throw on."

"Stop!" Shane growled.

Cormac's infectious grin spread over his face. "Stop having

sex with your mom? I can't do that, Shane. She's the mate of my heart."

"Please?" Shane's growl became another groan. "At least put some clothes on before you come out here. I like you, Cormac, but I can't take your naked ass in my kitchen."

"My ass isn't naked. I'm wearing boxers." Cormac lifted the robe to reveal teal blue shorts with white hearts on them.

Shane's hand met his eyes again. "Shit, I have to get out of here."

Four bears living in a small house in the heart of the Las Vegas Shiftertown was three bears too many. Bears liked solitude. Shane never found any.

Still covering his eyes, Shane staggered toward the back door ... and ran smack into another bear Shifter with a meaty *thunk*.

"Steady." Brody, Shane's younger brother, caught him by the shoulders. He pulled Shane into a brief hug and gave him a big pat on the head. "You can't run off by your lonesome today. We're needed."

"What for?" Shane smoothed the hair Brody had ruffled, though his brother's truncated hug had made him feel somewhat better. Shifters liked touch—it was calming. From the right Shifter, anyway. Anyone touching without permission got a fist full of bear claws coming at them.

"Graham's wolves are causing trouble again." Brody stepped around Cormac with a grin at his attire and grabbed an empty mug off the counter. Coffee from the old-fashioned percolator pot soon sloshed into it. "Same old thing. They're demanding more autonomy for wolves. Wolves shouldn't have to listen to Eric, should have their own closed-off section of Shiftertown. Yadda, yadda—you've heard it before."

Shane's irritation built toward rage. He wondered why the

bear inside him was acting like a cranky shit just waking from hibernation, but he hadn't had time to analyze his feelings. Being a tracker for the top bear in Shiftertown kept him busy.

"Why can't Eric and Graham take care of that?" Shane all but snapped. "It's early. I want to go for a run."

Graham was the leader of wolves who had been thrust unceremoniously into their Shiftertown, but Eric was the overall leader—the boss man, the big cheese. Nell, Shane and Brody's mom, was top bear in Shiftertown, but even she answered to Eric.

Shane's runs took place on the seven-thousand-foot-plus elevation of Mount Charleston, where he could shift to bear and pound through the woods. By himself. Bliss.

"Because Eric doesn't want the wolves to see him and Graham get into it," Brody said. "Those two have to be bestest buds. Unrest is handled by the trackers." He pointed to Shane and himself. "That would be us."

Shit. There went the morning.

Trackers acted as seconds and enforcers for the Shiftertown leaders, dealing with things the leaders didn't have time to take care of themselves. Shane worked directly for Nell, while Brody had been lent on a more-or-less permanent basis to Eric. Shane didn't mind the job most of the time, but this morning, it was damned inconvenient.

The majority of wolf Shifters who'd come here from northern Nevada were fine—Shane had made friends with several of them. Unfortunately, Graham still had some hotheads who were seriously pissed off that they'd been shoveled into this Shiftertown without being given a choice.

Shane didn't blame them for being angry, but he did blame them for trying to make everyone's life hell instead of figuring out how to deal with it.

Cormac set aside the empty cereal box and poured a quart of milk into the filled bowl. "Want me to come with you? We'll form a wall of bears and make them go home."

"In Mom's robe?" Brody snorted into his coffee mug. "It suits you, Cormac. Really does."

Cormac's laughter filled the room, which almost soothed Shane down. He could make anyone feel good.

"We'll bring Nell," Cormac offered. "She can scare them into hiding in their basements and never coming out."

When Mama Grizzly decided to do battle, anyone she faced ran for the hills. Literally.

"Nah, we can handle it," Brody said with confidence. He drained his coffee mug and slammed it, empty, to the counter. "They're just a bunch of smelly wolves. Come on, Shane."

Shane glanced longingly at the refrigerator, which was full of sausage and eggs waiting to be cooked, tamped down his anger, and heaved a long sigh. Breakfast, like his run, would have to wait.

"Call me if you need me," Cormac said cheerfully as he took up the giant bowl and shoveled in the first spoonful of cereal.

———

Freya found the cold of Mount Charleston's upper slopes refreshing. Here, she could almost imagine peace and safety, as when she and her twin brother, Rolf, had been cubs, blissfully ignorant of what the future would hold.

She hiked down a hill among soaring pines, her boots landing in muffled thuds on frozen pine needles and leaves. January down in the desert was a pleasant sixty-five degrees, but this elevation held freezing temps. The city in the valley teemed with crowds, while this part of the mountainside was thankfully devoid of people.

As she'd traveled south from San Francisco, through mountains and across the desert toward her destination, she'd heard there'd been more snow than usual this year. The major road up Mount Charleston had been plowed, but many side roads were shut off by drifts. Ice hung from the trees, and the entire mountainside was bathed in silence.

Freya needed this time alone with her thoughts while she pondered her intentions. She had a meeting later this morning with the person whose card she'd found among Rolf's things. This woman might be the key to finding him or might know absolutely nothing about Rolf's whereabouts. Either way, she had to try.

Maybe the woman had offered Rolf a place of refuge. He'd been restless lately, always worried that humans would figure out he and Freya were Shifter and turn them in to Shifter Bureau. He'd craved someplace his true nature wouldn't hinder him, but at the same time didn't want the two of them rounded up and herded into a Shiftertown.

It was tricky, trying to pass for humans in their world. They'd learned to assimilate, taking classes to learn various things to do with computers that would gain them employment. She thought Rolf had made his peace with their existence a while back, but her brother was always seeking a better way to live. A month ago, he thought he'd found it.

He'd told Freya this with a flash of smile in his wolf's eyes the night they'd met for decadent deep-dish pizza at their favorite Italian place near Washington Square. *This is gonna be awesome, sis.*

And then he'd been gone.

Once it became clear he was actually missing, she'd

checked all his favorite places to roam, like the redwood forests north of San Francisco, and found nothing. Nothing but the black card with the single phone number.

Freya hid her pain and worry as she sniffed the cold air. She'd risked coming this close to the Las Vegas Shiftertown, where she'd learned Graham's clan had been relocated, for the chance of any information about Rolf. The choice of meeting places hadn't been hers, but Freya had agreed.

As long as she stayed on the mountain, she'd be fine, she told herself. Shifters weren't allowed to go far from their Shiftertowns, right?

Freya's wolf, who sometimes had more sense than her human brain, growled a warning. She ceased her spinning thoughts to notice what her instincts were trying to tell her.

A fetid stench rode on the wind. It wasn't strong, but when Freya gave her scent sense over to her wolf, she knew something bad was out here with her. Something savage, something not right.

Not the person she was meeting. The woman, Althea Webster, was fully human. Freya had checked on her, though obtaining the information had been almost impossible. Freya still didn't know why Rolf had been in contact with her.

Her inner wolf told her she'd be safer right now if she shifted. Freya gave in, but not before she carefully removed her clothing and buried it with her backpack under a pile of dead leaves.

Icy wind blew down the mountain to roar through the ponderosa pines. It blended with Freya's snarls as she struggled into her wolf form.

She landed on large gray wolf paws, shook herself out, and took off over the snowy forest floor.

———

Shane stood shoulder-to-shoulder with Brody as they faced a line of wolf Shifters in human form who were big, muddy, half-hungover, and belligerent.

Just what Shane needed today.

Graham McNeil, the leader of this motley bunch, was also big, muddy, and belligerent, but he was stone-cold sober. He never let himself get too drunk, knowing he had to keep half a Shiftertown of Lupines in line.

Though Graham wanted everyone to believe he led by intimidation and fear, he could be compassionate. Shane had seen that in him more than once since Graham had moved to the Vegas Shiftertown. Never tell Graham he was nice, though. He didn't like it.

"See if you can talk sense into them," was Graham's greeting to Shane and Brody.

"Not negotiating with fucking bears," one of the wolves growled.

The man shut up quickly when Graham rounded on him and pinned him with a hard stare.

"Let me put it this way," Graham stated. "If Shane and Brody hand you guys over to me again, you're not going to like it. My mate might need to warn me I'm getting out of line. You know that only happens when it's truly bad. Right?"

The Lupines were angry about whatever had their pants in a twist this time, but not so mad that they wanted Graham to discipline them. They shut up, but sullenly.

This was Shane and Brody's tracker job today. Placate these assholes and prevent Graham from having to get in the Lupines' faces. Then maybe, just maybe, Shane could have some breakfast.

They stood on the dusty ground in the middle of the common area behind the houses. A few Shifters had turned their backyards into gardens of dry-climate flora, some of which were already blooming. Spring came early in the high desert. Any other day, Shane might admire the contrasting colors, but the clump of pissed-off wolves ruined any of the beauty.

Graham gazed steadily at his Lupines for a few more seconds, then he turned his back and marched away. He headed toward his house across the strip of ground without a goodbye and without looking back. Graham knew how to make an exit.

Brody, who was in a much better mood than Shane this morning, quietly studied the collected wolves. The fact that the Lupines hadn't simply dispersed in disgust meant Graham was seriously upset with them.

"So, what's the trouble, boys?" Brody asked in his good-natured way.

Shane knew he wouldn't be able to add anything without making the situation worse, so he clamped his mouth shut.

"Mates," the Lupine who'd declared he didn't want to negotiate with bears said. Name of Leopold Dunham—Leo to whatever friends he had—had scruffy black hair and mean gray eyes. "We need some."

"Don't we all," Brody responded with a laugh.

Mates were what kept Shifters sane. Even Graham, as volatile as he could be, had a mate who calmed his rampages with a single touch. Graham was probably chuckling with Misty now over how he'd managed to dump this morning's problems onto the bear brothers.

"The only reason we agreed to come to this shithole is we

thought we could find mates here." Leo spat on the ground. "Now Eric is saying his females are off limits."

Shane doubted Eric had put it that way. Eric's sister would have whacked her brother up the side of the head for calling the women under Eric's watch *his females*. Eric's mate would have quietly cheered her on.

What Eric had likely meant was that these Lupines couldn't simply scoop up any woman in Shiftertown and make off with them.

Also, Leo hadn't *agreed* to come to the Las Vegas Shiftertown, nor had Graham or any of his Lupines. Shifter Bureau had decided Graham's Shifters had to move in with Eric's, and there was fuck all anyone could do about it.

"Let me get this straight," Shane broke in. "You're mad because Eric didn't round up every female Shifter in this Shiftertown, shove them at you, and say *pick one?*"

"You can talk," Leo sneered. "Eric's sister shit all over you and then shacked up with a *human*. What a bitch."

A red mist descended behind Shane's eyes, and the angry bear who'd been rumbling inside him climbed to the surface.

"Don't speak about Cassidy like that," Shane stated flatly. "Not ever."

Brody cut in, his good humor still in place. "Yeah, her *human* mate can tase you until you can't walk, let alone worry about any kind of mating."

"Humans suck," another wolf growled. "We should take out her mate, and then that would be another female free for us."

"Sure," Brody said. A rising wind that smelled of rain ruffled his grizzled brown hair. "Go ahead. Kill Cassidy's mate and destroy her mate bond. Then see what she does to you."

A few of the wolves moved uneasily. Cassidy was a tall,

strong, Shifter Feline who could take on any wolf-man without breaking a sweat. Her mate, Diego, wouldn't go down easily either. He might be human, but he'd been a cop and now ran a private security company. He knew how to fight. Diego had gained Shane's—and most Shifters'—respect.

"I wouldn't say too loudly around Graham that humans suck either," Brody continued. Graham's mate, Misty, was human, and Graham made sure no one gave him grief for it.

More uneasy movement. Maybe Brody's half smile and reasonable comments would soothe these Lupines down and send them sheepishly home.

Ha, ha. Wolves going sheepishly home.

"We were promised mates," another wolf said. At his statement, the others straightened up again, the determined light brightening in their eyes.

Yet another Lupine took up the argument. "If Eric and Graham don't bring them to us, we'll take them for ourselves. Even they can't interfere with a Shifter and his mate once they're bound."

Technically true. A leader, no matter how powerful, could not mess with a Shifter's mate. That rule had been put in place centuries ago, to keep pack alphas from simply snatching up every female they wanted, whether the women in question were mated or not.

Shane's anger soared. These guys were talking about force-claiming Shifter females like it was their right. To hell with being diplomatic.

"It's a Shifter woman's choice whether she mates with you, dickhead." Shane made a show of looking around the empty stretch of the common area. "Funny, I don't see a horde of them throwing themselves at you. Maybe they're just not that into you."

Leo stepped forward, his face as hard as Graham's ever was. "Just because you're too chicken-shit to take who you want doesn't mean you can stop us from doing it."

Shane put himself in front of Brody, who was still trying to be relaxed, and met the Lupine straight on. "This isn't the old days, dog-breath. You don't grab a female and sequester her until she's too tired to fight you. Especially not in this Shiftertown. Unless you want all your limbs broken. By her. And by me."

"Eric is trying to keep them for *his* Shifters," the Lupine next to Leo argued. "We need mates, and Eric doesn't want us to have them."

The other wolves surged forward, the statement logical to their hungover brains.

Brody tried to patiently explain. "The ratio of men to women in this Shiftertown is like five to two. We outnumber them, my friends. Whether we like it or not."

Apparently, these wolves did not like it. "We don't mind sharing," one quipped from the back.

"Oh, right." Shane couldn't keep quiet and let Brody negotiate. "So not only are you going to tell every Shifter woman in this town they're fair game but that you're going to pass them around?"

"Yep," the second wolf said, as Leo remained in a silent stare-down with Shane. "We'll cut you in, if you're with us."

The others growled in serious agreement.

"Graham will never go for that," Brody pointed out.

"Fuck Graham." Leo took a step back from Shane, claws sprouting from his fingers. "He's done as leader. We'll take his mate, and we'll take Eric's, and then every other female in this town. They're *ours*."

Shit.

These weren't just a bunch of disgruntled Lupines, Shane realized. This was insurrection.

"You heard what Graham said." Brody's tone was too unworried for Shane's comfort. "If we need to bring him back out here, he's not going to go easy on you. How about you go home, sleep it off, and think about it once you've had breakfast?"

Something Shane wasn't going to get, he had the feeling.

The Lupines surged forward. "You'll never make it to Graham's place," Leo promised. "You'll be dead."

In a heartbeat, the group surrounded Shane and Brody and attacked them in force.

CHAPTER TWO

Shane found his arms full of half-shifted wolf as Leo leapt at him. Shane roared his anger, which became a bear snarl as he began to change.

Shane's long-sleeved gray shirt ripped as brown fur exploded on his arms, and his jeans split at the seams to release his powerful back limbs.

Damn it. I really liked *that shirt.*

Cloth fell in shreds to the ground as a thousand pounds of grizzly filled the space. Leo realized he was in the grip of razor-sharp bear claws and now scrambled to get away.

Shane tossed him aside. He suppressed his instinct to tear out the wolf's throat, because Graham would kill him if he did that, and Eric probably wouldn't stop him.

Then the Guardian would stick his sword into Shane's dead body to release his soul, and his family would hold a ceremony to send him to the Goddess. Nell would be very upset. She and Brody would go after Graham in revenge, and the whole Shiftertown could erupt into war.

Therefore, Shane suppressed his bear's urgings and settled

for throwing Leo to the ground and spinning to face the onslaught.

More Lupines came at him, less worried about the balance of power in Shiftertown and more interested in venting their spleen. Shane and Brody, now also bear, stood together in a solid wall of fur, fighting off wolves with swipes of their huge paws.

Leo, on his feet again, launched himself under Shane's reach and latched his teeth into the fur on the side of Shane's neck. Shane roared his displeasure, swinging his massive head around in an attempt to dislodge the wolf. The stupid thing held on, as Lupines could do.

Three others lunged at Shane, separating him from Brody. Shane's irritation quickly became rage, the berserker bear he'd been trying to suppress bursting to the surface. When it took over, it wouldn't matter that this little battle would cause Eric, Graham, and Nell to confront one another as enemies, and that the safety of all Shifters hung in the balance.

Shane's bear just fought.

Yet another wolf jumped on Shane, five of them trying to take him down. Shane spun his huge body, throwing off a couple of wolves with his momentum, but the other three, including Leo, grimly hung on. Brody was having the same problems and couldn't help.

Nothing for it. Shane would have to start maiming and hope he didn't kill anyone. The wolves snarled and fought, already far gone in madness. Shane's earth-shaking bear growls mixed with theirs in crazed response.

A sudden shotgun blast boomed through the chaos.

The part of the grizzly that was still Shane thought, *Oops, they woke up Mama Bear.*

Two of the wolves dropped from Shane's side. The last one —Leo—held on fast.

The quiet thunk of a tranquilizer gun sounded, and Leo went limp. Shane gave one final shake of his great head, at last dislodging the asshole.

The trouble was, the tranq dart had gone all the way through Leo's foreleg and nicked Shane. Most of the tranquilizer spent itself in the wolf, but enough leaked into Shane's blood to make his joints rubbery.

Shane swung around, snarling, to face Eric Warden, who held the tranq rifle ready to fire again.

Shane's legs gave out, and he sank to his belly with a grunt. When Eric saw that neither Leo nor Shane was getting up, he moved the rifle to another target.

Nell had fired into the air. She always loaded her shotgun with beanbag rounds, but the noise and the terrifying sight of the large, brindle-haired Nell, rage on her face, was enough to stop any Shifters in their tracks.

"Graham!" she bellowed. "Get these wolves under control, or you and I are going to have a problem."

So much for not letting the unruly Lupines see their leaders fighting.

Graham, who'd returned at a run, stepped up to Nell, she as tall as he was, meeting her enraged dark gaze with his gray one.

"That's what your sons were supposed to be doing," Graham snapped.

Nell, not intimidated, leaned into his face. "Who the hell decided to send my boys after your half-feral wolves? Dish out your own discipline, McNeil."

"It was my idea, actually." Eric's mild tones cut through Nell's and Graham's hostilities.

Eric's Shifter was a snow leopard, a beautiful animal. Even those who loathed Felines admitted that. In human form, he had dark hair, jade-green eyes, and plenty of hard muscle. No matter how dire the situation, Eric always spoke as though he was simply having a casual conversation, his voice soothing everyone down.

His unruffled demeanor took effect on Nell and Graham. Both turned to him, tense stances relaxing.

Graham's wolves picked themselves up from where they'd dropped when Nell's gun had gone off and shifted back to human form. They stood in a clump, breathing hard, knowing they were in deep shit. Leo remained wolf, sound asleep and snoring.

"I wanted Shane and Brody to talk to the Lupines," Eric explained. "Solving things between them, instead of having to be bashed on by their leader. I'd have explained, but I didn't want to wake you up." Eric scanned the Lupines, none of whom dared meet his gaze. "They're more annoyed than Graham or I realized."

The wolves wouldn't look at Nell either, and most especially not at Graham.

"Yeah, I see that," Graham conceded. "When it's about mates, things get dicey."

Eric continued. "I assumed that since neither Shane nor Brody are mated, they'd have mutual grounds for discussion. My apologies, friends." He flashed a grin to Nell, Shane, and Brody. "Next time, I'll send my sister."

Even Graham's lips twitched at that. While the Lupines had hotly boasted they'd take Cassidy away from her human mate, everyone standing knew damn well she'd wipe the floor with them. No one challenged Cassidy.

The small amount of tranq dissipated enough so Shane

could heave himself to his feet. He was groggy and nauseated, or maybe the nausea came from the sight of the Lupines, shaggy-haired and naked, who clumped together, awaiting Graham's displeasure.

Shane shook himself out, sending dust and dried grass over the nearest Lupine, who winced but didn't say a word.

Then Shane slowly compressed himself into his human form. Shifting when he was enraged was easy—changing back took time and a painful rearrangement of bones, muscle, and tendons.

For some reason, everyone stared at Shane while he struggled to rise to his human feet. Brody had already shifted, but no one had ogled *him*.

Shane leaned down and plucked his shirt out of the mud. He held it up, scanning the holes which had rendered the fabric so much gray scrap.

He hurled it back to the ground in fury. "Fuck this shit," he declared. "I'm out of here."

Without waiting for Eric or Graham, or even his mother, to agree to let him go, Shane turned his back on them all and marched toward the small one-story house he called home.

It was dangerous for a Shifter to deliberately turn away from powerful alphas like Graham, Eric, and Nell but no one tried to stop him. He figured they must understand his frustration, and a small part of him felt some gratitude for that.

Cormac, thank the Goddess, had shucked the pink robe and was in jeans and a sweatshirt by the time Shane returned. Cormac's dark hair was damp, indicating he'd recently stepped out of a shower. He looked Shane up and down with his sharp blue eyes but made no comment on his unclothed state.

"I heard Nell fire," Cormac said. "I figured she has it under control?"

He voiced the question confidently enough, though Shane sensed his need to rush out and make sure his mate was all right. Shane admired Cormac's self-discipline to let Nell go be her bad-ass self without running protectively after her.

"She does. Eric and Graham are out there too." Shane began to calm under Cormac's good-naturedness.

"Want breakfast?" Cormac offered. "I'm ready for some pancakes." Apparently, a whole box of cereal hadn't been enough to curb his appetite.

Shane let out a breath. "I'm not hungry anymore. I'm going for a run. Tell them not to come after me."

Corman gave him a sympathetic nod. "You want to be alone."

"Damn straight." Shane moved past Cormac to his tiny bedroom where he pulled on clothes from his used pile. It was laundry day, and the shirt and pants he'd shredded outside had been his last clean ones. At least he always kept clean under-wear on hand for emergencies such as these.

Re-dressed, he filled a small backpack with what he'd need, then returned to the kitchen and grabbed a giant bottle of water from the refrigerator.

"Want to take my truck?" Cormac offered. "It's good for off-roading."

The man would melt Shane with his generosity. "Nah, I'm not going far. See you, Cormac."

"Be careful, Shane."

The advice was offered in all seriousness. Shane grabbed his keys from the set of hooks where all the vehicle keys were kept in this house and headed for the back door.

"I'm always careful," Shane told him. "Don't wait up."

Before Shane could exit, he felt Cormac's warmth behind him. Without warning, the big man enfolded Shane into his embrace. Shane stiffened at first, then began to soften under the magic of Shifter touch.

"Waiting up is what parents do," Cormac said, voice muffled by Shane's big shoulder. "Even stepparents."

Shane's heart swelled with the love his family constantly surrounded him with, one that made a valiant attempt to cool down his inner bear. He hugged Cormac in return, then the two parted with a mutual thumping of backs, and Shane was gone.

———

MOUNT CHARLESTON WAS A SHORT DRIVE FROM Shiftertown, but it might have been a world away. Shane soon left the dry desert of creosote, Joshua trees, and dead winter grasses, and began to wind his way through white-boled aspens, bristlecones, and ponderosa pines.

The air was sharply cold but scented with the comforting odor of pine forest. Snow lay in patches between the trees and formed low walls on the sides of the plowed road. Clouds, gray with unshed precipitation, scudded overhead, hugging the highest peaks of the Spring Mountain range.

Eric's mate, Iona, had a cabin in the area she let other Shifters use. Tempting, but Shane was finished with anything civilized for the moment. The cabin was a house with all the comforts, a sweet place to take a load off, but Shane was too restless for that this morning.

He had his own secret spaces up on this mountain. He slowly bumped his small pickup down a single-lane road, making for his favorite spot. This road had been only cursorily plowed, and Shane's truck banged over hard ruts and slid on icy patches.

He could have taken Cormac up on his offer of the larger, higher-clearance pickup, but that would mean worrying about getting the vehicle home soon in case Cormac or Nell needed it. By driving his own truck, Shane could stay out here for days if he wanted.

He'd have to check in if he wasn't returning for a while, though. Once upon a time, a goon had kidnapped him and upset his whole family, so Shane would definitely text Nell if he wasn't coming home today. He didn't need his mother freaking out and Shiftertown searching for him en masse. Again.

When Shane reached the end of the road where his favorite hiking trail began, he parked the truck, climbed out, and inhaled deeply. Silence met his ears as the scents of the forest filled him.

Now *this* was more like it.

Shane stood still for a time, enjoying blissful solitude. This tiny road was way off the beaten track and officially closed in winter. A quick scan told him that no humans were nearby on a back-country hike. The woods were empty, giving Shane his much-needed privacy.

He lifted his backpack from the passenger seat, shouldered it, locked the pickup, and struck out into the woods. Shane always put distance between himself and his vehicle before he undressed and shifted. That way, if a park ranger waited at his truck when he returned, the ranger wouldn't see a naked man racing toward him, cursing because he'd left his only clothes in the pickup.

Shane trudged along the faint track until the trees well obscured him from the trailhead. There, he set down the backpack and began to strip. *Stupid wolves owed him a shirt,* he growled to himself, regretting the loss of the comfy one they'd made him ruin.

Shane stuffed his clothes into the backpack, buried it deep beneath dead leaves and pine needles, and straightened up, stretching in relief.

He laughed out loud, knowing no one could hear him, then he yelled invective at Graham's wolves for the hell of it.

Laughing again, Shane let his bear come.

Shifting twice in one day could be painful, but Shane put up with it as his muscles and bones struggled to readjust themselves. In a few moments, he landed on his bear paws, thick fur rippling as it settled.

Shane let out a roar, a warning to all the little creatures nearby that a grizzly walked among them.

Yes, yes, he knew that a grizzly was technically considered a brown bear and not a different species from all the other brown bears in creation. *Grizzly* just sounded so much cooler.

Shane finished showing off, lowered his head, and began a leisurely lope between the trees. The lope became a run, and then a charge.

The human part of Shane whooped in joy as he careened through the woods, expertly swerving around trees and plowing through undergrowth. Shane was huge, he was strong, and he was the only bear around.

Non-Shifter bears didn't live in this mountain range, so he had it all to himself. Wolves didn't live here either, thank the Mother Goddess. Other predators did—mountain lions and coyotes, to name two—but they were wise enough to steer clear of Shane.

Shane zigged and zagged, more or less following the trail, but letting himself go wherever. His bear instincts, including his terrific hearing and incredible sense of smell, would return him to the truck when he was ready.

Which wouldn't be for a good long time.

He let out another roar, spinning on a patch of ice to race off in another direction. This was a hell of a lot more fun than facing down Graham's cranky Lupines, any day of the week.

Shane was miles from his parking spot when he became abruptly aware that he was not alone.

He caught the unmistakable stink of something feral and savage. Two strides later, a huge gray shape came out of the trees and hurtled straight into him.

CHAPTER THREE

Shane staggered with the impact and went down in a crash of fur, claws, muddy snow, and pine needles.

He rolled to his feet a second later, but the wolf who'd attacked him locked its teeth around Shane's throat and hung on tight.

Damn, stupid, damn, fucking ...

This wolf wasn't a wild one. It was far too large and too agile to be a normal wolf, plus it was dumbass enough to attack a Shifter bear.

Shane realized three things as he tried to paw the wolf off him. First, the Lupine wasn't one of Graham's, nor was it from any other pack in the Las Vegas Shiftertown.

Second, no Collar glinted on the wolf's neck to deliver punishing shocks for its attack.

Third, she was female.

What the total fuck ... ?

The questions went out of his head as the Lupine's teeth ripped needles of pain into Shane's throat.

He hadn't been able to take out his annoyance on Graham's wolves—even his berserker bear had known he couldn't hurt them without consequences.

This Lupine, un-Collared and likely feral, was a different matter. Shane could bash it as much as he liked, then take its broken body to Shiftertown to be healed if it could be or sent to the Goddess if it couldn't. Shane's Collar wouldn't stop his violence, because last year, he'd had it replaced with a convincing fake.

The only thing preventing Shane from bringing his paw down on the wolf's neck and crushing it was that this Lupine was a lady. Shane was a gentleman that way.

Being female wouldn't stop her from trying to murder Shane though. Female Shifters could strip the flesh from the bones of their attackers and then stomp the hell out of whatever was left.

The female of the species is more deadly than the male, went the line in the old poem, and it was true. Shane always wondered if Kipling had been acquainted with Shifters.

If Shane didn't stop *this* female of the species, he realized, he'd be dragged back to her den as a bear rug.

The bear inside him told him to conquer her, make her his, and then give in to mating frenzy. The Lupines weren't wrong that Shifters needed mates, and hadn't Shane been waiting long enough?

Shane's inner brain knew there was something wrong with this thinking, but his bear wasn't listening. He let out the roar of an alpha, which could halt any Shifter of lesser dominance in their tracks.

Didn't work on this she-wolf. Not only did she tighten her grip on his neck, she started raking claws into Shane's flesh.

A wolf could keep its jaw locked around its victim until

either prey or predator were dead. Shane didn't feel like waiting around for either to happen.

He stopped trying to dislodge her and shifted his weight to land on top of her instead. The wolf didn't loosen her hold, but Shane was big, and soon he felt her struggling.

He pressed down until she had to release his throat to gasp for breath. A wolf whimper emerged and then a snarl, as though she was pissed off about being afraid to die.

Stop, Shane commanded her in the Shifter way. Shifters weren't telepathic, but body language and growls said much. Animals were great at communicating, especially among their own species.

This woman wasn't a bear, but she seemed to understand. She quieted under him, then to Shane's dismay, she began to shift.

She struggled with it. Shane lessened his weight on her without lifting off completely—he knew better than to trust her.

She growled and cursed with the change, which for some Shifters could be painful. At long last, her human form took shape enough for her to speak.

"Get *off* me." She shoved at him with ineffectual hands. A human was never going to lift a Shifter grizzly.

Without moving, Shane shifted back to his human form. As he lost fur and shrank down to his bulky human body, his reaction to her began to change. They were no longer animals battling for dominance in the woods, but two people, very naked, lying alone together on a bed of leaves.

With any luck, she'd be gnarled and hideous, not enticing at all. Or maybe so young she'd be little more than a cub, kicking in Shane's protective instincts instead.

Shane gazed down at her.

Nope, not hideous, and definitely not a cub. The instincts kicking Shane now were more primal than protective.

A human man might not find her attractive, which would make him an idiot. The woman had a square face with a blunt chin and a long nose, hinting at that of her wolf. Her hair was currently so full of dirt and leaves Shane wasn't certain what shade it was. Her skin was also plastered with mud and dirt, with lighter patches where her clothes had been.

Her eyes, on the other hand .... They were a cross between yellow and luminous gray, a beauty in them that caught him in their depths.

Shane stared down at her for a mesmerizing moment while she glared rage up at him.

"Stop." Shane repeated the word in a low rumble, taking the sharpness from it. "I don't want to hurt you."

"Leave me alone, *Shifter*." She spat her answer. "I'm busy."

"Hey, you attacked *me*. I was running through the woods, minding my own business, and a feral wolf comes flying at me. What was I supposed to do?"

"I am *not* feral." She screamed the word between her teeth as though stating it emphatically made it true.

Shane gripped her shoulders and leaned closer. "Why else would you attack a bear Shifter three times your size if you're not feral?"

"I thought *you* were." Her scowl told him she was sorry to be wrong. "Maybe I was defending my territory."

"This isn't your territory. I've never seen you here before, and believe me, I'd notice. If this is anyone's territory, it's mine. If you'll quit fighting and tell me who you are, maybe I can help."

Her glare intensified. "I don't think so. Help me what?

Become a civilized Shifter like you? With a Collar?" She poked at the silver and black chain around Shane's neck, then quickly drew her finger away as though it burned. "Locked in a Shiftertown, where you should be now. I thought you must be feral, running around here on your own."

"I do what I want," Shane growled. Well, mostly. "Who the hell are you? What pack are you from? Why aren't *you* in a Shiftertown?"

She wore no Collar and from all evidence, never had. Her throat, under the dirt, held no scar indicating that a Collar had been infused into her Shifter's flesh. Shane wanted to run his fingers across her skin, enjoying the smoothness of the Collar's absence.

"Because I'm not stupid enough to be in one of those," she snarled. "Where I have to answer to a leader who's not even in my pack or my clan, who thinks I can't choose my own mate."

She snapped her mouth closed, as though fearing she'd said too much.

Interesting. She spoke as though she was familiar with Shiftertowns but had somehow managed not to be rounded up into one. It was true that when humans had slapped Collars onto Shifters close to thirty years ago, some had managed to evade capture.

An entire secret compound of un-Collared Shifters lived in the middle of Texas, led by a white tiger called Kendrick. Shane wondered if this woman had been one of those Shifters. Maybe she'd run away from Kendrick's group or one like it.

"You have a name?" he demanded. "Mine's Shane."

She didn't want to tell him. She wriggled under him in annoyance but finally answered grudgingly. "It's Freya."

Shane waited but she didn't give him more than that. The

single name had been dragged out of her, and she wasn't about to reveal anything else.

"Nice to meet you, Freya. If I let you up, you promise you won't try to rip out my throat again?"

Freya's lip curled. "Your Collar tastes nasty."

"Is that your way of saying yes? I'm not letting go until you give me your word."

"My word?" Freya stared at him as though he'd lost his mind. "You'd take my word for it?"

"Sure. Why not?"

"Because you think I'm feral. I don't wear a Collar or bow to a Shifter leader, so I can't be trusted."

"Don't do my thinking for me," Shane said in a hard voice. "Makes me nuts. I'll take your word as a Shifter, period. You don't attack me, then we'll figure out what to do."

Freya ceased struggling, but Shane wasn't foolish enough to think she was submitting to his will or any such bullshit.

"Okay then," Freya said with a glower. "I give you my word. I won't attack you, as much as you deserve it."

Shane believed her. Freya, whoever she might be, was desperate, scared, and using belligerence to cover her fear, but she'd already learned she couldn't best a bear Shifter with physical strength.

She'd try to get away by cunning instead. He'd have to watch her.

Shane, Goddess save him, wanted to help her. Stupid Shifter instincts.

He carefully released her but seized her hands as he stood and heaved her up beside him. Freya found her feet with swift agility. Once they were both standing, he slowly let her go.

Shane became more and more aware, as they regarded

each other warily, that he and Freya were both nude, and she had curves that would stop traffic.

Shifters didn't pay much attention to nakedness when they first shifted into and out of their animal forms—too much going on at that moment to worry about it. But once the change was over, and human hormones began to wake up, they noticed in a huge way.

Freya studied Shane in distaste. "Are all bears as big as you?"

The question had no admiration in it whatsoever. "Yep," Shane answered. "The ladies too. You should see my mom."

Freya's eyes flickered from golden to gray and back. "You have a mother?"

"Most Shifters do." Shane decided to keep things neutral and not interrogate her about her own family, as much as he wanted to. "Don't you know any bears?"

"I grew up with Lupines. No other species."

"Goddess, you poor thing. But at least you didn't have to put up with Felines." Shane flashed her a grin he hoped would soften her, but she remained rigid. "I have a cabin nearby. Want to go get warmed up? There should be food there too."

Freya's eyes flickered again at the mention of food, the yellow glowing more strongly.

"Why would I go anywhere with you?" she demanded. "For all I know, you have a dozen more bear Shifters waiting there to lock a Collar on me."

"There aren't actually that many bears in our Shifter-town," Shane said without heat. "There's me and my mom, Brody, Cormac—he's my stepdad—Peigi down the street, a few more bear Shifter women I helped rescue a while ago, and a couple of their cubs. That's pretty much it."

"You *rescued* them?" Freya eyed him in disbelief. "You mean you put Collars on them and shut them in a Shiftertown. How is that a rescue?"

"They'd been in a very bad place." Shane let his voice grow somber. "Now they have houses to live in and are surrounded by people who care about them. And no, we didn't put Collars on them."

Shane had no idea why he admitted this last bit of information. If Shifter Bureau ever found out Shifters had learned how to substitute Collars with fakes, they'd lose what little freedom they'd carved out for themselves. *If* they weren't simply terminated as a danger to the public.

But for some reason Shane wanted to reassure Freya. Prove he wasn't an asshole Shifter bowing to Shifter Bureau's dictates.

"I don't want your houses or your rescue," Freya declared.

Her eyes told Shane differently. She was searching for something, though this wolf wasn't pathetic and whimpering. She might be dirty and disheveled, but she was strong and able. Likewise, she had immediate hunger but wasn't starving.

"There's no one at the cabin, I promise you," Shane said. "My leader doesn't even know I'll be going there." Not quite a lie—Cormac would have guessed, but he'd only tell Nell and Eric if there was absolute need. "I'm offering because, sweetie, you really need a shower."

Instead of growing offended, Freya sent him a sardonic glance. "Well, no shit."

"How long have you been running around up here?" Shane tried to keep the question casual, as though they were acquaintances who happened to bump into each other, naked, in the woods.

"None of your business." Freya again clapped her mouth closed, studying him as though debating what to do. She could easily spin around and sprint off into the trees, and Shane might have a hard time catching her. Lupines could be fast, especially if they had a head start.

After a time, Freya heaved a sigh. "All right. Show me this cabin where I can shower."

Shane noted Freya didn't say *take me there*. That would imply she was under Shane's power, being led where he wanted to go. *Show me* indicated that she was in control, telling Shane what to do. The words also implied that she would decide, once there, whether or not to go inside.

Shane shrugged his big shoulders as though he didn't care one way or another and gestured for her to walk beside him. Not behind him—he wanted to indicate he didn't regard her as a submissive, and besides, this way he could keep an eye on her.

He was slightly surprised when Freya fell into step with him without further argument. She had some kind of agenda, he knew, and going along with him now just became part of it.

"Where are your clothes?" Shane asked. "Mine are on my way to my pickup. But the cabin isn't far. We can walk."

He added the last part hastily as Freya's eyes narrowed in suspicion. She was not about to get into a vehicle with him.

"I know where I left them," Freya said. "Cabin first."

Okay, interesting. She trusted following Shane to an unknown cabin more than she trusted him with the location of her stuff.

Shane would have to figure out why later. For now, she needed a clean body, a quiet place to rest, and food to eat.

Who she was, why she was here, and what she was up to

would keep. Shane, as much as his bear growled at him to shake answers out of her, had learned the value of taking his time.

"Suit yourself," Shane made himself say.

He continued through the trees to the place he'd left his backpack, ready to march the mile or so beyond that to Eric's, leaving his truck to wait patiently for his return.

———

Freya wasn't certain why she chose to follow this Shifter, this bear, deeper into the woods. But his mention of a shower and a meal had the tired wolf inside her salivating.

She justified her response by the fact that Shane obviously wasn't the feral thing she'd scented in the woods with her. When Shane had come along, she'd thought he was the terrifying animal roaming this place just out of sight, and in her agitation her wolf had attacked first.

Freya had realized at once that he was a Collared Shifter, anything feral in him quashed long ago, but it had been too late for her to release him and race away. He'd never have let her, anyway.

At least Shane hadn't immediately tried to kill her. He could have—she'd felt that power in him. Nor had he dashed for the nearest cell phone to call Shifter Bureau and have her picked up.

Freya traveled without identification. Well, she had a fake driver's license a guy in San Francisco had fixed her up with a long time ago, but it wasn't Shifter identification. She had nothing that indicated her clan or her pack, or even her family, *who are long gone anyway,* she finished with familiar pain.

But Shifter Bureau was canny. They'd come up with an

app—so Rolf had told her—that let them figure out if a person was a Shifter or not, and then which Shifter they were and where they were supposed to be. Showing up on the app as an un-registered Shifter would get her arrested, if they didn't kill her outright. Then what would happen to Rolf, wherever he was?

She'd decided to take advantage of Shane's gullibility to clean herself up and eat, so she could reach her appointment fresh-smelling and clear-headed. She'd find some way to elude him when she was ready. Freya had spent a lifetime hiding out from Shifters, and she wasn't about to stop now.

Shane moved deftly along, light on his bare feet as he followed no discernable path. He'd retrieved a backpack he'd hidden but didn't stop to dress. Freya wasn't noticing his tight backside and firm body at all. Was she?

She couldn't afford to get involved with a Shifter, no matter how good-looking he was. He was a Collared Shifter, and not even a Lupine. Her enemy in all respects.

Shane abruptly halted. Freya forced her gaze past his muscular body and saw a house set among a thick stand of pines.

It rose two stories, walls sided in polished wooden boards, with a wraparound porch on the first level. Curtains hung in all the windows, and a porch light, shining in the dim winter morning, welcomed them.

Freya stilled in surprise. She'd pictured a rudimentary cabin in deep woods, battered and abandoned. Shifters weren't allowed lovely homes on the side of Mount Charleston.

"Our Shiftertown leader's mate, Iona, owns it," Shane said as though understanding her confusion. "Technically, her human mom does, but Shifters are welcome to use it whenever."

He stepped up to the porch, retrieved a key from a niche high in the wall, and shoved the key into the polished lock.

"Come on in." Shane threw open the door. "Make yourself at home. I won't bite." He grinned, his mouth full of white teeth. "Much."

CHAPTER FOUR

S hane stepped inside and flicked a wall switch, flooding a comfortable-looking living room with warm light. Tempting her, like he knew it would.

She should not go in there, Freya's wolf warned. She should spin around and flee, let Shane catch her if he could. Bears were strong, but wolves were fast.

On the other hand, Freya was tired and hungry, and Shane was right. She was a mess. Traveling to Las Vegas, looking for Rolf in all points between, had taken longer than she'd thought. She'd had to resort to living rough as her wolf when her money ran out. Not having a bed to sleep in for a few days had taken its toll.

"Bathroom is upstairs, right off the landing," Shane was saying as Freya made her feet cross the threshold. He dropped his backpack on the floor next to the door, as though not wanting its dirty canvas to touch the living room's pristine rug. "Clean towels in the bathroom cupboard. Bedroom on the left has some clothes that might fit you. Iona's Feline though, so if the scent bothers you, well ..." He opened his hands in an apologetic gesture. "That's what happens when your Shifter-town leader, his sister, his mate, et cetera, are cats. You gotta put up with the smell."

He spoke as though being locked in a Shiftertown with a leader who wasn't even his species was one big joke.

Freya hesitated at the foot of the stairs, wondering if Shane would rush up behind her and drag her to a bedroom to do what Shifter males did to fair-game females.

Then again, why would he bother with a bedroom? He could take her to the floor now or do it on the stairs. He also could have ravaged her in the woods, when he'd won their fight.

He *had* won, though Freya wouldn't admit it to him. He'd pinned her, and she'd never have been able to get away if he hadn't let her go.

Without looking at her, Shane unzipped his backpack and dumped its contents onto the rug. He pulled out a pair of sweatpants, which he quickly pulled on. Then he moved to the fireplace, where he knelt to light kindling that had been left waiting with carefully laid logs.

Freya couldn't stop herself gazing at Shane's well-muscled back, which bore scars from long-ago battles, plus a few more recent scratches she hadn't made. That and his nicely formed backside, now covered with the thin fabric of his sweatpants. The human in her appreciated the sight, and a basic need awoke.

She made herself turn away, clutch the carved newel post, and launch herself up the stairs.

The bathroom, as promised, was the first door at the top of the staircase. Freya skimmed inside and shut the door behind her. In the living room below, she heard Shane start belting out a Stevie Ray Vaughn tune in a loud baritone.

Freya had to smile. Shane's voice was warm and rich, but damn, he couldn't carry a tune in a bucket.

Freya locked the door, though the flimsy button lock wouldn't stop Shane if he wanted to burst in. She heard him continue to sing downstairs—or what passed for singing—even after she turned on the water in the glass-doored walk-in shower stall.

A shower had never felt more luxurious. Bath products lined up on the shelf ranged from generic men's shampoo and soap to scented body wash, shampoo, and conditioners for women. Freya lathered up guiltily with fine-smelling soap, hoping Eric's mate—Iona, Shane said her name was—wouldn't mind.

Shane had mentioned Iona's mother was human. Did that mean Eric was mated to a half-Shifter? Freya had met a few half-Shifters in her travels, who kept their Shifter identities fiercely secret. They'd feared Freya when she'd realized what they were, but she would never betray them.

A half-human woman had decided to mate with a Shifter and go live with him in a Shiftertown? Was she nuts?

As much as Freya loved the hot water on her sore body, she finished as quickly as she could. The towels she'd found were thick and fluffy, more luxury. The floor of the shower was now covered with the mud and dead leaves that had been on her body, so she spent a few minutes cleaning that.

A peek out the bathroom door showed no Shane in sight, though his voice still carried from somewhere downstairs. Freya nipped into the bedroom next to the bathroom, closing and locking that door. Clothes hung in the closet, as Shane had indicated, jeans and shirts, shorts for warmer weather, and sweatshirts and pullover sweaters.

Freya chose things in sizes closest to hers. She didn't want to wear another woman's undies, so she pulled on the clothes over her bare, damp body. She'd retrieve her own things soon enough.

By the time Freya exited the bedroom, Shane had switched to crooning *The Lion Sleeps Tonight* in a crazy falsetto. The big goof.

Trying to disarm her, Freya's caution told her. Making her laugh so she'd not notice her danger until the chains landed around her.

Freya found an unused hairbrush in the bathroom drawer, along with a few toothbrushes still in the package. For guests? How many of those did Shifters entertain up here?

Still, it was nice to comb out her hair and brush her teeth. Now she was clean, refreshed, and ready for her appointment to maybe learn of her brother's fate.

She left the bathroom to the sound of Shane's continued wailing. Freya would take him up on his offer of food and then go. Even if he'd brought her here to confine her—or other things—Freya would ditch him at the first opportunity.

She'd gotten away from tougher Shifters than Shane the bear, including the ones who'd tried to trap her before. She'd not let Shane stop her, no matter what she had to do.

———

SHANE GLANCED OUT OF THE KITCHEN WHEN HE HEARD Freya on the stairs, and the warbling song died in his throat.

The phrase *you clean up nice* was the understatement of the century.

The grime had fallen away to reveal Freya's sun-kissed skin and dark brown hair highlighted with silver—the mark of her gray wolf.

She wasn't as tall as other female Shifters Shane knew, though she would be tall for a human woman. Shane had noticed her ample chest and curvy hips while they'd stood unclothed in the woods, and the sweatshirt and jeans, a little tight on her, outlined her body in a delectable way.

Was he going to do the honorable thing and simply help her, like a good tracker would? Or would Shane's mating frenzy rise and make him want to keep her here?

Forever ...

No female had touched the primal beast within him since ... well, they never had. He'd once hoped Cassidy Warden would be his mate, but looking back, he realized that the mating frenzy hadn't instantly sprung to the surface when he'd been around her, like it was doing now with Freya. Interesting.

Or, maybe Shane was just horny. It had been a while. Freya looked *very* nice as she paused at the bottom of the stairs. The way her body moved inside the clothes told Shane she didn't have anything on underneath them.

Freya watched him hesitantly. He saw hunger in her eyes, but for food, not for Shane.

"I've whipped up a feast of sandwiches," Shane said. "Not a lot of fresh food here, but there's always sandwich stuff in the freezer. And frozen meals. And a microwave."

Freya left the stairs and headed for the kitchen, as though propelled by her empty stomach. Shane made sure she didn't have to pass close to him as she moved to the large table where Shane had laid out enough sandwiches to satisfy several starving Shifters after a group wrestling match.

"Iona's mom keeps all this food for Shifters?" Freya asked in amazement as she viewed the spread. Shane had thawed bread and several kinds of lunch meat, dressed up with the condiments that were always in the refrigerator. "She must be a saint. I'd think a human woman would be furious that her daughter paired up with a Shifter and refuse to give them anything."

"Just means you haven't met Iona's mom," Shane said. "Anyway, Eric pays to keep the place stocked. Only fair, since Shifters use it a lot."

"So Eric is the saint," Freya said in all seriousness.

Shane snorted a laugh. "You haven't met him either."

Freya didn't answer as she piled sandwiches on a plate. She shot Shane a wary glance when he approached, but she sat down at the far end of the table, planted her elbows on it, and started to eat.

Shane set a cup of fresh-brewed coffee next to her. Freya abandoned her sandwich to seize the mug and take a long swallow. Must have been a while since her last caffeine fix.

He slid into the chair on the opposite end of the long table, which was made to hold a Shifter family and lots of cubs taking a break on Mount Charleston. Plenty of space between him and Freya.

Shane snatched up a roast beef sandwich and then piled a heap of thawed blackberries next to it. Freya lowered her cup and stared at his plate in obvious bewilderment.

"Bears are omnivores," Shane said. "I can't imagine a meal without a lot of berries. Or honey. We like that too." He sent her a grin, hoping to coax a smile onto her serious face.

"Wolves like meat." Freya removed a sliver of iceberg lettuce Shane had added to the turkey sandwiches and dropped it to her plate. "Cheese isn't bad either."

She took another large, hungry bite, closing her eyes as she chewed.

"How long has it been since your last meal?" Shane asked.

"A couple of days." Freya opened her gray-gold eyes and fixed him with a wolf stare. "I ran short of money."

"Are you living on the road? Or, since you're Shifter, in the woods?"

"None of your business." Freya scowled as she swallowed another bite. "If you must know, I've been staying in motels when I can. I eat at whatever diner is attached to the motel—some are surprisingly good."

"No kidding. I love diner food."

"As long as they bring you lots of berries?" Freya asked, her eyes showing something approaching humor.

"With whipped cream." Shane popped a blackberry into his mouth.

"Figures." Freya fell silent as she finished her first sandwich and started another. Shane followed suit.

"You can stay here a while, if you want," Shane said after a time.

Freya stilled, sandwich in mid-air, and stared at him in incredulity. "What?"

"I said, you can stay—"

"I heard you. I'm having a hard time believing you're offering out of the goodness of your heart."

Shane shrugged. "Why not? The place is well stocked, as you can see. Eric and Iona won't mind, once I explain—"

"No." Freya half rose in her vehemence. "You're not telling Eric anything about me. You never met me, never saw me."

Shane made a show of adding another slab of cheese to his sandwich, as though paying no attention to her reaction. "Who are you running from? I guarantee that Eric will protect you. *I* will protect you."

"I don't need protecting." The answer was automatic, as

though Freya said this often. "Why would you anyway? You're not my pack or clan. You're a *bear*."

"I'm a tracker. Also, I'm my mom's second. That means I help take care of all Shifters in Shiftertown."

Freya sat back down, her apprehension high. Shane kept on eating, as though they weren't discussing anything important.

"I'm not from your Shiftertown," Freya pointed out.

"Doesn't matter." Shane tried another casual question. "What Shiftertown did you get assigned to?"

Freya tapped her bare throat. "No Collar, remember? I decided Shiftertowns weren't for me."

Shane hid his skepticism by tossing a few more berries into his mouth.

A Shifter didn't decide whether to join a Shiftertown or not. Humans had rounded up all known Shifters, documented them, Collared them, and assigned them to a collection of houses known as a Shiftertown. Freya hadn't been given a Collar, which meant she hadn't been rounded up, but she'd dropped hints that she knew what Shiftertowns were like. Curious.

She had to have been on the run ever since. She'd try to pass for human, but she'd have to move on as soon as local humans grew suspicious at her very slow aging. Shifters lived a long time.

"Our Shiftertown isn't so bad," Shane said. "Well, wasn't until Graham came along, but it still is pretty good. Okay, except for this morning, which was why I decided I needed a break. Graham's a good leader, if you can get past his attitude."

Freya started when Shane mentioned Graham's name and bowed her head over her meal as he went on, very carefully not looking at him.

Made sense that she'd have heard of Graham, as she was a Lupine. The entire Lupine world must be aware of Graham McNeil, who thought he was in charge of said world.

Shane expected Freya to state her opinion of him. Most Lupines wished Graham at the bottom of the ocean.

Freya pretended to not be interested at all, to not have noticed that Graham's name had even come up. Huh.

Freya popped the last crust of her last sandwich into her mouth and checked the digital clock on the microwave. She finished the bite and rose.

"Thanks, Shane. This was nice of you. I'll return the clothes when I can. I have to go now."

She was out of the kitchen and at the front door before Shane had time to blink. Reminded him how fast Lupines could move.

Bears could move rapidly too, when they chose. Shane was a step behind her when Freya's hand touched the doorknob.

"Why the rush?" he rumbled.

Freya glanced back at him. "I've got places I need to be. Shifters have lives outside of Shiftertowns, you know."

"Sure, they do. But you've been living rough for days, you said. Don't be in such a hurry to leave. Rest here for a while."

He kept the suggestion gentle and friendly, but Freya sent him a look of vast impatience. "I need to get going. I have an appointment." She appeared to immediately regret this admission.

Shane didn't like the sound of that. "Appointment with who? Where? Let me drive you."

Freya quickly opened the door. "Like I said, what I do is none of your business. I don't need a ride."

"We're miles from any town. Even a Shifter will be tired running all the way back to Las Vegas."

"Who says I'm going to Vegas? See you, Shane. I appreciate you not killing me."

Again, the flash of humor he'd glimpsed in her surfaced. Before Shane could respond, Freya shot out the door.

Shane was right behind her. "Seriously, you're trusting someone who sets up an appointment in the middle of nowhere?"

For answer, Freya simply waved a hand and headed at a run into the trees.

Shane growled with a mixture of irritation and worry as Freya swiftly disappeared into the woods. She was right, of course. It was none of his business what an un-Collared Lupine not from his Shiftertown got up to.

He should let her go. If Freya ran into an ambush by Shifter hunters, that was her tough luck. Hunters were allowed to kill Shifters who wore no Collar and had escaped being herded into Shiftertowns. Fair game. Her own fault, Shifter Bureau would say.

Damn, damn, damn.

Shane skimmed back into the house, banked the fire, and turned out the lights. He strode out again and locked the door, returning the key to its hiding place before he started after Freya.

She'd quickly vanished, but Shane wasn't called a tracker for nothing. He found her scent trail almost immediately. In seconds he was in bear form, his clothes in a bundle on his back, as he followed her to her mystery date.

CHAPTER FIVE

Freya was going to be late. She cursed herself for lingering to enjoy a shower and the meal, but on the other hand, she'd needed to bathe and eat. This Althea person might be less than receptive to Freya if she looked like a desperate fugitive.

Getting a meeting with the woman had been difficult enough—she'd had to rely on those who secretly helped rogue Shifters in the human world. This was how she'd found a man to make her fake ID a long time ago. A few encrypted messages later, and Freya had an interview set with Althea at a winter resort on Mount Charleston.

She hoped that Althea hadn't grown tired of waiting and departed. Though Freya wasn't certain she trusted a human who was so secretive, this was really the only lead she had about her brother's whereabouts. If she missed Althea, Freya was back to square one.

Freya had retrieved her own clothes from the woods, but decided to retain Iona's sweatshirt and jeans, which were clean and whole, for her outer layer. She'd also donned the padded jacket she'd hidden after brushing off as much of the leaves and dirt as she could.

Thus attired, she strode along toward the ski resort, replaying her conversation with Shane in her head.

Shane's mention of Graham had unnerved her, but she thought she'd hidden her reaction well. Shane hadn't said anything more about him and had gone on stuffing a very large sandwich into his mouth. With berries.

Bears were weird.

Knowing Graham and his wolves were in the valley below this mountain made Freya nervous. What happened if Shane ran straight to Graham to announce he'd met an un-Collared Lupine called Freya?

Didn't matter. Freya would talk with Althea then put a vast distance between herself and Shiftertown before Graham became aware of her presence.

It's a shame I have to run, came a thought out of nowhere. *There's something about Shane.*

Freya halted for a stride to examine this startling idea. Shane was the first Shifter she'd met in years, and definitely her first bear. She caught herself thinking of Shane's hard face and dark brown eyes, pleasant to look into. Behind his soft stare, he had strength and a shrewdness that was there for anyone who bothered to look. He was funny too, but Freya understood that his sense of humor hid a sharp mind.

She pressed the image of Shane firmly aside. Her encounter with him had been brief and was behind her now. A bump in the road of her life, one she was heading away from.

Why was that thought brushed with so much regret?

She forced herself to pay attention as she neared the ski lodge. The resort was crowded on this snowy Sunday, and the lines for the lifts were long. Even so, this place was remote enough that Freya could escape into the wilderness if she needed to. On the west side of this range was open country with few roads, where her wolf could easily evade a chase.

Freya had agreed to meet Althea here only after researching the location, liking both its popularity and isolation.

She strolled along the path at the end of the ski runs, hoping she looked like any of the other day-trippers who'd come up to Mount Charleston to enjoy the snow.

The resort was unnervingly normal. People moved to and from the lodge, some with anticipation of fun on the slopes, others ready to finish the sporty stuff and relax with a steaming latte or hot chocolate.

Kids on small skis took lessons in the practice area from patient instructors. The children were bundled up in tiny puffy jackets and adorable knit hats, and for a moment, Freya paused to smile at them. They were much more clumsy than Shifter cubs would be as they tried to balance on the skis, but they sure were cute.

A pang laced Freya's heart. When she'd run from the mate-claim, she'd given up her chance for her own cubs. A difficult choice. Then again, considering who her cubs' father would have been, it had been the right decision.

Still, watching these little ones made Freya realize what she'd missed. In her wanderings, she'd made friends with women who had children, and she'd enjoyed spoiling their kids, but it wasn't the same. In Shifter packs, cubs were everywhere, taken care of by the entire group. There was protectiveness and love in a wolf pack, even in Graham's, that she'd never found elsewhere.

But there also could be restrictive rules and a stifling

atmosphere, especially when one was in the pack but outside it at the same time.

A couple of little girls waved at Freya, responding to her smile, and she waved back. Before parents could begin to wonder at her interest in their children, Freya strode on toward the large wooden lodge.

Her meeting wasn't inside it—Freya continued past the buildings and around to the back. Here, at the far end of a huge, mostly empty parking lot, several black SUVs waited. Tall trees loomed behind the vehicles, marking the edge of the resort and the beginning of deeper woods.

As Freya approached, one of the SUVs' front passenger doors opened and a woman of medium height stepped out. She had dark hair cut short, the style like a sleek cap on her head. She wore black pants, flat-soled boots good for the slushy parking lot, and a thick dark blue jacket.

She'd donned black-rimmed sunglasses against the snowy glare, which was a little disquieting. Freya didn't like not being able to see a person's eyes.

The woman, presumably Althea Webster, nodded to two men who'd descended with her, they also in winter-appropriate clothes and sunglasses. The men wore earpieces, though Althea did not. All three waited silently for Freya to approach.

Freya did so, with caution. As much as she wanted to hear what Althea had to say, she agreed with Shane that she should be careful. That was why she'd agreed on this place to meet. Plenty of exits. No human in an SUV could catch a wolf on the run in dense woods.

Before Freya could come within claw-striking distance of the woman, the two men stepped forward. Not to block Althea entirely, but if Freya attacked, she'd have to go through them first.

"State your first and last name, please," the woman said. Her voice was smooth, cultured, and utterly calm.

Most human women had to fight for any kind of superiority in their male-dominated world, but Althea seemed to have achieved it. She exuded confidence, a knowledge that she ruled her own kingdom.

"Freya McHugh," Freya said. "Am I addressing Althea Webster?"

"First error." Althea's sunglasses glinted. "Never give a person a name and ask them to agree to it. Very easy for that person to say she is the trusted ally you are to meet, when she is in fact, your enemy."

"Good point," Freya said. She'd spent much of her life trying to hide her true identity. "Do you have some ID?"

A smile flickered across Althea's mouth. "Do you?"

"A human driver's license," Freya said. "But it's fake." Someone like Althea would probably figure that out the minute she looked at it, if she didn't know already.

"I appreciate your candor." Althea nodded once, which made sunlight dance on her glossy hair. "I am, in fact, Althea Webster, though now you'll have to take my word for it."

Freya shrugged, attempting to be nonchalant. "I could ask around about you if I'm worried."

"You could. You would not learn much. Tell me, Ms. McHugh, why do you want to work with me?"

Freya had obtained this interview with the pretense that she might be looking for employment with Althea's private security company. Freya's contact had assured her that the woman was currently recruiting. Freya had feared that if she asked about Rolf without seeing Althea face-to-face, she wouldn't get an answer.

"I don't, actually," Freya said. "But my brother did."

Silence. Althea fixed her attention on Freya, her expression betraying nothing.

Freya was well beyond the reach of the two guards, who carried tasers prominently in their belts. Freya had to wonder what other weapons their thick jackets concealed.

Her skin prickled, the cold seeping through her coat and Iona's warm sweatshirt. She'd scented Feline on the clothes, as Shane had told her she would, but now that scent grew stronger.

Freya doubted Iona's sweatshirt was coming alive. Her gaze shot to the closed back doors of one of the SUVs, its tinted window preventing her from seeing through it. Her hackles rose.

"You have a Shifter in there," she announced.

Not Rolf. The Shifter wasn't Lupine. This was proof that Althea either hired them, or captured them.

Althea sent Freya a fleeting smile. "Very good. Your senses are sharp, I see. Ewan." Althea directed her command at the SUV. "Come on out."

Nothing happened for a moment, then the door of the vehicle opened, and a tall, dark-haired Shifter in jeans and a sweatshirt slid out to land on motorcycle-booted feet. He wore sunglasses as well but hadn't bothered with a coat.

He was a Feline all right. If Freya hadn't identified his scent, she would have pegged him by his attitude. Cats thought they owned the world. She didn't recognize him, and Ewan showed no recognition of her, only regarded her with a blank sunglasses-stare.

Freya *really* hated it when she couldn't see a Shifter's eyes. He could be plotting anything behind those opaque lenses.

Ewan didn't wear a Collar. Another rogue Shifter, she

guessed, who'd sought employment with humans who were rogues themselves.

The Feline's presence explained the strong Shifter scent, but not entirely. There was another Shifter layered over that, more than could be explained by Ewan's presence or Freya's borrowed clothes. Freya studied Ewan, but he didn't seem to be aware of any other scents but his own and Freya's.

Did he know, or was he not as sensitive to Shifter presence as he should be?

Freya recognized the unique signature as it came closer, one she'd never known before today.

Bear.

Oh, for the Goddess' sake, what the hell was he doing here?

He'd followed her, of course.

Freya schooled her expression to not give away her sudden apprehension, but Althea was astute.

"Everything all right?" Althea's question had an edge to it.

"Sure," Freya said, hoping her voice didn't shake. "Wolves are always wary around a Feline."

Ewan's brows waggled. "We aim to please, sweetheart."

That was another thing about Felines. They were all wise asses.

Althea wasn't pleased that Ewan had spoken, but if she'd expected silent Shifter guards, she didn't understand Shifters. Felines couldn't keep their mouths shut.

And bears, apparently, couldn't mind their own business.

Freya pulled herself together and sent Althea a stare as cool as the ones trained on her. "I'm fine."

"So, you decided to trick me into this meeting, not to work for me, but to find out if I hired your brother." Althea's voice was ice cold. "I'm not in the habit of disclosing my roster."

Freya hadn't really expected her to answer directly. "I'm not here to betray you, or him. I just need to know."

"Do you?" Althea scoffed. "Why should I risk my business, and possibly my life, to tell a rogue Shifter anything?"

Ewan huffed. "Seriously. Lupines are pushy."

Althea's slight turn of head toward Ewan made him close his mouth, and some of his belligerence faded.

Wow. A human woman who could make a Feline behave. Wonders never ceased.

Of course, if Althea had such power over an arrogant Shifter male, what kind of discipline must she employ to keep her people in line? Did she have Rolf, cowed and waiting somewhere for her to let him out?

Ewan hadn't recognized Freya's scent, which he likely would have if he'd known Rolf. Members of Shifter families resembled one another in more than looks. Ewan might be holding back, but Freya doubted it. Her flicker of hope began to fade.

"Answer my question, please," Althea continued to Freya. "Why should I tell you?"

Freya had the feeling Althea was encouraging her to come up with a good argument. Freya had worked out in her mind how she would persuade the woman, but the presence of Shane lurking in the woods scattered her thoughts.

Would he charge in here demanding to know why Althea was toting around an un-Collared Shifter, and why she was meeting with Freya? Would he threaten to tell his leader, Eric? And even worse, Graham?

"I'm only looking for information," Freya babbled, the words not as eloquent as what she'd prepared. "My brother vanished, and I need to know if it was voluntary or not."

One of the guards near Althea stared off into space, as

though listening to something on his earpiece. The second guard stiffened, obviously hearing the same thing, and the first bent and whispered to Althea.

The woman turned her attention back to Freya, her mouth thinning. "It seems we have a watcher in the woods."

Shane. Crap.

Freya shrugged, trying to convey that the intruder had nothing to do with her, but Ewan whipped around, sniffing the wind.

"Holy shit," he said. "What is a *bear* doing out here?"

The guard who'd whispered to Althea disappeared under the trees, and soon shouts sounded behind the SUVs. After a few tense moments, five guards, including the one who'd stood with Althea, came around the SUVs, driving Shane forward. One held a tranq rifle, and two of the others had automatic shotguns.

Freya's heart tripped in sudden fear. She had no doubt that these guys could kill Shane without remorse. Why hadn't he run?

Ewan watched with derision as Shane was marched into the middle of Althea's circle. He was far larger than the men who surrounded him, but Shane had his hands raised as he moved unconcernedly in front of the guards.

"So." Althea pinned him with her sunglasses stare. "Who are you, and why are you listening in on a private conversation?"

Shane's response should be that he'd been taking a walk, doing his own thing, when her goons had surrounded him. He should say he didn't know anything about Althea, or her organization, or had heard any of her conversation with Freya. He should say he'd move along and never tell a soul what he'd seen at the end of this parking lot.

Instead, Shane beamed Althea a huge smile and then turned the same one on Freya.

"Baby," he boomed, his voice rumbling through the snow-clad trees. "There you are. I've been looking all over for you. What are you doing out here, risking your life to talk to a bunch of mercenaries?"

CHAPTER SIX

S hane belted out the question while Freya glared at him with her gold-gray eyes, clearly willing him to turn around and get the hell out of there.

Not going anywhere, sweetie. These guys and this Althea were trouble—he'd smelled that long before he'd reached the edge of the parking lot and peered around the SUVs.

Plus, there was a mangy Feline in their midst. Ewan, Althea had called him. Shane knew exactly where that cat's thoughts had been going—he'd broadcasted strongly that he wouldn't mind Freya under him, no matter that she was a mere Lupine. Ewan's unconcealed lust made Shane want to punch his face. Which he would, when he had the chance.

"Who is this?" Althea, the coolly crisp woman in charge, demanded of Freya.

Freya should deny any knowledge of Shane's existence. If she were wise, she would do so instantly. Then Althea would order her men to tranq Shane and dump his sleeping body somewhere while they vanished into the blue—probably with Freya.

Of course, they might not stop at simply tranquilizing Shane. They could very well kill him. No one but Shane's family and friends would worry about a dead Shifter.

"Before you shoot me, I should tell you that you do *not* want my mom on the warpath," Shane said. "Your entire army would crumble before her."

Althea completely ignored him. "Well?" she asked Freya. "What should I do with him? Keep him? Or make certain he tells no tales?"

Clever woman. Shane was Freya's problem, and she'd make it Freya's choice.

Freya could say the word, and these guys would snuff him. Shane saw it in their faces, especially that of the Feline who regarded Shane with the intense focus of a cat ready to take down its prey.

What would Freya have to lose by giving them Shane? Nell would come after Althea and her crew, sure, recruiting anyone she could along the way, but she'd know nothing about Freya. And that was only if Shane's body was ever found. The annoying Feline here could advise them on how to get rid of Shane completely, might even have a Guardian in his pocket who could render Shane dust with no questions asked.

Freya had no loyalty to him. Shane had given her food, clothes, and brief shelter, but she'd accepted reluctantly and had fled at the first opportunity.

Shane could only watch her, leaving it up to her what to do.

Freya gazed back at him, hers the only eyes exposed in this little group. Shane saw worry and indecision warring in them, fear for herself, and also fear for him. Something squeezed in his heart, even as his snarky bear said, *Aw, sweet.*

Althea was growing impatient, but she remained quiet, letting Freya battle with her conscience.

Freya released a heavy sigh and screwed up her face in exasperation. "He's my ex," she said to Althea. "He follows me everywhere. I *told* him to stay away, but here he is. I'm sorry."

The surprising lie rolled easily from her lips. Shane made sure nothing flickered on his face to give it away, but Ewan wasn't fooled. Shifters had difficulty lying—scent betrayed them.

"Hold on," Ewan began.

"You want to Challenge?" Shane asked before Ewan could tell Althea that Freya was full of it. "Would be fun."

"He's not—" Ewan tried again.

"Her mate, no," Shane finished. "I wish. But if you don't believe her, you can scent her on me. Or will when I'm in your face, rearranging it for you."

"I'm not afraid of a *bear*," Ewan declared.

"You should be." Shane lost his grin, bringing on the air of danger that was never far from a grizzly. "You haven't fought one before, have you?"

Ewan sneered, but Shane had his answer in Ewan's sudden trepidation. No, he hadn't.

Althea ignored them both, her attention all for Freya. "Who else knows of this appointment?" Her question was deadly cold.

"No one," Freya said quickly. "I promise you. I didn't even tell him." She jerked her chin at Shane. "He followed me."

Which was the absolute truth.

"I figured she was in a hurry to get to something danger-ous," Shane said to Althea. "Looks like I was right."

"Dangerous for *you*," Althea said to Shane. "I have a

choice now, you see. Kill you or recruit you. I could always use another Shifter."

"Tranqing me and leaving me in the woods is out then?" Shane asked. "That was going to be my favorite option."

"You already know too much about us," Althea said. "My organization isn't a deadly secret, but I'd rather not have people harassing me."

"Murdering Shifters won't keep folks from your doorstep," Shane pointed out. "I mentioned my mom."

"Yes." Althea's voice was colder than the winter air. "Touching."

"Plus, my brother and stepdad and every other Shifter in the Vegas Shiftertown," Shane went on calmly. "A lot of heat for you."

"No one will know what happened." Althea's confidence made Shane suspect she'd disposed of unwanted Shifters before. "But I want it to be Freya's choice, not mine."

Shane wondered why. Testing her, maybe. What was Freya doing, anyway? Trying to join Althea's team?

"Bet you wish you'd given her more presents," Ewan sniggered to Shane.

"How about you dump this loudmouth?" Shane suggested to Althea, jerking a thumb at Ewan. "I could beat him to a pulp for you."

That provoked a laugh from Ewan. "Sure, Ursine. I'm not afraid of a tamed Shifter with a Collar. He tries any aggression with me, and that Collar will shock the hell out of him," he added to Althea.

"So I've heard." Althea trained her gaze on Shane. "Why don't you and Ewan give us a demonstration? That is, if Freya agrees."

Freya watched all this with a blank expression, but Shane

sensed her quickened breath and rising body temperature, despite the dozen feet that separated them. He'd deliberately put himself between her and Ewan, not wanting the Feline to read her. The guys with weapons thought they'd guided Shane to this exact spot, but it had really been the other way around.

"It's okay, babe," Shane told Freya. "I can take this shithead."

He tried to convey his assurance to her, which wasn't feigned. Shane had been dealing with Graham's near-feral wolves and other disgruntled Shifters for years. Today's skirmish had been annoying but not unusual. Someone was always scheming to take out Eric or Graham and be leader in their place.

Not to mention the wrestling sessions Shane had been doing with Cormac. Cormac was a skilled fighter, and he'd been teaching Shane and Brody all he knew.

Freya was studying Shane. Shane liked her eyes, the golden highlights holding secrets he wanted to learn.

Would Freya coolly say she didn't care if the two male Shifters killed each other, or would she wonder in vicious glee who would win? Or be afraid for Shane, her supposed ex?

Her intervention calling him her ex was brilliant, and heartwarming. She'd been worried for Shane. Pretending he was a harmless irritation, not a threat, was her way of protecting him.

"Shane is a good fighter," Freya said to Althea. She put just enough grudging respect in the statement, making Shane want to laugh. "Do you think it would be a fair match?"

Ewan scoffed. "Don't worry about me, honey."

Shane said nothing. Althea fixed her attention on Freya alone, ignoring the bantering of two males trying to out-alpha each other.

This contest was entirely between the two women. Had nothing to do with all the guards or even Shane and Ewan. This was Freya's audition.

Shane was also aware that no matter what happened, things would not end well for him. If he fought Ewan and his fake Collar didn't go off, these humans would learn that it was possible for Shifters to somehow get around their Collars' restrictions. They might capture Shane to study this effect or betray him to Shifter Bureau if Althea thought this beneficial.

Or, Shane could suppress his instincts, let Ewan kick his ass, and wait for Althea's mercy—or Freya's if Althea continued her tactic of making Freya decide. Althea's calm assurance that no one would know what had happened to Shane if she had him killed was chilling.

He could also play along and let Althea recruit him, if that was Freya's choice. He could find out about this so-called private security firm and then report to Eric once he got away.

But Shane wouldn't leave unless Freya came with him. He didn't trust this human woman with her cool voice, her tamed Shifter, and her guards with too many weapons. Shane had only met Freya this morning, and she was a *Lupine*, but she was more vulnerable than she knew.

While Freya debated what to do, and Ewan watched with the arrogance only Felines could manage, Shane made his own decision.

He couldn't indicate his plan with body language because Ewan would suss that immediately, so Shane simply acted.

He barreled forward, forcing his shift as he went, until he was charging at Freya in his half-bear, half-man form.

The sudden appearance of a massive half-Shifted bear, clothes tearing from him, gave Shane the seconds he needed. The guards hesitated a hair too long, and even Althea snapped no orders. Freya watched him come, open-mouthed, more astonished than afraid.

She had spirit, his lady. Shane ran smack into Freya, lifted her from her feet, and hurtled with her into the woods.

Did Freya scream and flail like a damsel in an old movie? No, she seized his giant arms and demanded, "What the fuck are you doing?"

Shane didn't waste breath answering. He heard Althea cursing behind them, her cool finally splintered. Clicks told Shane the guards had rifles ready. Ewan was laughing, which broke off into a furious snarling—maybe Althea had told one of the guards to tase him.

A quiet thunk of a tranq gun going off was followed a split second later by the sting of a dart pricking Shane's side. He pulled the dart out of his fur, tossed it to the leaves ahead of him, and crushed it with his powerful foot as he ran on.

It took a lot of tranquilizer to bring down a bear, especially in his man-beast state. Althea's goons had probably loaded enough to knock out a Lupine or Feline—non-Tiger ones, that is. Bear hadn't been on the menu today.

Even so, the small amount that bit into Shane slowed his stride.

"Second time today," Shane growled in his half-beast's guttural tones. "*Damn* it. I should have stayed in bed."

"I wish you would have," Freya grappled at his giant paw-hands. "Are you going to put me down anytime soon?"

"No can do, sweetheart."

Shane heard pursuit, but unless Ewan shifted and sprinted after them, Shane would easily outpace them. He headed away from the resort down a trackless slope between the trees, where the big SUVs couldn't follow.

A bullet twanged against a tree, bits of bark showering

down. Althea's voice rose in fury at whoever had fired. She wanted Freya alive, apparently. Probably didn't care too much about Shane, though.

Freya continued to struggle, but she wouldn't make a dent in Shane's strength if she didn't shift. Shane kept a tight hold on her as he wound along an ever-varying route back to his pickup.

He wished now he'd taken Cormac up on his offer of his big F450. With his own truck, Shane would have to stick to graded roads and hope that Althea and her gang didn't figure out which ones. Not that there were that many ways down this mountain. Speed was their biggest ally.

As the noise of Althea and her men faded, Freya ceased fighting, but Shane didn't loosen his grip. He suspected she was conserving her strength to get away from him later.

Shane sensed no wildcat loping after them, so Althea must not have ordered Ewan to pursue. Didn't mean she would give up the chase, only that she saw no point in using Ewan, who might not be that easy to control.

Shane's pace began to slacken. The tranq, on top of the one he'd taken this morning, was encouraging his body to wind down and take a nap. It became harder to hold on to the frustrated Freya, but he didn't want to release her, not yet.

Somehow, he'd have to shove her into the truck and keep her there. Short of zip-tying her feet and hands and locking her under the cover in the truck's bed—both of which she'd escape from in a heartbeat—he'd have to trust her to sit quietly in the cab while he ran around to the driver's seat. This would be tricky.

He heard no pursuit by the time he thankfully caught sight of his pickup, the roof gleaming in a chance beam of sunlight.

Shane slowed to catch his breath, but Freya didn't try to break away from him.

Waiting for the right moment, Shane concluded.

Around them the woods were quiet, except for the rushing noise of Shane crashing through the underbrush around the pickup.

Freya said nothing when Shane finally set her on her feet on the passenger side of the truck. He shrank down to human form, his ragged clothes settling on his body.

Second set of clothes screwed today. Shane would have to start keeping a spare wardrobe in his back seat.

He leaned both hands heavily on the truck around Freya. Hemmed in by his body, Freya glowered up at him, more anger than fear in her eyes.

"If you want to run back to them, I probably can't stop you," Shane said in the harsh timbre of his bear-beast. "Take my advice, though, babe. Ditch them."

"I was going to." Freya jammed her arms across her chest, which formed a nice cleavage in her sweatshirt's neckline. "I was going to tell her to let you go, and then I'd walk away too."

"Yeah?" Shane dragged in a long breath, battling lethargy from the tranq. "What makes you think Althea would have said, *Sure, no problem. See ya?* She might now be ordering her crew to get rid of both our bodies."

"It was worth a shot," Freya said in irritation, but her eyes flicked from his evasively. She was telling the truth, but not entirely. "If she threatened me, I planned to take off. Her human goons can't outrun a wolf."

"Her Feline Shifter can."

Freya shrugged. "I figured that if Ewan went after me, you'd take him down. If he went after *you,* then I'd have a chance to get away."

Shane studied her to see if she was joking. Maybe she was. Or not.

"Good strategic thinking," Shane said. "No wonder Althea wanted you. Who the hell is she?"

Freya met his gaze again. "I admit, I don't know much. I found a card for her security firm and made this appointment with her."

"Huh. I'd like to hear all about it."

"I can't tell you much more than that."

Hmm, back to lies. Or at least not the full truth.

They regarded each other, Freya's mouth a tight line. Shane tried to ease his breathing but didn't want to calm down too much. His adrenaline was helping him fight the tranq, so he needed to keep it high.

"This isn't the place to discuss it." Shane dug out his keys, which luckily were still in his ripped-up pocket, and unlocked the truck. He could hot-wire the pickup if he had to, but replacing keys was a bitch. He swung open the passenger door. "Offer you a ride?"

Freya eyed him warily. "Where to?"

"Anywhere you want." Shane held the door as though they were on a date. "Promise."

Freya hesitated a long moment. Shane saw her weighing the pros and cons of taking his offer of transportation, her body heat increasing as she debated.

He liked her scent—lemons and a hint of ginger. So much better than those of the male Lupines he'd had to deal with today.

"All right." Freya, to his surprise, slid quickly into the pickup. She yanked the door from his hand to slam it shut.

Shane wasted no time in getting himself around the truck and plunking into the driver's seat, where he shifted all the way to human again. The rearview mirror showed that he looked awful, his face sweaty and dirt-streaked, with shreds of what used to be a black sweatshirt clinging to his arms.

"I say we get off the mountain," Shane said as he started the engine and pulled carefully across the slushy ground. "I know a lot of people in Vegas. Any one of them can help you."

"I can go my own way." Freya drew up one leg and folded her arms around it, studying the trees as Shane bumped the truck back to the road.

"Accepting help doesn't mean you're weak," Shane told her.

She skewered him with glittering eyes. "You sound like a motivational app."

"Wouldn't know. I don't have a smart phone." Now *he* was telling half-truths. Shifters weren't supposed to own state-of-the-art technology, but they had enough human friends who supplied them with all kinds of tech-y stuff.

"I always have contingency plans," Freya said. "So, you can let me off wherever I decide is a good place."

Her voice shook a little, betraying her uncertainty. Shane had the feeling she was realizing that contacting Althea maybe hadn't been the best move in whatever direction her life was going.

"If you say so," Shane said.

"I do appreciate what you've done." Freya's voice softened. "The shower and clothes, I mean. Not the bursting into my appointment and fouling it up."

"I had a bad feeling about them, and you did too." Shane saw by her flush that she agreed. "Besides, who would want to work with a Feline shit like Ewan? He would probably try to mate-claim you, just to prove he could."

Freya's flush grew deeper. Yeah, she'd figured that as well.

Shane steered onto the dirt road that descended toward the main one, and they jolted along in silence for a while.

Why she bothered lying about why she was meeting Althea, Shane didn't know. He'd have to—

His thoughts broke off as a flash of black SUV filled up Shane's rearview mirror.

"Fuck."

The SUV's front seat held Althea's guards. Another SUV was pulling to a halt on the paved road in front of Shane's pickup. Freya gasped, her foot coming off the seat and her eyes widening.

Shane didn't slow. "Hold on to something, sweetheart."

Freya whipped her head around to stare at him. Her eyes grew even rounder, then she grabbed the dashboard and held on tight.

Shane slammed the gas pedal to the floor and careened his truck toward the SUV waiting just ahead.

CHAPTER SEVEN

Freya let out a yelp as Shane accelerated straight toward the SUV. Did he mean to ram it? The SUV was twice the size of Shane's pickup, and while this vehicle felt sturdy, she didn't think it could survive the collision.

She braced for the impact and felt her wolf start to take over—it had better survival instincts.

At the last minute, the SUV at the intersection furiously reversed, tires sliding on snowy asphalt. Shane brushed by its front end with an inch to spare and raced along the descending mountain road. The SUV started after them, a second one pulling in behind it, and then a third.

Shane took the hairpin curves of the road with amazing deftness. Freya hung on, closing her eyes anytime they slid too near an edge before Shane pulled the truck around the next corner.

The SUVs followed without trouble. Freya expected the lead driver to cut in front of Shane or run them off the road, but he never did. Cars were climbing up the other lane, more skiers heading for the lodges, and snowbanks made the road still narrower. The driver risked a head-on collision if he pulled out, and prudently did not. Althea and her men were chasing them *safely*.

"Why didn't you run?" Shane kept his eyes on the road, hands turning the wheel with precision.

"I didn't want Althea's guards to shoot me." Freya braced herself as the pickup went swiftly around a 180 bend. "I planned to walk away slowly, remember?"

"No, I mean when I put you down by the truck just now. You could have turned wolf and sprinted off."

Freya wasn't sure why herself. "Would you have come after me?"

"Probably."

Shane spoke affably, no threat in his voice. Stating a fact.

Freya squeezed her eyes shut as they slid on a patch of ice. Shane competently straightened the wheel as though it was no big deal.

"Maybe I wanted a ride into town?" she ventured.

"Or you were having second thoughts about what you were doing."

Freya couldn't deny that. She hadn't wanted to climb into one of Althea's SUVs, especially not the vehicle containing Ewan, maybe to never be seen again. Freya had the feeling that if Althea considered her a threat, she wouldn't be allowed to simply stroll away, no matter what the woman did or didn't know about Rolf.

"Althea didn't look happy when you dragged me off," Freya observed.

"Nope." Shane took another corner with death-defying bravery and spun them out onto Highway 157 that led back to town. "Plus, she's not thrilled that I now know about her and her band of thugs."

"She might have tried to hire you." Freya glanced back at the SUV that was easily keeping pace with them. The other danced behind it.

"I doubt it. I think she figures a Collared Shifter is useless to her, unless she wants a bunch of boxes carried." Shane took his gaze momentarily from the road to shoot Freya a wink. "Lots of people ask me to help them move."

The way he phrased it: *She figures a Collared Shifter is useless to her* told Freya that Shane knew Althea's conclusion to be wrong. She thought about her own tussle with him earlier, and how his Collar had remained silent, no reaction to his violence.

"Why didn't you agree to fight Ewan?" Freya asked. "It wasn't because you thought you'd lose."

Shane shrugged. "He can probably give good battle, or he wouldn't be working for Althea. But I've already had to fight a bunch of rowdy wolves today—besides you, I mean—when I really just wanted some time to myself."

Freya knew bullshit when she heard it. "You didn't want to do a round with Ewan, because Althea would wonder why your Collar didn't go off."

Shane flashed her a glance. "Oh, the cute Lupine is observant," he said to the air.

"Why doesn't it work?" Freya asked. "Is it defective, and you hope Shifter Bureau won't notice?"

"It's a long, long story, sweetheart." He checked the rearview again. "Right now, I need to ditch these guys. We'll talk later."

He wouldn't get the chance to tell her the story, though, because Freya was leaving as soon as Shane found a safe place to stop. Even if he reneged on his promise to drop her off wherever she wished, she could simply jump out at any intersection once they were in the city. Traffic could snarl badly there, providing her plenty of opportunity to get away.

The highway leveled out, the curved road straightening. The pines ended abruptly, bushier trees taking their place. In another minute, all the trees and the snow had completely vanished, to be replaced by desert scrub in pale sandy soil.

Shane increased his speed. Traffic had picked up, this road being the main drag between Mount Charleston and Las Vegas. The lead SUV remained right behind Shane, but the driver still didn't pass or try to force them onto the side of the road.

Althea was picking her moment, Freya decided.

While Shane was driving faster, he wasn't flooring it. His speedometer read a steady pace, well within the speed limit. A highway patrol car passed them going the other way, not even glancing at the pickup and its companion SUVs.

"If you speed up and a cop pulls us over, Althea will have to abandon the chase," Freya suggested.

"If cops pull us over, they'll wonder why a Collared Shifter in shredded clothes is running around Mount Charleston, far from his Shiftertown. Then they'll wonder who you are and why you're with me. Wanna risk it?"

"If you didn't live in a Shiftertown, it wouldn't be a big deal," Freya countered in exasperation.

"If I wasn't from this Shiftertown, I wouldn't have been on the mountain this morning to help you," Shane said in a reasonable tone. "As it is, I really don't want to deal with Shifter Bureau on top of the day I'm already having."

Freya had to concede the point. Hopefully Althea's guys would attract the attention of the highway patrol or the Clark County sheriff, which would solve the problem. Sleek black SUVs full of men in sunglasses were more suspicious than a man and woman in a small pickup, even with Shane's torn shirt.

"What are you going to do then?" Freya asked.

"Try to lose them when I hit the freeway."

Freya hoped he could. She sat back, a little less tense now that the mountain grades were done, but her heart was still pounding.

Once Shane shook off Althea, Freya would have to decide what she'd do next. She had no other lead on her brother's disappearance. Filing a missing person report wasn't an option, in case the police figured out Rolf was a Shifter and sent the case to Shifter Bureau. Rolf wouldn't be a missing person then —he'd be a fugitive Shifter. Fugitives could be shot and killed without redress.

Shane had said he knew people who could help her. He'd said *people*. Didn't mean they necessarily were Shifters.

No. Freya cut off the thought. She needed to stay away even from humans who were friends with Shifters. She'd thank Shane for his help and walk away. When she got back to her job and could sort herself out again, she'd send Iona's clothes to her or else money for her to buy new ones.

Freya would find a way to survive. She'd been doing that for the last twenty-five years.

They neared the freeway. Trucks whizzed along in both directions amid the glitter of many cars. Clouds had gathered above the desert floor, gray and threatening. Winter in southern Nevada could bring torrents of rain in the lowlands, which would become snow for the slopes on the mountains.

Shane slowed to take a ramp onto the freeway. Althea and her goons were right behind them. Shane swerved through the dense traffic, soon putting a few eighteen-wheelers between him and Althea's vehicles.

"These guys are good," Shane said almost admiringly as he kept an eye on them.

Freya turned to look out the back window. The three SUVs were several cars behind them but keeping pace.

Shane continued, "They're following without hanging right on my ass. My guess is they'll stay with us until we try to hide on some back street in town. Then they corral us and scoop us up like stray sheep."

Freya straightened in her seat again, her fears mounting. "What can we do? I don't know the area well, don't have any ideas on where to go to ground. Which was why Althea picked this place to meet, I guess."

"She wouldn't have met you somewhere of your choosing," Shane pointed out.

"I'm aware."

"But it's your lucky day," Shane said cheerfully. "I do know the area better than anyone, and like I told you, I have a lot of friends in town."

"I don't want to endanger them," Freya said quickly.

"Sweetie, they live for danger. And it sounds like you didn't have a backup plan. Good thing you met me, right?"

"I'm still debating that," Freya growled.

Shane let out a laugh and abruptly took an exit. They'd reached the encroaching developments at the base of the mountain, which had heavily trafficked main roads. Shane slid through the lanes easily enough but grunted in frustration when he checked his mirrors again.

"They are going to dog us 'til the end," he announced. "They're waiting for us to run out of gas or something. Then they'll have us."

"Shit." Freya sent another fearful glance out the back window. The three SUVs were keeping up without hurrying. The dark vehicles hid their passengers like the sunglasses hid Althea's eyes and exuded the same confidence.

"They want to play hardball, do they?" Shane said with determination. "Well, there's one place they can't chase us, let alone catch us."

"Where?" Freya demanded, then she realized what he meant.

Shane's grim amusement returned. "Shiftertown, baby."

Freya hunkered down in the seat, her past, present, and future slamming together to trap her like bars on a cage.

"Just let me out somewhere," she pleaded. "I'll run. They'll chase me. Or at least they'll split up and give you time to get home."

"Are you nuts?" Shane asked in amazement. "Only place you'll be safe now is with me and my family in our Shiftertown. No one comes in without Eric's permission. Althea's goons will have to go through a lot of Shifters to get to you, and I guarantee, they won't succeed."

"No! I can't!" The words burst out of her, and Shane frowned.

"I'm not going to bring Shifter Bureau down on you or anything like that," he said in a gentle voice. "Don't worry. You stick with us until you have somewhere else to go."

He made it sound so easy. Freya's life was anything but.

"Graham McNeil is there." Freya clenched her hands in her lap, struggling to keep her wolf contained.

Shane sent her a puzzled glance. "Yes, I said so earlier. He's co-leader with Eric. He acts like a hard-ass, but he's actually a good guy. And a little easier to deal with since he mated."

"He has a *mate*?" Wonder of wonders. Freya shook herself.

That was a long way from the point. "Shane, I can't go to Graham's Shiftertown."

"Honey, we don't have a choice." Shane gestured to the rearview mirror. "If they catch us anywhere but Shiftertown, we're screwed. It's the only place we'll be safe." He continued changing lanes in nerve-wracking zigzags, as though the matter were settled.

"Shane," Freya said in desperation. She hadn't wanted to tell him her truths, but he was giving her no option. "I can't go anywhere near Graham or his Shifters."

Shane kept his eyes on the road. "Why? Because he's Lupine? I know he thinks he's the god of Lupines, but he has nothing to do with you."

"Yes, he does." Freya's throat closed, but she forced the confession out. "Graham is my pack leader. I ran away from him years ago. If he finds me, he'll force me back to him, back to what I was trying to get away from." Tears choked her voice. "Please, Shane. Don't let Graham McNeil know I still exist."

CHAPTER EIGHT

S hane's hands jerked on the wheel, and the truck spun on an oil patch before he righted it.

Freya had transformed from strong young woman who'd nearly kicked his ass to a frightened ball of anguish. She pulled her feet to the seat again, wrapping her arms around her legs and burying her face in her knees.

What in the hell had McNeil done to her? Shane's protective rage mounted, his distrust of Graham and his Lupines stirring from where he'd tried, not very successfully, to suppress it.

Shane glanced into the rearview mirror at Althea and her bullyboys and found them still hanging on. They'd spaced the SUVs strategically so that two flanked Shane's pickup from behind, while one smoothly glided past to be somewhere in front of him.

"He's never mentioned you," Shane stated. Never since he'd known Graham and all his Lupines had he heard of a stray one called Freya.

"No?" she sounded surprised.

"No. But like I said, we have no choice." Shane spoke in

the no-argument tone he'd perfected as a tracker. "First, we get free of this lady and her trigger-happy guards, then we worry about Graham. Which you don't need to do."

Freya's head popped up. "What are you talking about? He's my *pack leader*. I ran away from him. He'll sequester me and punish me, and there's not a thing you can do about it. His Shiftertown is the worst place you can take me."

The defeat and fear in her voice ramped up Shane's protective instincts still more. While Shane didn't really think Graham would be brutal to Freya, what did he know? Graham could be pretty ruthless with his Lupines, but he'd had to be, to keep his nearly wild Shifters together and safe.

Shane wanted to reach for Freya, pull her into his arms, and comfort her. Impossible dodging through heavy traffic at forty-five miles per hour.

"Things have changed, sweetheart." Shane hoped he sounded reassuring. "If I tell Graham to keep away from you, and Eric backs me up, Graham can't do shit to you."

Shane mentally crossed his fingers as he spoke. Eric might not take Shane's side. He might explain, in his laid-back way, that Graham had a legal right to deal with his own pack problems, without interference.

On the other hand, if Eric saw how afraid Freya was of Graham, he'd be less likely to back Graham, no matter how much the Lupine leader blustered.

Then there was Misty, Graham's sweet-as-honey mate. She'd never let Graham come down on Freya for running away all those years ago, would she?

"When did you leave his pack?" Shane asked Freya as he continued to head inexorably toward Shiftertown's gates. "Before the Collars, I'm assuming. You never wore one."

"Graham tried to protect me from those—he did for others

too, who were barely past being cubs when Shifter Bureau came for us." Freya's fingers went to her bare throat. "They hadn't gotten around to Collaring us all yet. Other packs were moved in, and there were a lot of them, which slowed down the process. A Shiftertown was being put together near Elko for all the packs, with Graham in charge. Everything started to go wrong for me then. In the confusion, I took the opportunity to run."

"Can you be more specific?" Shane demanded. "*Everything started to go wrong for me* is kind of vague. I need to know what I'm heading into."

"No." Freya hunkered down. "Not because I want to hamper you, but because I really don't want to talk about it. Not now. Just let me out of the truck. *Please.*"

She stayed in a tight ball and didn't move. At least she wasn't stupid enough to open the door and roll into traffic while he was moving at a good clip. But he'd keep an eye on her.

Shane swung onto the back road leading to Shiftertown's gates. The SUV that had been ahead of them missed that he'd turned and braked abruptly, but the two behind them closed in without a problem.

"Here's what's going to happen," Shane said. "I'm driving straight home and telling my family what you just told me. You'll be under our protection, and trust me, Graham doesn't want to mess with us."

Freya lifted her head. Shane didn't like the despair in her eyes, wanted to jam his fist into Graham's face for putting it there. He decided right then that he'd erase her worries forever. It would take some doing, but it would happen.

"Please, Shane."

The tremor in her voice broke his heart. Shane slowed as

he approached the open gates in the chain-link fence, all three SUVs now on his tail.

Shane sent Freya a big bear smile. "Trust me, sweetheart. I've got this."

She stared at him with fear, dismay, and old anger warring in her gray-gold eyes. Shane held her gaze, his truck steadily heading for the gates as though it knew where to go.

"Seriously," he said softly. "I promise."

A swallow moved Freya's throat. She very quickly nodded her head, but she really had no option now.

Shane's truck slid between the gates, the three SUVs barreling toward Shiftertown after him.

Though the road ahead of Shane was empty of other vehicles, that didn't mean there were no Shifters around. The Warden family was milling about their yard, the cubs playing. Xavier, Cassidy's human brother-in-law, kicked back on their porch. He must be taking a rare day off.

Brody sauntered out from behind the bears' house as though ready to greet Shane. Peigi was taking her group of foster cubs for a walk—which meant running, romping, and screaming chaos. Reid was with her. Better and better.

Shane cranked down his window. "Shut the gates!" he yelled to anyone within hearing range. "Trouble at my six o'clock!"

Pleasant recreation time vanished in a heartbeat. Xavier was on his feet and off the porch, his taser coming out of its holster. Peigi's cubs and the Warden's boy instantly headed for shelter, while Brody and Eric, who'd rapidly emerged from his house, sprinted for the gates.

Reid vanished in that unnerving way he did, materializing again right next to the gatepost. He slammed the chain-link gate seconds before the lead SUV reached it.

The vehicles fishtailed to a halt. Eric had ceased running and now strolled toward them with Brody as though Eric meant to ask the drivers if they needed directions.

Nell came out of the house at a swift pace, moving to join Eric in protecting her Shiftertown. Cormac, who'd followed, pivoted toward Shane's pickup.

"What's going on?" Cormac asked. He spied Freya in the front seat, and Shane saw him putting the clues together. "I guess you two should come on inside."

Freya had frozen in place, as though entering Shiftertown had turned her into a statue. Cormac opened her door for her, but she wasn't moving.

Shane reached the passenger side of the pickup and held out his big hands for Freya.

"We'll go into our house," Shane said. "No one will mess with you there."

Cormac, no fool, had already realized Freya was Lupine, wearing Iona's clothes, and terrified. "Don't worry," he said in his soothing tones. "We have your back."

Cormac knew how to calm people. Freya's rigid posture eased somewhat, and she shakily took Shane's hands. Shane smoothed the backs of her fingers, trying to flow comfort into her.

Shane helped her out of the truck, and she stood up, very close to Shane. Shane wanted to put his arms around her and hold her until her fear went away, but he suspected she'd only twist away from him if he tried.

Shane led her, one step at a time, up the short sidewalk to the house.

The bears' home was long and low, built in the 1950s, when breezy porches were more important in a hot climate than ornamentation. Pillars lined the ground-level veranda that stretched the length of the house, chairs and loungers large enough for bears scattered up and down it. Wind chimes that Nell loved silvered the air.

Freya glanced at none of this. She kept her wolf eyes straight ahead, as though he directed her through a dark tunnel.

Cormac sprang ahead of them and opened the front door. Freya followed Shane across the porch and over the threshold, drawing a long breath when her feet touched the tiled floor inside.

"Have a seat," Cormac said. "I'll get coffee. Unless you prefer tea?"

Freya said nothing, her gaze now flicking around the room.

"Coffee," Shane said, recalling how she'd drunk it deeply at the cabin. He guided her to the large, overstuffed chair farthest from the windows and eased her down to it. He dragged a smaller chair next to her and planted himself on it.

Cormac arrived with the coffee. "Here. Get that into you."

Freya took the mug, relaxing a little bit more. "Thanks. I'm all right."

She was still very scared, but no longer paralyzed. Freya sipped the coffee, as grateful for it now as she'd been at the cabin. The wolf must like her java.

"You're safe here," Shane said to her. "I know you don't believe me, but you are."

Freya swallowed another mouthful of coffee. "Graham ..." She broke off as though she could barely stomach saying his name.

"Has no authority in our house," Shane stated.

Cormac's brows rose, but he asked no questions. He looked from Freya to Shane and back before nodding. "I'll go see what's up with the guys who were chasing you."

He hadn't asked about that either. Cormac's philosophy was that when a person wanted to explain something, they would, in their own time. He had no need to pry.

Nell would definitely pry, but right now, she was explaining to the men in the SUVs why they should leave. Shane could hear her strong voice all the way in here.

Cormac headed for the front door and out, a cold draft blowing through the living room before he was gone.

"This is *our* territory," Shane explained as Freya took another swallow of coffee. "Mine, my mom's, Brody's, and Cormac's. Even though Graham's arrogant and alpha, he knows better than to annoy a bunch of cranky bears."

Freya at last looked up from her coffee. "I hope you're right," she said in a hushed voice.

She must be imagining Graham on the doorstep, backed by his mangy Lupines, demanding Shane and Nell turn Freya over to him. Graham might have tried something like that when he'd first arrived in this Shiftertown, but he'd learned that it was in his best interest to keep the peace.

"Graham can't enforce pack law if Eric and my mom say no," Shane continued. "The fact that you're in Graham's pack doesn't mean he wields absolute power over you. Maybe in the old days, but things are different now."

Freya didn't agree, that was clear. If she'd left before Shifter Bureau had locked Graham's Lupines into their Shiftertown, she'd have no idea what Shifters had been forced to concede in order to survive. Even Graham had figured out that the old ways didn't work anymore.

Also, Eric wasn't a dickhead and would never give a scared female over to Graham against her will. Neither would Nell.

And even if they'd wanted to, Shane wouldn't let them.

There was a bright flash and a rush of air outside the front door, the wind chimes jangling. Freya jerked her head up. Next came silence, followed by a polite knock.

"Come on in, Reid," Shane called.

The door opened a crack, and Stuart Reid peered in, his unnerving dark eyes like windows to a starless night. "They're going. You two all right?"

"Yep," Shane told him. "We're good."

Reid, a tall, lean man with wiry strength, entered the house. His dark hair was mussed, his rangy form hugged by jeans and a windbreaker against the January breeze.

Freya went rigid, her nostrils flaring as she caught Reid's scent.

"Not Fae," Reid said immediately, in the tone of someone weary of explaining himself. "*Dokk alfar.* Long story."

Reid hated Fae more than Shifters did. They'd destroyed his home and family and banished him for centuries. He'd finally managed to get back to Faerie recently and, with the help of Peigi, had kicked some Fae ass, which he'd enjoyed.

"The mercenaries are gone," Reid told Shane. "Eric explained to them that your friend here was off limits, and that they weren't welcome in Shiftertown. They didn't argue. Just drove off." He sounded surprised.

"Their leader probably decided dealing with all of us wasn't worth the trouble," Shane said. "She seemed like a smart ice queen."

"I'm sorry, Shane," Freya said with sincerity. "I didn't mean to bring this to your doorstep." Some fire returned to her eyes. "Of course, if you hadn't followed me and then half-kidnapped me, they wouldn't know where you live now."

"Like hell I was letting them take you," Shane returned. "I got a bad feeling about them, and you did too."

"Yes." Freya's jaw tightened. "But I have a worse feeling now. You brought me to a *Shiftertown*."

Reid listened with interest. "I can see you two have a lot to discuss. Shane's right, though," he said to Freya. "Shiftertowns are safe places in which to hide from humans. Ironic, but true. Do you want Peigi to come over?" He directed the question to Shane.

"Peigi," Freya repeated. "Shane said she was another bear."

"She is," Reid answered. "And now my mate. She can assure you this is the best place to be, if you still have doubt."

"Oh, I have a lot of doubts," Freya stated with a nod of her head.

"Maybe later," Shane said to Reid. "She needs to meet my family first."

Reid gave him one of his fleeting smiles. "I get it. I'll leave you to it, then." He turned for the door.

"The *conventional* way," Shane said quickly.

Reid rarely laughed, but he chuckled now and walked out the door, closing it before he stepped off the porch and walked away. Shane heard his dry laughter recede along with his footsteps.

"He can teleport," Shane said once he was gone. "Really creepy when you first see it."

Freya's brows went up. "Is that what caused the microburst on the porch?"

"Yep. At least he was nice enough not to teleport directly into the living room. You might have peed yourself."

"I wouldn't have peed myself," Freya scoffed. "But speaking of that, can I use your bathroom?"

"Sure. First door on the right." Shane pointed down the

hall. "Don't bother trying to climb out the window. It's too small."

Freya rolled her eyes as she rose to her feet and strode down the hall in indignation. The bathroom door slammed behind her.

Shane didn't mind her derision. Better that than the absolute fear she'd exuded when he'd driven her into Shiftertown.

The pheromones in this house were calming—those of a loving mated pair and their fun-loving sons. Freya was relaxing, which meant she'd soon try to figure out a way to escape back to the wide world.

Not yet, Shane vowed. Not until he was sure Althea had no real interest in Freya, and that Graham wouldn't try to drag her back to him as soon as Freya set foot out of this house.

———

Shane was right about the bathroom window, Freya saw. The horizontal slot was narrow and small, the window more for ventilation than light. A cat might slither out of it, but not an adult woman or a Shifter wolf.

Freya washed her hands and splashed water on her face, then drew a deep breath as she regarded herself in the mirror. She was wild-eyed, her hair tangled, like her wolf's.

But her initial panic was ebbing. Shane truly believed he'd protect her from Graham, though Freya wasn't certain how much power he'd actually have against her pack leader—Graham had always seemed unstoppable.

At any other time, Freya would be touched by Shane's worry for her. It had been a long while since someone had wanted to take care of her. She and Rolf had always looked out for each other, but she'd had no one else to lean on.

She could hear the echo of her brother's voice, see the warmth of his eyes. *It's you and me, sis. Our own little pack against the world.*

However, there were many more Shifters in this town than Shane. There was Eric, their leader—presumably he'd been the tall Feline who'd come out to thwart Althea's goons. Plus, the blue-eyed bear called Cormac who'd kindly given her coffee. He seemed concerned, but he wasn't in charge here. Freya sensed that. He was a buffer zone, not a leader.

Then there was the very weird man who stank of Faerie but insisted he wasn't Fae. Who could teleport.

This day was getting crazier by the minute.

Freya dried her face and hands on a deeply soft towel, hung it up, and left the bathroom.

A cluster of voices rumbled in the living room. Freya halted at the end of the hall, but there was nowhere for her to run or hide. Both front and back doors of this house lay beyond the voices, and she didn't know which windows might open in the bedrooms behind her.

Drawing a resolute breath, she stepped once more into the living room.

Freya found herself facing four large bear Shifters in human form, all regarding her intently. Shane, the friendly Cormac, another who looked enough like Shane to be his brother, and a woman with a strong body and eyes that pierced Freya's defenses.

"Welcome to our home, Freya," the woman said, the deep timbre in her voice the female version of Shane's. "Now, tell us everything."

———

CHAPTER NINE

"Now I know how Goldilocks felt," Freya said, trying to joke. There was a mama bear and a papa bear, but the two baby bears were enormous, full-grown men.

Shane stepped forward, putting himself between Freya and the stares of the others. "Come and sit down, sweetie."

"I'd rather stand," Freya said quickly. Easier to take on the four of them if she wasn't sitting in a chair peering up at a circle of faces. Of course, they were all taller than she was, regardless. She already had to tilt her head back to look at them.

The woman moved past Shane. "I'm Nell, honey. I'm leader of all the bears in this Shiftertown, and no, Graham can't come in here and take you off my territory. Trust me, he doesn't want to go toe-to-toe with me."

"Or me," the brother, Brody, said. "Shane says we need to have your back, so we have your back."

Nell slid her hand through the crook of Freya's arm. "Brody's right. Let's have a seat and discuss this."

She led Freya into the living room and a long sofa. Freya

found herself powerless to resist, or maybe she simply didn't want to expend the energy. She'd save her strength to fight or flee later.

Nell sat, pulling Freya down next to her. Cormac disappeared into the kitchen and returned with a refill of her coffee. He handed the mug to Freya, then settled himself in the chair Freya had vacated. Brody took another chair, sitting on the cushion's edge. Shane remained standing, positioning himself near the door like a sentry.

Nell had deep brown eyes, like Shane's, which held both compassion and steel. Her thick hair was dark with lighter highlights, very much like Shane's, though Shane's was so short the effect wasn't as stark.

Cormac, in contrast, had dark hair and eyes of brilliant blue. Freya dimly wondered if he were a different kind of bear than Shane and his family, who were grizzlies.

"Shane tells me you are in Graham's pack," Nell said. She'd unlinked from Freya but remained very close to her, which was oddly comforting.

"Was," Freya corrected.

"Are still," Nell said. "You might run away, but you're still connected. Packs have a bond, just like bear clans do."

"I won't go back to him," Freya declared, her agitation rising. "I'm happy to leave you all and figure things out on my own again."

Nell gently squeezed her arm. "I don't blame you. But you're not leaving. Not yet. It's safer here."

Freya's moment of sharp fear dissipated at Nell's touch. The magic of an alpha, her wolf whispered.

"You didn't want to talk about it in the truck," Shane said. He had his hands behind his back, a formidable barrier to anyone who might try to enter the house—or to leave it. "But we need to know. You said Graham protected you from the Collars. What *didn't* he protect you from?"

Freya truly didn't like to speak of it. Rolf had understood— he'd never brought up the subject once they were free of Graham and on their own.

She'd been so young, just past her Transition, uncertain of herself and what she wanted. She'd been forced into a choice, which hadn't really been a choice. Young female orphaned wolves weren't supposed to disobey.

"A mate-claim." The words tumbled from Freya's mouth before she could stop them. But, what the hell? The wolf in question might be dead by now or have been relocated to another Shiftertown far away. "I told you, Shane, that when Graham's Shiftertown was being built, other packs were brought into the area, with Graham put in charge of them all. A Lupine from another pack mate-claimed me. I tried to turn it down, but no one was going to let me. His family set up the Sun and Moon ceremonies whether I liked it or not."

Nell's eyes went hard. "Graham did nothing?"

"He couldn't really." Freya had tried to be fair to Graham as she'd thought things through afterward, but it was difficult. "He was having a hell of a time keeping all the Lupines from killing one another. Lots of enemies now had to live together. My mate-claim was a minor concern. I knew I could never fight the Lupine who wanted me and win. So, I took off."

"What about your own family?" Nell asked in her firm but compassionate tone. "How are you related to Graham?"

Freya gulped a breath. "My father was Graham's cousin. He and Graham shared a grandfather. But my mother and father died when I was a cub. They never had enough to eat, and when my father was shot by hunters, he wasn't strong enough to fight to stay alive. My mother went into a decline once their mate bond was broken. She took me and my brother to Graham with the last of her strength, and that was it. Graham promised to look after us. We both would have been okay, eventually, if Shifter Bureau hadn't come."

Freya had gone over the story so many times, stuffing the pain and sorrow into words to explain her situation.

She hadn't told the tale to many, though. When pretending to be human, she greatly modified the details if she related the matter at all, but the emptiness was still there.

Waves of sympathy poured from her listeners, to her surprise. Also surprising was that she felt them so strongly that she sagged into the sofa. She wasn't used to such a rush of palpable emotions.

Shane's brows drew together. "Your brother. Is he here? Still with Graham?"

"No." Freya's throat tightened. "Rolf ran away with me. He couldn't stop the mate-claim, but he could help me escape from it. We took off and eventually ended up in the Bay Area, where we've stayed, in various parts of it, ever since. I'd never have made it, if not for him." Tears stung her eyes.

"Is he still in the Bay Area?" Cormac asked. "Waiting for you?"

Freya shook her head, tears threatening to fall. "He disappeared about a month ago. I've been searching for him ever since. I found Althea's card in his apartment, the only thing I'd never seen there before. It took me a hell of a long time to get in touch with her—she doesn't exactly advertise. I wanted to know if he'd gone to work for her, voluntarily or not. Or if she knew where he'd gone."

She swallowed a sob as she finished. Freya had pushed her frantic worry into the background, having wiped her past from her mind long ago, knowing it was the only way to move forward. Now, with these four bears regarding her in compassion, Freya felt something within her break.

She was going to melt to the floor and cry, become a blubbering mess on Shane's living room rug.

The couch sagged on Freya's other side, the bulk of Shane warming her. Without a word, he put his arms around her and pulled her close.

Freya didn't want to lean into him, but her body had other ideas. She closed her eyes as she sank into his warmth, some of her pain ebbing.

Women who didn't know much about Shifters spoke about them with excitement, saying they could arouse at a touch, were walking sexual dreams.

Shane's strength against Freya, even though his arms were tight around her, didn't shout that he wanted her in his bed right now. His touch brushed solace into her, caring, a need to protect. This was the part of Shifters humans didn't understand.

Freya wanted to turn to Shane, bury her face in his shoulder, let him brush her skin with gentle fingers. He *could* be gentle—she'd already experienced that, even though he was a fearsome fighter.

Something murmured to her that everything was all right now. Freya only had to surrender, to stop running, cease battling.

She didn't have confidence in the voice, as much as she yearned to. But it was tempting to snuggle into Shane's arms and let him chase all the bad things away.

"You'll have to talk to Graham," Nell said, edging reality through Shane's sheltering embrace. "He'll know you're here by now. But don't worry, honey. You won't face him alone. You might feel like Goldilocks, but these bears are taking care of you. Graham won't oppose me."

"Or me," Shane rumbled.

"He'll argue," Brody predicted, heaving himself out of the chair.

Shane shrugged, moving Freya in a wonderful way. "Let him."

"Are you feeling up to it?" Nell asked Freya. "You've had a fright this morning, and I don't just mean running into my son." She shot a grin at Shane. "You can rest and eat if you want. Drink something stronger than coffee if you need fortification. Shane, she'll have to take your room. *You* can sleep on the couch."

Shane's laughter vibrated beneath Freya. "I don't mind. My bed's big, Freya. You'll like it."

The hint was there that it was large enough for both of them. Brody coughed, stifling it with his hand over his mouth.

"Later, Shane," Nell said in exasperation. "Let the poor woman rest before you get all mate frenzied on her."

"I'm not getting all mate frenzied," Shane retorted. "I'm just trying to help."

"It's all right," Freya heard herself saying, amusement returning. "Doesn't bother me."

Shane tugged her closer. "No? Good."

"Because she's obviously already resisted you," Brody said. "You didn't come in here wrapped around each other, which means you struck out, Shane."

Shane lifted a pillow from the sofa and chucked it at his brother. Brody deftly caught it and threw it back at Shane who grabbed it out of the air just as easily.

The teasing and laughter lent Freya strength. She forced herself to sit up, leaving Shane's arms, which proved to be harder than she thought. "I might as well get it over with," she said with a sigh.

If she faced Graham before she could think about it too much, she might be able to keep her head up and not collapse into a trembling heap.

"Are you sure?" Nell asked quietly.

"Yes." Freya clenched her into fists. "Before I talk myself out of it."

Nell started to rise, but Cormac forestalled her. "I'll go."

The other three bears nodded as though he'd made a wise decision. Without a good-bye, Cormac headed through the kitchen and out the back door.

When it closed behind him, Freya shuddered and barely stopped herself calling him back. The die was cast.

"Still think you should eat something," Nell said.

Freya laughed nervously. "Bears. They think food will solve everything."

"It does solve everything." Shane remained close beside her, his strong leg against the length of hers. "You felt better when I fed you at the cabin."

"I hadn't eaten in a while." Freya touched Shane's large hand, intending to push him away, but she found herself stilling, seeing no reason to move.

"Tell you what," Brody said. "You and Graham have your talk, then we'll bring out the grills and fix a mess of burgers. It's time for lunch, right?"

"With berries?" Freya asked, attempting an innocent expression.

Shane winked at her. "She's catching on."

Before this wonderful lunch happened, Freya had to confront Graham, which made the cub she'd been howl in despair. She'd felt that despair when her mother had left them alone, she and Rolf clinging to each other in fear. Then dismay when the great gray wolf had taken them in, his gruff ways frightening to the little twin cubs.

It hadn't been all bad with Graham, Freya knew. As pack leader, his schedule meant babysitting had been left to other Lupines, including Graham's trackers and several females who had cubs of their own. None of them had had much extra time for Freya and Rolf, who had grown closer together, taking care of each other.

Freya's feelings about Graham had always been mixed. On the one hand, he'd been very protective of her and Rolf, coming down hard on those who thought they should be killed because they were too much bother.

On the other, he'd had a full plate already with keeping his half-feral pack together. There hadn't been time for hugs and small indulgences that most cubs had, little time for play. She and Rolf had been forced to grow up fast. *Stick with me, sis*, Rolf had said often to comfort her. *We'll be okay.*

Shane kept himself comfortably against her. Freya should shake him off, but she somehow didn't want to. Maybe thoughts of her bleak cubhood were making her revel in the warmth of Shane next to her, in the strength of his touch.

Sure, that could be it.

Freya's breath caught when she heard Graham and Cormac approach the house. It was difficult *not* to hear Graham, who spoke in the same loud and unchecked voice she remembered from her cubhood. She rose, Shane joining her instantly.

"This had better be good, Cormac," Graham was saying testily. "I'm busy. Have Lupines to discipline for trying to kick bear asses."

Cormac laughed, the sound making the air inside the house lighter. "Kick bare asses. Good pun, Graham."

"What the fuck are you talking about?"

Yep, that was Graham. He had a sense of humor—somewhere—but a person sometimes needed an itemized list to explain jokes to him.

A light, female voice responded. "You understand him, Graham. You're being obtuse on purpose."

"Shit. Now my mate is calling me obtuse, as if I know what *that* means."

"She means ..." another Lupine, this one much younger than Graham, tried to say.

"Dougal, put a sock in it. Cormac, you had better tell me what the fuck is so important—"

The kitchen door opened, and Cormac strode inside. A young woman with dark hair in a ponytail followed him.

Graham, twenty-five years older than when Freya had last seen him, but still formidable, hesitated on the doorstep. No Shifter would enter another's territory without express permission. Though Cormac had asked them to come over, this was Nell's house. Graham and the younger Lupine had to wait on her sufferance.

Graham peered past Cormac into the living room, and his gaze fell on Freya. Any irascible words died as his lips parted in shock.

Freya took a step toward the kitchen, Shane right beside her. "Graham." Her voice was cracked, uncertain. "It's me."

Graham launched himself inside, barreling past Nell and Brody as he rocketed straight at Freya.

Shane was there like a barrier, but Graham whipped around him with Lupine speed. He grabbed Freya before

Shane could stop him and spun her from her feet, crushing her in a suffocating hug.

"Freya McHugh." The voice in her ear was hoarse with emotion. "My little cub, you're all right. Thank the Goddess, you're all right."

CHAPTER TEN

Emotions tumbled through Shane as Graham enclosed Freya in a fierce but relieved embrace.

Graham had been that worried about her, had he? The Lupine leader had never mentioned Freya or her brother, or any missing wolf for that matter. Now Graham pulled Freya in like a long-lost daughter, his eyes squeezed shut as though he fought tears.

Shane admitted that not speaking of Freya had been a good way to protect her. If Shifter Bureau ever realized Graham's pack was two members short, not only would they give Graham a ton of grief, but they'd tear the world apart trying to locate and possibly destroy Freya and her brother for simply existing.

Freya's hands had half lifted behind Graham's back when he'd grabbed her, and they froze there, as though she was uncertain whether to hug him in return. As the embrace went on, she eventually relaxed and rested her hands on his broad back.

Graham been the only father figure she'd really known, Shane realized. Goddess, how traumatic *that* must have been.

After a long time, the bears watching in silence, Graham eased from Freya. He rested his big hands on her shoulders, his fingers shaking.

"After so many years," he said, voice thick with tears. "You're all right Freya-cub."

"Not a cub anymore," Freya answered softly.

"You always will be to me." Graham abruptly released her, his habitual scowl creasing his face. "You were in the area, and you didn't bother sending me word?" His gruffness returned full force, Graham embarrassed he'd been caught being sentimental.

Freya's defiance flared. "I didn't know until recently that you were in Las Vegas. I thought the pack was still in Elko."

"Long story," Graham rumbled. "You wouldn't have sent word even if you'd known exactly where I was, would you?"

"To be honest? No." Freya folded her arms, her scowl starting to match Graham's. "Can you blame me?"

Graham rounded on Shane. "The minute you had her, you should have called me."

It was always difficult to meet Graham's gaze—the man knew how to turn on the dominant wolf. In fact, Graham rarely shut it off.

This time, Shane stared straight at him. He was mildly surprised he could do it.

"I don't work for you," Shane stated. "And it didn't occur to me that Freya was in your pack. No resemblance, no scent marker. She didn't tell me she knew you at all until we were almost to Shiftertown."

"*Any* Lupine should be brought straight to me," Graham snarled.

"Back to the part where I don't work for you," Shane said.

"The hell—" Graham began but was cut off by a gentle voice behind him.

"And Graham is very grateful to you, Shane, for keeping her safe," Misty said. "Isn't he?"

Misty was not very tall, the slightness of her frame emphasized by the giant bear Shifters and big Lupines around her. Misty, however, had a power all her own. Graham, unbelievably, snapped his mouth closed and subsided at her interruption.

Misty turned to Freya. "Don't worry, sweetie. There's plenty of room in our house for you until we get this sorted out. That is, if you don't object to a few unruly cubs."

She referred to two little wolves, Kyle and Matt, who were adorable but willful little shits. Nell sometimes babysat them, and only she and Misty could keep them in line. They didn't listen to Shane or Brody, or even Cormac for that matter, and they sure as hell didn't listen to Graham.

"Nope," Shane said before Freya could speak. "We've already decided. She's staying here."

Graham's temper blazed again. "You don't make decisions about one of my pack."

"As Freya said, she's not a cub anymore." Shane folded his arms and glared back at Graham. "She doesn't have to obey you. We don't roll that way in this Shiftertown."

Graham opened his mouth to roar his opinion of Shane's assessment, but Freya stepped in front of him.

"I'm going to take Nell's offer of hospitality," she declared quietly. "At least until I figure out what I want to do."

"There's no way a bunch of bears can protect you like I can. I'm your *pack leader*," Graham roared.

"How's Leo?" Freya asked, her tone too casual. "Did he move to this Shiftertown too?"

Graham, red in the face, spluttered. "Yes. He's—he's still a shithead."

"Mated?"

"No."

"That's why I am going to stay with Nell." Freya closed her mouth in finality.

Nell grinned. "Fine by me. You lose, Graham."

Shane went rigid at the mention of Leo's name. Leo Dunham was the asshole who'd led the rebellious wolves this morning. It just figured he'd done something scummy like mate-claiming Freya, which had sent her fleeing.

Any questions now would make the tension in this room worse, so Shane kept silent. Freya's face was tight with bad memories, and Graham looked about to explode. Questions would come, but they'd have to come later.

"Freya stays on our territory," Shane said firmly. "Until she decides otherwise."

Graham had the toughest stare of any Lupine he had ever met, but Shane stood still and took it.

"I won't let anything happen to her," Shane said.

"Neither will we," Nell joined in. "You just keep Leo away from her."

Graham turned to Freya with a growl. "It's his right to know why you refused the mate-claim."

"Bullshit," Shane burst out. "Freya was so repulsed by this guy that she took off on her own, knowing you couldn't stop him. The last thing she needs is to see him again."

"Shane," Nell said in a matter-of-fact tone. "That's actually true. By Shifter law, the one denied the claim can ask why."

Fuck Shifter law, Shane wanted to shout. He held on to his temper with effort. "Maybe, but does it have to be right now? We were chased down Mount Charleston by pissed-off mercenaries into a Shiftertown where Freya did *not* want to go. At least let her have lunch and a nap."

Graham scowled again. "It's whenever Leo wants it to be. His choice. I can't do anything about that. If Freya still refuses the claim, then he leaves her alone forever. That's also Shifter law."

"Don't tell him for a while then," Shane suggested.

Brody huffed. "With Shiftertown gossip the way it is, he probably already knows."

As though Brody's words were prophetic, a quiet knock sounded on the kitchen door.

The sound was too genial to come from an irate wolf demanding entrance. Shane recognized Eric's touch. He always approached Nell's territory cautiously and with respect, which was one reason Nell conceded to his overall Shiftertown leadership. She hadn't yet conceded to Graham's.

Cormac, the most neutral party in this room, opened the door.

Eric stood on the doorstep, calm expression in place, as though he'd come over to borrow a cup of sugar. Leo hovered, enraged, behind him.

"Come for another ass-kicking?" Shane couldn't stop himself from asking him.

Nell stood next to Cormac, the two forming a barrier. No one would get through that back door and into the house.

The chill of Freya's fear rushed to Shane, but she didn't shrink away or run—she stood resolutely, skewering Leo with a stare worthy of Graham.

"I came for my mate," Leo snapped. He was as unkempt as he had been earlier that day. Did these Lupines ever shower?

"This morning you were complaining because Eric wouldn't let you have the pick of females in this town," Shane reminded him. "Eric had to tranq you to shut you up."

"That was before I knew my own mate was in town."

"She refused the mate-claim," Brody broke in. "Means she's not yours. Never was."

"Sure, by the new rules." Leo spat on the ground—making sure the spittle landed a long way from the doorstep, Shane noted. "By the old rules, she was mine when I claimed her."

Eric spoke in his mild tones. "The old ways are done, my friend. The new rules prevail in this Shiftertown."

"I claimed her under the old rules, and they stand." Leo peered around the bears to Freya. "Come on," he said to her.

Shane watched Freya's fear vanish in a slap of outrage. "Is anyone going to let *me* speak?"

Nell turned to her, eyes holding sympathy. "You're right, honey. This is your call, and yours alone."

"Not here," Leo snarled. "She comes to Graham's territory, and we have this out."

"No." Freya stood firm. "Here's the deal, Graham. I'll talk to Leo and tell him why I refused his claim—which I still do, by the way— on one condition."

Graham regarded her in some surprise but gave her a nod. "Let's hear it."

"You help me figure out exactly what happened to Rolf. He's gone, and you're going to do everything you can to assist me to find him."

———

Freya waited breathlessly while Graham regarded her in shock. "What do you mean he's gone?" Graham demanded. "Gone where?"

"That's what we need to find out." Freya left Graham working through what she'd just told him and turned to Leo.

Shane remained at her side, a warm and solid bulwark against the onslaught. Freya drew courage from his strength, and also from the sudden wave of *fuck this shit* that had washed through her when Leo had commanded her to obey him.

Leo hadn't changed at all—he was still a scruffy wolf with hard muscles and a mean look in his eyes. When Leo and his pack had joined the group, he'd tried to rally those in Graham's pack to his side, had thought he should be leader of the new Shiftertown. Only someone like Graham could keep Leo in line.

Freya had expected to still be terrified of Leo, even after all these years. She was wary, yes—Leo was not a kind person, and he expected anyone less dominant than him to submit totally to his will.

When Freya had come out of her Transition, she'd been scared and unsure of her place in the pecking order. Leo had tried to take advantage of her uncertainty.

However, the moment Leo had mouthed his imperious *Come on*, Freya had realized with a jolt that the order had changed. Leo was no longer dominant to her. That comprehension made the wolf inside her howl with glee.

Not only subordinate to Freya, but *very* subordinate. Freya's wolf knew without a doubt that she could crush Leo underfoot with little effort.

She couldn't relax, though, not entirely. Leo was only a stickler for hierarchy rules when he agreed with them.

"Please get out of my sight," Freya said clearly to Leo and then switched her focus to Graham. "This is my statement to my pack leader. I reject Leo Dunham's mate-claim, under the light of the sun, the Father God, and before witnesses."

"You don't know what you're talking about," Leo snarled at her. "We need mates, you're fair game, and I staked my claim on you long ago."

"She's not a piece of property." Shane's rumble had deepened, a bear who was at the end of his patience. "She rejected the claim. Too bad, so sad for you. Seek a mate somewhere else."

"So you can shag her?" Leo demanded. "Is that what this is all about?"

"No." Freya kept her chin up. Any interest she'd had in Shane and his very attractive body wasn't the point here. "I don't want to be your mate, all right?"

Leo's eyes narrowed. "Fucking bear has twisted your head around." He pinned Shane with a hard gray gaze. "Fine, then. Shane the Stupid Bear, under the light of the Father God and before witnesses, *I Challenge*."

CHAPTER ELEVEN

The Shifters went still, even Graham falling silent. Freya stared at Leo in surprise—he had to be out of his mind. Leo had once been a good fighter, and Freya didn't see any sign of him weakening, but she'd had a taste of what Shane could do when provoked.

There was no reason for Leo to Challenge. Freya had already said no, and she didn't belong to Shane either. This was Leo's egotistical way of proving he was still in control—of his life, of his place, of Freya.

Shane's laughter boomed into the sudden quiet.

"Are you serious?" Shane's dark eyes danced. "I already beat your ass once this morning. You'll never survive a Challenge against me."

Leo didn't lose his belligerent confidence. Freya saw cunning in Leo's eyes, which worried her. In a fair fight, Shane could best him, but the Leo she remembered had fought dirty. Freya doubted that twenty-five years had changed him.

"You didn't beat me," Leo said to Shane. "Eric tranqued

me and took me out of the fight." He glowered at Eric, who ignored him.

Freya recognized that Eric, the relaxed man in distressed jeans and a black T-shirt, tousled dark hair and green eyes, held all the power in this room. Even Graham, as blustery as he was, did not have as much dominance as Eric. Close, but not quite.

Eric could stop Leo's threat with a word or even a flick of an eyebrow. He didn't. He was watching the conflict play out, as though he'd decided that Graham's pack and Nell's family needed to make their own decisions.

Only a Shifter confident of his power would do that. Eric knew that no matter what happened, he'd have it all under control in the long run.

"You need to answer, Shane," Graham stated.

"No," Freya said quickly to Shane. "Don't."

Shane shrugged. "I can take him, sweetheart. Don't worry."

"It isn't that." Freya drew herself up. "I refused his mate-claim. That should be enough. Leo winning a fight won't change my mind."

"She's right," Nell put in.

Leo bristled. "I'll beat him down just because I don't like him, then."

"Answer the Challenge, Shane." Graham's growl was low. "If you don't, I'll never hear the end of it."

"We have three leaders here," Nell pointed out. "What do we say? Follow the rules? Or, I can take Leo somewhere and soak his head until he cools off." Her toothy smile told Freya she'd enjoy every minute of that.

Eric finally spoke. "We follow the rules. A Challenge has

been issued. Freya has said the outcome won't influence her choice, but an unmet Challenge is a powder keg waiting to go off."

He didn't bother raising his voice. Nell and Graham nodded without argument, taking Eric's word as final.

Shane flexed his fingers. "I accept. Happy to. As the Challenged, I pick the venue. Fight club?"

"Done." Leo gave Shane a steady look. "Make your peace with the Goddess, bear."

Freya appealed to Nell. "Stop this. Please."

Nell regarded her with understanding. "No one fights to the death anymore, honey. First rule of the fight club. Graham and Eric are right, though. The outcome of the fight will settle the tension between Shane and Leo, so it goes ahead. This is about more than you."

Freya sensed that. She also saw in Leo's eyes that he was determined to win, no matter what he had to do to gain a victory.

"Freya." Graham's rumble broke her thoughts. "Walk with me."

He turned and made his way out through the kitchen. Any Shifter in his way moved aside for him, including Leo, but Shane leaned to murmur into Freya's ear.

"You don't have to obey him anymore."

A tingle traveled down Freya's spine. Shane's breath was warm, his words, soothing. He was the only one in this room who seemed to perceive how hard this reunion was for her.

"It's all right, I want to talk to him," Freya answered. "To ask him a thing or two."

"Okay, but I'm going with you."

Freya warmed still more. "I don't think that's what he has in mind."

"Tough." Shane put a large hand on her shoulder. "The least I can do for a Lupine who attacked me out of the blue is to protect her from Graham."

Freya for some reason wanted to laugh. "Fine, but if he gives you trouble, it's your own fault."

Shane shrugged. "I'll take the chance."

He steered her through the kitchen, following Graham's path. Leo, predictably, made a move toward Freya, but Eric all of a sudden was in his way.

They exited through the back door, Shane's hand still on her shoulder. Graham waited in the middle of the yard, his eyes narrowing when he saw Shane.

"I meant I wanted to talk to her alone," Graham said.

"You want her, you get me," Shane returned. "Live with it."

Graham rumbled a growl, but to Freya's surprise, he didn't argue. Without further objection, he turned and started off along the common area behind the houses.

Freya followed. Shane, no longer guiding her, strode right behind her.

Graham led them all the way down the common until he'd passed the last house and a cinder block wall that separated it from the desert beyond. Not far past that was the chain-link fence that marked the boundary of Shiftertown. A clump of olive trees that had been planted here, leaves dark green on spreading branches, hid them from any passing Shifter.

Beyond the fence, a swath of desert reached toward the mountains where Freya had recently had her aborted meeting with Althea.

Graham gazed in silence into the desert. A new development was spreading a few miles away, bare stud walls rising against the blue of the late morning sky.

Would people buy homes that close to Shiftertown? Or were humans growing so used to Shifters that they thought nothing of living near them?

After a moment, Graham turned abruptly. His face had lost its belligerent creases, and Freya saw, to her astonishment, that his eyes were moist.

"Freya." Graham lifted his hands as though he wanted to reach for her but balled his fists and held them back. "I thought I'd lost you, little cub."

He'd called her "little cub" since he'd opened the door of his ramshackle house outside Elko and found her and Rolf on the threshold. *What am I going to do with you, little cubs?* He sometimes said it with fond exasperation, sometimes roaring in frustration.

Freya tightened. "I had to leave. Leo wasn't taking no for an answer."

"I know." Graham sounded tired, defeated. "I was glad you ran. But it was hard not to come after you."

Freya recalled the frantic fear of the night they'd crept away, trying not to wake Graham or whatever Lupines might be passed out in his living room any given day. Graham's ferocity attracted those who wanted his protection—they'd hang out at his house rather than face the more aggressive Lupines waiting to be put into a Shiftertown.

She'd wilted in relief when she and Rolf had made it to open country outside the roundup area in Elko. They'd had to dodge Shifter Bureau patrols and local law enforcement, all the while fearing that a pack of wolves would soon be on their trail.

"You *wanted* me to go?" Freya asked in shock.

"It was the only way. I might have had to kill Leo to keep him off of you. Those in the other packs—hell, in my *own* pack

—might have used it as an excuse to turn against me. I told my cop friends to make sure you got through without Shifter Bureau finding out."

"Seriously, you let them go alone?" Shane demanded in anger. "Two cubs barely past their Transitions, wandering in the human world by themselves?"

"They weren't alone." Graham's usual aggressive self returned. "I had friends and acquaintances all over northern Nevada and California looking out for them. Why do you think you found somewhere to live so quickly?" he asked Freya.

Freya recalled the kind middle-aged woman who'd given them a ride as they'd hurried along the side of the highway. She'd been to Elko to see her grandchildren, she'd said, and was happy to drive Freya and Rolf as far as Reno. She even suggested that one of the hotels was hiring and paid somewhat decently.

Not a coincidence then. Both Freya and Rolf had been hired by the hotel restaurant's manager, no questions asked, which had given them a place to start.

Freya breathed out. "I didn't know. I wish I had."

"I wasn't going to let anything happen to my little cubs," Graham said, voice gentler than Freya had ever heard it.

"Damn." Shane's tone held reluctant admiration. "Never knew you had actual compassion, Graham. You hide it so well."

"Don't spread it around." Graham's famous scowl returned. "The minute my Lupines think I'm soft is the minute all hell breaks loose."

"I get it." Shane nodded in all seriousness. "Your secret is safe with me."

"Good."

"Why didn't you tell me?" Freya rubbed her arms against a sudden chill breeze. The clouds that had gathered hadn't yet released their rain, but the wind was cold and damp. "I was as much afraid of you as I was of Leo."

"Same reason I'm not telling them now," Graham answered. "Most of the packs were against me being made Shiftertown leader, as you know. If they'd found out where you were, they might have used you to get to me. I couldn't risk it." He quieted. "I'm so sorry, little cub."

Freya nodded, her throat tightening. "I understand." She'd seen how his own pack had been a handful, and they had already accepted Graham's leadership. "I do, in my head. The young wolf I was is going to take longer to come to terms with it."

"I know." Graham sounded regretful. "I've been keeping an eye on you all these years, or trying to at least. But you're saying Rolf disappeared? What the hell happened?"

"I don't know." Freya's frustrated fears pushed their way forward again. "He'd recently started a job at a software development company in Mountain View, testing code or something. He didn't show up to work about a month ago. They called me, asking if he was sick or hurt, and I had to tell them I hadn't seen him."

The few human twins she'd met had told her that sometimes they could sense when each other was hurt or in trouble, even if they lived on opposite sides of the country. She had the same with Rolf, but much stronger. She'd known in the back of her mind, even before his team leader at work had called her, that something was wrong.

Once when she and Rolf had been cubs, playing hide and seek in the vast lands outside Graham's ranch house, Rolf had vanished. Freya had known instinctively he hadn't simply been hiding. She'd searched long and hard, the evening becoming night, until she'd heard his cry from far, far away. Not out loud, she'd realized after calling for him a few frantic moments. Inside her head.

She remembered vividly how she'd run through the scrub and gravel toward the voice, finally finding a hole in the ground. An old mine shaft, she'd learned later, into which Rolf had fallen when he'd gone to hide.

It had been far too deep for her to navigate herself. Freya had returned to the ranch and tearfully confessed to Graham what had happened.

Graham hadn't bellowed at her, as she'd expected. He'd fetched rope, grappling hooks, and Chisholm, his second, and followed her back into the wilderness. Freya had pinpointed Rolf's position exactly, and Graham had climbed down into the shaft to lift him out and carry him home.

Graham had saved his yelling for the next morning, commanding her and Rolf to never go beyond a certain perimeter around the house without him—*ever*.

Freya took a breath, throwing off her memories, and continued. "He'd moved to a new apartment there—Mountain View is south of San Francisco, near Palo Alto, and I've been living in Golden Gate Heights. I like the park nearby." Freya paused with a wistful smile. She'd also been close to the recreational area on the coast, where she'd been able to go wolf and run at night. "We always do something together on the weekends, but that weekend we hadn't. I thought maybe Rolf had met someone—he didn't say that, but he dropped hints that his life was going to change. I was excited for him and kept expecting him to call and tell me about it. He never did."

Freya's heart felt hollow. She had no sense that Rolf was dead and gone but on the other hand, he simply wasn't there anymore. It was as though part of herself had vanished, and she wasn't certain she could breathe without it. "Do you think Shifter Bureau found him?" She voiced one of her greatest fears.

"No," Graham said without hesitation. "I'd have been notified if they had—and probably interrogated. Or the information would have showed up in the Guardian Network. That means Neal—the Guardian here—would have known about it, and he'd have told me."

"The Guardian Network?" Freya asked.

Shane answered before Graham could. "A mojo-magic database that all Guardians can access. It has information on every Shifter everywhere and knows more about us than Shifter Bureau ever could. It's kinda creepy."

Graham nodded in agreement. "The Guardians know that you and Rolf were once in my custody. If Rolf had been taken by Shifter Bureau, Neal would find out."

Guardians—the Shifters whose swords ushered Shifter souls into the afterlife—could be cryptic and enigmatic. Some were downright odd. But also, they could be very kind. The Guardian of Graham's pack had been three hundred years old and hadn't minded two new cubs crawling over him and asking him questions. He'd finally died before she and Rolf had gone, but she didn't know who the next Guardian had been.

Shane was behind her again, keeping the cold breeze at bay, like a bastion against everything bad.

Dangerous to think of him that way. Freya couldn't stay in this Shiftertown—even if she didn't fear discovery by Shifter Bureau, she wanted to continue her search for Rolf. The thought of leaving Shane behind, though, of never seeing him again, sliced sudden pain through her heart.

She turned from Graham to find Shane's dark eyes on her, something questioning in their depths.

Shane bulked larger than Graham, who'd always been a tower of might to Freya as a cub. Graham was an alpha—an in-your-face, never-forget-I'm-dominant alpha. But now, with Shane holding Freya's gaze, Graham faded into the background.

The corners of Shane's mouth twitched, as though he guessed the direction of her thoughts.

Freya forced her attention back to Graham. "I need to find my brother."

"I agree," Graham said. "We'll put our best trackers on it. We'll find out what happened, don't worry."

His reassurance didn't put Freya's mind at ease. Graham had always declared he'd fix everything, and as a cub Freya had believed him.

After she'd passed her Transition, becoming an adult in Shifter terms, she'd realized that while Graham could often solve a problem by threatening it, sometimes he couldn't. Freya's naivety had fallen once Shiftertowns had loomed, plus her life with humans had taught her much about reality. Sometimes bad things couldn't be banished.

"He means *all* the trackers," Shane told her. "His, Eric's, Mom's. Your brother won't stay lost for long."

Freya wanted to let them ease her fears, but she was too wise to real life. Her only comfort from the beginning was that if Rolf had been in an accident or hurt somehow, the police or a hospital would have called her. They'd both listed each other as their emergency contact. But she'd heard nothing. The void was very hard to take.

"I'm just glad I found you, little cub," Graham said, voice softening. "Or, you found me."

The super-strong Graham, who'd guarded her and Rolf from the outside world as well as his own Lupines, now looked haggard. Leadership of half-feral Shifters had taken its toll. Graham had worked hard to keep his wolves safe, and even now, he couldn't rest.

Freya went to him, unable to stop herself. He was the only father she'd truly known, and she wanted to comfort him. Graham gathered her into his strong embrace.

He'd been like this when she was a cub—a barrier between her and the night. Graham had been frightening, but he'd scared off all the bad things from Freya and Rolf too.

Freya sensed Shane step close to them, his protective watchfulness coming in waves.

Graham simply held Freya in a fatherly hug. The wolf cub in her felt his paternal relief that she was all right. Maybe the passing years and having a mate had softened Graham, or maybe he'd always been this caring, and Freya had been too young to understand that.

Shane was even closer to them by the time Graham released her. He pretended to ignore Shane as he squeezed Freya's shoulders.

"Come on, little cub." Graham's voice was gruff with emotion. "Let's go home."

It's not my home, Freya wanted to say, but she'd fight that battle when had to.

Graham kept his hand on Freya's shoulder to lead her back along the line of houses. Shane walked tight against Freya's other side.

A crowd of Lupines had gathered near Shane's house, with Nell, Cormac, and Brody holding them at bay. Misty was talking to the wolves, gesticulating as though trying to reassure them.

Eric stood on the edge of the group, hands resting on his narrow hips, like a referee waiting to break up any ensuing fight.

Graham peeled himself from Freya and strode forward, his voice already ringing. "What the hell?"

The wolves gave way before him, but they didn't disperse.

Shane stuck close to Freya. "I won't let them hurt you, trust me," he said rapidly, as though he expected Freya to panic. "Neither will my family."

"You're not Lupine." Packs didn't like outsiders interfering with their business. They must really *hate* having Shifters from other species telling them what to do.

"Doesn't matter," Shane said. "Shiftertown dynamics are a little bit different. Graham's wolves need to learn that."

As they neared the growling Lupines, Graham's shout came clearly to them. "The fuck you tell me my decisions."

Leo had decided to confront Graham, though he couldn't quite look Graham in the eye. "It's pack law." He jerked a thumb at the gathered wolves. "I say the mate-claim is good. If she turns it down, then you need to declare her fair game for everyone else. We need mates—you know we do. And cubs."

Freya heated with anger, the dominance she'd felt when she'd defied Leo flaring again. Once upon a time, a female who was declared fair game could be claimed by anyone in the pack, sometimes several at a time. She would be expected to bear cubs with different fathers for the good of the gene pool. That had been before females had decided that they'd had enough of being used as incubators at asshole males' pleasure and rebelled.

Shane stood solidly in front of Freya. "This isn't the wild, dickhead," he told Leo. "We're not half-feral, scratching for a living in the desert."

"Doesn't matter." Leo's eyes bore the red tinge of an enraged wolf—one who was still working off a dose of tranq. "We've been penned up here against our will. The only way we'll tolerate it is if we get to have mates. She's one of us." He thrust a forefinger at Freya. "The mate-claim stands. Or else."

Graham towered over him. "Don't you ever give me an ultimatum, scumbag. I'm your leader, and my decisions are final."

While Leo flinched under Graham's admonishment, his stance retained defiance. He'd push for the claim, Freya realized in dismay, and if he won enough support among the Lupines, Graham would be hard-pressed to keep control. Even Eric, who watched with a calm that belied his power, couldn't stand against frenzied Shifters.

The best thing Freya could do was get out of here. She was good at slipping away unnoticed, fleeing before anyone realized she'd gone. Maybe she'd contact Althea again, apologize for the screwup, and see if she could get near the woman to continue her quest to find Rolf.

She could even take a job with Althea herself and hide behind hardened mercenaries with weapons for a while. Of course, she'd have to deal with the creepy Feline called Ewan, but there was only one of him versus the fifty-plus Lupines in this Shiftertown.

Shane ruined Freya's plans for vanishing by drawing her to his side and planting his arm around her waist.

"Before you start a rebellion, Lupine, I'm going to put an end to all of this." Shane's hold tightened on Freya as the wolves, including Graham, turned to him in annoyance.

Shane let his voice ring out. "Freya McHugh, under the

light of the Father God and before witnesses, I claim you as mate!"

Freya rocked on her heels, her breath deserting her. She instantly opened her mouth to tell Shane he was crazy, but all that escaped her throat was a dry wheeze.

Shane grinned down at her then at the stunned crowd. "I bet you all saw that coming. Am I right?"

CHAPTER TWELVE

No one moved, no one spoke. Shane's family, the Lupines, and Graham all regarded Shane in shock, but he didn't know why they should be surprised.

As soon as he'd said the words, something inside him clicked. This was *right*.

Freya faltered under his touch, as though she might crumple to the ground, but a quick glance showed him that she was in no danger at all of passing out. Freya glared up at Shane, her golden wolf eyes sparkling in fury.

Well, why shouldn't Shane mate-claim her? The Goddess looked out for Shifters, even in their captivity, plus all the shit that had happened to them over the centuries. She made sure they found their true mates, formed mate bonds, and everything else. Right?

Freya's scent with its gingery bite slipped through him, as though the wolf in her reached to the bear inside Shane. Freya the human might want to rip him apart, but Freya's wolf responded with a tiny flare of mating frenzy. If wolves purred, Freya's would be doing it.

At the edge of his awareness, Shane heard Leo spluttering. "He can't ... Not right ..."

"Shut it," Graham said. "He can do what he wants, even if he's a fucking bear."

Shane quieted, directing his words to Freya alone. "You don't have to answer now."

"Oh, you're letting me have a choice?" Freya widened her eyes. "How nice of you."

"Seriously." Shane gently squeezed her shoulder. "Take your time. In the meantime, my claim keeps everyone off your back."

Freya wriggled out from under his hand. "You mean everyone except *you*."

Shane couldn't stop his grin. "I'll try to restrain myself."

It would be hard, he already knew. Mate frenzy bubbled up inside him, the primal call to take his lady into his arms and let them both go crazy. The instinctive need to reproduce, released as soon as the mate-claim was made and accepted, pounded through him with brutal suddenness.

But he'd leave her alone. Leo had driven her away with his mate-claim, and Shane wasn't like that asshole.

Freya studied Graham, Leo, and the angry Lupines behind them with her head up, her mouth set in a firm line. She turned to survey Shane's family, who'd spread out in a defensive formation between the wolves and Freya.

Waves of her frustration, fear, and anger slapped at Shane, but Freya was resilient. She drew herself up and faced him.

"All right," she said firmly. "I'll take your offer of sanctuary while I think about your mate-claim."

Shane acknowledged a bite of disappointment that she didn't accept right away. His intent had been to give her space to be safe and decide what she would do, without Graham,

Leo, or even his own family messing with her. The fact that the mate-claim got his bear excited was just a side effect. Right?

Freya's tone brooked no argument. Leo started to object anyway, but Graham turned around and decked him on the jaw.

"You had your chance," Graham growled as Leo rubbed his face. "Now shut up and go home."

Leo snarled, but Graham had pulled that punch. Leo would have been on the ground, unconscious, otherwise.

Leo shot Shane a vicious look. Shane expected him to say something like *This isn't over,* but Leo turned and marched away in silence, pretending it was his choice to go.

About half the Lupines fell into step with him. The others lingered, probably deciding that continuing to support Leo was no longer worth it.

Good. Maybe the pack would pound sense into the idiot, and Eric wouldn't have to send Shane and other trackers to intervene again.

Nell somehow managed to draw Freya from Shane. "Come on, sweetheart. Let's go inside. I'm getting tired of all this testosterone."

Freya's defiance lightened under Nell's touch. Shane's mom knew how to give aid without condescension.

Shane had to let them go. Of course, he would—Freya needed peace and quiet, not Shane hovering over her badgering her to accept his mate-claim. He'd give her all the space she needed. *Wouldn't he?* he directed at his bear.

The bear in him growled in sullen response.

"Shane." Eric gave Shane a minute tilt of his head. He wanted a word.

Shane watched Nell guide Freya into the house. Did Freya

glance back longingly at Shane? Thank him with her beautiful eyes for his intervention?

No, she did not. She strode next to Nell and through the kitchen door without so much as acknowledging Shane's existence.

Misty went to Graham and wrapped her hands around his flame-tattooed bicep. It was almost comical how rapidly Graham unwound when he looked down at her. The man was stupidly in love with his mate, the lucky bastard.

Shane ignored Brody's knowing grin as well as Cormac's understanding one and joined Eric.

"Yeah, boss?" Shane kept up a light tone. Never admit he was serious about that mate-claim, nope, not Shane.

Instead of answering, Eric started off in his nonchalant amble toward his own house, and Shane could only follow.

He hoped no one else was home at Eric's. It would be easier to explain his motives without a bunch of Felines watching him with wide-eyed interest.

No such luck. As soon as Eric opened the door, Shane saw them all waiting inside. No one had done anything as blatant as stare out the window, but Shane knew the entire Warden family was very aware of what had just transpired.

Iona, Eric's mate, with dark hair and light blue eyes, sat cross-legged on the couch, their cub, Callum, on her lap. Callum, at two, had his mother's eyes and black hair and his father's unruffled demeanor.

Iona was a panther, a black leopard, while Eric's Feline form was snow leopard. Callum could already shift into the cutest coal-black cub the world ever saw. They'd all been surprised he'd done it so soon, since he had some human blood, but Shifter cubs were unpredictable. At the moment, Callum's pudgy limbs were human shaped, while he watched Shane with cool blue eyes.

Next to them on the couch was a small girl, Amanda, who had Cassidy's face and Diego's eyes. She waved a happy hello to Shane, and he fist-bumped her in return.

"Good thinking, Shane." Iona exuded warm approval. "Was that my sweatshirt your new mate is wearing?"

"Yeah." Shane felt himself blushing for no reason. "I told her to borrow something from the closet at the cabin. Her own clothes were filthy. And she's not my new mate. Not yet."

Iona's smile held wisdom. "Give her time. *I* sure needed it."

"Yeah, I remember," Shane said with a touch of amusement. Iona had resisted Eric with all her strength.

Eric bent to give Iona a lingering kiss that revealed his love for her more than words. He rubbed the top of Amanda's head, gave Callum's a gentle kiss, and continued into the kitchen.

He expected Shane to follow him. Shane gave Iona a pained look and did so, ignoring Iona's chuckle.

Cassidy and Diego waited for them at the kitchen table. The remains of a vast breakfast were spread around them—Diego was a hell of a cook, and the Warden family let him have mastery in the kitchen.

Once upon a time, Shane had hoped that the tall, green-eyed Cassidy would indicate she'd accept a mate-claim from him. But Cassidy had never encouraged him, and Shane had resigned himself long ago that they'd be friends only. When Diego had come onto the scene, Shane had known he no longer stood a chance.

Diego and Cassidy had obviously shared the mate bond from the start. Shane had given them his blessing and let

Cassidy go in his heart. He'd grown to like Diego, who was smart, canny, resourceful, and an all-around decent guy.

"Diego," Eric said, bypassing any questions the eager couple might throw out about Shane's mate-claim. "I need to know everything I can about a private security company run by a woman named Althea Webster. Shane will fill you in on the details."

Instead of bristling at Eric's abrupt order, Diego looked interested. "I think I've heard of her. What do you know, Shane? I can have Xav do some searching." Xavier, Diego's younger brother and his partner in DX Security, was good at coaxing info out of the vast information network.

Eric asks, we all jump to obey. Shane had never resented that before, but today, he chafed with impatience. He wanted to rush home, to make sure Freya was all right and that she didn't hate him too much.

"Not a lot," Shane answered with outward calm. "Freya might have more information about her, but probably not much. Althea has a Shifter in her ranks, a Feline called Ewan. No Collar. The Guardian Network can probably tell you about him."

Diego made a few notes on his tablet, which was never far from his hand. "Anything will be helpful. Knowing Xav, he already has a dossier on Ms. Webster's company. He likes keeping tabs on our competition."

Shane helped himself to a cup of coffee from the half full pot, pretending he was at his ease. His nerves grated and jangled, which cooling coffee would not help, but he took a sip and tried to appear as his usual affable self.

Diego listened thoughtfully as Shane described what he'd seen of Althea's crew. In spite of his current agitation, Shane didn't leave out a single point, even if it seemed insignificant. A tracker provided all the intel he could so his leader could make decisions and do his job.

"Interesting," Diego said when Shane finished. "I have to wonder about Ms. Webster's goal. To provide competent teams for her clients? To make a shitload of money? To achieve world domination?"

"She was pretty secretive," Shane said. "Not happy I turned up."

"Why *did* you turn up?" Cassidy asked. She regarded Shane steadily—she had always seen straight through him.

"I didn't like the idea of Freya meeting them alone," Shane said with candor. If Cassidy and family thought Shane would be embarrassed about his protectiveness to Freya, he'd have to disappoint them. "Something smelled off."

"Something seems off to me too," Eric agreed. "Those guys in the SUVs gave up nothing and turned around pretty speedily. Did Freya tell you she was in Graham's pack?"

"Not at first." Not until they were almost on top of Shiftertown, but Eric didn't need to know absolutely everything about Freya. She had her reasons for doing what she did, good ones, even if Shane didn't know what they were.

"Surprised me." Eric's statement was delivered in a mild tone, but for Eric, that was betraying outright shock. "McNeil never mentioned her."

"Pack leader being a pack leader?" Diego suggested. "He didn't want anyone to know he had strays. Shifter Bureau would be all over that."

"I agree—it was smart." Eric sounded only slightly admiring, which to anyone who knew him was high praise. Eric had always held his feelings close to his chest—shrewd in a man who had to keep a Shiftertown of Felines, Lupines, and bears together.

"Well, she's here now," Shane said with a hint of a growl. "Under my family's protection."

Cassidy looked amused. "We know, Shane. Don't worry. We won't be insisting Graham's leadership outweighs a mate-claim. Because it doesn't."

She slid her gaze sideways to Diego, who moved a little closer to her. Their love for each other filled the space between them.

"You have to be prepared for her turning you down," Eric warned Shane. "Then she'll be fair game, unless Graham is prepared to lock her in his basement. His Lupines are getting out of hand, but they aren't entirely wrong. Mates would calm them the hell down."

"You are not sacrificing Freya for the good of Shiftertown," Shane said immediately. "I'll go to the mat with you on that one."

Eric fixed him with an unblinking gaze, while Cassidy and Diego watched with interest.

Shane's sudden aggression shouldn't surprise them. It was natural for a Shifter who'd just made a mate-claim. Unnatural for Shane, who'd never opposed Eric since the day he'd come to live in this Shiftertown.

But then, mates changed everything.

Freya had changed everything. With her wolf eyes and sassy tongue, her courage and her resolve, she'd reached into something within Shane and tied it in knots.

"I'd never dream of it," Eric said, deadpan. "But Graham will be hard-pressed to protect her if she refuses the claim."

"Then I'll have to convince her I'll be one hell of a mate." Shane met Eric's gaze with an assuredness he didn't feel. "Besides, she's smart enough to realize she's safer in my house than she would be with Graham. She won't turn me down until Leo has been rendered null as a threat."

"Which you plan to do at the fight club," Cassidy stated. No surprise she already knew all about that too.

"Yep." Shane nodded. "I will kick his sorry ass and leave him to limp home."

"Be careful, Shane." This came from Diego. "Not because I don't think you can take him, but because Leo's cunning. He'll try to cheat." Cassidy and Eric nodded, in total agreement.

"Fully expect him to." Shane plunked his empty coffee cup to the counter. "As long as he doesn't ruin any more shirts for me, I'll go easy on him. I'll knock him out right away and let his friends carry him home."

Eric and Cassidy exuded confidence that Shane would do exactly as he stated. Diego, the only human in the room, was more cautious, which was why Diego was good at his job. He didn't get cocky.

Shane knew he'd do well to emulate him.

They were being too nice to her. Freya was exhausted, wilting under the care of Cormac, Nell, and Brody as they sat her at their kitchen table and shoved a pile of sandwiches at her.

Freya tried to explain that she'd eaten plenty at the cabin and was fine, but the bears insisted that she'd experienced a lot of stress between then and now and should down a bunch more food.

Any other time, she'd be amused at their logic, but Freya was tired, stunned, and uncertain what to do.

Shane's mate-claim had jolted her. Even while she understood that the claim would shield her from Leo and even Graham if necessary, the fact that Shane had made it still scared the hell out of her.

Not because she was afraid of Shane. When she'd attacked him in the woods, thinking he was the source of the wrongness she'd sensed in the mountains, she'd quickly understood that Shane would not hurt her. He was tough, strong, and a good fighter, but he'd thwarted her attack without injuring her.

Then he'd helped her up, taken her to the cabin, let her bathe without invading her privacy, and fed her. When she'd slipped away to her meeting, Shane had followed—in concern for her safety, not because he'd wanted to trap her.

Graham, though his worry for her as a cub had been real, had restricted her. For her own good, she'd realized as she grew older, but she'd been alternately frustrated and angry. Graham hadn't been as strict with Rolf, because Rolf was male. Rolf would have to battle it out to find his place in the hierarchy after his Transition, Graham had explained when Freya had objected to his unfairness. That Freya would have to as well hadn't seemed to bother him. But then, Freya would probably find a mate who would take care of her.

Nell, Cormac, and Brody seemed uncertain what to do with her, but they were trying to make her feel welcome.

Brody had crushed her in a hug the moment Shane had walked off with Eric. Freya had barely been able to breathe with her face squashed against his broad chest. "It will be so great to finally have a sister," he'd rumbled. "Even a wolf one."

"Don't smother her with compliments," Cormac had said. He'd gently disentangled her from Brody and wrapped her in a softer hug. "Welcome to the family, honey."

Nell had also embraced her, but more cautiously. "I

acknowledge and respect the mate-claim," she said formally. She'd clasped Freya's shoulders when they came out of the hug. "Shane's been through a lot. Let him down easy if you refuse the claim, all right?"

"I'll try," was all Freya could say.

After that they'd pressed grilled ham and cheese sandwiches at her, along with a ton of potato salad and a large bowl of blackberries.

"Where do you get fresh blackberries in January?" Freya had to ask.

"Friend in Mexico sends them to me," Cormac said. He tossed berries into this mouth with his fingers. "He's a half Shifter, a bear. No one knows it. Plus, he's a hell of a good farmer."

"How can no one know it?" Freya had spent her life evading too much scrutiny. She and Rolf had moved fairly often within the Bay Area so no one would start wondering why they looked the same after twenty-odd years. They'd shared an apartment until a few years ago, when their jobs took them in different directions and commuting would have been difficult. She'd missed having Rolf near every day, but their work opportunities were too good to pass up. Freya couldn't imagine staying somewhere long enough to run a successful farm.

"Half-human Shifters have an easier time hiding their true natures," Cormac said. "He lives near Huatulco, down in Oaxaca. A beautiful area."

"You've been there?" Freya asked in surprise. All her life she'd only heard about limitations on travel for Shifters.

"I visit him from time to time." Cormac shrugged, unworried. "I know a guy and his wife who sail down there from San

Diego. They let me hitch a ride. How do you think I get all these berries back here?" He winked at Freya.

So much for Collared Shifters practically living in cages. Shane ran free on Mount Charleston, and Cormac sailed to and from southern Mexico whenever he felt like it.

"We're careful," Nell said, noting Freya's expression. "But we don't let Shifter Bureau have it all their own way."

Freya was beginning to understand that.

She'd never spent time with Shifters who weren't half wild. While Nell, Brody, and Cormac ate heartily, as did all Shifters, they spoke to one another with fondness. Though they exchanged teasing banter, there was no constant argument.

Graham had always been growling at his seconds or at Lupines who came to him with some grievance or demand. They'd been respectful, but not friendly.

Freya thought about the sweet-voiced Misty. How did she fit into Graham's brutal world?

Shane hadn't returned by the time Freya finished the meal —or at least got it through to the bears that she was full. Whatever Eric had taken him to do kept him away.

Freya found herself craning to look out the window, trying to catch sight of him. Each time, she snapped herself back to the conversation. Why did she care what Shane was doing?

Her skin itched in a way that was starting to drive her crazy. The irritation wasn't on the outside of her body, Freya realized when she rubbed her arms in annoyance. Something inside her burned, and she caught herself again and again watching for Shane's return.

This had to stop.

The windows darkened with early nightfall, but Shane still hadn't come home. Rain had begun late in the afternoon, and now it pattered steadily on the roof. Outside this snug house, the temperature dropped, the night chilling. Even the desert could be cold and dreary in January.

Freya gave up, told her hosts good-night, and went to bed.

Nell had fixed up Shane's room for her, putting clean sheets on the mattress and setting out towels for her to use in the bathroom. Freya recalled Shane's grin when he'd said *My bed's big, Freya. You'll like it.*

The bed was indeed huge, she saw when she entered, taking up most of the small bedroom. The mattress sagged a little, holding the impression of Shane. It also held his scent.

There had to be something wrong with her. Freya had often slept in beds previously inhabited by humans, closing her eyes, and ignoring the lingering stamp of them. Tonight, though, she tossed and turned, punching the pillows, and willing her body to cool.

Not used to the desert, she thought. She'd lived for the last two and more decades in northern California, with its rugged coast, high mountains, and swaths of woods among rolling hills. She was used to foggy hills, not flat, cold openness.

Her drained body at last dropped into slumber, but it wasn't restful. Freya dreamed she was in wolf form, with Shane as bear chasing her through endless woods. Shane's bear soon tackled her, easily taking her down. Instead of fighting him, as she'd done on the mountain, Freya rolled over and welcomed him.

In the dream, the wolf nipped at Shane and licked his muzzle, her tail wagging like a silly dog's.

Shane gave a sudden snarl, and the grizzly grew into a massive monster, his body enveloping Freya's. He'd swallow her whole, she thought in panic, and she struggled in earnest to get away. Shane laughed and held her harder, knowing she couldn't break free.

Freya yelped and came awake, her own voice jerking her from sleep.

She dragged in a breath and hugged the covers to her, trying to stem her panic. The blankets smelled of Shane, which didn't ease her rocketing heartbeat.

The door creaked open and faint light silhouetted Shane against the hallway beyond.

"Freya?" The question held nothing but concern. "You all right?"

CHAPTER THIRTEEN

Shane hovered in the doorway, waiting for Freya's reply, barely keeping himself from rushing to her and gathering her into his arms.

Once Eric and Diego had finally finished picking his brain, Shane had returned home to find the house dark and silent. Bears went to sleep early in the winter.

He'd bunked down on the couch, very aware Freya was a short way down the hall in his bed, then had been jerked from his fitful sleep by Freya's cry. Instantly he'd come to his feet, the blanket falling from his bare legs, and charged to his bedroom. At the last minute, he made himself stop and open the door without hurry.

"I'm fine," Freya whispered. Her voice shook, and the dim light from the hall showed her clutching the covers like a cub seeking safety.

Shane closed the door but didn't turn on the light. His Shifter sight let him see her perfectly fine in the dark.

He seated himself on the end of the bed, sensing that right now he needed to keep his distance.

"Lot of scary shit today," he said. "Chased by mercenaries, reuniting with Graham, and then that asshole Leo being himself. And you met me and my family." Shane let himself laugh. "Scariest of all, right?"

Freya sent him a wavering smile. "Not really. I think I like bears."

Shane pressed a hand to his chest. "Wow. I converted her after one day. Like my brother always says, *Once you go bear, you never go back.*"

Freya's smile steadied. "Then again, you're all really full of yourselves."

"Oh, and Lupines aren't? You never, *ever* take yourselves too damn seriously."

Shane swore he saw her blush. "Because Felines and bears try to push us around," she said with a hint of steel. "Just because our legs are thinner than yours, or something."

"I don't mind if they are." Shane glanced at her bare foot and ankle protruding from the blankets. "I like your legs."

Freya jerked her foot back under the covers. "Not helping me sleep, Shane."

"Compliments don't relax you? Mmm, I gotta work on that."

They were both brittle, throwing out feeble humor to keep from talking about what they needed to discuss.

"You didn't have to make the mate-claim," Freya said abruptly.

Okay, so much for not talking about it. "Best thing to do in the circumstances." Shane tried to sound reasonable and not like he wanted to haul her into his embrace and promise to protect her forever. "Do you want Leo insisting his claim is legit? Or Graham to grow so fed up that he tells you to accept him to keep the peace?"

"Of course, I don't want that." Freya made an impatient noise. "But you put me in a bind."

"Not really. This is what you do." Shane tapped off his points on his broad fingertips. "Hang out here, pretend to contemplate my claim as a legitimate offer, then I bust Leo's chops, and Graham sits on him. Once he's under control, you reject my claim and go on your merry way."

It cost Shane a lot to say those things. Yesterday morning, he'd never wanted to see another Lupine again. Now he didn't want to let this one go.

"As simple as that?" Freya rumpled her hair, which tumbled over one eye. Adorable.

"Sure. Meanwhile, eat your fill of Cormac's great food, put up with my brother's jokes, you and my mom braid each other's hair ..."

Shane felt the bed tremble with laughter. At least he could distract her with stupid jokes.

"You say I can go." Freya became serious again. "But will Eric let me?"

"Eric?" Shane blinked in surprise. "Eric's not into confining Shifters. He's happy for any who get away from Shifter Bureau, and he'll help you as much as he can. He's looking into Althea and her company, by the way. That's where I was all afternoon, talking to Diego and Xav. They're going to find out what she's up to and maybe see if she knows anything about your brother."

Freya drew her knees to her chest and hugged them, her expression telling Shane she was afraid to hope. "Can they?"

"Sure. Diego and Xav are amazing. Diego was a cop for a long time, and he knows how to find out things. Xav is a computer wizard. Even the Guardian consults him."

Freya looked puzzled. "Why would a Guardian consult a

human? To ask about the best way to stick his sword through a Shifter's heart?"

"Funny. Guardians are like the world's greatest hacker geniuses, but Xav sometimes puts them to shame. So says Neal. Neal Ingram. He's our Guardian. You'll like him—he's Lupine."

Freya's brows went up. "You're fine with a Lupine Guardian?"

"I don't know about *fine*, but you gotta go with what's what, in Shiftertown." The Felines and bears had not been happy when it was announced that Neal was the Guardian for the whole Shiftertown, but they'd all grown used to him. Neal, quiet and enigmatic like most Guardians, was an honorable guy.

"He's not one of Graham's Lupines," Freya said. "How are *they* with the situation?"

"They have no choice, is how they are with it," Shane answered. "Shifter Bureau wouldn't let Graham have a Choosing for a new Guardian when his died, so they had to accept Neal as it."

"Our Guardian was a good man." Freya's voice softened. "I was there when he passed on—Graham had to ask a Guardian in another pack to send him to the Goddess. I didn't realize Graham wasn't allowed to have a Choosing."

"That's what he told us," Shane said. "Not that he likes to talk about it."

"Why was Graham forced to move here anyway?" Freya asked. "It was hard enough for him in Elko. He was facing a war."

And didn't have time to take care of a scared young wolf and her brother just out of their Transitions, Shane supplied silently.

"Because humans are stupid about Shifters," he answered. "They don't realize that putting different groups of us together seriously messes with the order of things. Fortunately, Eric and Graham knew how to be reasonable about it."

"Graham?" Freya said in disbelief. "Reasonable?"

"That took a while, I admit. Misty helped."

"She is so totally not who I expected Graham to end up with." Freya rested her head on her knees. "What happened there?"

"They fell in love." Shane opened his hands. "It was a beautiful thing."

"Have you ever fallen in love?" The question held true curiosity.

Shane had once thought so with Cassidy, but those feelings were long ago and far away. "I don't know. Have you?"

"No." Freya answered without hesitation.

"You're pretty positive about that."

"I was too young when I lived with Shifters. After I left, I didn't want to commit to any human. Too dangerous."

Why was Shane elated by this answer? Not because she'd been living in a precarious situation—that made him want to hurt anyone who'd threatened her—but because she hadn't felt a spark for anyone.

Great, he was triumphant about her non-existent boyfriends.

As they'd talked, Shane had ended up a little closer to her. He wasn't certain when or how that had happened. Freya simply watched him with her wolf's eyes without flinching.

"Maybe the two of us weren't meant to fall in love before this," Shane found himself rumbling. He tried to stop the words—what an inane thing to say. "Maybe the Goddess has her own plans."

"Sometimes I think the Goddess looks out for me," Freya said. "I got away from the pack and Leo, and I lived a relatively good life. Rolf got into software development, and I went into graphic design." She smiled. "We worked in the same company for a while, but he was recruited by another, and then the startup in Mountain View. He was in high demand. Maybe as good as you say the Guardians were."

"You like graphic design?" Shane asked.

"I do." Freya lifted her head. "I don't know how arty I am, but I love playing with patterns and colors, putting elements together to form something that feels *right*. I mostly work on magazine ads, both print and online, sometimes do posters for sales conventions. Doesn't matter what it's for— when everything comes together, it's like a song. I took vacation I'd been saving up to look for Rolf, and I hope I can go back to it."

Like a song when she smiled, as well. The hint of it now warmed his soul.

Goddess help him, when had Shane become so sappy?

She'd just said she wanted to get back to her old life. The one without Shane in it. That should smack the sappiness out of him, but it didn't. Probably because he was an idiot.

They were side by side now. Had Shane moved, or had she?

Freya had, Shane realized. She'd swung her legs over the side of the bed to sit next to him.

"Hey," Shane said softly. He touched her hand, and when she didn't pull away, twined his fingers through the backs of hers.

"Hey." Her response was shy.

Shane leaned closer. "I'm not sorry I mate-claimed you."

Freya didn't pull away. "Okay."

"You' re supposed to say, *I'm not sorry you mate-claimed me either, Shane.*" He put on a falsetto as he said her line.

Freya shook her head, her warm hair brushing his shoulder. "You are such a shit."

"Yeah, I get that a lot."

Freya's legs were still tangled in the blanket, Shane's bare from his boxer briefs down. His T-shirt clung to his chest, his skin warm even in the winter.

Their hips and thighs touched, hands remaining entwined. Something hot and electric flowed into Shane and wound around his heart.

He brushed back her thick hair from her face, gazing down into her wolf's golden eyes. Freya had beauty he'd never experienced before, one that pulled him to her even when he'd been shut in Eric's house away from her.

Freya studied him without trepidation, letting him skim his fingers along the smooth curve of her face.

She didn't protest at all when Shane leaned down and kissed her.

Freya's mouth was warm, sweet, and worth kissing. Shane scooped her closer, and she deepened the kiss, hands finding his shoulders, the back of his neck.

Shane felt the connection inside him again, the one that had kicked in when he'd made the mate-claim.

This was right, good, the Goddess's plan.

Sure, whatever. Shane shut down the poetic side of his brain and let the physical one take over.

Freya's tongue drew fire, and Shane let her explore. She tasted of blackberries, a sign she'd been dining with bears. He smiled to himself as he enjoyed it, fingers touching the corners of her mouth to open her more to him.

Freya started to pull him down to her, then she drew back

with a sudden gasp. Her eyes widened as she stared at him as though she had no idea how her mouth had come to be sealed against his.

Shane tried to convince himself to carefully settle her back on the bed, pull the covers over her, and get the hell out of this room.

Not one part of his body obeyed.

Well, they could stare at each other all night, or—

Freya launched herself at him, her next kiss scorching. Shane fell backward onto the mattress, a sweet armful of Freya on top of him.

She kissed him as though she couldn't get enough of his mouth, tongue, lips. Shane held her steadily with his big hands, her squirming rubbing in a nice way against his very stiff cock.

Her hair was silky warm, her mouth wonderful. Shane's knee moved between her legs, and Freya moaned in her throat.

This could turn into mating frenzy very fast.

Who was he kidding, it *was* mating frenzy. Only reason why she'd stopped rolling her eyes at him and started frantically kissing him.

Again, Shane told himself to slide her away and leave the room, and again, his body wouldn't obey.

Why not? the bear inside him growled. *Mating ceremony's only a formality.*

Yeah, but ...

Shane slid his hand behind Freya's hair, ready to ease the kiss to a close, but Freya broke it abruptly. Her breath came rapidly, her mouth trembling.

"We shouldn't do this," she whispered. "I'm not ready."

Shane rubbed his thumb across her moist lower lip and didn't answer, forcing himself to calm the hell down.

Freya sent him a shaky smile. "You're supposed to say, *I'm not ready for this either, Freya.*" She mimicked Shane's baritone.

Laughter bubbled up inside him. She was going to be an amazing mate.

"I've been ready since you smacked into me in the woods," Shane said. "Crazy wolf who shifted into a beautiful woman."

He saw her flush in the darkness. "Why didn't you ravish me then? Or *try* to, anyway." He caught a flash of her wolf's bravado.

Shane shrugged, continuing to enjoy her satin hair beneath his fingertips. "I'm a great guy."

"Yeah? I think it was because I looked like shit."

Shane's instant interest in her in the woods hadn't cared, but he shrugged again. "If you want to think so."

"I need to wait." Freya took up her earlier theme. "To find out how all this plays out. I don't want to get my heart tangled in a relationship, and this relationship right now is only a convenience. For both of us."

Shane wasn't sure about that, but he'd go along with whatever she said. At least, until his cock decided to give up. He wasn't thinking too straight right now.

"And I truly am totally exhausted." Freya went limp on top of him, her head resting on his shoulder. "I need to sleep."

If she thought her warm weight on him would soothe Shane down, she was mistaken.

But, as Shane had just told her, he was a great guy. Her attraction to him tonight was mate frenzy, triggered by his claim and her need for a safe haven, but Freya's hunger had now abated, leaving her tired and relaxed.

Shane forced himself to sit up, scooping Freya up and depositing her on the bed beside him.

"Tell you what." Shane rose, shook out the covers, and settled them over her. "You get some sleep, and we'll argue about it in the morning. Maybe all day tomorrow. Or all week. As long as it takes."

He heard himself babbling, but his nonsense words seemed to ease her. Freya yawned.

When Shane turned away, thinking he'd grab a quick and very cold shower, she caught his hand.

"Stay?" The request was quiet, hesitant.

Shane debated his answer only for a moment. Then he stripped back the sheets and scrambled quickly into the bed, dragging the covers over them both. Freya had snuggled down on her side, resting her head on her bent arm on the pillow. Shane spooned against her back, one hand on her hip, and gazed down at her.

"Good night, my Freya," he whispered.

Silence. Freya's eyes were closed, and her chest rose and fell with a long breath.

"You're supposed to say, *Good night, Shane*."

No answer. Freya drew another breath, her body releasing into much-needed sleep.

Shane stayed awake in their nest, enjoying her nearness as rain drummed on the roof, sleep eluding him for a long time.

Xavier Escobar frowned at the computer screen. He was the last one working tonight at the small office complex that held DX Security, staying late to unravel the puzzle that was Althea Webster's private security firm.

Shane had provided a good description of the woman, her guards, the Shifter with her, their weaponry, and their vehicles, including license plate numbers. Shifters had formidable powers of observation, and Shane was one of the best. He never boasted of his ability, but it was there.

Xav would get Freya's take on Althea's setup tomorrow—as in, how Freya had contacted her and fixed the interview, though Xav had already learned a lot about that process. If a person wanted to hire Althea, or go to work for her, they called a phone number on an otherwise blank black card that could only be obtained by referral.

The seeker was then put in touch with someone else who would arrange the meeting with Althea. There were many layers between the woman and the world.

He'd come across intriguing information after he'd returned from Shiftertown this evening, which was why he was sitting in the office so late, the window above his desk black with night and streaked with rain.

Althea had started inquiring about something very interesting, in encrypted emails that Neal had found and Xav had decrypted. He was reading the startling details when the back door opened.

Instantly, Xav killed the light and turned off his bright computer screen. This office was very secure, which was why he didn't worry about sitting alone in the night on a quiet backstreet in Las Vegas.

On the other hand, someone had just managed to get past the complicated lock on the rear door and was moving through the office as though they knew exactly where they were going.

Emergency lighting was always on at low intensity in the hallways, and this outlined the intruder, who paused in the hall outside Xav's office.

Xav tightened, but he switched on the light again.

"Lindsay," he said in a neutral tone. "What's up?"

Lindsay Cummings was heat personified. She was Feline, her wildcat a lynx, which was small and lithe. Lindsay in human form sometimes resembled a cat, with her narrow face and pointed nose, sleek golden hair, big green eyes, and a smile that could knock a man out at ten paces.

She liked to wear tight clothing, as she was now—jeans that hugged her hips topped with a bright pink fuzzy sweater. She loved to dance, and to laugh and shriek while doing it.

Lindsay was also gentle, kind, and amazingly compassionate, especially with the orphaned cubs she and Cassidy took turns looking after.

On the other hand, Lindsay could party like nobody's business. Xav had more than once awakened on the floor of his apartment after an all-night bar crawl with Lindsay—alone, his shirt gone, his mouth on fire, and no memory of how he'd gotten there. One morning when he'd peeled open his eyes, wondering why his wrist burned so much, he'd found a small tattoo of a cat's face on it. No idea where it had come from.

Xav had considered having the ink removed but ultimately

decided to keep it. A souvenir of a night that must have been wild.

"Working late?" Lindsay leaned on the doorframe in a provocative pose. "What does a girl have to do to get you to call her? Run a secret mercenary agency?" She cocked her head. "Hmm, there's an idea."

Xav rocked back in his chair without turning the computer screen on again. "How did you get in here?" he asked as though merely curious. "There's a pretty sophisticated lock on that door."

Lindsay shrugged, the sweater rippling with her lush body. "I watched you open it the other day and memorized the code."

Xav had to laugh. "Thank you for reminding me I should change my code every day. I'm lazy about that."

The tension he'd sensed behind her sexy stance eased. "So, you're not mad at me for stalking you?"

"I didn't say that. Were you stalking me?"

"Well, yeah." Lindsay sauntered into the office and rested one hip against his desk. "You never call. You never text. You don't even send suggestive emojis."

Xav suppressed a grin. "Shifters aren't supposed to have phones that can receive suggestive emojis."

"Shifters aren't supposed to do a lot of things." Lindsay hoisted herself to sit on the end of his desk and crossed her long legs. She wore high-heeled boots that were good for the winter rains as well as for looking great on her feet.

"I've been busy," Xav said, then added quickly, "That's the truth, not an excuse. Diego has had me hopping on a couple of projects, and then Eric gave me a quest today that's eating all my time. Believe me, I'd rather be out dancing with you."

"You still can be." The sparkle in Lindsay's eyes promised

another crazy night. "Vegas is a twenty-four-hour town. Something's always open."

Xav grinned. "Like tattoo shops?"

Lindsay reached for his hand and turned it over, brushing her fingers over the tatt on Xav's wrist. Xav had gone to a tattoo artist to have the ink finished in several shades, including giving the cat lovely green eyes.

"This was your idea, you know," Lindsay said. "You insisted on a lynx."

Xav attempted to ignore the hot tingles running from his wrist down his spine to his cock. "I don't remember it at all, but I believe you."

Lindsay caressed the lines, and Xav's blood heated to furnace level. Good thing it was somewhat dark in here. The desk light didn't push the night back much.

"What do you say?" Lindsay asked casually. "Let's blow this joint and go out on the town."

Xav let out a sigh of true regret. "I can't. Eric wants a dossier on this mercenary woman, and I can't give him an incomplete one. He'll know."

"So, you're not going out with me because you're fascinated by another woman?" Lindsay's tone was teasing, but her voice held some strain.

"Althea is pretty interesting," Xav said. "Though not in the way you mean. Her dad founded her mercenary company, and she took it over when he died. From what I'm reading, all her dad's cronies assumed she'd sell the business once she inherited it, or at least have one of them run it for her while she stepped to the sidelines."

"Because she's a woman," Lindsay said in understanding. "Lots of humans think like that."

"She surprised them all." Xav turned on the computer

screen and scrolled through his report. "She fired a lot of people she called dead weight, and then she expanded. Not rapidly, just slowly and steadily. Now, she has some of the best strategists in the world working for her. Her troops always complete their missions successfully."

"Good for her," Lindsay said with true admiration. She leaned to peer at the screen. "Though the idea of private human armies running around makes me a little nervous. What if someone hires her to take out Shifters?"

"From what I've learned, Althea's choosy about which clients she takes on. No slaughtering villages of families so that mining companies can claim the land. Instead, she helps those villages get rid of ruthless dictators or clears out drug lords so people can get back to farming or whatever they do without having to worry about dangerous guys."

"Aw." Lindsay skimmed the words Xav had typed. "A *nice* mercenary."

"Well, to a point," Xav said. "She's had army camps completely taken out, recruiting the best of the survivors to work for her and ransoming those she doesn't want."

"Ah." Lindsay sat up straight. "Again, I hope she doesn't come after Shifters."

"I don't think she will." Xav clicked open another tab and scrolled through more information. "She seems to like Shifters, and wishes she could recruit more. Probably why she let Freya contact her."

"Poor Freya." Lindsay's compassion emerged. "Cassidy shared what Eric told her, plus I saw some of what was going on out my window. Freya looks like a sweetie who needs some fun. Cass and I should take her out with us, am I right? I think Shane will be good for her, though."

"From what I understand, she wasn't thrilled with his

mate-claim."

"She'll come around." Lindsay sounded confident. "Bears are great in the sack. So I've heard," she added with a smirk.

Xav was surprised by the sting that washed through him, which he quickly suppressed.

He was under no illusion that Lindsay was a saint. Shifter women weren't admonished to be chaste until their mating—after their Transition, they could take up with whatever male they wanted without censure. No Shifters were condemned for having cubs without a mating ceremony, and such cubs weren't considered illegitimate. When Shifters found their mates, they took any cubs the other had as their own. A nice system, Xav had always thought.

Lindsay, though, didn't like to talk about her previous conquests with Xav. Did she worry he'd be jealous? Or worry that he wouldn't be?

He *was* jealous, of course. Xav had no claim on Lindsay, and they hadn't agreed to be exclusive, but that didn't mean Xav didn't wish things were otherwise.

"Let's hope Shane's really good for her," Xav said, keeping his voice light. "I'm thinking she'll be safer with him than anywhere else."

"It's hard being a Shifter." The words were soft, Lindsay's usual verve fading. "We're so strong but so vulnerable at the same time. Whenever the world changes, we're in danger all over again."

Xav knew Lindsay meant not only being Shifter but being a single female Shifter. He'd seen male Shifters glare at Lindsay as though not understanding why she hadn't chosen one of them yet. As though her entire life should be based on choosing a mate.

Graham's Lupines wanted mates, and like the group Diego

had told him about growling around this morning, they were starting to make this a point of contention.

Xav looked up at Lindsay, her eyes the same green as those of the cat on his wrist. "You won't be in danger as long as I'm around."

Lindsay gazed back at him in stark hope, which she quickly masked. Or had Xav only imagined her expression?

"Oh, the big bad human is going to look after a Shifter, is he?" Lindsay raked her fingers through the air and let out a *Rowrr*. "I have claws, honey."

"I have a taser," Xav pointed out. "And a lot of cool toys that will keep those Shifters down."

"Ooh, toys." Lindsay pretended to look fascinated. "You can tell me all about them one day."

Xav hit the combination of buttons to shut down his computer and heaved himself off his chair. "I'll give Eric his report in the morning. How about you and me find someplace to dance?"

Lindsay hopped down from the desk. "Now you're talking."

She wound her arm through Xav's and let him lead her through the dark office to the door she'd sneaked through. Outside, the night was cold, stars hard white in the sky.

Xav escorted Lindsay to his car, his body thrumming. He knew they'd do nothing but dance and drink tonight, but Xav would relish every moment of simply being in her electric presence.

FREYA POPPED HER EYES OPEN TO FIND SUNLIGHT flooding Shane's room. What had awakened her was not the sun, she realized after a hazy moment, but a slight draft when someone had opened the bedroom door. That someone was Nell.

Nell stilled as she took in Shane curled up around Freya under the covers, the big man still fast asleep. Nell regarded them both with enigmatic brown eyes, then she slowly withdrew, closing the door with barely a sound.

Nell hadn't appeared unhappy that Shane and Freya lay snuggled together. In fact, she'd looked pleased.

As soon as the door shut, Freya hurriedly sat up and reached for clothes. Her own were still stuffed in her backpack on the other side of the room, so she picked up Iona's sweatshirt and jeans from where she'd left them on the chair next to the bed.

When she sat back, sweatshirt in hand, it was to find Shane gazing at her with intense brown eyes, his heartwarming smile in place.

"Hey."

"Hey, yourself." Freya's anxiety briefly evaporated, and she leaned to brush a kiss to his lips. The spark that leapt inside her was raw. "Your mom was just in here. I'm going to talk to her."

She expected Shane to grow alarmed or argue her out of it, but he lay back, lacing his hands behind his head. His large T-shirt hugged his delectable body. "Good idea."

Freya longed to snuggle down against his side again and sigh happily. Equally, she wanted to go out into the kitchen and have a massively large breakfast. Running around in the woods, being reunited with Graham and his wolves and then unexpectedly mate-claimed made a woman hungry.

Shane didn't elaborate on why it was a good idea to talk to Nell. He only watched without comment as she tugged on the clothes and left the room. She glanced back before she closed the door, and he sent her an encouraging smile.

Freya stopped in the bathroom to wash her face and brush her teeth with the toothbrush Nell had set out for her. She tried to get her hair in some kind of order. Giving up on that last, she went in search of Nell.

Shane's mom wasn't in the kitchen. That room was empty when she entered it, and there were unfortunately no signs of cooking.

A movement in the backyard took Freya outside to spot Nell, dressed in a thick coat, jeans, and hiking boots, wandering from the house down the common area. Wind rumpled her grizzly-bear hair, but the rain had gone, the sun shining brightly in a sharp blue sky.

"Don't worry," Nell said as Freya approached her. "I'm not going to haul you over the coals for sleeping with my son."

"Nothing happened," Freya said quickly. She fell into step with Nell who seemed in no hurry to get anywhere. "We talked." And kissed. Kisses that had unlocked the closed-off spaces inside her.

"I know. I said *sleeping*. Walls are thin in a Shifter house, honey. At least some of them are." Without explaining that cryptic statement, Nell continued her walk.

"Did you want to speak with me?" Freya asked when Nell said nothing more.

"I did. Thought we could have a chat without so many Shifters around." Nell rolled her eyes. "I love my family, and even like my neighbors, but it can get a bit much."

"I understand, growing up with a twin-brother wolf-Shifter." Who had to still be alive. Hadn't he? "You're pretty dominant, though."

"Yep. I'm third in dominance in this town. Eric and

Graham are about equal as first, Cassidy is second, along with Iona—though Iona's status is a little different as leader's mate—and then me. I was fourth, after Eric's son, Jace, but he found his mate in Austin and lives there now."

Freya had heard about the Austin Shiftertown, run by a family of lion Shifters. She knew where all the Shiftertowns were located—in North Carolina, Montana, New Mexico, across Texas, up into North Dakota. Anywhere remote had Shiftertowns, though the Austin one was smack in the middle of a city, as was this Shiftertown.

Shifters in the cities had been given neighborhoods nobody wanted, but with new developments springing up, like the one Freya had seen in the distance yesterday, encroachment was becoming a problem.

Freya knew Nell had explained the hierarchy to Freya as a kindness. Shifters finding themselves in strange groups usually had to learn the hard way where they fit in. Nell hadn't mentioned Shane, but as son of the top bear in town, he'd be well-respected. Didn't mean he'd be high up himself, because dominance was individual, but being in a strong family didn't hurt.

Freya had no idea where she'd be in the hierarchy here. She'd been barely past her Transition when she'd fled Graham's pack, before her place had been determined. She remembered her flash of knowledge that she now far outranked Leo, but other than that, she didn't know where she belonged.

"I didn't only bring you out here to explain who's who in Shiftertown," Nell said. "If you stick around, you'll learn it. I wanted to tell you about Shane."

To explain to Freya what a great mate he'd be? Or to tell her to stay away from him?

"I had to raise him and Brody on my own after their father died," Nell began. "Two little cubs, and me with no idea what to do with them."

Freya could picture it vividly, Nell young and heartbroken, with Brody and Shane cute but unruly bear cubs. Her own mother had faced the same thing and had chosen to give up her cubs to the strongest man she knew.

"But they were good kids and helped you out?" Freya asked with optimism.

"No, they were little shits." Nell chuckled. "They kept me hopping, I can tell you. I did whatever was necessary for them to be safe. Moving to Shiftertown was one of those things I had to do. Don't think that was an easy decision."

"*You* didn't make the decision," Freya said, her outrage stirring. "Shifter Bureau told you to go, and you had to."

"This is what you don't understand, Freya." Nell's tone was patient. "*You* ran, which was understandable, and I know Graham made sure you got away to safety. He must have had to stand on his head to do that, but he did it. But even he realized that banding together in Shiftertowns, combining our strengths while pretending to comply with Shifter Bureau's rules, was our best way to survive."

Freya regarded her with some surprise. Graham and his Lupines had been furious about the new regulations for Shifters, and many had said they'd resist them, using force if necessary.

"How did Shane feel about moving to Shiftertown?" Freya asked.

"He hated it. He and Brody both. They wanted to fight, to go back to the woods and eke out an existence. But I knew our future was living in the human world. This is the beginning."

Some humans really liked Shifters, Freya had learned by

living among them. Not only Shifter groupies with their almost fanatic fascination with them, but those who believed humans and Shifters should live together in harmony. Freya thought they were dreamers, but maybe one day ...

"My sons are fine with it now," Nell went on. "More accepting, at least. Brody works for Eric as his tracker. Shane works for me, as my second, but I lend him to Eric a lot. And Graham sometimes. Trackers are our eyes and ears, our fighters when we need someone to fight for us. Leaders can't always engage, which I don't like, but makes sense. We'd be battling for our places every day. Trackers help keep the peace."

"Your own little army," Freya said. "Like Althea's."

"A bit." Nell shrugged. "But trackers don't get paid. They work for us because they love us."

Freya looked for humor in Nell's eyes and found none. She was serious.

"What about Cormac?"

Nell's face softened. "Cormac is a big sweetie."

"Is he a tracker?"

"He's more of a negotiator," Nell said. "You might have noticed that everyone relaxes when Cormac's around."

Freya had seen that. "You're lucky," she said with conviction.

"I know, honey. It wasn't as easy with Cormac as you might think. There were issues we had to work through, but yes, I am lucky." Nell's little smile told Freya more than words how much she adored him.

Some humans believed that mating for Shifters was only a sexual pull—the mating frenzy—but Freya had seen true bonds form even between Graham's wildest wolves. That mate bond was love and something beyond it—something worth striving for.

"Shane at one point thought he wanted to take Cassidy Warden as his mate," Nell startled Freya by saying. "I'm telling you this bluntly, because it's only fair you know where things stand."

Freya tried to suppress the pang Nell's announcement sent through her. Of course, Shane would have had past relationships, and Cassidy, who Freya had glimpsed in Eric's yard yesterday, was beautiful. It was no surprise that Shane, or any Shifter, would want to pursue her.

Freya's head told her that while her heart burned in response. The wolf inside her lifted its hackles and growled.

"What happened between them?" Freya asked in a casual tone, hoping the wolf's fury didn't show.

The twinkle in Nell's eyes told Freya she wasn't fooled. "Shane never made a mate-claim with Cassidy. Cass took another Shifter, called Donovan, as mate, who was then killed. A great tragedy." Nell's amusement fled. "We feared Cassidy would die herself, she went through so much grief. But then she met Diego. Shane knew it was never meant to be between him and Cassidy. He's been over it for a while now, and he and Diego are good friends. But you need to know."

"I don't expect to form the mate bond with him," Freya said quickly. "In fact, I won't stay here long enough for any sort of bond to form. I appreciate you taking care of me, and I'll repay you somehow, but I'll be leaving soon. I want to resolve things with Graham, then I have a brother to find."

Nell regarded her with something like pity. "You're young, Freya. Resolution takes a long time—sometimes it never comes."

Freya worked to suppress her dismay, but she knew Nell

was right. Her ideal scenario was that she and Graham would talk again, Leo would figure out he needed to back way off, and she'd take Graham's promised help and find out what had happened to Rolf. Once he was located, she and Rolf would go back to San Francisco and resume their lives.

She'd have to reject Shane's mate-claim before she went. But Shane had made the claim only to expedite the situation, hadn't he? Shane wouldn't care one way or the other what Freya did once she was gone. He might even be relieved he wouldn't have to go through with an actual mating ceremony with her.

Freya thought of the power in Shane's hard kisses last night, awakening a longing she hadn't known she'd possessed, and confusion swirled through her.

If she rejected the claim and went back to her old life, she'd never find out what she could have had with Shane. Even the thought of hugging him in farewell and walking away made her hollow inside.

Nell was watching her closely, but before Freya could form a response, the dark-haired Reid came out of a house down the row and sprinted toward them.

Nell watched him come in surprise. "What's he running for? He usually teleports when he wants to get anywhere in a hurry. Or maybe he doesn't want to scare you."

Reid slowed as he neared them. He'd been going full out, but he wasn't even breathing hard when he stopped in front of Nell.

"Graham's sending me out." He flicked his midnight gaze to Freya, his eyes unreadable. "Leo has disappeared," he said flatly. "He vanished in the night and hasn't returned."

"Couldn't you have put a tracker on the asshole?" Shane demanded of Graham in irritation.

Ten minutes ago, he'd sat up with a start when Brody had barged into his bedroom, his brother not surprised to find Shane there. Without explanation, Brody had dragged him out the front door to meet Graham, barely giving him time to pull on a pair of jeans.

Shane had been warm and happy wrapped around Freya, not really minding when she'd slipped off to talk to his mother. He'd see her at breakfast, enjoy watching her lift a blackberry to her lips, curling her tongue around it ...

"I *am* putting a tracker on him," Graham said with his usual growl. "You."

"Very funny. I meant on his phone or something."

"I usually do know where all my wolves are at any given time," Graham snapped. "Leo's gone off the radar."

Shane believed him. Once upon a time, humans had stolen some of Graham's Lupines, including cubs. They'd been returned safely, but since then, Graham had kept an extremely close eye on those under his protection.

"What does it matter if one of your asshole wolves decided to go on an all-night bender?" Shane's growl matched Graham's. "He'll drag himself home hungover and be too sick to fight the Challenge. Which means he forfeits. Saves me some time."

Graham's scowl couldn't disguise the concern in his gray eyes. "I don't give a shit about the Challenge right now, Shane."

"All right," Shane conceded, trying to rein in his temper. "You wouldn't be worried for no reason. Why are you so sure something's wrong?"

"Leo's kind of an idiot, that's why. Leo's brother, when I pressed him, said he was talking about those mercs you took Freya away from, the ones Eric is researching now. He went up to Mount Charleston to find them, who the hell knows why."

With Leo, it could be anything. To ask them to eliminate Shane? Or did Leo know something about Freya's brother's disappearance?

"Why does he think he can locate them?" Shane's alarm and anger merged. "Freya barely knew how to contact Althea. And why does Leo assume they'll have gone back up the mountain?"

"He's not very smart," Graham said. "Probably figured he'd pick up their scent where you met them, or at least the that of the Feline you mentioned. I already sent my nephew to scout around. He reported that though he hasn't found Leo, he's sensed something else very weird."

"Crap."

Graham's nephew Dougal was young, but he'd been

trained by Graham, who was one of the best fighters around. If Dougal said something was wrong, something was wrong.

"Exactly," Graham said. "So, I need you, Brody, and Reid to go check it out."

"Why not some of your Lupines?" Brody asked him. "They know Leo better than we do."

"Because I need the best of the best on this. Eric agrees."

Graham likely added the last because he knew Shane wouldn't budge unless it was clear that Eric sanctioned the search. When Graham had first arrived in this Shiftertown, he'd fought having to okay missions with a Feline, but since then Graham had learned the wisdom of not pissing off Eric.

More surprising was the fact that Graham had just called Shane, Brody, and Reid the best of the best. Graham always spoke the truth as he saw it—he wasn't using flattery to get his way. He really meant it.

"All right," Shane said. "If you're concerned, then I am too."

Graham acknowledged this with the barest nod. "Take Neal with you."

Shane's unease grew. Graham wouldn't ask for the Guardian unless he feared Leo was dead.

"Sure thing," Shane said, subdued, and Brody nodded somberly.

Shane's bleak mood dissolved when a humming in his blood told him Freya was nearby. He turned to see her, Nell, and Reid striding toward him where he stood with Graham.

Sleeping next to Freya last night had been satisfying, but it hadn't been enough. Shane had made the mate-claim to cool things down in Shiftertown, but it was turning *him* into a searing mess.

Freya halted close to Shane, her proximity sending his

heartbeat off the scale. "Reid says you're going out looking for Leo," she said. "Be careful—Leo might be leading you into a trap."

The fact that she was anxious for him made Shane want to grin like an idiot. He forced himself to speak normally. "Graham doesn't think so. That might have been Leo's original intent, but now it appears like something bad might have happened to him."

"Want me along?" Freya asked. "I know Leo's scent, as well as some of his tricks."

Shane didn't want her out of his sight, but he shook his head. "Better not. Graham thinks it's dangerous. Which means it is, because Graham isn't afraid of anything. Stupidly so, sometimes."

"Standing right here," Graham said with a soft growl.

"Trying to emphasize the hazards," Shane told him.

"I'm more worried about you." Freya looked surprised at her own admission. "You text us the minute you know anything, all right?" Her eyes took on the glare of a she-wolf who expected her wishes to be commands.

On impulse, Shane cupped her face in his hands and kissed her mouth.

Freya started, but not in distaste. Her lips softened beneath his, a woman who wanted this kiss. Shane closed his eyes as he savored it.

Graham loudly cleared his throat. "Meanwhile, one of my wolves is in dire peril."

Shane ignored him. He took his time easing away from Freya, who released him with reluctance.

"*You* stay out of dire peril while I'm gone," Shane told her.

Freya rested a hand on Shane's chest, where his heart rocketed. "Be careful," she said softly. "I don't like this."

"I don't either. But it's my job to flush out the bad stuff." Shane lifted her hand and kissed her fingers. "I'll be back soon, and we'll party."

Freya's expression told him she didn't believe his glib reassurance, and Shane didn't believe it either, but what the hell. He was just happy she'd agreed to remain here, where Nell and Graham could look after her.

There was a reason Shifter leaders stayed put and sent out the trackers to uncover the danger. The leaders needed to guard the more vulnerable, in case that danger came home. Trackers were expendable.

No one ever said that, but Shane knew it to be the truth. He and the other trackers were the scouts, the spies, and the first line of defense. They had to be tough, fearless, and have nothing to lose.

Shane realized this morning he'd now found something he didn't want to lose.

Freya smiled shakily as she let him go. Shane ignored Graham hovering impatiently, Nell watching in interest, and Reid, as impatient as Graham but with more understanding, to gaze into Freya's eyes and touch her smooth cheek.

Then he gave Freya one last, brief kiss, sent his mom a grateful glance, and waved for Reid to join him as he strode away to become a fearless tracker once more.

"She'll be okay, bro." Brody gunned the big pickup Cormac had insisted they use, taking Shane, Reid, and Neal at breakneck speed down the freeway to the turnoff toward Mount Charleston.

Reid, who couldn't teleport to a place he'd never seen,

hung on to the back of Brody's seat, his face set in grim lines. Neal hulked next to him, the big Lupine barely fitting in the small space. His large sword, sheathed, lay across his lap, the tip over Reid's knees.

Reid looked like he might puke, but whether because of proximity to High Fae magic or Brody's driving, Shane couldn't say.

"I know." Shane tried to reassure himself. "Mom won't let Graham bully her or anyone hurt her."

"Cormac won't either."

Shane, as usual, felt better just thinking about Cormac, who took care of people without belligerence. He might not have the prominence Nell did, but everyone seemed to do what he wanted without resistance.

"When I get my hands on Leo, though ..." Shane left the thought hanging. If Leo was alive and well, Graham would punish him thoroughly, yes, but Shane's anger soared beyond logical proportion.

"There's still the Challenge," Brody reminded him.

"That's true." A fair fight in the ring with referees wasn't what Shane had in mind, but he knew he'd have to take it.

"I don't understand the Challenge at all." Reid's strong fingers gripped the upholstery as Brody roared off the freeway to the winding mountain highway. "A woman accepts or rejects the mate-claim, and that should be it."

"Should be," Brody said, sounding reasonable. "But Shifters have always complicated things."

"No kidding," Reid said dryly.

"Do not tell me *dokk alfar* live simple and straightforward lives," Brody said. "I've heard differently, mostly from your mate."

"We have our rituals," Reid admitted. "But when it comes

to taking our partner for life, it's private. Between the two of us."

"Uh huh." Brody tried unsuccessfully to smother a chuckle. Reid and his mate, Peigi, had gone through a lot before they'd figured out they should stay together.

Shane shut out their banter, which was created through nervousness. Neal, the silent type, said nothing at all. Refreshing.

Shane watched the scenery he'd flashed past the other way yesterday as they'd fled Althea and her goons. Althea had given up going after Freya once Eric and other Shifters had intervened—or had she?

Had she chased Shane and Freya down the mountain to keep them from talking about her merc group? Or for some more sinister reason? And did she have anything to do with Leo's disappearance?

Freya was safe in Shiftertown, Shane repeated to himself. Her biggest threat there had been Leo, who'd decided to take himself to the mountains and get into trouble. She'd be fine with Nell, Cormac, Graham, Eric, Cassidy, and Diego hovering around her.

The cranky bear inside Shane wanted to jump out of the truck and run back to his mate. He'd wrap himself around her, closing them off from the world.

He caught himself with his hand on the door, ready to thrust it open. His fingers sprouted bear claws, and he felt fur springing up on his arms.

"Easy." Neal's voice was quiet in his ear. "You doing tracker shit is the best way to keep her from danger."

The fact that Neal, a mateless Guardian, understood Shane's dilemma best of everyone in the vehicle increased Shane's respect for him.

His fur vanished, and his claws receded. "Thanks," Shane whispered to Neal.

Neal nodded once and sat back as though nothing had happened.

Once desert had given way to tall trees, gray clouds, and snowbanks, Brody pulled off onto an unpaved side road. They'd passed few vehicles on the way up the mountain—it was Monday, and most people in Las Vegas were back at work, their kids in school. The resort would be quiet now as well.

Graham must have given Brody the direction to where he'd find Dougal—Graham hadn't bothered to tell Shane. Brody drove with confidence along a half-muddy, half-icy track, halting where it petered out.

A flash of padded orange jacket rippled between the trees, then Dougal stepped out to meet them.

The young Lupine's breath steamed in the air. "Glad to see you guys."

For Dougal, who shared his uncle Graham's arrogance, to be happy that two bears, a Guardian, and a *dokk alfar* had come to his aid meant something seriously wasn't good.

"What's up?" Shane asked as he hauled himself from the truck. Brody joined him. "Any sign of Leo?"

"I think so."

Dougal looked so troubled that Shane's tension heightened. "You *think* so?"

Dougal had filled out since his post-Transition leanness, and now bulked with muscle. He'd become a younger version of Graham, though without his uncle's solid air of command.

Reid unfolded his long body from the pickup, and Neal climbed out, the sword on its strap over his shoulder. The two waited wordlessly for Dougal to explain.

"I mean that I picked up his scent." Dougal shuffled his

weight from side to side with his usual restiveness. "But the closer I got, the more I smelled something else."

"Smelled what?" Reid asked him.

"I can't describe it. I thought it was another Shifter, but ... I've never encountered anything like it."

This was getting better and better. "Can you point us to where you were?" Shane asked him.

Dougal gave him a disdainful look, his bravado returning. "I'm not so chickenshit I can't lead the way. Come on. See if you can keep up."

He set off at a lope into the trees. Shane jogged after him, Reid, Neal, and Brody behind him.

Mist clung to the forest floor, tendrils of it stirred by their passing. The temperature had dropped since yesterday, but Shane felt it only marginally as the bear inside him began to heat his blood.

Or maybe that was from his burgeoning mating frenzy. Shane knew he needed to focus on the task at hand, but his thoughts were continually pulled to Freya's head resting on his chest in his bed, the warmth of her body against his, the sound of her soft breathing in the night.

After all these years, and all this loneliness. *Freya.* The Norse goddess of love.

Also of warriors fallen in battle. Shane needed to remember that before he grew all poetic.

They skimmed through undergrowth, as silent as smoke, the ground damp where the snow hadn't penetrated beneath the trees. Nothing moved. The animals that lived on the mountain had either gone dormant or were hiding from the predators in their midst.

Dougal maintained a rapid pace until he reached a small

clearing. Stumps showed where someone had cut a firebreak, the undergrowth cleared out here as well.

"This is where I found it." Dougal halted at the edge of the clearing, the others stopping beside him.

Shane wrinkled his nose, already smelling what the younger man had. "Rank."

Neal let out a soft wolf snarl, Brody's bear one echoing it.

Reid didn't have a Shifter's sense of smell, but he also made a face. "What the hell is that?"

"Shifter, but not right," Shane said. Brody and Neal nodded their agreement.

"It isn't Leo," Dougal said with confidence. "I grew up with him—I'd recognize his scent. But I think Leo fought with whatever this is."

Finished speaking, Dougal moved out across the clearing, scanning the ground as he went. He moved like a wolf, as though he'd forgotten he hadn't shifted.

"Here." Dougal straightened, his body rigid. He pointed to a hollow depression in a cushion of pine needles and dead leaves.

Shane joined him, the other three following cautiously.

Shane smelled the blood before he spied it on the leaf detritus. He also saw bits of dark gray-and-white fur that littered the hollow, plus small shreds of cloth that he identified as blue denim. Someone had shifted, ripping through their clothes as Shane had yesterday morning.

"*This* smells of Leo." Dougal gestured at the spot. "He was here. He fought something."

"What?" Brody asked. "Another Shifter?"

"Good question." Shane grew quiet as he contemplated the evidence. "Did you find a trail?" he asked Dougal.

"Possibly." Dougal gestured deeper into the woods. "But I wanted backup."

"Wise." Shane knew Dougal must have been truly spooked to call Graham and ask for help.

Shane unlaced the hiking boots he'd donned for the trek, preparing himself to shift. They could track much better in their animal forms.

This had nothing to do with Althea's mercenaries, Shane suspected. Ewan's scent hadn't been like this. He was Feline and obnoxious, but a fairly ordinary Shifter.

Shane finished undressing, hiding away his clothes as Brody was doing, and shifted.

His bear form came a little more quickly today, the animal in him bracing for their unnerving errand. The stench was now thick to his grizzly nose, far stronger than it had been in his human form.

Shane recognized the smell from experience—not the specific Shifter in question, but the general sense.

Feral.

Shane's body language and fierce growl expressed the word.

Yep, was Brody's reply.

Neal had remained human, but Shane could tell his wolf hackles were up. The hilt of his sword let out a faint *ting.*

Only Reid was safe from the onslaught of scent, but his dark eyes glittered as he surveyed the woods around them. One hand brushed back his winter jacket to reveal both a taser and a Glock. Good thinking, to bring both.

Dougal, who'd finally become wolf, started off with Lupine speediness, expecting the others to follow.

Shane had been told that bears lumbered, mostly by Felines who could hit the ground sprinting. Bears *strolled,* he'd corrected them. Why waste all the energy only to end up in the same place as the racing Felines? Bears saw interesting things along the way when they took their time.

What Shane rarely explained was that bears could charge when they wanted to, faster than a wildcat or wolf could comprehend. Bears put power behind that run, and whoever they hurtled themselves *at* was in deep shit.

Dougal's wolf paws flashed, his tail flicking as he ran. Shane moved unwaveringly, and he heard Brody coming behind him in a similar gait.

Reid, with his long legs, dashed ahead of the bears. He sometimes ran marathons, usually coming in first, and Shane saw why today. The *dokk alfar* could *move*.

Dougal halted so abruptly that Shane almost ran into him. He stopped himself in time, Brody growling softly as he did the same. Reid became motionless between one heartbeat and the next and unsheathed the Glock.

"*Kaghthak*," Reid said softly.

Shane had no idea what that meant—a *dokk alfar* swear word, he guessed. He slowly rose on his hind legs to see what Reid and Dougal were staring at.

It was Leo, or what was left of him. He'd shifted into his half-wolf, half-man form, the strongest of the shapes a Shifter could assume. His clothes hung in shreds, as did the fur on his body, long strips of it exposing bloody flesh.

One of his ears had nearly been torn off and lay beside his head, attached by a single thread of skin. Leo's eyes were half open, though his face was a caved-in mess.

Neal reached them, his startled exclamation changing to a whispered prayer to the Goddess.

Shane moved past Dougal and Reid, trying not to breathe through his nose. The feral smell was strongest here, along with the bodily fluids Leo had ejected as he fought his losing battle.

To Shane's amazement, he saw Leo's chest rise and fall.

He's still alive, his stunned mind told him, and he raced forward to aid his enemy.

CHAPTER SIXTEEN

Freya did not like the empty feeling that weighed on her after Shane sped away in Cormac's pickup. He'd sent her a cheery wave, but a tight ball formed in her stomach, one that had nothing to do with all the food she'd consumed the day before.

It was logical that she remain behind with Nell, but the wolf in her wanted to tear off after the truck, like a dog chasing a car down the road.

She paced restlessly behind the house, wondering what she'd do with herself until Shane returned.

Freya's edginess went well beyond feeling cooped up in a Shiftertown. That was part of it, but a sharp need had risen in her, one that wanted to find Shane, put herself between him and his enemies, and beat off anyone who tried to hurt him.

"Want to talk about it?" A soft voice stopped Freya mid-pace. Misty, Graham's improbable mate, watched Freya from a few yards away.

Misty was a small-statured woman but curvy and unashamedly plump. Her dark brown hair had been twisted into a knot that managed to appear styled if simple, and she wore a sweatshirt with a screen print of a howling wolf on it. She'd pushed up her sleeves, revealing a delicate tattoo of a blooming rose on the inside of her right arm.

"Nothing to talk about." Freya knew she was being curt, but her nerves were frayed. "Shane's doing his job. I'm not a tracker. No reason for me to follow him."

"Sure." The corners of Misty's warm brown eyes crinkled with her smile. "Keep telling yourself that. I know how it is, believe me. Being leader's mate is no picnic, especially when Graham's drawn into bad stuff. And at times things have been truly bad."

"Have they?" Freya surveyed the houses around them, whose overall atmosphere was calm and serene. Cubs played in yards, watched over by any Shifter who happened to be outside. "I thought everyone was safe and happy in Shiftertown."

Misty acknowledged Freya's bite of sarcasm. "I didn't understand either, before I came here. I pictured everyone locked down at night or brainwashed to believe they were content. My first sight of Shiftertown was Iona and Eric's mating ceremony—a true eye opener."

Freya had witnessed a few mating ceremonies growing up, though she'd been a cub and hadn't understood the ritual fully. "Pretty raucous, was it?"

"Shifters dancing around like crazy, many of them naked?" Again, the eye crinkling. "Raucous is a good word for it. I remember Graham watching the others, seeming lost. He didn't belong here, and he knew it."

"Graham? Lost?" Freya couldn't imagine Graham being anything other than his overbearing self. "He looks fine now. As confident as ever."

"Yes, but that took time. He was so worried about his wolves, especially the cubs, who had to fit into an already full Shiftertown. Plus, he had to figure out how to deal with Eric, who was going through mating frenzy for Iona. Then Graham and I started going out, and that was *really* confusing for him."

"I'll bet." Freya hadn't yet recovered from the shock of Graham's choice of mates. "He never had anything good to say about humans."

"I never knew Shifters could be so compassionate, or so intense." Misty's eyes filled with open love for Graham. "He's been through hell, and he's taught me so much." She paused. "He told me about you."

"Did he?"

Graham seemed to have kept Freya's existence hidden from everyone else, though of course his own pack knew about her and her disappearance. That they'd all stayed loyal to Graham and said nothing about Freya both surprised and warmed her.

"He said mates should keep no secrets from each other. Graham has told me a lot." From her expression Freya guessed he'd revealed some things she'd rather not have known. "But don't worry. I never told a soul. Mates do keep secrets—*for* each other."

"Thank you." Freya's gratitude came out sincerely.

"I'm glad to finally meet you." Misty held out her hands, and Freya took them without hesitation. The mate of a pack leader held power that had nothing to do with dominance, which would be different for Misty as human anyway.

Freya squeezed Misty's fingers, seeing strength that her softness belied.

"Let me introduce you to some of the newer members of the clan." Misty tugged Freya to walk beside her. "Just because you're mating with Shane doesn't mean you're out of Graham's pack. You're still family."

"Technically maybe," Freya said. "I've been gone a long time."

"Doesn't matter," Misty answered firmly. "Graham enjoys being a father figure to all the cubs in his pack. He'll never admit that, of course, even under torture."

"Of course." Freya had to laugh.

She remembered how Graham had scared her and Rolf at first with his loud voice and the way he could growl. But they'd both soon come to realize Graham would never hurt them. Ever. He was protective, caring, and even loving, though he'd hide it with every breath.

At one of the larger houses, Misty stepped onto the porch and opened the back door into a sunny kitchen.

Two small boys were perched on a long countertop, a large tub of ice cream between them. The lads were busily relieving the tub of its contents and didn't notice Freya and Misty enter.

Both whipped around when Misty cleared her throat, spoons still in the tub. Two little faces smeared with chocolate and marshmallow became stricken with guilt.

"Sorry, Misty," one of the boys said. "We didn't know you'd be back so soon."

Misty shook her head as she studied them. "You know the rules. Come down from there."

Both boys slid from the counter, and as they hit the floor, they morphed into wolf cubs, clothes falling away.

They were thicker-bodied than most wolf cubs, but they wagged their tails hard, gamboled into Misty, and then ran at Freya. They put noses to her boots and jeans, sniffing, sniffing.

"Oh, they're adorable." Freya crouched on the tile floor,

ruffling ears and stroking heads. The cubs yelped in joy and launched themselves at her to lick her face.

"Matt and Kyle," Misty said with fondness. "They're twins. It's easier to tell them apart when they're not wolf." Misty carried the half-eaten tub of ice cream to the table then fetched two bowls from a cupboard. "At least they used spoons this time."

Freya sat down, cross-legged, nearly knocked over by the enthusiastic cubs. They continued sniffing, back ends swaying from their energetic tails.

"I'm a twin too," she told them, her heart squeezing as she felt the absence of Rolf. The announcement was met with even more tail wagging. "Do they live here?" Freya asked Misty.

"Oh, yes. Graham took them in when their parents were killed."

Graham would have, Freya realized. She recalled the day when Graham had glared down at her and Rolf, two terrified little cubs realizing they'd been left in his care. *I suppose you're staying with me now,* he'd growled.

Even with this cranky declaration, Graham hadn't fobbed Freya or Rolf off on another wolf family and didn't leave the house without making sure they were being looked after. He hadn't demanded absolute obedience from either of them, or anything like that. He'd been a casual foster father sometimes, but never cruel or bullying, nor did he expect anything in return for his hospitality.

These cubs were relaxed and happy, currently consumed with curiosity about Freya. Their worry when Misty had caught them with the ice cream was remorse at being caught, not fear of punishment.

Shifters were different from humans, from the ground up.

The privacy Freya had built around her life to keep humans from getting too close would mean nothing at all with Shifters. Every clan and pack had their secrets, but overall privacy was an alien concept. Shifters had always lived as a community.

Shiftertowns apparently were just an extension of the prides, packs, and clan systems they'd always had. Freya would have to adjust her perceptions if she stayed—but why was she even thinking of staying?

Worry for Shane zoomed back at her. She'd felt the weirdness in the woods, and now Shane was out there, tracking it down. Without her.

As though they sensed her anxiety, the two cubs climbed onto Freya's lap, their exuberance easing. One of the wolves continued to lick her face, but the swipes became comforting kisses.

"They're very special cubs." Misty poured hot coffee from an old-fashioned pot into mugs but leaned against the counter, waiting to offer it. "They've saved my life more than once. Graham's too. They're more magical than other Lupines. Guards, Graham says they're called."

Freya's brows went up. She'd heard of Guardians, but not Guards. "What does that mean?"

"I'm not entirely sure. A friend of ours, Ben, another very magical person, told us about them." Misty paused, as though she considered how much to reveal. "According to Ben, they were created to guard the highest of the Fae, like generals and even the emperor. We take good care of them, and they take care of us."

Freya continued to stroke the little wolves, who had draped themselves over her thighs, eyes closing as they used her warmth to send them to sleep.

"They're sure cute, whatever they are."

Misty brought the coffee to Freya, who took the mug, being careful not to spill the hot liquid on the cubs.

"Graham would love it if you stayed," Misty said as she put the lid on the tub of ice cream and returned it to the freezer. "Though he says he'll understand if you don't want to."

Freya sipped the coffee, which was very good, but she couldn't be soothed, not today. "Please understand that this is hard for me. I never meant to come here, never meant to see Graham and his pack again."

"I think you *did* mean to come here." Misty resumed her slouch against the counter, but her eyes held wisdom. "Whether you realize it or not."

Freya made an exasperated noise. "You mean the Goddess sent me here to reconcile with Graham? I don't think She interferes that specifically in our business."

Misty shrugged. "You never know. Sometimes the universe drives us toward events that shape our lives."

"Now *you* sound like a motivational app." Freya's irritableness softened when one of the cubs blinked up at her with sleepy eyes. How could she stay crabby with these little guys warming her?

Misty laughed, a compassionate sound. "It's the only explanation I can find for why I turned up at a Shifter groupie bar—somewhere I'd never have gone on my own—and met Graham when he took the stool next to mine. How did we both end up in that random place on that random night?"

She had a point. "Graham sat down next to you, and you didn't run away screaming?" Freya asked in amusement.

"I thought he was hot, to be honest." Misty's eyes took on a faraway light. "I could tell he was unhappy. Not just because he'd had a bad day, but deep behind that. I saw a lot of pain and frustration in him. It touched me, somehow."

"Graham's a complicated Shifter, that's for sure." Freya took another thoughtful sip of coffee then met Misty's gaze squarely. "I'm glad he found you. Or you found him. He needed someone."

"He did," Misty said. "And I needed him."

Freya had never imagined Graham's mate would be a soft-faced, sweet-voiced human woman called Misty, but maybe Misty was right. The Goddess, or the universe, sometimes put people where they needed to be.

The cub who'd been watching her thumped his tail once, as though pleased Freya had caught on, and drifted back to sleep.

———

NEAL INGRAM HOVERED BEHIND SHANE AND REID as they bent over Leo's motionless body. Neal didn't draw the sword, to Shane's relief, which meant he thought there was hope.

Dougal's voice rose in pitch in his anguish. "We have to get him home."

"Reid?" Shane glanced at the man. "I know it's a long way, but can you take him?"

Reid nodded. "Should be able to. I've never been inside his house, so I'll have to materialize outside it. Or do you want him at a hospital?"

"Doubt a hospital could help," Brody said somberly. "Neal? What do you think?"

Neal's leather jacket creaked as he straightened up. "Hospital won't help him. He needs a Shifter healer."

"Want me to text Zander?" Shane offered.

Brody's brows went up. "Whoa, you're on texting terms

with the elusive Zander Moncrieff? He never answers his phone anyway, bro."

"He seems to know when it's important." Shane's phone was with his clothes, so he couldn't start texting immediately. "I think you should take him to Graham's house. Leo's brothers might use this as an opportunity to edge Leo out of his place. He'll be safer with Graham."

Dougal stared at him. "They'd do that?"

Shane, with more experience of Shifters through the years, nodded. "Unfortunately."

Reid didn't wait for more debate. He stepped past Shane, crouched down, and very carefully put his hands under Leo's bloody body.

Awareness flickered through Leo's eyes, and Shane saw horror when he realized what Reid was going to do.

The air around Reid heated, and Shane stepped hastily back. A hot wind burst through the woods, and then Reid and Leo were gone.

"Shit," Dougal said, now sounding exactly like Graham. "I *hate* when he does that."

SHANE TEXTED ZANDER AFTER HE PULLED ON HIS clothes, but as Brody predicted, the polar bear who was the best healer anyone knew, didn't answer. Shane tried again as Brody steered the truck back onto the icy dirt road, Dougal on his motorcycle falling in behind them.

Neal had the backseat to himself this time, but he did not relax. He drummed his fingers on jeans-clad thighs, impatient with the slow movements of the pickup. He needed to be with Leo in case the man expired.

Shane longed to tell Freya what happened, but he didn't have her number. Something he'd have to rectify. He sent a message to Cormac instead, knowing he would relay the information to those who needed it.

Brody had to take it easy until they got to a paved road, then he sped onto the highway. As they wound down the mountain, out of forest to desert again, Shane's phone vibrated with a reply from Zander.

On it, was the brief message, and nothing more.

Shane's impatience on the journey was for a different reason than Neal's. He tapped his feet against the floorboards while Brody took them down the street and through the gates then nearly tore himself out of the pickup when Brody pulled to a stop at their house.

Freya stepped calmly out of the front door and into the yard to meet him, neither hurrying nor hesitant, as though this was something she did every day. Shane's heart turned over when he realized she'd been waiting for him.

Shane went to her and enfolded her in his arms.

Freya started, then her embrace flowed around him, her whisper warm in his ear. "Hey. You okay?"

He was now. Feeling Freya against him, inhaling her scent, hearing her voice, unknotted Shane's fears and apprehensions. The small pains from his run through the underbrush in the woods, which he'd ignored at the time, evaporated and were gone. He buried his face in her shoulder and hung on.

Brody huffed as he went around them. Shane heard a mutter of "lawn ornaments in my way," but he sensed Brody's satisfaction. A new mate in the family was a welcome addition, and Brody liked Freya. Shane knew that without Brody saying a word.

Shane eased from Freya, happy that she kept hold of his arms. "Cormac tell you what's going on?" he asked.

Freya nodded, her golden eyes huge. "Nell and Cormac went over to Graham's to see if they could help. Reid said they'll need a Shifter healer. I didn't know there was such a thing."

"A couple of them out there." Shane caressed Freya's shoulders, meaning to be comforting, but he couldn't stop himself drawing comfort from her in return. "One, a full-of-himself polar bear. Another is a sweet half-Shifter from Austin. If polar bear doesn't show up soon, I'll ask her, but I'm not sure she can help in this case."

"Reid didn't say much about Leo's injuries. Are they that bad?"

"Put it this way—I was surprised he was still alive." Shane rested his forehead against hers. "I'm sorry, Freya."

"Why? You didn't hurt him." She hesitated. "Did you?"

"No, sweetheart. When I best a Shifter, I do it in a fair fight. Whatever did that to him ..." He shuddered. "It wasn't good."

Shane felt Freya tighten under his touch. "I smelled something bad out there while I was killing time waiting to meet with Althea. That's why I attacked you, remember? I was afraid you'd take me out me if I didn't disable you first."

"You thought you'd disable *me?*" Shane asked incredulously. "What if I *had* been a feral bear Shifter? You'd have been in so much danger." He didn't like the thought of that.

"I realized you weren't right after we started the fight." Freya slanted him a smile that made Shane wish they weren't in the middle of the front yard. "You smelled a lot better than a feral."

"Aw, thanks. Wait a minute. *Right* after we started? Why

did you keep going, then? Instead of saying, *Oops, sorry. Didn't mean to shred your fur.*"

"Why didn't *you* stop?" Freya's eyes sparked with something between amusement and outrage. "You even accused me of being feral. Are you saying I stank?"

"Well ..." Shane had started to enjoy the scuffle, especially the lying on top of her part. "You did need a shower, remember?"

Freya slipped from his grip with mock indignation. "Oh, thanks a lot, Shane. And you want me to be your mate?"

Shane's large hands tightened on her shoulders. "I let you take that shower, remember? Next time, maybe I could join you."

The flash of need in her eyes was unmistakable. Freya shut it down before it could flare, but Shane saw it.

Mating frenzy. The same that was stirring inside him.

Shane's phone buzzed. He tried to ignore the persistent vibration, but Freya didn't let him. "Someone's texting you."

"Yeah, might be Zander." Shane checked the message, then grimaced. "It's Eric. He wants a meeting. Xav found something, he says." Shane shut the phone off and clasped Freya's hand. "This time, you're coming with me."

CHAPTER SEVENTEEN

Freya walked beside Shane to Eric's house, her smaller hand in his large one.

If anyone had told her a month ago that she'd be in a Shiftertown, ready to visit a Feline's home and wanting to stick close to a bear, she'd have laughed herself sick. She'd have shared the prediction with Rolf, and he'd have doubled over in mirth.

Her eyes stung. Rolf had to be okay. Just had to be.

Shane led Freya onto Eric's front porch and announced through the screen door that they'd arrived. Eric and family would already know, but it was courteous to tell them.

The leggy, blond Cassidy opened the door one-handed, her other arm cradling a girl of about four with dark hair and beautiful brown eyes. Both mother and daughter regarded Freya with Feline curiosity.

"Freya, welcome." Cassidy's voice was pleasantly velvet. "I'm so happy to meet you. Blessings on the mate-claim."

"She hasn't said yes, yet," Shane reminded her. He

released Freya to slide into the house first, Shifter fashion, and continued to the living room.

"Mmm." Cassidy remained on the porch with Freya. Her eyes held something Freya couldn't read, but she sensed that Cassidy understood Freya's dilemma. "This is Amanda."

The pride in her voice was unmistakable. Freya smiled at the girl. "Hi, Amanda."

"Hi," Amanda said brightly. She wrinkled her nose. "Wolf."

Freya laughed. "That's right. But I'll try to keep it under control."

Amanda considered this. "Okay." She wriggled to get down, and Cassidy set her on her feet. "Want to see my downstairs room?" she asked Freya.

Cassidy's eyes widened, and Freya realized what Amanda had just offered. The cub didn't mean the place where she slept, but her secret room somewhere under the house. A true honor.

"Maybe later," Freya said quickly. "But only if it's all right with your mom."

Before Cassidy could answer, Amanda said, "It will be. Matt says you're nice." Her nose wrinkled again. "He's a wolf too."

"She's such a Feline," Cassidy said, her pride still evident. "Go play with Callum now. I have to talk with Uncle Eric."

"Too much talking," Amanda announced. "We can see the room later, Freya." With that, she scuttled off the porch and into the side yard, calling for Callum, who Freya assumed was Eric and Iona's cub.

"Love you, sweetie," Cassidy called after her.

"Love you too, Mom." Amanda tossed it off over her shoulder, but Cassidy glowed.

Freya's regret that she'd had no chance for cubs decided to kick her again. Of course, now that Shane had offered the claim ...

No. Freya needed to answer him with her head straight. No wishful thinking and no decisions made in the height of mate frenzy.

Sure. That should be so easy.

"Come on," Cassidy said. "Let's squeeze in."

"I absolutely do not have to see the downstairs," Freya murmured quickly to Cassidy. "Promise."

Cassidy made a little shrug. "We'll see." She sailed from the porch into the living room. "You can start now."

To Freya's surprise, Eric had waited for them. On the sofa, sitting hip-to-hip with Eric, was the dark-haired Iona. She bathed Freya in a warm smile and patted the empty cushion on her other side.

Freya had assumed Amanda and Callum were being watched over by one of the Shifter parents who lived in this house, but Diego stepped close to Cassidy, his arm stealing around her waist.

"Peigi's out there." Cassidy noted Freya's concern and waved in the direction of the backyard. "And Lindsay. Cubs are well looked after."

Unease flashed over the face of the man who must be Xav when Cassidy mentioned Lindsay. Freya felt a flicker of curiosity about that.

She took the offered seat next to Iona, though she would rather be with Shane, who'd parked himself at the front window. Shane was half turned away from the room, gazing out at the street like a guard. Which he was, Freya realized. A tracker, still on duty.

Nell and Cormac entered through the kitchen, as did

Brody, who joined Shane. With them was Reid, who stationed himself at a side window. Graham was absent, but Leo was at Graham's, so he'd have stayed there to help him.

Even without Graham, the living room was full, but Eric, lounging on the sofa with his feet up, did not suggest they move into the yard where they could spread out. Freya guessed he wanted as few Shifters to overhear as possible. Peigi and Lindsay might be watching over the cubs, but Freya would bet that they'd also been recruited to keep inquisitive Shifters away.

"Xav has a report," Eric said. He gestured for Xav, the attractive man who much resembled Diego, to begin.

"I've found out a lot about Althea Webster and her band of merry men," Xav said. He gave them a quick summary of how she'd inherited the business from her father and was determined to make it into a thriving concern. She didn't take jobs that hurt innocents, from what Xav could determine, and some that even helped the downtrodden.

"She finds clients through word of mouth," Xav continued. "Someone will mention something in a bar, and one of her agents stationed there will call a number. If that agent is given the go-ahead, he or she hands the interested person the black business card with nothing but a phone number on it. That phone number leads to another agent, and so on. Althea also has internet searches monitored, not only for ones on her business but for those looking for her kind of services. I was also able to get a bead on what *she* does internet searches for." Xav held up the electronic tablet he clutched, though Freya couldn't read what was on it from across the room.

"Yeah, this is interesting," Diego said. His tone held warning.

"Shifters," Xav said grimly. "Specifically, experiments done on Shifters in the past."

Iona's hand had been resting on Eric's thigh and now she laid the other one on his shoulder. Calming him, Freya realized. Eric's ripple of unease through the couch was palpable.

Shane glanced sharply at Eric then slid his gaze to Freya. The connection between them when their eyes met was startling. Freya drew in a quick breath, the fire in her heart flaring.

Mating frenzy? Or something else?

She forced her attention from Shane and back to the conversation, noting that everyone in the room, Diego included, had tensed mightily.

"*Why* is she so interested?" Iona demanded. Her blue eyes had gone hard with fury, a Shifter woman ready to defend her mate.

"A question I can't answer," Xav said. "Althea's done research on the kind of chips that were put into Eric and also various drugs that were pumped through Shifters, and their reactions to them."

Even Freya had heard of the experiments performed on Shifters when humans first realized that supernatural creatures walked among them. Shifter Bureau had tested Collars to get the shock reaction just right, had pumped Shifters with adrenaline to see how much they could take before passing out, and how much made them shift. There were other things, but Rolf had kept those from Freya, telling her she didn't want to know.

The experiments had stopped when anti-cruelty groups had begun to protest, but a lot of damage had already been done.

Xav's voice quieted as he continued, "She's especially interested in the experiments that made Shifters go feral."

No one spoke. One of a Shifter's greatest fears was entering the feral state, which meant loss of control over their mind, their instincts, and sometimes their bodies. They could switch to animal form and never return, losing themselves to their beasts forever.

Or they might simply go insane, attacking anyone and everyone, including those they loved. Mates, cubs, sisters, brothers, parents—family ties and even mate bonds ceased to have meaning when a Shifter went feral.

All Shifters hovered on the edge of this state, a fun gift leftover from the High Fae who'd created them centuries ago. Feral Shifters could fight without any fear whatsoever, a tactical advantage to those Fae chieftains who'd used them as Battle Beasts in their brutal wars.

Of course, feral Shifters couldn't always remember who they were supposed to be fighting. They'd slay their enemies and then turn around and go after the Fae who'd put them on the battlefield. It had only been a matter of time before Shifters organized and battled their way free of their Fae masters, ending up in the human world, and closing the gates to Faerie behind them.

Rolf had enjoyed historical research, learning all he could about both Shifter and human societies. That is, when he wasn't kicking back in pubs with the friends he attracted with his charm, and laughing hard with Freya over absolutely nothing.

Her breath caught on the pain in her heart.

As though he knew her thoughts, or at least their direction, Eric said quietly, "Freya, you have a missing brother who contacted Althea, and there's a feral running loose on the mountain..."

All eyes in the room turned to Freya, making her flush.

"My brother was not the feral in the woods," she said quickly. "I know his scent, and that wasn't it."

"Are you sure, honey?" Nell asked, voice gentle. "Once we've gone wild, it's different."

Freya shook her head. "It can't be *that* different. Shane would always know Brody, wouldn't he? Even if Brody went feral?"

"She has a point," Shane rumbled. "He'd be as much a pain-in-the ass as he ever was."

"Hey." Brody gave his brother a pretend punch on the shoulder.

"Could the feral be one of Althea's crew?" Diego asked. "She was up there with some of her guys plus another Shifter —Ewan. Maybe she either let the feral loose, or he got away from her."

"Ewan wasn't feral," Freya said, and Shane nodded his agreement. "Or even heading that way, I don't think."

"Not even close," Shane added. "Just your average annoying Feline." Instead of taking offence, the Felines in the room relaxed slightly, Iona laughing.

How different their reactions were to those of Graham and his wolf pack. The Lupines she'd grown up with had been touchy, always ready to scrap with one another. They'd never let a bear into their midst to make fun of them.

"So," Eric said. "What you've discovered, Xav, is that Althea is avidly researching experiments that turned Shifters feral, and there is a feral Shifter on the mountain where she was recently. This feral, whoever it is, attacked the hell out of Leo and nearly killed him. Might still have killed him—any word on Zander?"

Shane checked his phone and shook his head. "Just the one text back. He'll be here." His confidence was unfeigned.

"For now, I'd like to get Althea in front of me and ask her a few questions," Eric said.

"Maybe not in front of *you*." Iona's voice, though quiet, held caution.

Eric sent her a conceding glance. "You could be right." It cost him to admit this, Freya saw. "Because researchers did those kinds of experiments on me," he explained to Freya. "My mate is telling me I wouldn't be objective."

Eric revealing this weakness to a Lupine and an outsider surprised the hell out of Freya. Graham would never tell his wolves if he'd been a test subject.

But Eric wasn't that kind of leader, Freya had come to understand. He laid himself bare and then let Shifters take him as he was without compromise. Considering he'd held this entire Shiftertown together for twenty-five years indicated that he was powerful indeed.

"Good thing I know someone who will be," Eric continued.

Another round of silence fell. Everyone seemed to know who Eric was talking about. Freya sent Shane a questioning look, but he only gave her a minute shake of his head.

"I wouldn't call him objective, actually," Shane said to Eric.

"But he can get answers," Brody said.

"And he has way better backup than any of us do," Shane said.

A ripple of amusement went through those present. It was irritating for Freya not to be in on the joke.

"None of this matters if we don't know where Althea is," Shane pointed out.

"Xav?" Eric prompted.

"She has offices in several locations," Xav said. "Los Angeles, Seattle, Dallas. She went back to the Dallas office last night."

"Handy," Eric said with approval.

Freya wasn't certain why. Dallas was a two-hour flight or a twelve-hundred-mile drive from Las Vegas, and Shifters—Collared ones in Shiftertowns, anyway—weren't allowed to fly.

"I'll call him," Eric said, though again he didn't mention names. "I hate to say this, because putting my friends in danger is not what I want to do, but we have to go back up to the mountain."

"And find the feral," Shane finished.

Eric nodded. "We need to get him under control and figure out what he knows—especially if Althea has anything to do with him, anything at all. Also, to help him ... if we can."

He did not voice what would happen if they couldn't. A feral Shifter who was too far gone would have to be killed, for its own sake as well as others' safety. It was a worry every Shifter carried deep inside them.

"Shane, take Brody, Reid, and Neal," Eric ordered. "Dougal too, if he's up to it. But don't let him get hurt trying to prove himself."

"Sure thing, boss," Shane said without argument.

Freya got to her feet. "I can go with Shane." She faced Eric before anyone could interrupt her. "I scented the feral before, and I might be able to recognize it. If he knows where Rolf is, or if he shared the feral's fate, I need that information. I don't want to wait for it."

Eric didn't change expression. "I fully intend for you to go with Shane. He won't be as focused if he's worried about you here, no matter how much Nell and I promise to protect you. I don't need any fuck-ups with this."

Shane didn't look surprised. "You're right—I'd be seriously

unfocussed. Then you'd get in my face, Mom would get into yours, and all hell would break loose. Let's keep it simple."

Nothing was simple at all, but Freya didn't comment.

She hadn't meant to go to Shane, yet for some reason, she ended up next to him, close enough to touch. To her dismay, she watched her own hand reach for his, but fortunately, Shane's phone buzzed at that instant, and she dropped her arm to her side.

Shane's face tightened when he read the message on his illegal too-tech-for-Shifters phone. "Zander's here," he announced.

CHAPTER EIGHTEEN

Zander proved to be a massive man who emerged from a comically small taxi in front of Eric's house. He exchanged jovial words with the driver, the two of them joking like best friends, then he reached into the car to help a young woman emerge.

She had a dark braid of hair down her back and storm-gray eyes. A Lupine, Freya knew immediately. The young woman smiled a greeting at those who'd gathered in Eric's front yard before she withdrew a long, leather-wrapped bundle from the taxi's backseat. She cradled it carefully and went to join Zander.

They were mates. Their body language and the tender glance Zander gave her shouted that fact. Freya felt a faint shimmer of magic coming from the bundle, and she stiffened in shock.

"Sword," Shane whispered to her. "Yep, she's a Guardian."

Well, well, well. Times had changed indeed if a woman had made it through the Choosing for a Guardian. Guardians had always been men, despite the fact that a female Fae had been responsible for all the magic in the original Sword.

The taxi driver gave Zander and the woman a final wave, and then turned the car around to head out of Shiftertown.

"Are humans in this city happy to give Shifters rides?" Freya asked. Rolf had told her that many taxi and ride-share drivers would refuse Shifter fares and sometimes report them to Shifter Bureau.

"Not usually," Shane answered. "But Zander can talk anyone into doing anything. Anyone except Eric," he added in a murmur. "Watch."

Zander, who wore a long black duster coat and had two pure white braids strung with beads framing his face, spread his arms. "Greetings, Vegans."

"Zander," Eric answered in a neutral tone, then ignored the big man and turned to the woman. "Rae Lyall. Welcome to my home." He took Rae's hands in his and pulled her into a careful hug. Zander hovered like a thundercloud, but Eric continued the embrace one Shifter gave to another to show they wouldn't attack. "Please greet your father for me."

"He sends his love." Rae spoke in a smooth alto as Eric released her. "Are we in time?"

"He's still alive." Eric stepped back, somber. "But in a bad way. His injuries are extensive, I must warn you."

"If they weren't, Shane wouldn't have summoned me," Zander said. He turned to Shane and did the arm-spreading thing again. "Shane! How are you, my second-favorite grizzly?"

"Doing well, my least favorite polar bear."

Zander laughed. The two men slammed together in a Shifter embrace, hugging as though they were the closest friends in the world.

"Who is your first-favorite grizzly?" Freya asked Zander when they parted. Polar bear Shifters were rare, but that explained his white-blond braids and very black eyes.

Zander gazed down at Freya from his great height, and the wolf inside her stilled. For all his ebullience, Freya saw in him a vast mixture of sorrow and compassion. It was as though he'd looked upon too much suffering in the world. If he was a healer, then he had.

Freya sensed all this in the instant before Zander's eyes shuttered. "My favorite grizzly is Nell, of course," he boomed. "How are you, you beautiful thing?"

"Too old and wise to fall for your flattery, Moncrieff." Nell sent him a severe frown but couldn't hide her amusement.

Next to her, Cormac openly grinned. "She's my favorite grizzly too, Healer."

"As it should be." Zander returned his attention to Shane and Freya. "Who is your mate, Shane? You should have told me. I would have brought a mating ceremony gift."

"I haven't accepted his claim," Freya said quickly. She wondered how Zander knew about it. She doubted Shane would have mentioned the mate-claim in texts asking him to come help Leo. "I'm Freya McHugh, by the way. I'm only visiting."

"Of course, you are." Zander gave her a knowing nod.

Freya saw Zander note her lack of Collar. He didn't wear a Collar either.

Zander touched his neck, as though she'd asked a question about it. "I have a fake one, for special occasions. But fishing at Tahoe isn't where I need it. If you're wondering how we got here so fast, Marlo was fishing with me and flew us here. He's not so skilled a fisherman, but he knows how to keep the beer stocked."

Everyone laughed, though the laughter was strained. It was uncertain whether Zander could save Leo. While Leo had never been popular, any Shifter suffering and dying was a tragedy, a loss for both his family and his community.

Rae cut through the banter by laying her bundle on the ground and pulling Freya into a gentle embrace. Freya smelled pine and warmth—Lupine scents—and sensed the wolf inside her. The sword beside them let out a shimmering hum.

"It likes you," Zander said. "*I* like you."

He waited for Rae and Freya to part before he hauled Freya into a huge bear hug. The embrace wasn't sexual or possessive, but a welcome into Zander's and Rae's circle. Shane hovered, but without any jealous anger, happy that Freya was meeting his friends.

When Zander released Freya, he held her by the shoulders while she caught her breath. He peered down into her eyes, as though understanding everything about her.

"Keep him in your heart," he said, his voice surprisingly quiet. "That way, no matter what happens, he'll never be gone."

Freya's lips parted. Was he talking about Shane or her missing brother? Had Eric or Shane filled him in?

Zander grinned at her confusion then swung around and faced the gathered Shifters, fists in the air.

"Laters, peeps," Zander boomed. "Eric, lay in the brews. I'm going to need them."

With that cheerful statement, he strode off in the direction of Graham's house. Rae had lifted the sword while Zander had made his loud farewell and now fell into step beside him.

"Does he know about Rolf?" Freya asked Shane. "How much did you tell him?"

"I didn't say a word." Shane moved to her, surrounding her

in his comforting warmth. "He likes to act like he's crazy, but Zander is very perceptive. He can read people. He's not telepathic, but he just seems to know when you're hurting."

Freya edged closer to Shane, unnerved that she wanted to be next to him as often as possible. "I should go with them. Leo's never been my favorite person, but he's one of Graham's pack. Not blood-related, but family all the same."

"Yeah, we should make sure he's all right." Shane's arm brushed the length of hers, as though he shared Freya's need to be close.

While Freya hadn't said the words that would complete the mate-claim, she knew that mating was more complicated than the rituals Shifters had created for it. The animals inside them knew exactly what their human brains took longer to acknowledge—a connection that would soon be impossible to break.

Before they could start off after Zander and Rae, Eric called out from his front porch.

"Shane. Speak to you a sec?"

Shane heaved a sigh from the soles of his motorcycle boots. "Go on, Freya. I'll catch up. A tracker's work is never done."

A few days ago, Freya had considered herself capable and independent, traveling the length of California alone and sleeping outside as wolf for some of it. Now she hesitated over the distance to Graham's house a few doors down.

Not that she was afraid. She simply didn't want Shane out of her sight.

Eric waited, not without understanding, but his word overrode Freya's needs. Shane sent Freya an apologetic glance before he turned from her and jogged toward Eric.

Freya squared her shoulders, told her wolf to stop growling, and made for Graham's home.

———

Everyone was inside Graham's house by the time Misty let Freya in through the kitchen.

"They're upstairs," Misty said. "Leo's in a bad way. Graham is not happy."

Her understated way of saying Graham was devastated, Freya guessed. Graham was gruff and bellowing, but when any of his Lupines were hurt, he moved heaven and earth to help them.

"I need to go up," Freya said.

Misty drew a breath, likely to tell Freya she shouldn't, then she nodded. "First door at the top of the stairs."

Freya thanked her and left the kitchen, climbing the stairs through the quiet house. She had no illusion that she could assist in any physical way, but when a Shifter was hurt, even the presence of others could help.

Graham would need her more than Leo would, Freya suspected. Another broken link in the pack would be felt across it. She could at least heal the one between herself and Graham.

The bedroom she entered was large but crowded. Graham stood at the foot of the bed, his arms folded, glowering at the bloody human-shaped body that was Leo.

Freya hadn't seen Leo brought in, and now she swallowed a lump in her throat. The abrasions from claws and teeth were so thick she could barely see an inch of untouched skin. Leo's eyes were closed, his face icy pale. One of his hands had changed to a wolf paw, but lay limply on his stomach, as though he'd lost all energy to continue the shift in either direction.

This Shiftertown's Guardian, Neal, sat on a chair too small for his bulk, his sword resting across his knees.

It was humming, a palpable sound. Rae's sword, now out of its bundle and strapped to her back, hummed in return. Graham's scowl went to the blades, as though their noise offended him.

Zander removed his duster to reveal a T-shirt with several different fish species printed in a line down his back. Pain and compassion warred on his face as he gazed down at Leo.

"It's bad," he murmured. "Sweetheart?" he said to Rae.

Rae unsheathed her sword. Freya hoped she wasn't about to relieve Leo's suffering by sending him to the afterlife, but Rae merely held the sword out to Zander.

Resting his big hand on the silver hilt Zander sank to his knees. He placed his other hand on Leo's wolf paw, and then he began to chant.

The words sounded ancient. They were unintelligible to her, though she could sense the prayer to the Goddess in them.

She went to stand at Graham's side. "Will they truly be able to help?" she whispered.

Graham answered in a low voice, "No idea. If they can fix him, then Zander will be in pain for a long time, and Leo will still be an asshole. If Zander *can't* fix him ..."

They'd have a sad ceremony to the Goddess, and Leo's brothers would mourn. They'd possibly blame Freya's return for his injuries, or maybe Shane. Things could get bad.

Freya slipped her hand into Graham's. "Even if I don't stay here permanently, I'll come back to visit you. I won't disappear again. I'm still part of your pack."

Graham's frown deepened, but he squeezed her fingers. "Don't make promises you might not keep, little cub. We'll decide what's best for you once we figure out this shit and get your brother back."

A typical Graham answer, but he wasn't wrong. They had a long way to go to resolve all their issues. But Freya standing here, her hand in Graham's, was a start.

Zander clenched the sword's hilt until his knuckles whitened, but he didn't cease chanting. His voice never wavered, but Freya heard a note of pain in it he strove to hide.

The wolf in her began to snarl, uneasy with the sword's humming and Zander's obvious agony. The air felt dense, too much magic clouding it.

Rae turned her head and looked at Freya. Freya read the same worry in her, the one that wanted to grab her mate and haul him out of there.

She had to watch this all the time, Freya realized. To see Zander go through whatever torture happened inside him that let his healing powers work.

Freya sent her a smile of sympathy mixed with respect. The magic in Rae's sword must aid Zander's ability, and keep him from falling apart entirely, but it was still difficult to witness.

Zander's voice grew louder, his deep rumble rising.

Slowly, slowly, Leo's wounds began to close. Freya blinked in amazement as strips of bloody skin wove together and the severed ear smoothed back to his head. Rae went down on one knee as Zander's hand began to slip from the sword's hilt, and she settled his grip on the sword once more.

Neal's sword thrummed on his lap, and he lifted his hands away as though he didn't know what to do with this response. Rae's sword answered, sounding almost gleeful.

Zander slumped more and more as Leo continued to heal. Finally, Leo drew a long breath, his paw changing to a human hand. His chest began to rise and fall with ease, a man asleep instead of one struggling to live.

Graham let out a relieved sigh a moment before Rae dropped the sword and caught Zander as he fell into her arms. Freya started forward to help, but a strong hand—Shane's—held her back. She hadn't heard Shane enter, but every part of her was glad he was here.

"She's got him," Shane murmured. "It's a Guardian-Healer thing."

Zander lay in Rae's embrace, eyes closed in utter exhaustion. Rae's sword continued to ring—*it* was happy.

Graham went to the bed and laid his hand on Leo's shoulder. Whatever anyone felt about Leo, there would be no hole in the world from his death today.

Zander's face was drained of color, the robust man now a collapsed wreck on the floor.

"Will they be all right?" Freya whispered as she let Shane lead her into the hall.

"Eventually." Shane shook his head. "Zander has a hell of a job. I think of that when I'm complaining about Eric sending me out at two a.m. to see what Shifters are yelling about."

"Don't downplay what you do," Freya said. "It's tough to keep the peace among Shifters living so close together. I'm surprised it's as quiet as it is here."

"Graham, Nell, and Eric command a lot of respect."

Freya ran her hand over his strong arm. "And they have competent trackers."

"Now, you're buttering me up." Shane sent her a grin. "Does that mean you like me?"

Freya snatched her touch away, annoyed with her lack of control. "Don't get too full of yourself. I—"

She broke off when she saw two little wolves emerge at the

top of the stairs. One morphed into the form of a boy. Matt or Kyle—Freya wasn't sure.

"Are you mates yet?" he demanded.

"Yes," Shane said, at the same time Freya said quickly, "No."

"You'll be mates," Kyle, or Matt, said with confidence. "You have to be. You need each other, for what is to come."

Freya stared at him. His last sentence had been uttered in a deeper voice, still his but with a resonance that didn't go with his tiny stature.

The boy regarded her with an innocent expression, as though unaware he'd intoned such a dire proclamation.

"Zander will be okay," he went on in his normal voice. "Rae's his mate. She heals *him*."

The other twin, who'd remained a wolf, let out a little howl of agreement.

Freya sank to her heels to rub the wolf cub's fur and ruffle the hair of the one who'd spoken. He shifted instantly to a wolf again, snuggling to her for his share of pets.

"You two are adorable," Freya crooned.

"They're little shits," Shane said. "But yeah. We love them."

Freya feigned amazement. "This from a bear. These cubs *must* be special."

Matt and Kyle yipped and howled, leaping around under Freya's hands, tails going wild.

From inside the bedroom came Leo's voice, very weak. "Will someone make those two brats shut *up*?"

———

Althea Webster entered her office at the top of a downtown Dallas high-rise at midnight and found someone there.

Two someones. She'd come in for a few hours of peaceful alone time to go through her plans, leaving her guards at the end of the hall. Her floor was always tightly secure.

Evidently not secure enough.

A man sat at her desk, the light from her computer screens illuminating a hard face and vivid blue eyes. His hair was very dark, with only a few strands of gray at the temples.

Though he was a big man, he was nowhere near as huge as the one who stood solidly behind him. *He* was clearly a Shifter, bulking larger than any human Althea had ever seen. The dim light showed that his hair was striped black and orange.

"Obviously, I need to have a word with my security team." Althea halted in the doorway, her path to escape clear behind her. "I know you, don't I? Or know of you."

"Dylan Morrissey," the man said without looking up. "This is Tiger. That is my son, Sean."

Dylan jerked his thumb at Tiger behind him. Althea jumped when another Shifter, lounging in a chair behind the door, sent her a lazy salute. She hadn't noted him at all, which was bad of her. Dylan must have positioned the very unnerving Tiger where he was in order to draw her attention.

Sean was a younger version of Dylan. A naked broadsword leaned against the wall beside him, and Althea swore it emitted a faint hum.

Althea spent a second or two regaining her composure, though outwardly it would appear she'd never lost it. She'd learned since childhood to conceal her surprise and anger, and most importantly, her fear. Many people thought Althea cold, but in truth she had plenty of emotions. She simply took great care that they couldn't be used against her.

"I've heard of you, of course, Mr. Morrissey." Anyone who knew anything about Shifters had. "I would be happy to speak to you if you make an appointment. As it is, I must ask you to leave. My guards can escort you out if you wish."

"Tiger would make short work of your guards, lass, and there's no need for that."

Althea believed him. "Did you come to hire me?" she asked. "Or to work for me?"

She managed to put a hint of amusement in her voice, while inwardly, she was wary. If these Shifters decided to attack her, kidnap her, or kill her, she could do little about it. Even the small pistol she kept in her purse wouldn't help against three of them. She had the feeling it wouldn't make a dent in the one called Tiger.

At the same time that she calculated her chances for survival, she made mental notes about how to prevent Shifters circumventing her security again. A few people would have to be demoted.

"Neither." Dylan laid his hands flat on her desk and regarded her without tension. "I came to find out why you're so keen on making Shifters go feral. And to stop you, lass. I can't be having that."

CHAPTER NINETEEN

Althea's legs weakened from both relief and fear, wanting to bend as much as she commanded them not to.

A chair bumped the backs of her knees, and a warm voice very like Dylan's said in her ear, "Sit down, love. You look all in."

Sean Morrissey was next to her—she'd never heard him move—one hand on her shoulder, the other on the chair he'd drawn to her.

Instead of arrogantly protesting she was fine, Althea sank into the seat. Sean released her from his grip, its absence making her suddenly cold.

The one called Tiger remained still, a massive statue in a San Antonio Spurs sweatshirt. Tiger didn't look like a Shifter who was a big basketball fan—he'd most likely worn the shirt because someone had handed it to him.

Tiger watched her with golden eyes that unnerved her more than any Shifter's gaze ever had. This one had walked through fire, Althea sensed, had seen and survived things most Shifters had not.

In spite of Tiger's obvious size and strength, Althea clocked Dylan as the most dangerous person in the room. The other two were formidable in their own right, but they answered to him.

She removed her purse strap from her shoulder with careful deliberation and set the bag squarely on her lap. She met Dylan's gaze, as difficult as that was, and decided to give him the bare truth.

"I have no interest in making Shifters go feral." Althea was pleased her voice was crisp and businesslike. "I am trying to discover who *is* making them feral and how I can stop them."

Several heartbeats of silence went by. She realized she'd surprised them.

Shifters were masters of hiding their emotions, but these three hadn't been expecting her reply. Dylan inhaled softly—testing her scent, she believed. Shifters could smell a lie.

Dylan gestured to whatever he'd pulled up on her screen. "It looks to me like you've found all kinds of methods that can be tried. Drugs, electric shocks, reprogramming Collars. Torture."

His voice chilled as he ran through the list. Althea understood that Dylan was on the edge of fury, and nothing good could come of his anger.

"I know." She crossed her slim legs, a sign to her listeners that she was comfortable, yet closing them off at the same time. "The information is out there for anyone who looks hard enough. Someone else has found it, and someone is creating feral Shifters. A rival of mine, very likely. When I tightened up my father's company, some of those I let go decided to set up their own private armies, and they try to get in my way on occasion—ruthlessly. I've already lost very good soldiers in conflict." She decided not to say exactly where the fight had taken place. It had been a disaster, and her men had barely made it out.

"You don't know who directed that conflict?" Dylan asked.

"No. Which annoys me." Althea had been angry, upset, and grieved by the loss of her men. She knew her soldiers individually—who they were and who they had been before they'd come to her. None of those who'd made it home had blamed her for the loss, but she blamed herself. She should have been more prepared.

"Hmm." Dylan's gaze flicked back to the screen. "Could be, we could help you find out."

He made it sound like an offer, but Althea heard it as a command. "What are you suggesting?" she asked.

"Share with me everything you know about these ferals and who their creators might be. Dossiers on these rivals, every speculation, every fact." Dylan's eyes went a lighter shade of blue. "I and my trackers will narrow down the possibilities and find the culprit."

"And then what?" Althea pretended the question was casual, mere curiosity.

"Then we deal with them."

The answer was flat and final. Althea suppressed a shiver.

"I don't think Shifter Bureau will let you deal with them," she pointed out.

"Shifter Bureau doesn't have to know."

Dylan's commanding tone was no longer subtle. His eyes held a cold hardness that told Althea he would not tolerate her turning around and summoning Shifter Bureau after this meeting. That if she did, it might be her last act on earth.

"I have no liking for Shifter Bureau," Althea stated. "Short-sighted idiots."

"And you're different?"

"Because I hire Shifters to be soldiers? I see the potential for Shifters to be useful members of society. They can teach us so much, enrich our lives." She shrugged. "Too bad Shifter Bureau can't see beyond their fear. If Shifters had wanted to wipe out humanity and take over, they would done so have long ago."

"True." Dylan gave her an approving nod. "But we are still dangerous. If we're not suppressed, who knows what we'll do?"

"Be terrific soldiers, leaders, and innovators," Althea said promptly. She'd always believed that without hesitation, though her father had not. His one blind spot. "You could show us how to be stronger."

"Mmm." Dylan made his noncommittal noise. "You'd harness the power of Shifters? Maybe we don't want to be harnessed. Maybe we don't want to teach humans anything."

"It would be your choice, of course." Althea returned his nod with a cool one of her own. "That is the point Shifter Bureau doesn't understand."

Sean and Tiger listened to this debate without changing expression or offering their opinions. Whatever they thought about Shifters blending with human society, they kept to themselves.

Dylan did another scan of her screens, probably memorizing every byte of data on it. Though Tiger never looked at the computer, Althea had the weird feeling he'd absorbed all its information as well.

"I find it interesting that you decided to meet Freya McHugh at the resort on Mount Charleston," Dylan said. "Very near the place a feral was running around. One that attacked and nearly killed a Shifter."

Althea's eyes widened before she could stop herself. "Freya? Is she all right?"

"The lass is fine and safe—she wasn't the one attacked. But she has questions, as I do. First, why Mount Charleston? Did you know about the loose feral there?"

"No, I didn't. I wouldn't have risked her life, or my own men if I'd known." She tightened her lips. "Freya had good potential. Wasted now, of course. She's stuck in a Shiftertown," she finished in disgust.

"You chased her and Shane to its gates," Dylan stated. "She obviously wanted to get away from you."

"It wasn't obvious at all," Althea snapped. "When Shifters come to me, it's because they need a job and know they can provide what I need. I wanted to give Freya a place to be safe, where a feral-making maniac wouldn't get hold of her." Her impatience increased. "Then that giant lug of a Collared Shifter brainwashed her into thinking she needed to be rescued and trapped in his Shiftertown. I was trying to save her from that. But I wasn't foolish enough to think I could best all those Shifters at the gate when we reached it. I hope Freya finds a way to escape them. She'll have a place with me if she does."

Althea had gone rigid as her answer became a rant. She made herself relax into the chair and take a long, slow breath. She hadn't become emotional in front of anyone in a long time, especially not anyone male. Dylan was compelling—she felt that from him in waves.

"Makes sense, Dad," Sean said. His voice was easy, calm, exactly what Althea needed to be right now. "Why would a Shifter run *to* a Shiftertown if she didn't have to?"

Dylan didn't answer him, his focus all for Althea. "What about her brother?"

Freya had stood in front of Althea and demanded she be

told where her brother was. "I don't know anything about him. Rolf never came to me."

"Your card was found in his apartment after he went missing."

"I have a record of my agent giving him my card, but that is as far as the association went. Not all potential recruits contact me. According to Freya, now he's missing." Althea took another surreptitious breath. "This troubles me."

"And me," Dylan said, voice dry. "And his sister too, of course."

"I'll put my best agents onto it," Althea said. Her right foot jerked the slightest bit, and she stilled it with effort. "He needs to be found."

The man called Tiger finally spoke, his voice reverberating through the room. "You think he might have been captured by the ones making ferals."

Althea tried to look away from Tiger's intense gaze and found she couldn't. "Unfortunately, I do."

"Then we will need access to your research," Dylan said. "Sean?" He beckoned to his son.

Althea sat up straight, uncrossing her legs. "You mean right now?"

Dylan's shrug was almost imperceptible. "No time like the present."

Sean moved to Althea's desk in answer to his father's summons, leather jacket whispering.

Althea opened her mouth to explain that her information was confidential, proprietary—no one could be allowed to look at it. But she realized she was not going to prevail.

Sean sent her a look of quiet understanding. Althea was struck by what a handsome man he was. She'd long ago decided that it wasn't worth it for her to be attracted or attached to any man, but she could see why she might be tempted to make an exception for Sean.

She knew something of the Morrissey family who ruled the Shiftertown in Austin. Sean had a wife—a mate, as Shifters called them. Althea had no intention of getting involved with a Shifter, but she acknowledged that Sean's mate was a very lucky woman.

Dylan rose, backing away from the desk to let Sean sit down where his father had been. Sean's broad hands went to the keyboard, his fingers proving skilled as they danced across the keys.

Althea could only watch as her data was sifted through— every file, every spreadsheet, every bit of information she'd collected through her years of running this agency. Her father had collected much before her. Now all opened to Sean.

Althea looked away from Sean to find Tiger studying her intently. In all her research, she'd never heard mention of him.

"It's all right," Tiger said reassuringly. "Sean will take good care of everything."

He said it with such comfort and conviction that Althea believed him. She found herself relaxing, though she wasn't certain why, while the Morrissey father and son competently robbed her agency of all its knowledge.

———

AFTER A RESTLESS NIGHT, FREYA FOUND HERSELF SITTING next to Shane in another pickup, heading back up Mount Charleston. Close to her other side on the front bench seat was Brody, the two bears sandwiching her between them. They rode in Cormac's large F450, but with Shane and Brody the size they were, there was very little room left for her.

The smaller back seat held Reid and Neal Ingram. The sheathed Sword of the Guardian hummed, not as loudly as it had when Zander had healed Leo, but it was there on the edge of Freya's hearing. She was surprised none of the others seemed to notice the faint noise, but maybe they were simply used to it.

Dougal rode behind them on his motorcycle, having flatly refused to ride in a vehicle with so many bears.

Zander and Rae had disappeared deeper into Graham's house after Leo's healing, to rest and recover. Leo had remained in bed. When Freya had looked in on him before she'd left the house, she'd found him wan. Weak.

Leo had acknowledged her with a nod of his head, but his arrogance had dimmed, and he'd made no mention of the Challenge he'd leveled at Shane. Freya wasn't certain he'd forget about it, but all the bluster had been taken from him.

Shane had avoided Freya for the rest of the evening. He'd gone to speak with Neal and Reid, going over plans for today, and only returned once the meal Cormac and Nell had put together was well in progress.

Freya had slept by herself that night, which had been lonely, but the arrangement had been better for her and Shane both. Mating frenzy might have goaded her into not resisting Shane, and she needed to resist. She had to find Rolf, who was out there somewhere, and until she knew what had happened to him, she couldn't think about Shane and a mate-claim that would confine her to a Shiftertown. Rolf had been her only family, the two of them their own tiny wolf pack for many years. She couldn't shove worrying thoughts of him out of the way to bask in ones of Shane.

At least that's what Freya told herself as she hugged the pillow, missing Shane's warmth. She knew full well that if she and Shane let themselves be alone, they'd succumb to frenzy and might never come out of it.

As Shane navigated their way up the mountain, he told them what Eric had relayed to him early this morning. Dylan Morrissey, of the Austin Shiftertown, had met with Althea and learned that someone, not her, was creating feral Shifters to fight for them.

The Shifters and Reid listened to this grimly. Freya continued to believe that the feral running around in the mountains wasn't Rolf, but her concern for him grew. Was this what had happened to him?

Shane drove them up the unpaved road close to where they'd found Leo, Dougal bumping slowly behind them.

It had snowed in the night, and the road was covered with a film of ice. The truck sliced through it, splashing mud and slush into the morning air.

Shane stopped at the end of the track. Brody, Neal, and Reid piled out in silence, Neal shouldering his sword. Dougal cut his engine, and a hush fell over the woods.

Any other time, Freya would find the quiet peaceful. The trees sighed in the breeze, and sunlight filtered through pine needles and the stark, empty branches of deciduous trees. Shane's warmth at her side stirred dark need within her.

"I know." Shane rested his gaze on her, the same longing in it that Freya felt. He drew a long breath. "Let's get this done."

Freya nodded. She started to slide across the seat to follow Brody out, but Shane briefly pulled her back to him, his arm going around her, and kissed her.

Freya's desires flared to life, blotting out the woods, the other Shifters, and their quest. Shane's mouth was firm, no longer polite. He opened her, tasted, and Freya hung on and tasted him back.

He conveyed he wanted so much more than kissing, and Freya wanted it too. Soon she'd not be able to fight anymore. Mating frenzy would consume her, and Freya would let it.

Her wolf gave a satisfied growl. *About time you caught on.*

Something thumped the front of the pickup. Freya jumped but Shane took his time ending the kiss.

"He's not going to give us any peace," Shane murmured as he brushed back Freya's hair, his touch full of heat.

Brody leaned on the hood of the pickup, unabashedly staring at them through the window. "Any time you two are ready."

"We should go," Freya said to Shane.

"Yep." Shane brushed a soft kiss to her forehead. "We'll find them, Freya. Both this feral and your brother."

"We will." If Freya said it like she believed it, it would come true, wouldn't it? "And then ..."

Shane's eyes filled with fire. "Yeah. Then."

He deliberately uncurled his hands from around her and opened the driver's side door. Freya quickly slid out of the passenger side, smoothing her jacket as she stepped into the cold air.

Brody continued to be amused as he watched her and Shane, but his mocking wasn't derisive. He seemed happy that she and Shane were lusting for each other, pleased for his brother.

She wasn't certain anymore whether she'd refuse Shane's mate-claim or not. Freya definitely didn't want to live in a Shiftertown for the rest of her life, but living on her own, without Shane, was no longer as appealing. She'd be back to her own life and free, but there would be an emptiness now. Meeting Shane had changed her, and she'd no longer be the same person she'd been.

Freya shook off her thoughts. Nothing could be decided until they found Rolf, however. She squared her shoulders, ready to search for the dangerous Shifter who might know where her lost brother was.

———

After several hours with no sign of any Shifter, feral or otherwise, Shane became convinced the feral had left the mountain.

"I don't like that idea," he said as the six of them gathered to confer. They'd searched in teams of three, Shane deciding any fewer in a group would be too dangerous. "Where has he gone? Down into Vegas? He could do a lot of damage there."

"No reports of any problems at the ski lodge," Reid said. "A lot of vulnerable humans there, but this feral hasn't attacked any."

Freya stood close to Shane, as though she liked being where she could touch him. They'd shifted for the search, leaving clothes hidden near the truck. Now that they'd shifted back, Freya's lovely nude body next to his was making it hard to concentrate.

"Maybe the feral isn't so far gone then," she said, arms folded over her lush breasts the others knew better than to ogle. "He knows humans are off limits, and besides, there's a lot of cubs with them." Her voice softened. "I'm glad he hasn't hurt the cubs."

"If he's in the desert now, this turns into searching for a needle in a haystack," Brody rumbled. "We'll need more help."

"Plus air support," Shane said. "Marlo?"

Neal gave him a nod. "He's still around. Waiting to take Zander and Rae home when they're ready."

"Well, Marlo might have to make a detour." Shane strove to keep his eyes off Freya's delectable body. "Let's at least try to pick up a trail. If the feral isn't here, we need to know which direction it went."

"If it's still alive," Neal said.

Trust a Guardian to inject a somber note. "True," Shane said. "Let's hope it's alive, not only for its own sake, but because anything that can kill a feral would be worse than it."

They shifted again to their animal forms, Freya searching with Shane and Brody, Dougal following Neal and Reid. Dougal didn't like Reid, but he respected the hell out of Neal, who would keep the young Lupine in line.

By the time the sun went down, the Shifters had found no sign of the feral's immediate presence. They'd picked up the scent a few times, only to have it peter out in different places in deep woods. The feral, Shane concluded, was very good at laying false trails.

Freya as wolf sat on her haunches once they regrouped, tongue lolling. Her wolf was beautiful—silky gray hair so thick she had a ruff around her neck. Her fur went well with her golden eyes, watchful under pricked ears.

She indicated nothing, but Shane sensed her fatigue. Freya hadn't had much rest at all since she'd arrived in Shiftertown. She'd valiantly continue, but it was clear, with the discouraging hunt, that she needed a break.

Shane shifted to human form. "Let me take Freya to Iona's cabin," he said to the others. "It's getting dark, which makes the search more dangerous."

While Shifters had terrific senses of hearing and smell, the feral would have the upper hand in its enhanced state. Shane hated to retreat to the city, however—it would be that much harder to pick up the scent in the morning.

Brody, also human once more, nodded thoughtfully. "You and Freya rest. We'll look around a bit longer, then report back to Mom and Eric."

Dougal's brows came together in puzzlement, and he opened his mouth to ask a question, but Neal overrode him.

"Yes, I think that's the best idea," the Guardian rumbled. "We'll be there after a while and then start again in the morning."

"Why will they be safe at the cabin?" Dougal demanded, determined to be heard. "We should stick together."

"No Shifter will go to Eric's cabin without an invitation," Brody said. "Eric's scent is all over it, and any Shifter will know he's an alpha. Not to mention all the overlapping scents of Iona, Cassidy and Jace, and our mom and Cormac."

"It's defendable, and we'll be around," Reid put in. "Freya should be safe." He sent Shane a reassuring look, but even Reid knew what might happen when Shane and Freya were alone.

"I guess." Dougal was past his Transition, but he still thought like a cub sometimes.

Shane led the way back to where they'd hidden clothing, Freya remaining in wolf form. She maintained it even when Shane dressed. He bundled up her clothes and strode ahead of her to the cabin.

He unlocked the door in the quietness of dusk, and gestured Freya inside. "Welcome, my love. If you stay wolf, don't get too much hair on the sofa. Iona will give me one of her disappointed looks, and I don't want that."

Freya, after giving him a disdainful wolf stare, strode in, her tail held at an arrogant angle. Shane chuckled and closed the door behind her.

THE WOLF IN THE DARKNESS EMITTED A SOFT GROWL. IT watched the cabin as lights went on in the windows, first downstairs, then up.

Light, warmth, comfort. Home. Mate.

All the things the wolf had forgotten. All the things it wanted again but had no idea how to find.

A pit of vast loneliness opened inside the wolf, who wanted to let it out in a mournful howl.

Suppressing the instinct, the wolf faded back into the darkness of the woods, settling down to watch and wait.

CHAPTER TWENTY

S hane immediately went to work building a fire. The air in the big living room was crisp and cold, the blaze he'd started a few days ago nothing but ash.

While engaged in this task, he heard Freya take up her bundle of clothes, then wolf claws on the stairs as she ascended.

She'd need to become human to work the doorknobs, Shane thought with some amusement, but only silence floated down from upstairs. Whatever she'd decided to do, she was being quiet about it.

Shane finished with the fire and entered the kitchen to brew coffee. Not until that was done did Freya reappear.

She stood in the kitchen doorway, fully dressed, including a padded jacket, as though she meant to go back out again. "I don't like hiding indoors while others search," she said.

Shane unhurriedly poured coffee into two mugs and held one out to her. "It's better to rest and regain strength. We don't know what we'll be facing out there."

Freya made no move to take the coffee. "You seem certain

we'll succeed." She let out a sigh. "I'm starting to be very discouraged. About finding Rolf, I mean. I sense him out there, I know it, but it's like he's drifting away from me." She blinked as her eyes moistened.

Shane set down the steaming mugs and went to her. "Dylan is also investigating with his team, as Eric told me. You and I are only part of a larger circle." Shane gripped her arms through the thick jacket, finding her warmth in spite of the layers of padding. "We'll discover what's happened to your brother, sweetheart. I promise."

"I'm tired, I suppose," Freya admitted. "But knowing he's alive and believing I'll ever see him again are two different things."

Shane caressed her through the jacket, trying to soothe. "But don't lose heart, Freya. We'll find him."

"I'm so afraid he's been taken by those men that Althea said are making feral Shifters. Rolf would get in touch with me if he could. Even when we're mad at each other, we still stay in touch, even if only to continue the argument. Something like this has never happened."

The fear in Freya's voice made Shane lose his resolve to keep away from her. He pulled her close, letting himself drop a kiss to her hair. "Let's hope not, love. But even if he has been taken, we have a secret weapon. We have Zander. He's cured ferals before."

"I want to believe everything will be all right. I truly do." Freya let out a rueful laugh. "Rolf would tease me for being so worried. He could make light of anything."

"If he's anything like you, I look forward to meeting him," Shane rumbled.

Freya pulled away to gaze at him with hungry eyes. "And I'm so distracted by this ... this *need* for you. It's like I'm burning up from the inside out."

"I am too." Shane's voice went soft, and he cupped her face. "Maybe we shouldn't resist so much."

He expected Freya to scoff at him, to accuse him of trying to coerce her into bed with him.

Instead, she slid her arms around him. "Maybe we shouldn't," she whispered.

She rose on tiptoes to kiss his lips, and that destroyed everything.

———

FREYA FELT THE CHANGE IN HERSELF AS THE KISS deepened. She sought Shane with hands and mouth, losing herself in him and to the mate frenzy.

Her jacket slid to the floor at the same time she clawed at Shane's sweatshirt, dragging it off over his head. More kisses, these frantic, as her own shirt came off. Next, her bra, and after that, they grappled to open each other's jeans, Freya shimmying hers off as Shane nearly fell over jerking his away.

In underwear alone, they came back to each other, kisses turning hot, wild. Shane's touch slid down her body, hands cupping her hips. He jerked her closer, his strength unrestrained, until they overbalanced.

Freya didn't fight it as they went down to the softness of the sofa, Shane's body supporting Freya's as they landed.

She barely noted where they were as she slid over Shane, seeking his mouth again. Her breasts met his chest, and his strong arms held her close.

Freya raised her head and gazed down at Shane. His dark eyes held hers, his short hair mussed from their play. A few days ago, she'd noticed how attractive he was, and now he was burned on her senses forever.

The observation lasted only a moment. Shane pulled her down for another kiss, his hands molding her waist before he slid them under the waistband of her panties. Freya gasped a moan as he moved fingers between her legs, finding and stroking the hotness there.

What was left of Freya's self-control splintered. She'd had sex before—a few truncated and not very satisfactory encounters with human men. She'd had to practically turn herself inside out to hide that she was Shifter.

Freya had soon concluded that seeking physical relationships with humans wasn't worth it. She understood abruptly now why those experiences had always left her disappointed. She'd never been able to let go, never had the yearning she now had for Shane.

His touch brought her to life. Freya cried out with fevered joy, a dark passion she'd never known winding through her. She heard herself shouting Shane's name, and his hoarse rumble in response.

Freya jerked at his boxer briefs, wanting to bare the hard cock she felt through them. She'd half shift and rip the underwear from him if she had to.

Shane released her to slide the fabric from his hips and then to pull hers down too. Freya laughed as they found themselves on the floor, the rug's softness cradling them.

Shane rolled onto her, bracing his weight to keep from crushing her. His smile warmed her through and rendered his face incredibly handsome. Freya touched his blunt cheekbones, traced his strong lips.

His entire body was delectable. Strong shoulders, hard

chest, firm abdomen, and the trim line of hair that pointed to his thick cock.

"You are beautiful," Shane told her. He brushed back her hair, drawing his fingers through it. "You look at me with those wolf's eyes, and I'm gone."

Shane's eyes, brown and soft, were the sexiest Freya had ever seen.

"Don't be gone," she whispered. "Be here with me."

Shane's fierce kiss ended the conversation. Freya felt his cock at her opening, and the floor seemed to spin. She held on to him, her head rocking back as he slid inside her.

What Freya had held back from her past encounters surged up and broke free, the wild thing inside her released.

She wound herself around Shane, squeezing him as he rocked into her. Shane groaned with his thrusts, every kiss scorching. The rug's friction burned her back, but Freya barely felt the sting.

She only knew Shane inside her, the two of them one. The glow from the fireplace seemed to take on a blue tinge, as though a nimbus surrounded them, but Freya was too far gone in frenzy to find that odd.

Shane kissed and nipped at her, and Freya laughed as she nipped him back. He growled like a bear, but remained human, and Freya forced her hands not to sprout claws.

Being with a Shifter was crazy and untamed, and matched the primal need inside Freya. She cried out as Shane brought her to the height of her desire, his own peak hitting at almost the same time.

They thrust together, heat to heat, the frenzy not subdued in any way.

When Shane collapsed, breathless onto her, Freya held him, searching for her own breath. Shane grinned down at her in a combination of dark passion and the mischievousness that was himself.

Freya laughed and then yelped as Shane slid inside her again, proving his own frenzy was just as strong as hers, and like hers, nowhere near sated.

———

THE FERAL WOLF IN THE WOODS LAID ITS HEAD ON ITS paws. It knew exactly what was going on inside the cabin, the pheromones from two frenzied Shifters not very subtle.

The crazed part of the wolf told it that they were vulnerable now and could be savaged, as it had done with the other arrogant fool of a Lupine.

The last shred of the wolf's sanity made it stay in the bed of leaves it had hollowed out for itself and keep watch. Guarding.

The two inside were mates—the glow of the forming mate bond was there for all to see. They would know of no danger until it was too late.

Or maybe the Lupine could see the mate bond because it had lost anything human it had ever possessed. It was pure wolf now. Things unclear in its human form were sharp now.

The two in the cabin would never be a threat. The Lupine skulking around yesterday had been. The feral wolf still knew the difference.

The wild joy inside the cabin increased the wolf's loneliness. It had felt these kinds of things before. With a mate of its own? There was no memory of that, which made it even more empty.

The Lupine had been robbed of all it had once been, which made it very angry. And very sad.

One day, the wolf knew deep inside, the anger and the sadness would win. And then the wolf would be dead.

Until then, it could keep watch over the two who were full of life, whose love for each other was just beginning.

———

Freya woke hours later, in the bed she and Shane had finally staggered to, when the door downstairs banged shut.

She knew right away that it wasn't a dangerous intruder barging in, because she heard Brody's rumble and Neal answering. Dougal loudly announced he was raiding the refrigerator for beer. Freya thanked the Goddess she and Shane had managed to scoop up their clothes before climbing the stairs for a round of frantic lovemaking in the bedroom.

Shane continued to sleep. His large chest moved, and a quiet snore emitted from his lips.

Freya smiled, her heart swelling. *Her mate.* She never thought it would happen to her, never thought a Collared Shifter in a Shiftertown would make her fall sloppily in love with him.

They had many things to work through, of course, but right now, such considerations were pleasantly hazy, giving Freya confidence that she could at last touch happiness.

Shane apparently had mastered the trick of sleeping through a houseful of noisy Shifters, because he didn't wake. Freya slipped out of bed, groped around until she found jeans and a shirt, and quickly dressed.

The sweatshirt she'd donned was Shane's, she realized as she left the room. Not only did it hold his warmth and scent, but the sleeves draped a long way over her wrists, and the hem hung almost to her knees.

Freya impatiently shoved the sleeves up her arms and went downstairs.

The three male Shifters stared with interest when they saw her, then pretended they had no idea she and Shane had been upstairs having the best sex of Freya's life. Reid eyed her without trepidation, his expression neutral.

Freya likewise behaved as though nothing significant had happened between her and Shane. She could be casual if they could.

"Did you find anything?" she asked.

Dougal upended a beer bottle and took a noisy slurp. "No. I should have come up here on my own. I can hunt better by myself."

"And you'd have ended up like Leo," Neal observed in his quiet voice.

"Okay, maybe." Dougal shrugged. "But we'll never find that feral with Reid around, stinking like a Fae." Before Reid could speak, Dougal rushed on. "*I know you're* hoch alfar, *but the feral won't.*"

"Fair point," Reid said. "But I'll stick with you in case I have to haul any of you to safety."

Dougal scowled and resumed his beer.

"This feral is very good at leading us up the garden path," Brody said. "Or at least in circles in the woods. I'd like to ask him how he does that." He sounded admiring.

"What do we do now?" Freya asked, discouraged. "Start again in the morning? Move the search from the mountain?"

"The trail's got to be somewhere," Brody said in frustration. "We might have to recruit Tiger. He's like a super Shifter. His specialty is finding people." He tapped the side of his head. "He's messed up inside, but brilliant. The only catch is we have to get Dylan's permission. Dylan likes to keep Tiger close by him."

"Is he the Shifter you were talking about who'd be Dylan's backup?" Freya asked. "When he went to talk to Althea?"

"He is." The deep voice behind her was Shane's. Freya felt all kinds of gladness as she turned to find him stepping off the stairs. "But if Dylan thinks it's necessary we find this Shifter, then he'll send Tiger. *If* Tiger decides he wants to, that is. No one really tells Tiger what to do."

"Except Carly." Brody chuckled. "Cutest thing you ever saw is a petite human woman wrapping Tiger around her little finger."

Like Misty and Graham, Freya thought. These big warriors needed the common sense and love of the human women to keep them sane.

I'm the opposite, she mused. *I need a massively strong Shifter with a smart-ass mouth and big heart for my sanity.*

The wolf inside her heartily agreed. Freya thought she heard a huff of agreement from another wolf, and she stilled.

The others had started for the kitchen, deciding that Dougal's idea of beer was a good one. Shane lingered, resting his strong hand on her shoulder.

"What's the matter, sweetheart?"

Freya shook her head, resisting turning and seeking his arms again. "I guess I'm hearing my brother in my mind. Knowing exactly what he'd say to me if he saw me in your shirt."

Shane, who'd found another sweatshirt in his size, grinned at her. "I'll explain to him that I can't resist the beautiful Freya, Lupine-ness and all."

Freya nuzzled the hand that lay on her shoulder. "Never thought a bear would smell good to me."

Shane vibrated with laughter. "We all have to make sacrifices." He bent to speak into her ear. "I'd do anything for you, I think. Even cover myself with Lupine-scented perfume if you want."

"Eww. Please don't." Freya loved that Shane could make her laugh. "You stay the way you are."

"Want to join the others?" Shane asked, voice low. "Or would you rather go back up and celebrate life?"

Freya wanted the life celebration with everything she had. The wolf in her started to dance in joy as mating frenzy boiled through her blood.

"We could do that," she said, sending Shane a coy glance.

He grinned and took her hand, the two preparing to race up the stairs.

Yes. Hold on to him.

Freya halted in mid-stride. The voice rang out in her head, but it wasn't hers or Rolf's.

Shane's grin died. "Freya?"

Freya slid her hand from his and went to the door. The voice had been ragged and hoarse, but the conviction from it was strong.

Before Shane could stop her, Freya unlocked the door. She opened it cautiously, but no one appeared. She stepped out onto the porch, Shane right behind her.

The clouds of the last few days had cleared, and dry, frigid air skimmed the trees. Moonlight, sharp and bright, filtered through the pine needles to light the space around the cabin.

Freya peered across the clearing, her gaze locking with that of a dark gray wolf that sat beneath the trees, watching her intently.

CHAPTER TWENTY-ONE

Shane followed Freya's line of sight and froze as he spied the wolf.

The two Lupines, one dark in the moonlight, one human and motionless on the porch, were staring at each other as though in recognition.

The wolf in the woods had a darker coat than Freya's silver-gray. Its eyes were light, almost blue-white, in contrast to Freya's golden ones.

This wasn't her brother. Freya's twin should look just like her, the way Matt and Kyle's wolves did.

Ergo, it must be the feral.

"Freya," Shane whispered.

"I know." Freya's voice was as quiet as his. "Don't spook it."

"Damn it, I need a tranq rifle about now."

Reid had one, but Shane would have to slide back into the house, find it, and get back out here before the wolf decided to vanish. Based on the difficulty they'd had tracking it today, it was good at that.

Freya took one slow pace forward. The wolf in the woods didn't move. Freya took another, stepping down to the top porch stair.

The wolf rose from its haunches.

"Don't even think about going out there and making friends with it," Shane said. "If it's not running, it's luring you into a trap."

"I don't think so." Freya didn't move her gaze from the feral as she spoke. "She's here for a reason."

Shane started. "*She?*"

"Yes." Freya's answer was a breath. "She's a female."

"*Shit.*" Shane stared at the wolf and realized Freya was right.

A wild female wolf's build was slighter than that of a male, though Shifter Lupines were closer in stature. But the way the wolf held herself, and that stare, told Shane what Freya had sensed right away.

Freya had soundlessly descended as he'd pondered and now stepped off the last stair to the ground.

"Damn it, Freya." Shane moved quickly to follow her, but Freya held up her hand, stopping him.

"Let me go alone."

"No way in hell am I doing that."

Freya didn't bother to argue. She walked forward, ignoring him.

The wolf waited, watching Freya put each slow foot in front of the other. Shane made himself remain motionless, fearing that a sudden move might make the feral attack Freya.

The fact that the wolf was female didn't mean she was any less deadly. Leo had barely clung to life when she'd finished with him.

"My name's Freya," Freya was saying softly. "Will you let me speak to you? I won't hurt you. Neither will Shane."

Shane was making no promises, but he kept silent.

The wolf stiffened, her head coming up slightly. Shane couldn't decide whether she understood or was so far gone she had no comprehension of Freya's words.

Freya took another step. If she went any closer, Shane was coming with her, even if it scared off the wolf they were trying to catch. The feral had torn up Leo good, and who knew what it would do to Freya?

The wolf watched Freya approach. Why it wasn't either running away or attacking, Shane didn't know, but he sure as hell wasn't letting it hurt Freya.

He'd seen what the loss of a mate had done to his mother, and her deep loneliness until she'd met Cormac. Shane had sensed her unhappiness, but he hadn't understood it at a visceral level until now.

He'd do anything to keep Freya safe, including blowing a chance to get intel on this Shifter and whoever had made it go feral.

Freya took another step.

Any decision to stay or go was abruptly taken from Shane as Neal barreled around the cabin from the back, sword ready, and hurtled silently toward the feral wolf.

Who of course instantly vanished from sight. Shane briefly heard paws on dead underbrush and then silence.

Freya let out a noise of frustration, but Neal didn't stop. He sprinted for the woods, fixed on the point the wolf had disappeared.

Reid popped into existence at the edge of the clearing, tranq rifle in his hands, then he followed Neal at a run.

Freya charged after them. "No. Don't hurt her."

"Aw, damn it." Shane was off the porch and after Freya in no time, and he heard Brody and Dougal behind him.

"What the fuck?" Brody demanded. "Did Freya just say *her*?"

"Run now, talk later." Shane had about caught up to Freya when she doubled her speed. Wolves could *run*.

Shane felt his bear coming. He managed to fling off his sweatshirt before his jeans split and the grizzly sprang after Freya, his boots and shreds of clothing scattering behind him.

Life was always less complicated when Shane was bear. His bulk and fur made the cold recede, and his paws covered the uneven ground with ease. The rancid stench of the feral wolf came to him, her fear ramping up the scent. He could hear her now, too, her steps no longer silent to his sharp hearing.

Most of all, he sensed Freya. She stayed human but ran lithely, keeping up with Reid without hindrance. The beauty of her, flashing in and out of the moonlight, made Shane's heart sing.

He'd made her his mate fully tonight. Never mind they hadn't yet stood in front of all Shiftertown, while Eric said the words to seal their bond. That was a ritual put into place to keep the peace among Shifters, but it had nothing to do with finding a true mate.

Shane felt whole, more alive than he'd ever been. The emptiness he'd carried around inside him for decades had gone, his love for Freya filling the space.

Of course, she hadn't yet accepted the mate-claim. When she found her brother, she might want to return with him to her life in the human world, where she could pretend not to be Shifter. A freedom, of sorts. Better than Collars and a Shiftertown, Freya had already said.

I'll cross that bridge when I come to it. Right now, they had a feral wolf to catch.

A high-pitched shriek made Shane double his speed. He'd lost sight of Freya, and fear for his mate galvanized him.

He broke through underbrush to find the feral surrounded. Brody had circled around through the woods and now blocked the wolf's path into the forest behind it. Dougal, who'd followed Brody, moved back and forth beyond him, agitated and edgy.

Reid held the tranq gun to his shoulder, trying for a clear shot. Neal occupied the space Reid couldn't cover, his sword out and ready. The wolf gazed at the sword in terror, and Shane realized that her shriek had been from fear of it and Neal.

Only Freya stood in a non-threatening posture, her hands up reassuringly.

"I won't let them hurt you," she said, voice steady. "I only want to talk to you. You need help, don't you?"

The wolf stood, stiff-legged, and let out a snarl, her light blue eyes tinged with a red glow.

Shane came to a stop next to Freya, catching the wolf's gaze. *You leave my mate the hell alone.*

The wolf stared at Shane for a startled moment, then her fury suddenly drained. She sat on her haunches, lifted her muzzle to the sky, and howled.

It was a mournful sound, full of despair. Heartbreaking.

Neal stepped toward the wolf and touched the sword to her fur. The howling turned to another shriek, then she spun to face Neal on all four paws, the snarls returning.

"What are you doing?" Freya demanded.

"The sword should help her," Neal said without taking his

eyes from the wolf. "The magic of the Goddess can restore sanity."

"Obviously, it isn't working," Freya said in a hard voice.

The wolf leapt away from Neal and whirled toward Brody, poised to hurtle over him to freedom. Brody rose on his hind legs, blocking her, while Shane surged forward, ready to tackle her.

The pop of the tranq rifle ended the hunt. The wolf cried out as the tranq dart thunked into her hip, and she thrashed, trying to fight the drug.

Freya ran to the wolf as her flailing slowed then died away with a pitiful whimper.

The air around the wolf shimmered. Her limbs changed and fur receded, until a bare woman lay before them, tangled in long, dark hair.

Freya caught the woman's filthy and bloody hands as she started to struggle. "It's all right," she said. "I've got you."

The woman's gaze flicked from Freya to Neal and then to Reid, her bewilderment changing to rage again. But her strength had gone.

She turned back to Freya and clutched Freya's hands in a feeble grip. "I trust *you*." Her voice was hoarse, the words barely forming. "Only you. You are ... special."

Before Freya could ask what she meant, the fight left her eyes, and the Lupine woman slumped to the ground, the tranq taking full effect.

Freya continued to hold her hands. "It's all right," she murmured, though the woman was now fast asleep. "Like I said, I've got you."

CHAPTER TWENTY-TWO

A long argument ensued about what to do with the feral Shifter.

Reid had teleported the woman back to the cabin, where they sat now, everyone human and dressed again.

Freya had insisted the woman be taken upstairs and put into a bed, and she'd gone up with her. Reid volunteered to stand guard over her, reasoning that he could tranq her again or grab her and take her to Eric if she woke and tried to get away.

Neal had gone up to stand at the head of the stairs, sword point down, like a sentinel in ripped jeans and a leather jacket.

Brody suggested they keep the woman tranqued until Eric and Graham could decide what to do with her. Shane wasn't sure whether he agreed or not, but they couldn't let her revert to wolf and savage everyone, especially with Freya here.

When Dougal declared loudly that they should just kill her and have Neal send her to dust, Freya burst downstairs in indignant rage.

"Is that really what you do to any Shifter in trouble?" she demanded.

Brody tried to play peacemaker. "Remember what she did to Leo," he said gently. "A feral Shifter is mostly dead already, Freya. Very few regain their sanity."

"If she gets loose in here, she could kill all of us without trying very hard," Dougal put in. "If she takes out Neal, who's going to send us to the Summerland?"

"She didn't actually kill Leo," Freya pointed out. "She could have, easily, as you say."

"She left him for dead," Dougal said. "Same thing."

Dougal had no love for Leo, but he'd want vengeance on a wrong done to one of Graham's Lupines.

"I agree with Freya that she deliberately left Leo alive," Shane said. "We need to find out exactly what happened there. I doubt Leo was walking along, minding his own business when she simply attacked."

"Of course, she did," Dougal insisted. "She's *feral*."

Freya shot Shane a sideways glance. Remembering how she'd attacked *him* without provocation, was she? He winked at her, and she snapped her attention back to Dougal.

"You are not killing her," Freya proclaimed.

"You think we should just let her go, then?" Dougal's tone was incredulous.

"No." Shane spoke in a firm voice. Dougal flinched but quieted. Shane turned to Freya. "We have to take her to Shiftertown, sweetheart. She'll die out here."

"How are we supposed to get her there?" Dougal asked in a calmer manner.

"Teleported and tranqued." Shane met Freya's stubborn gaze. "It's the only way."

"I know." Freya's eyes held anguish and anger. "But I wish—"

Whatever she wished was cut off by a wailing scream from upstairs followed by pounding footsteps as Neal and Reid charged into the bedroom where the feral lay.

Freya was up the stairs in a heartbeat, Shane a pace behind her. He heard Brody and Dougal follow.

The woman was standing up on the bed, clad in the night-gown Freya had found in one of the drawers. She clung to the headboard with one hand, the other held out in a defensive stance.

Her terrified gaze was locked on Neal and the Sword of the Guardian. She continued to keen, the sound splitting Shane's ears, while Dougal cursed with language worthy of his uncle Graham.

Freya darted past Neal and Reid to the bed before Shane could stop her.

"It's all right," Freya shouted over the woman's howls. "You're safe."

The light blue gaze snapped to Freya, and the screaming instantly stopped. The woman continued to clutch the head-board as her cries changed to wretched sobbing.

Shane grabbed for Freya as she climbed up on the bed, but Freya shook him off with surprising strength.

Freya knelt on the mattress in front of the woman without trying to touch her. "I won't let them hurt you, I promise."

The woman sent Freya a pleading look from behind her snarled hair. To Shane's surprise, she calmed somewhat, as though Freya's voice reached through her wildness.

"Get them out," she said, voice rasping.

"Not leaving you alone with her," Shane said instantly to Freya.

The woman whipped her attention to Shane, and he suppressed a shiver. He wouldn't want to meet that stare alone on a dark night.

"Mate," she said.

"Yep." Shane nodded. "Freya's mate."

For once Freya didn't argue that she hadn't yet accepted the claim. She said nothing, keeping her gaze on the woman.

"Mate ... bond." The woman lifted her grimy fingers and traced the air.

Shane started. The warm glow he'd begun to sense inside him gave a sudden throb. *Holy shit.*

On the other hand, why not? Shane had somehow known from the moment Freya had charged out of the woods and knocked him over that she filled the empty spaces in his life.

Mates. Together. Not in coercion, but in love.

Shane gave the woman a nod. Freya didn't see, as her back was to him, but the woman acknowledged Shane's agreement in satisfaction.

"What's your name?" Freya asked.

The woman's brows drew together in distress. She didn't know.

"It's all right." This time Freya did reach forward and laid her hand gently on the woman's nightgown-clad arm.

Shane tensed, ready to intervene, but the feral stilled. Her anguish eased a moment and wonder took its place.

"Special," she whispered to Freya. "What are you?"

"I'm Lupine," Freya answered, sounding puzzled. "A wolf. Like you."

"Not like me." The woman shook her head, her snarled hair trembling. "Not like *him*." She pointed a shaking finger at Neal. "Or *him*." The finger went to Dougal. "Special." Her certainty became tinged with confusion. "You should be two. Not alone."

"She's not alone," Shane said. "She has me. Her mate, remember?"

The woman shook her head again. "Not a mate. Two."

Freya gasped. "She means Rolf. I have a twin brother," she explained. "I can't find him."

"Twin. Yes." Determination flared in the woman's eyes. "You must find him. Must." She abruptly grabbed for Freya, who let out a cry as the woman's fingers dug into her arms. "Find him." She started to shake Freya, building into a frenetic panic.

"Reid," Shane barked.

Reid was already moving. He slammed the tranq dart in his hand to the woman's shoulder, releasing a full dose.

The woman screamed and clutched at Freya. "Don't leave me," she begged. "Please, don't let them—" The words broke off as the tranq took effect. The Lupine woman slumped to the mattress, landing half in Freya's lap.

Freya carefully disentangled herself and lowered the woman's body to the bed. "She knows about Rolf," she said in an excited whisper. "She must have seen him. How else would she know I have a twin?"

There could be any number of reasons the woman had fixated on Freya, Shane thought, but he didn't voice his opinion.

It was true they needed to question her. If she could help Freya, so much the better. Shane determined to defend the poor wild being from the entire Shiftertown until Freya had her answers.

"Come on." Shane held out his hand. "Let's get her home."

————

Freya rode in the back seat of the pickup with the feral woman, who had shifted to wolf in her sleep, as though seeking that state. Her head was on Freya's lap, and Freya stroked her matted fur.

After some debate they'd decided against teleporting. If she woke up, alone, in Graham's house, or Eric's, surrounded by strange Shifters, she might lose her last grip on sanity and go on a rampage. Cubs lived in both houses, and then there was Misty, not to mention the still-recovering Leo.

Reid assured them that the tranq would keep her out for the duration of the trip, though he left extra darts with Brody, who rode in the front seat with Shane. Reid then teleported back to let Eric and Graham know what was coming.

Dougal had departed on his motorcycle, toting Neal on the back.

Freya's mind whirled from all that had occurred. Finding the feral woman, the woman's instinct that knew Freya had become separated from her brother, and Shane ...

She glanced up, catching Shane's glance in the rearview mirror. She'd surrendered herself to him, and it had been wonderful.

Being a twin meant she'd always had someone in her life, another part of her. But she'd not had this full completion of herself, a *mate*.

It was hard for Freya to let people into her life—she'd learned to keep them distant to survive—but Shane fit. And somehow, she fit into his.

In spite of the Collars and the Shiftertowns and all the things she'd fled, being with Shane seemed the most natural thing in the world. He'd broken her from her shell, and Freya wasn't certain she wanted to crawl back inside any time soon.

Shane's smile in the rearview mirror lit all kinds of fires inside her. Maybe later, after they figured things out, they could sneak away from Shiftertown and come up to the cabin again. And then …

"Take it easy, bro." Brody gave a shout of alarm, and Shane jerked the pickup back into his lane. "Mate frenzy," Brody muttered. "Sheesh."

"Sorry." Shane sent Freya a grin in the mirror, not the least bit sorry.

They reached Shiftertown without further mishap. The wolf stirred as the pickup slowed in front of Shane's house but didn't wake.

Dougal had passed their truck on the road, entering Shiftertown before them. Neal and Reid waited with Eric in Eric's front yard, Cassidy and Nell not far away. Dougal wasn't with them—presumably he'd dropped off Neal and gone to fetch Graham.

Shane lifted the wolf from where she slumbered on Freya's lap and carried her toward the waiting group. Freya scrambled out and hurried to walk beside him.

"She's going to freak out when she wakes up," Shane said to Eric as he approached. "I suggest we take her to a room where she can't damage anything."

"With me," Freya said quickly. "She seems to be better when I'm there."

"Safest place is ours," Eric said. "We cleared out a space for Jace to go when his Transition got too much for him."

"Mmm." Shane backed a step. "Our place is set up for bears. Reinforced."

Neither of them suggested Graham's, no doubt because Leo was recuperating there.

If the Lupine woman disappeared into Eric's house, would Freya be allowed to talk to her? And would she go completely wild if she woke in a strange place surrounded by Felines? At least she'd already met Shane and Brody and knew their scent, plus was convinced Freya was Shane's mate.

Shane exchanged a glance with Freya, as though understanding her line of thinking, and began carrying the wolf toward his own house.

"Shane." Eric's voice went hard.

"Sorry, Eric." Shane kept walking. "Gotta do what's best for the lady. Take it up with my mom."

Freya hid a smile at the surprised look on Eric's face. Eric didn't argue, however, as though he actually did understand. He said nothing more as Shane carried the woman to his front porch.

Cormac opened the door for them. "I'll need this entire story. Downstairs?"

"Have to," Shane answered. "We're out of bedrooms upstairs."

Cormac led the way into the kitchen and opened a deep closet that served as a pantry. Shane had to turn sideways to carry the wolf in. Freya followed, neither Shane nor Cormac preventing her.

"I see we're almost out of syrup," Cormac mentioned before he pressed a hidden lever that swung the entire shelf unit at the end of the closet inward. He flicked on a light to reveal a flight of wooden steps.

They looked like typical basement stairs leading to the space where the water heater and various other home appliances would be kept. The walls were bare cement, and a single lightbulb illuminated the way.

Shane went first. He navigated the steps without mishap, his balance unaffected by the wolf he carried. Freya pattered down behind him, and Cormac shut the door at the top before trudging after them.

They emerged into a short, wide hallway with unfinished stud walls. A water heater, as well as a washer and dryer, occupied most of the space. A clothesline strung across one corner held several very large white T-shirts.

At the end of this space was a finished wall, blank and painted white. Shane paused and stared at a decal that had been stuck up on a stud beside it.

The wall shuddered once, then silently slid aside.

"I should have asked Mom before I brought you down here, Freya," Shane said as he strode forward. "But too late now. You can always walk around with your eyes closed if you want."

"Nell's fine with it." Cormac was right behind Freya as she stepped through the door, which quietly closed again behind them. "I'd have stopped you if she wasn't."

"She's my mate," Shane reminded him. "Family now."

He said it so easily. The wolf inside Freya made a contented noise, and she swore she heard Rolf's laughter. *About time you figured it out, sis.*

"Exactly," Cormac said.

They were in another hallway, this one wider and finished with painted drywall. Paneled doors of solid oak were set at intervals, with a double door at the very end.

Shane opened the nearest door to reveal a large, well-decorated bedroom with a big bed, a flat-screen TV on a wall, and simple but elegant furniture—dresser and nightstands, vanity table and bench, plus two overstuffed comfy-looking chairs in front of the TV.

Shane laid the wolf on the bed. She instantly curled up, tail over her nose, and drew in a long breath, as though she knew it was safe to relax.

Freya had always known about the secret places under Shifter houses, where Shifters kept their prized possessions— those who were lucky enough to have them, that is. Shifters lived a long time and had learned to accumulate things that would fund them through centuries when regimes and currencies changed.

That was why, when Cassidy's daughter had offered to show Freya her room "downstairs," Freya had quickly declined the invitation. Only the privileged few could descend into a Shifter's private cellar.

"But you're letting me down here," she finished her thought out loud.

Shane slid his arm around her waist. "Why wouldn't I?"

Family now, he'd said. Shane's family had done nothing but make her feel welcome, happy she might become Shane's mate.

"Graham's basement was full of motorcycle repair stuff," Freya said nervously. "We loved it. Rolf could build his own bike by the time he was fifteen. I helped him." She swallowed, the memory painful.

"It probably is still full of motorcycle stuff," Shane said with humor. "Though Misty might have had something to say about that."

"I'll bet," Freya agreed.

Cormac, who had been watching the two exchange banter, told them he was off to find Zander and slipped away.

"You should eat something," Shane said to Freya after he'd gone. "And get some rest. We didn't sleep much last night."

The reminder of *why* they hadn't slept much made heat surge in her. She tamped it down with difficulty.

"I don't want to leave her." Freya regarded the wolf, who slept on with slow even breaths. "If she wakes up …"

"She might try to escape," Shane finished. "I don't want her going through you to do it."

Freya shook her head. "I don't think she'll fight me. I seem to be able to keep her calm. Or somewhat calm anyway."

"Even so, I'm not leaving you alone with her. If you stay, I stay."

Freya couldn't stop her smile. "I'm all right with that."

"Whoa." Shane's arm tightened around her. "A big change from *get away from me, you annoying bear* when we first met."

"I never said that. Exactly." Freya leaned against his strong body, liking how he held her up.

"You thought it. At least, the wolf in you did."

"Sure, because bears have insta-love for Lupines."

Shane chuckled. "Maybe not, but it was close to that with you. Never looked at a wolf before and thought her so beautiful."

He'd melt her if he didn't quit talking. Freya let out a sigh, closing her eyes and absorbing the goodness of him. "I still don't know what I'm going to do, Shane."

"That's all right. You don't have to decide anything right away."

"I mean, even after we find Rolf." Freya couldn't bring herself to say *if* they found him. "I spent so much of my life running away from Collars and Shiftertowns that I don't know if I can simply accept them."

"*I* mean, take as long as you want to figure it out. Weeks.

Months. Years. I can skip Shiftertown and run around the world with you if it makes you happy. I'd never try to trap any Shifter here, and especially not my mate."

Freya looked up at him, startled. "But Shifter Bureau ... Eric. They won't just let you disappear."

"If you hadn't noticed, I'm not much for following the rules," Shane rumbled. "Eric isn't either, and my mom definitely isn't. Eric and Neal, with their hacker partner in crime, Xav, would cover it up that I was gone. They'll also cover up your presence here—I'm sure they've already done that." He turned her to slide both arms around her. "They've got my back, and I've got yours."

Shane followed his words by tilting her head back and giving her a long, slow kiss filled with fire and promise.

Freya shuddered with need as she kissed him back, absorbing his strength. The vivid memory of their crazed lovemaking on the cabin's living room rug flashed to her, renewing the fire. She'd felt more complete in that moment than she had in her entire life.

"Oh, you gotta be kidding me." Zander Moncrieff's incredulous growl filled the space behind them. "Can't you Vegas Shifters stay out of trouble?"

CHAPTER TWENTY-THREE

Freya leapt from Shane's embrace as Zander filled the bedroom doorway. Behind him was Rae, her sword hilt gleaming above her shoulder, amusement in her eyes.

Zander still looked haggard, in spite of his rest after what he'd done for Leo, and Freya sensed Rae's worry for him. She wished there was another way to help the feral wolf besides taxing Zander's strength.

"Maybe you should wait before you try to heal her," Freya said to Zander in concern.

A very young voice came from behind Zander and Rae. "You can do it, Zander. We'll help."

Matt and Kyle slid through the adults into the room and to the bed. They wore matching red long-sleeved T-shirts with the words "Here Comes Trouble" on them. Had Cormac let them in? Freya wondered, though she suspected the pair did whatever they liked, went wherever they wanted.

Zander crouched his bulk down to them. "Aw, that's nice guys, but ..."

"How did you two little monsters get in here?" Shane

interrupted, echoing Freya's thoughts. "That door lock is biometric."

Freya recalled Shane staring at what had looked like a decal on the wall, which must be an ocular reader.

Rae answered. "Cormac let *us* in. I didn't see Matt and Kyle behind us."

"Locks don't bother us," Kyle said. "Do they, Matt?"

"Nope." Matt nodded readily.

Shane frowned but he didn't pursue it. "Freya's right," he said to Zander. "Take your time. We can keep her tranqued until you're ready."

"You can't knock her out for too long." Zander rose. "That much drug isn't good for us."

"True, but going feral yourself because you connected with one isn't good for *you*," Shane pointed out.

"I've done it before," Zander said defiantly, but he wouldn't meet Shane's eyes.

"And how did that work out for you?" Shane asked.

"Yeah, all right, not good." Zander grimaced. "But I made it. Of course, I didn't have Rae then. She's my anchor now." He beamed Rae a loving smile, but Rae's expression told Freya she agreed with Shane.

"You didn't have us then either," Matt said. He pointed to the wolf on the bed. "*She's* a Lupine, one of us. We'll fix her."

To Freya's alarm, the two boys immediately swarmed up on the bed and knelt on either side of the sleeping wolf. Matt reached out a hand to stroke her side.

Freya readied herself to grab them, certain the woman would wake and strike out, but nothing happened. The wolf slept on, and Matt and Kyle glided hands gently along her fur.

"You'll be okay, now," Kyle assured the wolf. "Being feral is like having a bad dream. It will go away soon."

His childish optimism touched Freya's heart. Had she been that trusting once upon a time?

The wolf abruptly popped open her light blue eyes and jerked, snarling.

Freya started forward, but the wolf blinked, fixed her gaze on the boys, and stilled. Freya saw her deliberately control herself as they continued to pet her, the cubs not alarmed at all.

"Let Zander do this," Shane commanded them. He reached for the cubs to lift them off the bed, but Matt and Kyle evaded him, laughing, like it was a game.

The wolf lay still through this, as though she had just enough awareness to keep her from hurting cubs.

When Zander stepped to the bed, however, the wolf came upright and sent him a warning growl. Then she saw Rae, the Sword of the Guardian glinting on her back, and the growl became a long, terrible snarl.

Shane tried once more to grab the cubs, but they twisted from him, leaping fearlessly over the wolf to hide behind her.

"You'll be okay, wolf." Matt told the wolf. "Zander thinks he can heal you, but you're already fine."

"Let me be the judge of that. Rae isn't here to send you to the Summerland," Zander told the feral, his tones quiet. "She'll help me heal you. I promise."

The wolf rose slowly and stiffly on the bed, red tinging her eyes as her fangs showed under rippling gums. Matt and Kyle, undaunted, climbed right onto her back.

"No!" Freya lunged for them. The wolf sprang at Zander at the same time, and Freya, the wolf, and the cubs went down in a tangle.

They landed on the mattress, just barely. Freya tried to shove Matt and Kyle out of harm's way, expecting any moment to feel raking claws on her skin and teeth on her throat.

Instead, the Lupine howled and then trailed off into a series of whimpers.

"Oh, poor wolf." Kyle pet her as the wolf fell on her side, wide-eyed and panting.

Freya lifted herself away, Shane's strong hands helping her to her feet.

The wolf's fur shimmered, her claws and fangs receding as her human form took the beast's place. Kyle and Matt, in contrast, morphed to wolf, leaving their clothes empty and surprisingly whole.

The cubs cuddled into the wolf-woman's sides as she became human, and her arms went instinctively around them.

She gazed wildly up at Freya, Shane, Rae, and Zander, but the red tinge had gone from the woman's eyes, the primal rage she'd shown in the woods replaced by confusion.

"Oh, Goddess," she said in a perfectly lucid voice. "What happened to me?"

———

"You have any idea how she got cured without me touching her?" Zander demanded of Shane after they'd emerged upstairs and into the kitchen.

Freya and Rae had remained downstairs to help the wolf woman bathe and dress. Matt and Kyle, still wolves, had ignored all commands to leave with Zander and Shane.

"No." Shane yanked open the refrigerator and grabbed two bottles of beer, handing one to Zander. "I thought you would. One second, she's feral and about to tear into us, the next, she's back to sanity."

Her name was Keira Vaughan, she'd told them. She was from a Shiftertown in northern Idaho and had only a vague idea of how she came to be running around the slopes of Mount Charleston. She wore no Collar—the scar around her neck showed it had been removed.

"Ferals don't heal themselves." Zander moved to the living room and threw himself onto a chair. "Ah," he said after a sip of beer. "It's nice to visit a houseful of bears. You have right-sized chairs." He stretched out his booted feet and made himself at home.

They were alone up here. Nell, Brody, and Cormac must be next door arguing with Eric about what to do with the feral wolf.

Who was feral no longer. Keira now knew exactly who she was, who her pack was, and where she'd grown up, everything until the time she'd left her Shiftertown in the middle of the night. Things had gone fuzzy after that.

"She'll struggle to merge her memories to what she did when feral," Zander said. "That's what happens. She might recall everything, or nothing. Nothing would be kinder."

Shane couldn't argue. He knew it would be hard on Keira to remember being out of control and anyone she'd hurt along the way.

He plunked himself on the couch. "She kept saying Freya was special. That she trusted only Freya, not the rest of us, to keep her safe."

Zander frowned. "Interesting."

"Keira didn't worry about Matt and Kyle, either. She was gentle until she saw you." Shane huffed a laugh. "'Course, you do look like a crazy fiend sometimes."

"Thanks." Zander smoothed his stark white braids. "I try. But yeah, she instinctively knew not to hurt them."

"Matt said something like *Zander thinks he can heal you, but you're already fine.* He also said, *We'll fix you.*"

Zander shrugged. "Cubs being cubs?" He sounded dubious.

"Could they be healers?" Shane wondered. "Graham and Misty say they're descendants of very powerful Shifters from back in the days we were enthralled to the Fae. Maybe they had healing powers too."

"I don't know about that," Zander said. "I've spent my life avoiding anything Fae. I live in *this* world, I've found the mate of my heart, and the distant past is dead and gone." He spoke with finality.

"Except the Fae keep dredging up that past," Shane said. "Fae have been trying to capture or coerce Shifters to fight for them, to be their Battle Beasts again."

"Yep, I am aware. You think this mercenary outfit making Shifters feral has anything to do with the Fae? Eric and Graham brought me up to speed on that."

"Who knows?" Shane asked. "I wouldn't put it past the Fae to use human mercenaries to do their dirty work. Then again, I wouldn't put it past humans to figure out how to use Shifters for their own benefit. Fae might have nothing to do with it. I didn't scent anything Fae on Keira."

"I didn't either. What I mostly scented when I walked into the room downstairs—besides feral wolf—was a bear and a Lupine getting friendly." Zander's big face split with a grin. "Congratulations, Shane. I'll be dancing at your mating ceremony."

"Nothing's settled yet," Shane said.

The tactile memory of Freya under him, their bodies locked together, had tormented him all day, as had the beautiful image of Freya on top of him, her face soft with pleasure.

Zander's laughter broke through Shane's hot daydream. "Like I said, I'll be dancing. You two have already figured it out. You just need to say the words."

Shane hoped it would be that simple. He drank his beer in silence, the remembered heat of Freya starting to blot out all doubt.

———

"I don't remember much," Keira said. She sat crosslegged on the bed, dressed in sweatpants and a flower-print top much too big for her—one of Nell's. Rae and Freya had helped her shower in a large bathroom that had a massive standalone tub plus enormous shower stall with several shower heads, then found her clothes from Nell's wardrobe.

The wolf cubs had been banished from the bathroom and had fallen asleep on pillows on the bed while they waited for the adults to finish up.

Keira now had one cub on each knee, where they'd planted themselves as though they'd decided to be Keira's protectors. The little wolves drowsed, each opening an eye from time to time to peek at her.

"I ran away from my Shiftertown," Keira said. "That I do remember."

"We have something in common then." Freya was perched on the edge of the bed, while Rae lounged in one of the big chairs, her sword on the floor at her side. "I ran away too," Freya continued. "From a mate-claim I didn't want, plus the Collars."

"I was pretty far down in my pack, nearly at the bottom." Keira shivered. "Everyone's pretty keen on the hierarchy there."

"The Northern Idaho Shiftertown?" Rae asked. "I've heard they're sticklers for Shifter tradition. I'm from Montana. That Shiftertown is too, but they're adapting. It was a huge shock when I was Chosen as Guardian."

Keira nodded somberly. "You'd have been driven out of our Shiftertown. The leader says he's hard on us for our own good, but I think he just likes his power."

"I used to believe Graham was like that," Freya said. "In reality, he has a lot of compassion while he pretends to be a hard-ass. Although sometimes, he's not pretending."

"Lucas doesn't have any compassion at all." Keira scowled. "He's a Feline who doesn't like wolves, and my pack leader is too scared to stand up to him. My immediate family were mostly all gone before Shiftertowns started, and I was stuck into the Idaho one. I'm only distantly related to my pack leader, and he wasn't very interested in supporting me. I finally couldn't take it anymore and left. No one tried very hard to stop me."

Whereas Graham had made certain Freya and Rolf got away safely and were cared for along their journey. The difference between a good leader and one only interested in his status, Freya mused.

"How did your Collar come off?" Freya asked.

Keira pressed a hand to her throat. "I met a guy in Spokane who said he could get rid of it for me. I can't remember how I met him—through other Shifters, I think. There are more outside of Shiftertowns than I realized."

"And he removed it?"

"Yes." The word was hesitant as Keira skimmed her fingers across her scar. "This is where my memories get fuzzy. He ran a tattoo shop, and he had a hidden room where he helped Shifters get free of their Collars. I remember I was considering getting a tatt once I healed from the Collar removal, to celebrate my freedom." Her grin flashed, making her beautiful, before she sobered again. "He gave me some anesthetic, because the Collar coming off would be painful. I thought it would be something like lidocaine, but it totally knocked me out. When I came to, my neck hurt, the Collar was gone, and I had no idea where I was."

"Not in the shop anymore, I take it," Freya said.

"I only have flashes from then on. I was someplace large but partitioned off with thick walls. People gave me food and water, which I suspect was drugged, because I could never quite wake up. I tried to not eat or drink, but I'd get so thirsty, I couldn't stop myself."

Rae made a noise of sympathy mixed with anger. "We'll find this tattoo shop and make them sorry they met you."

Keira sent her a grave nod. "If I can remember, I'll tell you. I lost track of how long I'd been in my cell when they started injecting me with things. At first, I was terrified, but they never did anything but give me the shots when I was groggy from the drugged water. Then I started getting so *angry*. Finally, when someone came with a syringe, I went wolf and attacked him. I was instantly tased and tranqued. I thought for sure they'd kill me, but instead they moved me to a larger area, which was outdoors. It had high walls and a cage grating on top, too strong for me to tear out of. I had room to run, and I did that, I remember. A lot. After a while, I stopped caring where I was, as long as I could run, shift, eat, and attack whatever came at me."

"They were making you go feral," Freya said. She realized she and Rolf had been out in the world, vulnerable, just like Keira. But for luck and Graham, she and Rolf could have been taken, drugged, injected, turned into enraged animals too.

"I didn't realize what was happening to me," Keira said. "Somewhere inside, I was aware that I'd gone completely mad, but the rest of me stopped caring."

"Did you get away from them?" Freya asked. "Is that why you were running around on Mount Charleston?"

"I don't know." Keira shrugged, unhappy. "There were more Shifters in the compound, though I never spoke to any. They'd come and go—I know, because I'd stop hearing them and scenting them when they left. I fell asleep one night and then woke up in the woods. I didn't know where I was, or why I was there. I just knew I was alone."

"I sensed you," Freya said. "I was alone myself, and I knew a feral was in the woods with me. I first feared—or hoped—it might be my brother, but I realized it wasn't." She eyed Keira with trepidation. "You knew I was a twin. Did you know because you'd seen him—or scented him—before? Was my brother there, in that compound?"

Keira studied Freya for a time before she shook her head. "I don't know, but my wolf understood a lot of things I didn't. Maybe I did see him, or meet him, or sensed him. I wish I could tell you. I'm sorry."

Freya strove to hide her anguish, but Keira laid a hand on hers. This woman had been through so much, and she still had enough empathy to feel sorry for Freya. Freya's heart burned, and she nodded her thanks.

"Do you know where the compound was?" Rae asked as Freya tried to master her emotions.

Keira frowned in thought. "Not exactly. It was in deep woods, but not the one I was left in—Mount Charleston, you said it was? The trees and scents were completely different. I could see trees towering above the cage I was in. When I was taken out to run—supervised—I saw more pine trees but also some redwoods. I lived in northern California as a cub, and I know about redwoods."

"Do you remember fighting Leo?" Rae asked gently. "The wolf you tore up, though you left him alive."

Keira swallowed. "I saw him roving the woods. I didn't want to get too close, because I realized he was a Collared Shifter, but he must have scented me. He followed me and then attacked me."

"Are you sure *he* attacked?" Rae asked. "With you being feral?"

Freya sent Rae an incredulous look. "Leo? Of course, he would. Either to prove he could take down a feral or because he wanted something else from her."

"He was in wolf form," Keira said. "I think he wanted both those things. They'd given me training to fight, and once my wolf started it wouldn't stop until he was broken."

Freya squeezed Keira's hand as she started to shake. "You could have killed him, and you didn't. You stopped yourself in time."

"Barely," Keira breathed.

"But you did," Freya said. "Hold on to that. What I don't understand is that you followed Shane and me to the cabin, but you didn't attack *us*. Why not?"

"You weren't a threat." Keira's answer was instant. "The other Lupine—Leo—was. You were wrapped up in each other, and I saw your mate bond. I wasn't going to interfere with that."

CHAPTER TWENTY-FOUR

Freya stared at Keira as she said the words. "The mate bond," she repeated. The magical bond that went beyond mate frenzy and mate-claims, beyond even the concept of love. "Are you sure?"

Keira nodded. "Very sure."

Freya's wolf hummed in satisfaction. *I knew it.*

Mating frenzy did not always mean a bond, Freya told herself quickly, though a bond was always accompanied by frenzy.

So she'd heard. This was all new territory to her.

"You should rest," Freya, unnerved, said to Keira. "You've had quite a time."

Keira glanced around the cozy room. "Will they let me stay here?" It was a plea.

"I think so," Freya said. "Shane's family is letting *me* stay They're good people. I mean, for bears."

The three Lupines exchanged grins.

"Will I have to go back to my own Shiftertown?" Keira asked when the moment had passed. She stroked Matt's and

Kyle's little bodies as though they sustained her. "With a new Collar?"

"Why should you?" Freya demanded. "If you were unhappy there, I'll bet Eric—he's the Shiftertown leader— could make some arrangements for you to stay. Or go anywhere you want to."

"How can he?" Keira asked without optimism. "Shifter Bureau will have record of my disappearance by now. Who knows what they'll do to me when they catch me?"

"We won't let that happen," Freya assured her. "You can trust Eric. He and his family are also good people. You know, for Felines."

She hoped to make Keira grin again but only got a faint smile from her. "Or else they've brainwashed you," Keira said.

"Nah," Rae answered. "Zander trusts Eric and Shane, and believe me, Zander doesn't trust *anyone*. If you don't want to stay in a Shiftertown, Zander could find you a fishing boat to live on in Alaska. The winters are dark, but summer days last all night."

Keira's eyes widened. "Not sure about that."

Rae dissolved into laughter. "I'm teasing you. Zander's always trying to talk someone into looking after his boat while he's in my Shiftertown or running around the world healing Shifters."

"He healed me?" Keira asked.

Rae's laughter died. "No." She shot Freya a puzzled look. "Do you know what happened?"

"They did it." Freya gestured to the sleeping wolf cubs. "I think."

"And you." Keira gazed at Freya in awe. "When you tackled me, I felt the energy come from you as well as the cubs. The wolf inside me remembers that." She held Freya with her light-blue eyes. "I keep saying you are special, Freya. Very special. And I thank you for that."

———

"She believes you healed her?" Shane asked Freya as they walked together behind the houses later that evening, the sky already dark. "Or at least helped?"

Freya rubbed her arms. "Yes, and I don't know what to think."

It was cold, even with coats, but Freya had felt the need to be outside and away from Shifters staring at her as only Shifters could. Shane's family were waiting for her to accept Shane's claim, and Zander and Rae debated whether she truly had healing powers.

Keira was still resting in the basement. Nell had said, as Freya had hoped, that Keira could stay there as long as she wanted.

The cubs had remained with Keira, as though sensing she needed them. Freya wondered if Graham would march over and bellow for them to get their little butts home, as he'd done often enough with Rolf and Freya, or if he'd understand that they were comforting Keira.

"This ever happen before?" Shane asked.

He sounded worried, and Freya didn't like that.

"I think I would have noticed if I'd cured anyone," she said, trying to keep her tone light. "Might have tried to make a living at it."

"Hey." Shane halted and turned her to face him. "Not judging you, love. It's weird, and I want to help you figure it out."

"Oh, you think I'm weird now?" Freya tried to joke, but all that had happened made her shaky.

Shane slid his arms around her, pulling her close. "I think you're perfect." She felt his lips brush her hair. "That's why I'm persisting with the mate-claim. You take your time, but the claim stands."

Freya pressed her hands to his chest, but he didn't budge. "Stop," she whispered.

"Stop what, sweetheart? Hugging you? Or telling you you're perfect?"

"All of it." Freya's eyes stung. "I don't know what's going on with me, or what's happened to my brother, or why I'm falling in love with you. It's all ... very confusing."

"Falling in love with me?" Shane tilted her face up so she'd have to meet his eyes. His expression was shocked. "With me? A big goof of a bear no one wants?"

"How could no one want *you*? You're wonderful." Freya's tears came then, her body quivering with them.

Shane stared at her for another stunned moment, then dragged her up to him and covered her mouth in a long, fiery kiss.

Freya's need for Shane surged, pushing aside her fears. With that longing came a more intense heat that wove around her heart and began to still her shakes.

The kiss went on, warmth in the brisk winter evening. Freya lost herself in it, letting the chill of the night wash her clean her as she sought the goodness of Shane. Shane's large hands on her back warmed her through the jacket, the heat of his mouth intense.

A sharp gust made them both jump, laughing a little as they came apart. Freya thought Shane would turn her and steer her back to the house, but instead he guided her around the corner of the cinder block wall, which cut the wind somewhat.

There was nothing in the dark beyond the wall but desert, where dried grasses whispered in the steady breeze. Moonlight outlined bare stud walls of the new houses across the field and the mountains beyond that. No one to see them. No one to watch.

Shane had Freya against the wall before she could take in much of the scenery. He slid his hands under her coat, tugging her to him for another fierce kiss.

She felt her shirt stretch as Shane got his fingers under it, then the loosening relief of her bra opening. Freya had noticed other Shifter women not wearing bras—Iona, Cassidy, Lindsay —and she wondered if she should follow their example. Her hesitation about that told her she'd been living as human too long.

Shane cupped her breasts with his large hands, the bra no longer a barrier. At the same time, Freya sought the warmth inside his jacket, then his bare skin under his sweatshirt. A wild tingle opened her, hot liquid pooling between her legs. Freya recalled every detail of the crazed lovemaking at the cabin, and her excitement flared.

Shane ran his tongue down her throat, trailing fire. He paused to taste her, as though enjoying the fact that her neck bore no Collar. After that he bent to take each of her breasts in turn into his mouth, suckling, teeth lightly scraping.

Freya let out a groan as she fumbled at his belt buckle, struggling to unfasten his jeans and find him inside. His cock pressed the fabric of his underwear, hard and ready, and she enjoyed herself running her hand up and down it.

Shane made a raw noise in his throat, and he returned to kissing her mouth, the kisses now savage. The more Freya played, the more fierce his kiss grew, until he grabbed her wrists and yanked himself free of her touch.

They stared at each other, rapid breaths fogging in the cold air. Shane's eyes held desire but also a question. Freya's desire answered, and she gave him a slow nod.

Shane's smile lit the night. Excitement flaring, they managed to remove each other's clothes in a blur that Freya didn't remember. In a few moments she was up against the wall, her padded coat shielding her from the harshness of the concrete. Freezing wind slid around the corner to join the already frigid desert cold, but Freya barely noticed it.

She did notice Shane parting her legs, drawing them around himself while he slid straight inside her. Their faces were close together, Shane's softening in passion, his eyes like darkness itself.

Everything connected within Freya—the stars, the cold, Shane deep inside her, the giddy possibility of mate bond. Shane's thrusts shattered her, Freya melting into incandescence.

She cried out as the wild heat burst through her. Her wails rose into the silent sky, no one to hear it but the stars.

Shane's voice joined hers as he suddenly came, his hot seed scalding. Freya wound herself around him, the two of them one, mates, bonded.

The moment was the most perfect of Freya's life.

Freya loved him, and she knew that this love would never die. Shane had touched her life, her heart, and embedded himself there forever.

Her thoughts scattered as he pulled her up for another kiss, this one less frantic, afterglow embracing them.

"I want you to stay," Shane whispered. "Damn, I want you with me, Freya. But I won't trap you." His next kiss was rougher. "Like I said, you take all the time you need, and if you want to go, you go." He broke the kiss and traced her cheek, his fingers shaking. "Offer stands for me to go with you."

A very tempting offer. Freedom of the world, with Shane by her side. Sharing life by day and a bed by night. Joy for the taking.

Happiness so acute it made Freya shake.

"I'll stay for a while," Freya promised, her voice trembling. An easy pledge to make, because every day she remained with him made it harder to go. "Though maybe we'll find someplace warmer when we do this again?" She wasn't cold at all, but she couldn't resist the quip.

Shane's gaze sharpened, and Freya realized she'd said *when*, not *if*. "I'll take you up on that," he rumbled.

In the next kiss, fiery threads wrapped Freya's heart, and her wolf let out a whispered howl of triumph.

Keira had said she'd seen the mate bond—not simply sensed it in her feral state, but *seen* it. Freya didn't know whether that was possible, or whether she truly felt what she hoped she did. Mate bonds were tricky.

Not tricky, her wolf told her. *Love.*

Freya couldn't banish the voice, but hope gave her both strength and more fear. Joy was wonderful, but heartbreak could hover close behind.

She pushed those thoughts aside as she and Shane dressed again after a last, lingering kiss. By tacit agreement they headed home, hand in hand. Shane's very large bed awaited them there, and more moonlight.

———

Shane took his time walking with Freya back to civilization, or at least to the cluster of houses they called home. She snuggled into his side, and he kept his arm firmly around her.

They didn't speak. They didn't need to. Afterglow and mate bond conveyed everything between them.

Brody exited from the back door of Shane's house as they approached. "There you are, bro." He took in Shane and Freya entwined, and a grin spread across his face. "Now, what were you two doing out there?"

Shane's mood couldn't be broken by his nosy little brother. "None of your business," he said with good humor.

"It will be my business when there's cubs running around. Uncle Brody will always be babysitting, won't he?" He sounded delighted at the prospect.

"Jumping the gun a little," Shane said but anticipation flickered inside him. Freya, cubs, a home full of laughter. Exactly what he needed.

"Come on." Instead of heading into the house, Brody started off toward Eric's. "They're waiting."

Freya paused in surprise. "Why?" she asked. "What's up?"

"Althea, the mercenary lady, came to visit," Brody said. "She's got news. Eric wants you and Freya to hear it."

CHAPTER TWENTY-FIVE

Althea Webster, cool in a black business suit with her sleek hair in place, high-heeled boots on her feet, sat in an armchair in Eric's living room. Two bodyguards stood behind her. One was human, the other was the Feline, Ewan.

Ewan bared his teeth in what was meant to be a smile when Freya walked in with Shane behind Brody. Freya ignored him, but Shane moved to block Ewan's view of her.

Freya still thrummed from what she and Shane had done against that wall, when he'd broken through her barriers so thoroughly she could never raise them again. He'd offered her both freedom and the wild happiness of being with him, and Freya knew she was succumbing not only to him but her own desires.

Her wolf made a satisfied growl, the Lupine within her smug.

To Freya's surprise, Keira sat at the table in the dining area of the room, flanked by Rae, Cassidy, and Iona. She was obviously nervous but wore a determined look, as though telling herself not to flee.

Matt and Kyle played a game with square blocks on the floor near Keira's feet. While many human children their age were already immersed in online gaming, Matt and Kyle seemed to find the wooden blocks endlessly fascinating.

Cassidy's mate, Diego, and his brother, Xav, leaned watchfully on either side of the kitchen doorway. Freya saw the bulge of a taser in Xav's belt. Zander was also there, sharing a sofa with Eric, the two of them competing for who could appear to be the most relaxed.

Neal Ingram had parked himself in a corner of the dining room, as though watching over Keira and the cubs. Freya noted that Keira carefully did not look at him.

Nell, Cormac, and Brody filled the rest of the space, but remained standing, as did Shane and Freya.

Graham was not there, and Eric offered no explanation for his absence.

Althea gave Freya a severe once-over, disapproval in her eyes. For what? Freya wondered. Letting Shane spirit her away from their meeting? Or for obviously just finishing making wild love to him?

"Nice to see you again, Ms. Webster," Shane said. He gave Ewan a hard stare then ignored him.

Ewan emitted a low growl, which cut off when Althea raised her fingers ever so slightly.

Eric crossed his booted feet at the ankles. "She's come a long way because her news is important. I'll let her tell us all."

Althea clearly was used to being the one in charge of a meeting, but she remained cool as she began.

"I had a visit from your friend Dylan the other night, as you know. I told him then that a rival had defeated my men in a battle, but I didn't know who directed it. Yesterday, there was another battle between two private armies, though mine wasn't involved. One of the groups was wiped out. The entire army, I mean. Soldiers ripped to shreds."

The room went quiet. Eric was the only one without shock on his face, as he'd already heard the story, but rage flickered his eyes.

"Whose was the winning army?" Eric asked in his most quiet voice.

"It was run by a man named Mitchell Heaney," Althea said crisply. "He used to work for my father, but I dismissed him when I took over. He was too unmanageable. I hadn't heard he'd been recruiting Shifters, but Shifters definitely did this killing. I saw photos." A muscle twitched in Althea's jaw before she mastered it.

Ewan cleared his throat, and Althea gave him a brief nod. Permission to speak.

"It was Shifters, all right," Ewan said. "A few were killed on Heaney's side, though not many. They stayed in their animal forms after death. A couple of Felines and a Lupine."

Freya's heart constricted. A Lupine. Had it been Rolf?

No, Freya told herself. She'd have felt the emptiness if he'd died. A blow like that would have reached her.

Her inner wolf growled. *He's alive. Find him!*

"Did that troop have a Guardian?" Rae asked from the table. "Were the Shifters sent to dust?"

Ewan shrugged, unhappy. "I don't know."

"Where was the battlefield?" Zander asked. "Exact coordinates."

He meant to travel out there with Rae, Freya realized. To make sure the Shifter bodies were taken care of. Good. They didn't deserve to be left exposed. Freya had the feeling Zander would take care of any dead humans as well.

"On an island north of Malaysia," Althea said. "In the South China Sea. I can send you a map."

"Is Heaney's mercenary company based there?" Eric asked Althea.

Althea shook her head. "No. Mitch's compound is in the U.S. Out west here somewhere, is all I know." Freya caught a flash of irritation that she didn't know where exactly. "A lot of ground to cover, I realize."

Mitch, Freya noted she said. Not *Heaney*, or even *Mitchell*. This sounded personal.

"Keira said redwoods," Freya interjected. She glanced at Keira for confirmation and the woman gave her a nod. "That means California or Oregon. There's a place we used to go north of San Francisco with lots of redwoods. A little touristy, but beyond the tourist area, the woods get deep. My brother and I used to go wolf and run there."

She'd gone there to check it out when after Rolf had disappeared but found no sign of him.

"Let me contact Dylan," Eric said. "And we'll go hunting. Redwoods only grow in a small region these days. We'll find Mitchell Heaney and have a chat." The chill in his voice made Freya's skin prickle.

"Sounds fun," Nell said with gusto. "Can I come?"

"I prefer you accompany Rae and Zander," Eric said. "You'll be good there, I think. Also, someone needs to keep Zander in line."

"Sitting right here, dude," Zander said with a feigned growl.

"Where Nell goes, I go," Cormac said.

"I figured." Eric gave him a nod. "You two talk with Ms. Webster after this meeting and get the coordinates. I want her with me and Dylan to look for Heaney's compound. Graham will want to come, and I'll need Neal there too."

In case they found Shifters in such bad shape they had to be put out of their misery by a Guardian, he meant.

Neal glanced at Keira before he nodded at Eric. Neal had been a man of few words since Freya had met him, and he said nothing now, but his eyes spoke volumes. He was ready to find the man who'd turned Keira feral and explain to him why he shouldn't have done that.

"I'm going." Freya met Eric's gaze, though she knew she shouldn't. She was not of his clan, his species, or even of this Shiftertown. He ranked high above her, but this was about her brother. Her family, their pack of two. "Don't try to talk me out of it."

"Wouldn't dream of it," Eric said. "If we find your brother among Heaney's Shifters, and he's gone feral, he'll be easier to deal with if you are there."

Eric's succinct words on the surface weren't comforting, but Freya found them reassuring. He knew what might happen and was preparing her for it.

"Not staying behind if Freya's out there," Shane stated.

"Graham will be there to look out for her," Eric said, leaning back into the sofa as though ready to take a nap.

Shane's eyes went flinty. "She's my mate, Eric. Deal with it."

Eric dissolved into laughter. "I'm teasing you, my friend. Of course, you'll be with Freya. I'm counting on you to keep her safe."

———

Keira felt safer once she was returning to the bear's house, escorted by Rae and Freya.

Ironic—there were Lupines in this Shiftertown, good ones, even Shane admitted that grudgingly—but she preferred to stay with the bears.

Keira should want to go to Graham, the Lupine leader, but she wasn't ready to face him yet. She'd hurt one of his wolves, and she didn't know what payment he'd exact for that.

For now, she wanted to hole up and hide. Nell had told her she could stay as long as she liked, and that act of kindness had left Keira near tears.

The Shifter who unnerved her most was Neal, the Guardian.

When she'd seen his sword coming at her out in the woods, she'd experienced an overwhelming sense of terror. She wasn't certain why, because he hadn't been trying to kill her or send her to the afterlife. He'd simply touched her, and the feral in her had gone wild.

Neal was behind them now as Keira walked the short distance from Eric's home to Nell's. Tall and quiet, he had a hard face and gray eyes that took in everything, assessing in silence.

"Eric could use your help," Neal said to her.

Keira jumped, but Freya answered before she could. "You mean tracking down this Heaney guy? A little too traumatic, I think."

"She might remember more when she gets nearer where he held her," Neal said. "Scents, sights."

"Like I said, traumatic." Freya was being very protective of Keira, which gave her a warm feeling.

"No, he's right," Keira heard herself say. "I could tell him if he's in the right area."

The wolf cub, Matt, who'd trotted out with his brother after Keira, ran in front of her. "You stay home, Keira. We'll get the bad guys for you."

Shane, who waited for them on the porch, heard. "You two aren't going anywhere. The last thing we need is to search for you after you run off."

"We won't run off," Kyle proclaimed. "We'll be good."

"Anyway, shouldn't you be going home by now?" Shane rumbled. "Misty worries about you."

"We want to stay with Keira," Matt said. He and Kyle pressed themselves to either side of her.

Keira did feel better with the two cubs around. She didn't know why, because they were so tiny, like two small balls of ferocity. Maybe it was their blazing self-assurance, the cubs too young for the world to have crushed out their confidence.

"You can't both go with us *and* protect Keira," Shane pointed out.

"Yes, we can," Matt declared. "I'll go, and Kyle will stay. That way, we both go and stay."

Keira wanted to hug the two little guys. "I'll be all right, Matt, I promise."

Matt shook his head, his lip protruding in seriousness. "This will work."

Keira stopped arguing. She was very lucky Shane and Freya had rescued her, and she knew it. What the rest of her life would be, she didn't know yet, but she'd found respite here, if only briefly.

When she looked back at Neal again, he was still watching her, his gray eyes enigmatic. Keira shivered, grasped the two cubs by the hands, and let them lead her to her safe haven.

———

Shane kept his eye on Freya as they arrived at the dirt-packed airstrip the next morning ready to begin the search. Eric was splitting them into teams for this mission, but they all had to start in the same place—at the remote airstrip and Marlo's plane.

In his younger years, the lanky pilot, Marlo, with his scruffy fringe of hair and scraggly beard, had run illegal substances into the country. "Pot mostly," he'd say. "None of the bad shit that people do now. Not my style."

These days, Marlo was happy to transport Shifters where they needed to go in his converted DC3 that looked rundown but easily flew all over the country. He knew how to keep well out of the way of Shifter Bureau and the police alike.

Other vehicles arrived behind Shane's, disgorging Shifters and humans.

Shane's team would be Freya, Reid, Xav ... and Matt. Graham had roared when he'd heard that.

"No way in hell," Graham had shouted at Matt, when he'd met up with Eric and Shane to discuss the mission. "I'm supposed to keep you two safe and out of trouble."

Matt, who'd become a wolf again, only gave Graham an innocent cub stare.

Misty had assured Graham that she'd keep Matt and Kyle home with her. But as soon as Shane had driven out of Shifter-town, a wolf cub had popped out from under his pickup's front seat and squirmed onto Freya's lap. Matt had then stuck his head out the half-open window and sniffed, sniffed, sniffed all the many scents.

"I'll watch out for him," Freya had said when Shane had jammed on his brakes. "It's too late to turn around, and he'd just stow away again if we went back."

Now, Graham caught sight of Matt and looked murderous.

"He wants to help," Freya had said quickly. "I really think he can."

Graham balled his fists and waved his arms around, as he liked to do, but in the end, Matt had his way. The wolf cubs generally did.

Althea would join the search, but she had her own plane, which took off from the Las Vegas airport, with a legitimate flight plan and everything. She'd agreed to pick up Dylan in Austin—somehow—and then join them for the search.

Shane, Xav, and Freya had studied satellite maps with Eric most of the night, both those freely accessible on the internet and the more covert ones Xav had access to. Shane and Xav narrowed it down to three areas where a camp converting Shifters could hide itself—in an area near Mount Shasta, in northern California; in a strip of land east of the Redwoods State and National Park; and in an area in coastal Oregon, just north of the California border.

All were remote enough that a camp could operate under the radar yet be close to redwood forests. Freya had showed them where she and Rolf used to go, but after that, she'd been quiet while they pored over the maps. She'd studied them intently, though, brushing her finger along the Oregon border.

Eric had started to assign Shane and Freya to the Mount Shasta site, but Freya had kept her finger on the border area and said, "I'd rather search here."

Eric had opened his mouth to argue, but Shane broke in. "If she says there, then there. I'm guessing you have some connection to Rolf, right?"

Twins were reputed to have that ability, and with Shifters, even non-twin Shifter siblings shared a bond. Matt and Kyle certainly did, seeming to read each other's minds.

Freya had nodded without taking her eyes from the map,

as though she could sense her brother within the drawn lines. Eric had shrugged, as though it made no difference to him, and agreed.

"Welcome aboard," Marlo told them cheerfully now. "Marlo Air jetting you to the middle of nowhere. Sit back, relax, and take turns looking out the window. No other entertainment, folks. There's a box of snacks in the back if you get hungry."

Matt heard the word "snack" and sprang up the stairs into the plane, his small paws scrabbling on the metal.

Freya, who'd gazed hesitantly at the old aircraft, abruptly hurried in to look after Matt, Shane right behind her. The others—Graham, Brody, Reid, Neal, Diego, Xav, and Graham's nephew Dougal—arranged themselves on the seats behind the pilot's chair or the ones along the walls farther in the back.

Since Matt had already charged to the rear of the plane to find the box filled with bags of chips, cookies, and crackers, Freya and Shane sat together there on a seat against the fuselage.

The plane shuddered as Marlo fired up the engines. He trundled to the end of the short runway and soon had them hurtling into the air. The plane lurched, and Freya clutched Shane.

"Good thing I don't get airsick," Freya said over the roar. "At least I don't on regular planes."

They bounced and slid as Marlo climbed through the clouds. Matt, his nose buried in a large bag of corn chips he'd opened with his teeth, didn't notice. His tail stirred a breeze.

Freya nestled into Shane's side, and he pulled her close.

When they found her brother—and Shane determined they would—everything might change. Freya had lived free most of her life, she and her brother being each other's support team. She didn't necessarily need a mate and a family of unruly bears living in a tiny house in Shiftertown.

What Shane was trying to tell himself was that Freya didn't need *him*.

He needed her, though. If she decided to go, she'd leave a gaping hole in his life that no one and nothing would ever fill.

He held Freya more tightly, and she turned a sweet smile\ to him. Shane kissed her, wondering if today's kisses would be the last they shared.

CHAPTER TWENTY-SIX

Freya's wolf senses heightened as she exited the plane that afternoon on a flat area near the Oregon-California border. They were the last to be dropped off, and Marlo climbed down once Freya, Shane, Matt, Xav, and Reid were on the ground.

Xav, who had paper maps for this remote area, unrolled one on the ground. They were terrain maps, with ridges marked in undulating lines.

"This is the most likely place for a hidden camp," Xav pointed to a space with markings that meant little to Freya. "Deep in the woods. No satellite photos show anything here but dense forest. Even infrared couldn't pick up anything. Could be because there's nothing there but dense forest, or because it's well shielded. It's worth a look."

"Yes," Freya said. "I think it is." She'd known it last night as she'd gazed at the maps, and she knew it now.

"Are your Spidey senses tingling?" Shane asked in her ear.

"Very funny." Freya scowled at him, though she appreciated Shane trying to lighten the mood.

"Spiderman isn't real," Matt declared. He'd become a human boy again, now dressed in sweatpants and T-shirt, things he could easily remove for Shifting. "Wolf Shifters are way better trackers."

"Not arguing with you there, buddy," Shane said. He gestured them onward. "Shall we?"

Marlo stayed with the plane, promising he'd have it ready to take off at a moment's notice, and the other five struck out on the trail Xav had indicated.

Freya assumed that someone would have to carry Matt—Shane's broad shoulders would be a good place for him—but Matt had boundless energy. He ran ahead, then back, then chattered to Xav, then scampered back to Freya to trot next to her.

The only person Matt seemed wary of was Reid. Whenever Matt came to close to Reid, he'd squeak and dart back to huddle next to Shane. Reid, who Freya had learned was raising a handful of orphaned Shifter cubs that adored him, good-humoredly ignored him.

Xav had distributed communication devices that were pretty high tech, in case they got separated, he said. Freya had to wonder where Xav had obtained them but decided it best not to ask. Xav tested the devices once they were snuggled into their ears, having each of them speak a test phrase. It felt odd to hear everyone through the earpiece, but Freya grew used to it as they walked on.

Marlo had circled the area some before he'd landed—the grimy window had showed nothing below them but endless woods. There were probably great places to camp and hike down here, Freya thought. Or to build a compound for turning Shifters feral.

It was nearby. Freya knew it, without knowing how she knew it.

She closed her eyes and stretched out her senses, searching for the faint connection to Rolf that had been with her all her life. Freya pictured his familiar face, so like hers, but with a masculine cockiness and a sunny nature that could always make her laugh.

Just as she feared she'd find nothing, she felt a pull to the east, as though someone called to her. The cry was faint and weak, but it was there.

Matt's small hand slid into hers. "Don't shut it out."

Freya startled. "You hear that too? Or sense it?"

"Not as much as you do. Kyle and I can always find each other."

Meaning she and Rolf could as well? If that were the case, why hadn't she found him right away?

There must be something else going on here. Rolf maybe was somewhere that could somehow block her from homing in on him. Anyone who could figure out how to cage Shifters maybe could keep them from communicating as well. It took Fae magic to do that, but Fae had helped humans before— assisting with the Collars for example.

The only change in *her* life besides Rolf disappearing was Shane.

His presence was hard to ignore. Shane, the large grizzly, had shouldered his way into her world and wasn't leaving.

Now, Freya didn't want him to.

The woods closed quickly around them as Xav and Reid led them down the faint track they'd found, the forest muting sound and cutting off most of the daylight. The Oregon winter sky was already densely cloudy, and the thick trees plunged the path into gloom. The ground was bare, but the air smelled moist and icy. Snow was on its way.

There was a soft click in Freya's ear, and Xav's voice came through. "I'm veering left. No trail here, so be careful."

Another click, then Reid. "I'm going ahead to scout. I can get back to you the easiest."

"*We* should scout," Matt said. "We have noses."

"So does Reid," Shane rumbled. "Technically."

"I mean *Shifter* noses."

"I know you do, bud, but I promised Graham I'd keep you out of danger. Which means you stay with me and Freya."

Matt heaved an exasperated cub sigh. "I don't mind staying with *Freya*."

Shane chuckled. "Neither do I."

Freya rolled her eyes at both of them, but even Shane's warm laughter sounded muffled in this thick forest.

The undergrowth became dense, but Shane cautioned them against shifting right away for easier going. A compound of feral Shifters would scent them coming a long way off, and who knew where their confused loyalties would lie.

"We'd scent them too," Freya whispered to Shane.

"True. And I don't."

Matt took a long sniff. "Neither do I. But we will," he finished with confidence.

Reid suddenly reappeared next to Xav ahead of them. Xav jumped. "Geez, dude. Warn me next time."

Reid paid no attention to his outburst. "There're signs that people have been out here. Can't tell if human or Shifter."

"Burned out campfires?" Xav asked. "Holes for tent stakes? That kind of thing?"

"Depressions in the ground, broken underbrush. Not much, just enough to show me someone went through, and possibly slept on leaves and pine needles." Reid scanned the trees around them. "I learned a lot of woodcraft growing up in Faerie. We always had to keep an eye on the bastards."

By *bastards*, he meant the High Fae, who'd been even more ruthless to Reid's people, Nell had told her, than they had been to Shifters. The Fae had at least wanted most Shifters to stay alive.

"We'll keep our eyes peeled," Shane said.

Matt stared at him in horror. "You're not peeling my *eyes*."

Amid stifled laughter, Freya explained the saying, and they pressed on.

About half a mile later, Freya's skin began to itch. It began as a tingle but grew to hot irritation fast.

"Is there poison ivy out here?" She rubbed her stomach under her shirt. "Poison oak?"

"Not that I've seen," Reid said.

"No warnings on any of my charts," Xav added.

"What is wrong with me then?" Freya closed her eyes, squirming in annoyance, and then she felt a flash of fire.

Don't fight it, sis.

Freya gasped and popped open her eyes. "Rolf?"

"What?" Shane was next to her in an instant. "What's wrong, baby?"

"I thought I heard—*ow*."

Freya jerked her arm from her stomach, where fur had sprung out. Her hands were now claws, raking her own flesh.

The wolf inside her was clamoring to come out.

Just do it. Help me!

"Freya." Shane's voice cut through her agitation. "Tell me what's happening."

"I heard Rolf calling." Freya threw off her coat and scrabbled at her sweatshirt but couldn't grip it. "I'm shifting."

"I see that. Wait a second."

"I can't. It's, it's ..." Her voice trailed off in a series of growls and squeaks—how embarrassing.

Shane helped skim off her sweatshirt with his strong hands, but it was too late for her pants. Suddenly Freya was wolf, kicking free of the torn jeans and hiking boots.

She'd never shifted this quickly or easily before. Freya shook out her fur, a howl building inside her.

"That's how you do it," Matt piped, and then he too became wolf.

Freya tried to suppress her cry. The sound would alert any enemy force and give away their position, but her wolf had other ideas.

Freya found herself on her haunches, her muzzle to the sky. A long, mournful howl ripped from her throat, floating up through the trees to echo back from the thick branches.

A second howl, much higher pitched, joined hers. Matt sat right next to her, his voice soaring.

"Shit," Xav whispered.

Reid said nothing at all. He stepped into the shadows of the trees, but instead of teleporting, he moved silently on foot into the gloom.

Freya drew a breath for another howl, but a very large grizzly abruptly knocked her over. The would-be howl came out a snarl, then she struggled under a mass of fur and muscle.

Freya.

The name burned into her mind from miles away. Rolf—it must be—but he sounded very different.

Will you get off me, you freaking bear? she snarled.

Shane's growl vibrated through her. *You gonna shut up, mate of my heart?*

Freya was struggling to listen, to pinpoint from where Rolf

had cried out—if it had been him at all—but who else would say her name?

She snapped her attention back to Shane. *What did you call me?*

Mate of my heart. Shane said it in bear body language, which Freya could understand perfectly, to her surprise.

Her worries fled for one glorious moment. Shane's weight was a comfort, not a burden, and his endearment wrapped itself around her.

Mate of my heart, she murmured. *I like that.*

Shane nuzzled her. *I like it too. Now we need to get the hell out of here.*

Freya agreed. If she and Matt had just alerted a compound full of feral Shifters with their howling, they didn't need to linger here to be found.

Stealth, she told her wolf. *Remember what that is?*

The wolf inside her laughed in excitement. It knew Rolf was near, and it reached out for the wolf that was its second self. Rolf was her pack, and she needed him.

Freya tentatively opened her senses again, searching for a sign of the other wolf as Shane heaved himself up from her.

Find me Freya. Please!

Freya scrambled to her feet, testing the wind for scent. Matt too was sniffing, his entire body expanding as he sucked in air.

Meanwhile, Xav had followed Reid into the shadows. Freya's comm, which had fallen from her ear when she'd shifted, crackled.

"Reid's found something. We'll ..."

The static surged, and Xav's voice vanished.

Shane abruptly shifted to his half-man, half-bear beast, a terrifying sight. His claws receded enough to lift the comms from the damp forest floor and replace one in Freya's ear and then his own.

"Xav?" he said in a guttural voice. "What happened?"

More crackling, before Reid came through, faintly. "Go. Go! I'll stay with Xavier."

Then nothing. Freya stared at Shane worriedly, another whine escaping her. She tried to shift to half-beast so she could talk to him, but the wolf wouldn't budge.

"Damn it." Shane stared into the woods where Xav and Reid had vanished, then motioned for Freya to follow him in a different direction. "Come on. Both of you. And no more howling."

Matt yipped once and scampered after Shane. Freya hesitated, torn between the pull to her brother and the pull to Shane. She knew Rolf was *there—that* way, a little to the right of where Shane had started off.

Shane moved swiftly, his bear bulk upright and ferocious.

Freya remembered a documentary she and Rolf had laughed over about people swearing they'd seen a Sasquatch. If any human caught sight of Shane right now, they'd be grabbing their cameras and fleeing over the hills, jabbering to anyone they encountered that they'd sighted Bigfoot.

She smothered a laugh, which would come out another yowl, and trotted after Shane and Matt.

———

SHANE RETURNED TO HIS ALL-BEAR FORM AFTER clearing a path through some dense undergrowth. He pushed forward, and Freya loped untiringly beside him. Matt kept up, dashing ahead then running back, then dashing ahead again.

Shane feared he'd tire, but the little cub seemed to be made of endless energy.

Shane wasn't certain exactly where he was leading them, but he didn't want them rushing after Xav to fall into whatever trap Xav might have sprung. Reid could get Xav out of danger easier than could Shane or Freya.

The safest place to go was back to the plane. Freya wouldn't like that, but Marlo could lift her and Matt out of here, while Shane returned to find out what happened to Xav and continue the hunt for the ferals. He wouldn't be above using a little tranq so Freya and Matt wouldn't realize where they were going until Marlo was airborne.

Freya suddenly veered from Shane, shattering his plans. She surged right, heading straight into thicker woods. Matt ran after her, yipping his encouragement.

No! Shane's bear roared. *Get back here.*

Did either wolf listen to him? Of course not. Shane let out a growl that would scare the crap out of anyone but the two willful Lupines and lumbered after them.

Where the hell are you going? Shane tried to project. When Shifters weren't looking at each other, it was hard to communicate. Bears could understand his rumbles but could wolves?

This way, Uncle Shane, came Matt's giddy response. *He's this way.*

Matt meant that Freya had found a connection to her brother somehow. Or at least, someone was making her believe she had.

Could you slow down instead of running straight into an enemy's arms? Shane snarled. *That's probably what happened to Xav.*

He still only heard static on his comm, which he hoped

meant Reid had teleported Xav out of range. But if that were the case, why didn't Reid return for Matt and Freya?

We'll rescue Xav too, Matt assured him.

No, you will— Shane broke off as Matt raced away, out of sight. *How did I get stuck with all these Lupines?*

Your good luck, Freya sent back to him. Shane swore her tail waggled, and not just the furry one.

Matt! Shane bellowed silently.

There was no sign of the cub, no sound of him either. *Damn it.*

I don't scent him anymore, Freya said worriedly as she fell back to trot beside Shane.

Great, Shane muttered. *Graham will slice me up and feed me to his wolves if I lose the little shit.*

Me too, Freya said.

No, Graham would land all blame squarely on Shane and declare he was owed vengeance. But that was fine. Shane wouldn't let Graham touch a hair on Freya's head.

To their immense relief, Matt soon bounded back toward them.

They're here, he projected. *I found them. Come on, come on, come on.*

Did he mean Reid and Xav? Shane thought. Surrounded by how many crazed abductors? *Found who?* he demanded.

Freya's brother, Matt said happily. *And the feral Shifters. This way. This way!*

CHAPTER TWENTY-SEVEN

Freya realized Matt was right before she'd taken three strides. She felt a tug, one she hadn't experienced this sharply since the time Rolf had fallen down the mine shaft when they'd been playing.

Graham's rage about that incident had come from fear, Freya knew now. He'd been shaky after he'd brought them home safely, doctoring Rolf's wounds with gentle hands. He'd sent them to bed, smoothing Freya's hair from her forehead before he'd left her darkened room.

Graham was far away now, searching with another team, but Freya had Shane, the strong, courageous, and determined grizzly.

The pull dragged her farther to the right. Matt corrected when he saw her turn, the cub knowing she felt the true direction to go. Shane, however, growled and grumbled.

But he didn't stop her. Shane was trusting Freya. It gave her a warm feeling.

The trees, which had shut out the snow with their thick

branches, abruptly thinned, then ended at the edge of a ridge. Freya skidded to a halt, her paws slipping on ice.

Matt flew right over the side. Before Freya could cry out in alarm, he scrambled up again. He circled Freya, tail going like mad.

Shane burst from the trees behind them, letting out a relieved breath when he saw they were both safe. Together, they approached the ledge and looked over.

The hill was steep but not sheer, conical fir trees marching down the rocky slope to a river valley beyond. Freya could see what looked like a boat dock in the far distance, a tiny thing. No boats were there in the winter chill, though the river flowed past its icy banks.

I bet you're going to say we have to go down there, Shane growled.

Down there and across the river, Freya answered.

The Goddess is laughing at me, isn't she? Shane rumbled.

It's okay, Uncle Shane. Matt circled Freya then Shane at top speed. *I won't let you drown.*

Will it do any good at all to tell you to stay behind? Shane demanded.

No, Matt answered without hesitation. He yipped, raising his nose to test the air.

Figures. Shane heaved a bear sigh. *All right. Onward. Goddess I'm going to have so much crap to pick out of my fur.*

Freya would have laughed any other time, but anxiousness crept through her. If the mercenaries creating ferals had Rolf caged, they'd see what happened when you messed with a Shifter's family.

Can we call for backup? she asked. She had no illusions that she and Shane could take on a band of mercenaries alone.

Xav and Reid were carrying the cell phones, Shane

answered. *And the comms are out of range. Best we could do is return to the plane and hope Marlo's still there.*

The afternoon had waned as they searched, and the sun—a ball of misty light obscured by clouds—was already sliding behind the mountains to the west. Long, blue-tinted shadows crawled along the hills and over the far bank of the river.

We might lose him if we go back. Freya feared she'd not be able to pinpoint Rolf again if they left the area. *My brother needs help.*

I get that. We can check it out, at least.

Freya blinked. She'd braced herself to argue with Shane and relaxed in relief when he simply agreed.

Shane moved in front of her to lead them. He picked his way down the hill, shoving larger rocks aside for the wolves or clearing deep patches of snow. Matt scampered along, tirelessly popping over boulders and scrambling around scrubby trees.

By the time they reached the bottom of the slope, Freya's paws were sore from the gravel and thorny dead grass, and her legs ached from constantly bracing on icy patches. Shane didn't complain other than emitting a barely audible growl, but Matt was as fresh as when they'd started.

Shane paused on the riverbank to scope out the other side. The current was fairly calm here, but the water still flowed quickly over rocks, thin chunks of ice breaking free and floating past them.

Far downstream another bear wandered from the trees and took two steps into the water to drink. Freya watched it catch their scent, jerking its head up.

It was a grizzly, but a wild one. It observed the bear and wolf that had invaded its territory, then turned and nonchalantly sauntered back into the woods.

Shane chuckled. *Bears never like to show fear.*

I don't know, Freya mused. *I've seen you and Brody when your mom yells for you.*

That's different. Shane then directed his thoughts at Matt. *Get up on my back, kid.*

I can swim, Uncle Shane. I do it all the time in the pool Graham blows up for us.

Not the same thing. Shane growled. *I'm not having you washed downstream and waste time looking for you and maybe having a bear decide you'd make a tasty snack. Up you go.*

Matt set his body in stubborn lines, but before he could argue, Shane seized Matt by the scruff and tossed him backward onto his broad back. Matt hunkered down and quieted, as though deciding riding on Shane was more fun.

Shane plunged fully into the river, and his stifled shriek floated back to Freya. *Holy Mother Goddess, that's cold.*

I thought bears never showed fear. Freya stepped delicately into the stream, agreeing that, yes, it was damn cold.

Not fear, Shane rumbled. *Common sense.* He continued plowing through the icy water, creating a wake behind him for Freya to follow. *Though my common sense is saying it wants to be snuggled in bed. With you.*

The warmth that washed through Freya almost cut the chill of the river. She hurried after Shane as he parted the water, the wolf knowing she'd follow him anywhere.

Matt clung to Shane's back as he waded and then swam across the river, Freya close behind him. On the far side, Shane heaved and bounded up onto the bank. Matt dropped off and shot out of the way as Shane shook himself, water going everywhere.

Freya waited until he was done before she scrambled up beside him. *You could hire yourself out as a lawn sprinkler.*

Very funny, my mate—hey! Shane yelped as Freya shook herself from nose to tail, spraying droplets all over him. Matt laughed from the shelter of a small tree. He was the only one who'd stayed dry.

Shane gave his fur a final ripple. *Where to now?*

Freya stood still as wind, chilling with the coming night, poured down the hill to them. It was cold, but in their wolf and bear forms they could forge a river and stand in the winter breeze to dry off with only a few grumbles.

Ahead of them was more woods, the ground rockier on this side, the scrub more sparse.

Freya faced the direction from which she'd felt the pull to her brother. It was still there, stronger now. *This way.*

Are you sure it's him? Shane asked. *Not someone messing with you?*

I don't know how they could be. Freya probed the connection, but it was insubstantial, dissolving as she reached for it. Only when she let it come without resistance did she feel Rolf's unmistakable presence. *It's Rolf. I'm certain.*

It's him, Uncle Shane, Matt put in. *Twins know.*

Shane tested the air and turned in the direction Freya indicated. *All right. Let's go pull his balls from the fire.*

Freya's gratitude swelled as Shane moved in front of her to lead. He'd been helping her since the moment he'd met her, been beside her to face her past. He'd listened to her story, believed her, and comforted her.

Why shouldn't she want a mate like him?

Matt trotted along beside Freya, the cub full of confidence and vitality, as the path took them into woods that grew deeper and denser. The trees here must be mostly old growth, with few harvested in this remote region. Now it was a protected national forest, if Freya remembered correctly from the maps they'd viewed last night.

They moved on without speaking, saving their energy for what might come.

The overpowering smell of feral Shifters hit Freya abruptly, as though a wall of scent had suddenly slammed into their path. Both Shane and Freya halted, gagging, and Matt said *Ewwww*.

Shane silently urged them forward. He lowered himself to creep along the ground, and Freya followed suit. The feral Shifters, with senses heightened by their primal state, would scent them quickly, even through their own stink.

At the same time, Freya and Shane had to be alert for whatever humans might be guarding the Shifters. Humans would carry weapons for both tranquilizing and for killing, knowing they wouldn't be safe around unpredictable Shifters without them.

Shane dropped all the way to the ground and stilled. Freya slunk beside him and sank to her belly. Matt, thankfully, stayed quietly next to Freya.

There. Shane indicated what he was looking at.

Freya might have missed it, even with her wolf senses. About fifty yards ahead of them among thinning trees was an oblong building made of stone—the same kind of stones that littered the ground around them. With no windows, it very much resembled a natural knoll. Camouflage netting had been draped over it to further disguise it.

As they watched, two human guards moved in front of the building as though on patrol. Both wore camo fatigues, and each held a tranq rifle. Radios rested on their shoulders, equipment belts around their waists, from which hung tasers and shock sticks.

The stench from the building indicated that the Shifters were in there. How many? Freya smelled Lupines and Felines —no bears—but there was so much scent blended together it was hard to distinguish individual smells.

Matt, Shane projected without moving. *Climb up on Freya. You stay there, no matter what happens.*

Matt obeyed without a word, which told Freya he was spooked. Shane sent a whispered command for Freya to stay put then he moved forward, keeping so close to the ground it was as if fur rippled through the underbrush.

Sis, are you coming?

Rolf's voice, desperate and close, rang through her head. Freya wanted to leap up and run to him, so much so that she forced herself to remain still.

You should be together, Matt said, his whisper in her head as quiet as Shane's had been.

We're trying to find him, Freya said, attempting to reassure herself at the same time.

I meant with Uncle Shane.

Freya started. *Kinda busy for that right now. We'll figure it out once we find my brother.*

No. Matt's voice rose in distress, and Freya realized in a heartbeat that he no longer was talking about the mate-claim.

Shane had moved out of sight behind the building. The two guards in front remained there—they hadn't seen him.

Then Shane's roar came to them abruptly and with it a clear word in bear. *Shit!*

Freya backed up until trees hid her from the stone building, then she skimmed the ground as she circled the compound, alert for Shane's scent and her connection to him.

The structure was larger than it looked, probably twenty yards long by about fifteen wide. Freya slid around it, Matt clinging silently to her, until she reached its other side. She sank down in the tall grass, peering through its stalks to get her bearings.

Large cages had been set behind the building, their bars woven tightly with thick wire. They were empty now, and no one was in sight.

Very quietly, Freya moved forward, her wolf making no noise at all.

A soft click made her freeze.

A man rose not ten feet in front of her, a tranq rifle aimed straight at her. No, not a man—a Shifter. A Feline with shaggy hair and white-blue eyes that were rimmed with red.

Feral.

The Shifter didn't move, and neither did the rifle trained on Freya. Freya's heart hammered, wondering whether he'd fire or not. The fact that he had a tranq rifle meant the humans trusted him, so he probably wouldn't be friendly.

A door slammed open, and Freya heard a peremptory snap of fingers. The Feline scowled and lowered the rifle.

Freya let out a breath of relief before a familiar scent rocked her.

Her brother Rolf stood on the doorstep of the stone building. A chill breeze moved his short, dark hair, which was brushed with the silver of his gray wolf. Rolf gazed at her with golden-gray eyes from a face she'd missed so much.

"About time you showed up, sis," he stated, his voice gravel-harsh. "Come on in. I have so much to tell you."

CHAPTER TWENTY-EIGHT

Shane was having problems of his own. Namely, five asshole Shifters who stared him down over tranq rifles, pinning him in place. They'd surrounded him, moving far more stealthily than any Shifter should be able to.

Shit, was all he'd been able to project before he rose into his half-beast form.

Feline and Lupine Shifters should wet themselves when confronted with a bear's half-beast, but these dudes only let their rifle muzzles follow him up.

"We came here to rescue you," Shane informed them. "Get you away from your human captors and back home."

He spoke resolutely, but a couple of the Shifters laughed.

"Do we look like captives?" a Feline said. "Don't think I want to be rescued by a mangy bear."

Shane really wished the comms worked. Something was very wrong here, and help would be useful right about now. He'd love it if Reid teleported in to take Freya and Matt to safety, but that would only work if Reid could get a fix on their present location.

Second best idea, satellite phone. Cells probably didn't have the range this far from civilization, even in this day and age, and humans now locked theirs with facial recognition or codes and shit. Satellite phone would be best. One of these guys must have one, or maybe someone inside the building would.

"So, what did you do?" Shane kept his tone casual and his claw-hands where they could see them. "Convince the humans you were on their side? Smart."

"Better than that," the Feline answered. "What happens when a human thinks he can control Shifters by removing their Collars and pumping them full of adrenaline?" He showed pointed teeth in a cat smile. "He finds out he can't."

"Did you kill them?" Shane tensed but held his position.

"Not yet." The Feline's smugness was annoying. "But they're out of commission. They didn't bring enough bosses to keep us in line, did they? Typical human mistake." A few Lupines guffawed in agreement.

A typical Shifter mistake to think Shifter Bureau wouldn't care that the humans in question had been doing something very illegal. Though humans weren't supposed to help Shifters out of Collars and let them fight in combat situations, the Shifters would be punished first. Humans—if they were still alive—second, and they wouldn't be given the harsh treatment the Shifters would receive.

Furthermore, if the human abductors turned up dead, these Shifters would be instantly terminated. Other Shifters in the area who had nothing to do with any of this might be as well.

"Where are they?" Shane asked. "Heaney and his followers?"

"Why do you care?" The Feline's grin vanished. "You here to rescue *them*?"

"Seriously?" Shane scoffed the word. "I'm not fond of humans who think they can use Shifters for their own gain. But I have to tell you, a pile of dead bodies isn't going to help your case."

"There are some Shifter bodies." The Feline growled. "No Guardian. Humans didn't care."

"Yeah, that was stupid of Heaney."

Shane shared the Feline's anger about that. Shifters couldn't be left to rot, their souls open to Fae capture.

"Tell you what, though," Shane continued. "I know where there is a Guardian. Or at least, I can call him. He traveled with me on what we thought was going to be a recuse mission."

"Which Guardian?"

Shane figured there was nothing to lose by telling them. All Shifters—rogue, feral, or happy at home—needed a Guardian.

"His name's Neal Ingram. He's with the Las Vegas Shiftertown."

"Yeah?" A Lupine with longer black hair that hadn't been combed in a while snorted a laugh. "Vegas, eh? He gonna dance for us?"

"Shut up," the Feline said irritably. "If he's with a Shiftertown, he'll report us to his Shiftertown leader, and we're screwed."

"Neal's only concerned about being a Guardian," Shane said. "Not with following human rules. He'll be more worried about getting to the Shifters in time." He hesitated. "What happened to the Shifters on that island near Malaysia? The ones that died there?"

The Feline flinched uncomfortably but kept his rifle

trained on Shane. "I told you, humans don't understand about Guardians."

"What happened to the human soldiers?" Shane asked. "On both sides?"

"You know, you seem to care a lot about the humans."

Shane held on to his patience with effort. "Because if they're found, there will be a lot of questions. Even if it's in a country that doesn't have special laws about Shifters killing humans, Shifter Bureau will get wind of it. Did that battle happen before or after you overthrew your human captors?"

The Feline said nothing, but the Lupine answered, his voice rasping. "Before. We won that fight for them, but they didn't give a shit that Shifters went down doing it. When we got back here, we took over the compound."

"There's another Guardian heading out to find those Shifters even as we speak," Shane said.

The Feline sneered. "What, you've got Guardians coming out your ass?"

"Shifters going feral and killing humans grabbed our attention." Shane stopped himself appending *asshole* to the statement. "You've heard of Zander Moncrieff? He's mated to a Guardian. They're going to the South China Sea to take care of the Shifters."

The Lupine lowered his rifle a tad. "You mean Rae Lyall? From Montana?"

"Yep."

"She shouldn't go," the Lupine said in alarm. "Too dangerous."

"That's why Zander's with her. You think anyone's going to mess with an insane polar bear?"

The Lupine looked only slightly reassured.

Shane filed away the information that this Lupine knew

Rae or of her but didn't press it. He flicked his attention back to the Feline. He was the leader of this little group, the one Shane would have to take out before the others would listen.

"What happened to Heaney?" Shane asked. "You have him in a cage or something?"

"You think you know a lot," the Feline stated. "Tell you what, I'll show you what's up. Then you can decide whether we really want to be rescued." He smirked. "Spoiler alert—we don't."

How the hell did this dickhead get to lead a patrol? Shane wondered. Answer, he was more dominant than others, and there hadn't been much choice.

"All right, show me," Shane said.

At the same time, a shrill whistle cut the air. The Shifters came alert, and the Feline aimed the rifle directly at Shane.

"Looks like you didn't come alone," the Feline snarled. "Get inside. If you try anything, you'll have five darts in you. Even a grizzly will have trouble surviving that."

Shane's heart thumped. The signal and the Feline's words meant they'd found Freya or Matt. Probably both.

Shane moved slowly, ready for an opening to grab a rifle or shock stick from a belt and drop at least one Shifter. The Shifters fell into close formation but stayed out of his reach, taking away his chance as they herded him to the stone structure.

In a deep niche in the rock wall was a narrow metal door that appeared to be very solid. One of the Shifters punched in a code to open it, blocking Shane's view of the keypad with his body.

Two of the Shifters went in ahead, keeping Shane covered while he stepped across the threshold. The Feline and the other two came behind him.

The inside of the building resembled a large bunker. A long corridor, made of concrete blocks, bisected it, with rooms opening on either side of the hallway. Shane glimpsed bunks in some of the cubicles as he went by and computers and electronic equipment in others. One room was a mess hall, empty now.

In the very center of the bunker was what Shane took to be the command center. Monitors had been hung up on the walls, with a few workstations beneath them so whoever did surveillance could review whatever information they received.

Two of the monitors showed the perimeter of the building, and two more broadcast views of the woods. Probably how the Shifters knew they were coming.

Shane was made to stand in the middle of this room, far from the computers.

A couple of the guards in here were human. Both men's eyes flickered when the grizzly-beast entered, but they kept still.

Probably how they'd survived the takeover, Shane surmised. They'd learned to control their panic around Shifters.

Another Lupine entered. He didn't have a rifle or other weapon, but his unfeigned confidence told Shane he was the leader of this motley bunch. He wore a sweatshirt over torn, stained jeans and motorcycle boots, but somehow this ensemble didn't make him look scruffy.

The Lupine had dark hair touched with silver, and Freya's eyes.

Freya, still in wolf form, entered directly behind him, covered by more guards. On Freya's back was the small form of Matt.

Shane growled, a low rumble that shook the room. The

golden-eyed Lupine stopped at the noise, but he showed no fear.

"You must be Shane," he said. "I'm Rolf McHugh. Freya's brother."

"What the fuck?" Shane demanded. "Freya, you okay?"

Freya sat down on her haunches. Matt slid from her back and moved to crouch between her front paws.

I'm fine, Freya responded. She sounded both angry and worried.

"What the hell happened here?" Shane asked Rolf. "We came to rescue you, but you look fine to me. Feral, sure, but fine."

Rolf huffed a laugh. "They captured me, Mr. Heaney and his humans. Caged me, tortured me until I went crazy. Just like they did to all the Shifters in this room." He sent the human guards a pointed stare. "I let these guys live because they never did anything to us, only followed orders. They're very good at following orders."

Both guards stood rigidly, though one looked a bit wan. They were glad to be alive but not happy to be here.

"What about Althea?" Shane asked. He saw no need to be subtle. "Freya found her card in your apartment."

Rolf shot Freya a glance that held a touch of remorse, but he shrugged. "I hated hiding my Shifter self. Freya and I were good at it, but it wears you down, and I was trying to find a better way for us both to exist. I heard about Althea's organization and thought I'd reach out. I'd check her out, and if she offered good terms, I could bring Freya in as well. I couldn't tell you, sis, because I had to swear myself to secrecy, or I wouldn't get a meet. I guess this guy Heaney had an ear out for Shifters who wanted to join her—I gather he used to work for her. His thugs got me the minute I stepped off the bus in the middle of nowhere for my meeting with one of her agents. Tranqued me from the side of the road."

Fury entered his eyes, which for a moment, pushed out any shred of sanity in them. Rolf blinked, fighting to master himself.

Freya regarded her brother with sadness in her gray-gold eyes. Whatever joy she'd experienced when finding him was now buried behind wariness. She wasn't foolish enough to pretend everything was fine and okay, when it wasn't.

Shane loved her.

"How'd you get free of Heaney?" Shane asked Rolf.

"He was careful." Rolf smiled, his wolf self very much evident. "Had guards all over, with tranq rifles and tasers, plus Heaney was good at brainwashing. Telling us we were better off without Collars—he blamed them for sending Shifters over the edge into feral. But, hey, I'd never had a Collar. My conversion exposed the truth—that he was using lots of drugs and torture to make us insane. Had nothing to do with the effing Collars. The Shifters getting killed on that island jungle pushed things over the top. I got the rest of the Shifters to join me, and we took over."

"Did you kill Heaney?" Shane kept the question casual. He understood Rolf's rage and agreed that Heaney needed to be stopped, but Shifters murdering him wouldn't help their cause.

Rolf's expression was chilling. "Everyone is still alive. More or less. Heavily tranqued, after we had a little fun."

Didn't sound good. If the humans recovered, they could testify that Shifters had hurt them. Shane wasn't optimistic about the humans' chances.

"So, what's your plan?" Shane asked. "Live out the rest of

your life in this bunker? Fun for a while, but I'd get bored. You get any reception in here? I'd want to watch the games."

He glanced up as he spoke, as though he could spy radio waves coming through the walls. Shane noted that there were cameras positioned around the room, but most had severed wires dangling from them. Shifters probably had disabled them not only to prevent Heaney from calling for help but to keep them from recording what the Shifters did in here.

"Cell phones don't work, no." Rolf looked amused. "No internet provider either. But we manage."

Satellite phones then, maybe a dish hidden somewhere to get TV signals. Probably a two-way radio somewhere as well.

Shifters in Shiftertowns weren't allowed state-of-the-art electronics, so they'd become very good at repair and modification of what they had. A radio would be useful to the Shifters for keeping tabs on the outside world, and it would be useful for Shane to call for help. He knew a few amateur radio operators in Las Vegas, friends of Diego's he could trust.

"You sing songs and tell stories?" Shane asked. "Sounds like fun."

"You'd be surprised." The corners of Rolf's eyes crinkled. He was more frightening when he pretended to be sane, Shane decided. "We're fine, trust me. Thank you for taking care of Freya and bringing her to me."

"I didn't bring her to you, friend," Shane said. "We're here to take *you* home. We'll have to figure out how to keep you out of Shifter Bureau's clutches, but I know people."

Rolf chuckled, an unnerving sound. The Shifters surrounding them had their gazes almost fanatically fixed on him, and the human guards had become statues.

"I'm not going anywhere," Rolf declared. "I've hidden my true nature all my life, but no longer. More Shifters will journey here to be freed and join us. Heaney had the right idea, but the wrong goal. He wanted Shifters to form an army, enslaved by him, to fight in his petty little wars." Rolf lost his smile. "The Shifters will form an army, yes, but of their own volition, to fight for *me*. For all Shifters. To get us free of the humans for once and for all."

The wild gleam returned to Rolf's eyes. "How about it, Shane. You with me?"

CHAPTER TWENTY-NINE

Freya kept herself protectively over Matt, who wisely remained beneath her, while her heart broke. The Lupine Shifter asking Shane to join him had the shape, voice, and eyes of her brother, but the Rolf she knew wasn't in there anymore.

Her twin brother, the other half of herself, who'd make her laugh when she was down, who loved the deepest dish cheesiest pizza one day and dove with enthusiasm into Indonesian food the next, was gone. The spark had gone from his eyes, along with the incurable optimism that had kept them going day after day while they struggled to live in human society.

In his place stood a ruthless stranger, one she didn't know. One she didn't trust.

That was what going feral did to a Shifter—removed their recognizable human side completely. Rolf was all wolf right now, in spite of standing up and wearing clothes—ones Rolf would never think to wear. He'd always been neatly dressed.

The wild strength Freya had glimpsed in her brother over

the years, and had sometimes felt in herself, had completely taken over.

This isn't right. Matt's distress came to her. *You're supposed to be together, be strong. Not like this.*

I know, sweetie. Freya tried to reassure him. *I'll keep you safe. Don't worry.*

She could tell Matt didn't believe her. He burrowed into her fur, trying to hide himself.

Rolf, with fearsome swiftness, switched his gaze to Freya and stared straight down at Matt. "Cute cub," he said. "Whose is it?"

He'd know by scent that Matt wasn't hers, or Shane's either.

He's an orphan, Freya said. *Like we were.*

For one instant, she saw the old Rolf shine through, the scared cub who'd put his arm around her when they'd been left on Graham's porch and told her they'd be okay.

"It's lucky you came here, kid," Rolf said to Matt. "Better than a Shiftertown, any day."

Matt found his courage and peered out from under Freya. *Graham takes care of me. He can kick all your asses. So can Shane.*

Rolf froze, his gaze hardening as it went back to Freya. "Graham? You went back to *Graham?*"

Freya kept her eyes locked on Rolf and sensed Shane step closer to her. The other Shifters moved to keep Shane covered.

Not on purpose, Freya answered swiftly. *But yes, I found him again. He took care of us, Rolf, when no one else would. He kept us safe.*

"He kept us confined," Rolf snarled. "Wouldn't let us discover our potential. Wouldn't let us be *us.*"

He made sure no other Shifters killed us or abused us. He

helped us get away when we ran, made sure we were taken care of. You think we just happened to find people who were nice to us?

Rolf's eyes narrowed. "He'd tell you that, of course."

If you talked to him, you'd understand.

"Sure, sis. And if I walk in front of Shifter Bureau's weapons with my arms spread, I'd understand what would happen there too." Rolf went down on one knee, putting his face on Freya's level. Matt lifted his wolf chin and glared at him. "Graham kept us under his thumb because he knew what we were. He couldn't afford to let us learn our true nature. We'd overthrow him in a second once we did, and he knew it."

Freya lost her patience. *Okay, bro, I've had enough of your crazy talk. The humans gave you some bad drugs, and it's terrible, and I'll help you. But don't condescend to me, because I'm not putting up with that shit.*

Shane's laughter came to her. *You are so awesome.*

Rolf stared at Freya a moment, then he burst out laughing. "Oh, I have missed you, my pain-in-the-ass sister. Shift and talk to me, and I'll tell you what I've learned about us."

Nope, Freya said at once. *Keeping my fur on.* There were too many Shifters around for her to stand as a naked woman in front of them. Shifters didn't care about nudity usually, but she wasn't taking a chance with these guys.

Rolf spun to his feet and snapped his fingers at a human guard. "Bring her some coveralls. Hurry up."

The guard silently exited. Shane, Freya noticed out of the corner of her eye, edged closer to the remaining human guard.

She kept her attention fixed on Rolf. *Tell me what you've learned, now,* she said in her bossy-sister voice.

Rolf shrugged, as if he didn't mind discussing this in front of his troops. "I've always known you and I were different, even when we were cubs. How do you think we've survived this long? Sure, Graham took us in, but we thrived. And when we ditched his ass and that loser who tried to mate-claim you, we thrived again. It should have been harder for us, but it wasn't. Why do you think that's true?"

Because we worked our butts off and didn't do anything stupid, Freya growled. *Because we looked out for each other.*

"Yeah, partly that."

You're like me and Kyle. Matt almost shouted it. *I told you, Freya. Keira told you too. You're special. Like us.*

Freya stared down at Matt. *What?*

Guards, Misty had called them. Wolf Shifters who'd been created to protect the highest among the Fae, she'd said, including their emperor. Matt and Kyle were descended from these ultra-strong warriors. They were twins—had all Guards been?

Matt was trying to tell her that she and Rolf were also descended from these Guards.

Keira, in her feral state, had sensed something about Freya. *You are ... special,* she'd claimed.

Holy Mother Goddess.

"Look inside you, Freya." Rolf stepped closer, blocking her view of Shane. "You know it is the truth."

Freya flashed through incidents in her life, such as when she'd been able to locate Rolf when he'd fallen into the mine shaft. How she'd known Rolf was here, instead of in the other areas Xav and Eric had identified as possible places to search. The strange glow that had surrounded her and Shane when they'd made love for the first time also took on significance. She'd immediately rejected Leo, knowing he wasn't the mate for her, but had not tried very hard to push Shane away.

She also knew exactly what Shane was doing as he

murmured something to the human guard. He was instantly away from the man, back within the circle of Shifters before they'd noticed he'd moved.

Rolf's gaze was fixed on her, willing her to accept that somehow, she'd inherited the DNA of Shifter Guards from long ago.

Explains how you were able to overthrow the humans here, she said carefully.

"Yep. Took them by surprise, let me tell you."

How do you know we're Guards? Freya asked him. *Or think we are?*

"Is that what we're called?" Rolf took on a thoughtful expression. "I hadn't heard that name specifically. Another Shifter who was a captive here when I arrived told me. He knew a lot about Shifter history—deep history from before the Shifter-Fae wars. As you are aware, I'm interested in history too. He told me about the Lupines who'd been bred to be super strong, super powerful, and said he thought I was one of them. I didn't believe him—like you don't believe it—but I realized when I felt the power rising in me, that he was right. Trust me, I had time to think a lot about it while the humans were pulsing me with shocks."

Where is this Shifter? Freya asked. *Can we talk to him?*

Rolf's face darkened. "He died. Was killed in the battle on that island. He was a good guy, even when he became a feral. His death sent me over the edge, I think. Once we were back in the compound, I broke my chains and wrecked my cage, then freed as many Shifters as I could before we had to fight Heaney and his mercs. I went kinda nuts and took most of them down fast. The other Shifters said my wolf became gigantic and even glowed. Scared the shit out of them, and me too, honestly." He sent a grin to the other Shifters, who nodded, some nervously.

The second guard returned, a folded garment in his arms. He brought it to Rolf, then backed away, stone-faced and seemingly nonchalant, but Freya scented his fear.

Rolf set the dark blue coveralls on the floor. "Turn around," he snarled at the other Shifters. "Anyone looking at my sister gets his head ripped off. Including yours, bear."

Shane chortled but complied.

Even Rolf courteously looked away as Freya shifted back to her human form and stepped into the coveralls. There were made for a human man but were only slightly too big for her.

What Freya had heard Shane ask the guard he'd spoken to was where their radios were located. The guard had told him. No one else had noted this request Freya had sensed through her ties to Shane, not even Rolf.

Freya zipped up and settled the coverall. She wished she had something for her feet, which were now cold, but that was a minor worry.

If Shane managed to call for help, would Rolf and his feral Shifters try to kill them? These were Shifters she'd come to like and respect—Brody, Neal, young Dougal. And what would they do to Diego and Xav?

"All right," she said brightly. "Done."

Freya thought Matt might shift to his small boy form, but he remained wolf. Instead of trying to hide behind her, he remained where he was, glaring at the Shifters as they turned around again.

"It's good to see you, Freya." Rolf came to Freya and opened his arms for a hug. "I've missed you."

Freya allowed the embrace. She'd so longed to share this

with her brother, exchanging comfort as they always had, but now she was wary.

When Rolf wrapped his strong arms around her, however, for a brief moment she could forget the insanity in his eyes, that his usual bonhomie had changed to a strange, disparaging humor. In this instant, he was her brother, the cub who'd survived to adulthood with her, who'd celebrated triumphs and held her during their tragedies.

He was in there somewhere, Freya knew. He'd suffered an ordeal, like Keira had, and needed to heal.

Rolf had turned his rage to vengeance, but feral Shifters didn't last. They burned out, and when they were done, they died.

Freya ended the embrace first, but Rolf kept hold of her shoulders. "Join us, Freya. It won't take much to release your strength, and then we can take on the world. You and me. Like old times. What do you say?"

Freya didn't want to know what he meant by *It won't take much*. Much what? Drugs? Torture? Electric shocks? All three?

She was uncertain how to answer. Should she resist? Or go along with it and try to break him out when he trusted her more?

While she debated, not liking either solution, Shane cleared his throat.

"I hate to intrude on this touching family reunion, but can you tell me where the head is? I seriously need to pee."

Shane pasted on an inane expression as Rolf turned to stare at him in annoyance.

Shane continued. "Please don't tell me to embrace my animal nature and piss in a bucket. That's just gross. This place must have a bathroom."

Rolf closed his eyes briefly then pointed abruptly to two of the Shifters guards, the Feline and the Lupine who'd brought Shane inside in the first place. "You and you—take him to the latrine."

"Latrine," Shane repeated with a grin. "So military of you."

"Just go," Rolf snapped.

Freya said nothing at all. She kept her gaze on Rolf, pulling his attention back to her and away from Shane.

Stay here, Shane sent to Matt, who might decide he needed to go to the bathroom too. *Keep her safe.*

Not going anywhere, Matt assured him.

Good lad.

Shane allowed the two Shifters, their tranq rifles ready, to lead him out. The human guard who'd told him how to get to the radio room quietly followed.

The guards herded him down the long hall to a bend at the end. Shane remained in his half-beast form, which meant he had to duck his head under the low ceiling. The place hadn't been designed for eight-foot-tall half-bear, half-man Shifters.

They passed the radio room, which wasn't much more than a small closet. It contained a stack of transceivers next to a desktop computer, and shelves piled with electronics supplies behind all that. Shane made sure not to turn his head when he glanced into it.

"I always knew my mate was special," he said conversationally to the other Shifters. "Now I find out she's sister to the leader. How cool is that?"

He grinned at the Lupine and the Feline, who strove to not appear nervous about escorting him. They must believe that with Freya and Matt more or less hostages in the main room, Shane wouldn't try anything, but they were still edgy.

"Yeah, you got lucky," the Feline said, his arrogance undimmed. "She's pretty hot. You know, for a Lupine."

"Nothing wrong with Lupines," the Lupine returned. "You don't know what you're missing."

The Feline chortled. "Hey, if one like *her* was interested in me, I wouldn't mind trying it."

They rounded the corner, and Shane saw that the bathroom—the latrine, as Rolf called it—lay at the very end of a short corridor. There was no door in the wide opening, which showed how much Heaney had trusted his soldiers.

Shane stepped inside to find the bathroom surprisingly neat and clean. A line of urinals occupied one wall, with sinks on another, and stalls in the very back. White subway tile gleamed around the room, and the taps and spigots were fairly new, nothing rusty.

Shane swung to the Feline as soon as the two Shifters were in the doorway behind him. "Were you looking at my mate when she shifted?" he demanded. "You were supposed to keep your eyes to yourself."

The Feline shrugged. "No, but could you blame me if I was?"

Shane let his affability fall away. "Seriously, are you talking about my *mate*?"

"Shut up, dickhead," the Lupine said quickly to the Feline.

"Too late." Shane made a lightning grab for the Feline and slammed him face-first into a urinal before either could react.

The Lupine belatedly raised his rifle but fell like a stone when the human guard fired a tranq into him.

The Feline, with his cat reflexes, bounced from the urinal and came at Shane, claws out. Shane, who'd had plenty of practice battling Felines at the fight club, knew how to duck. He got under the Feline's reach, seized him by the throat, and threw him into the wall.

Before the Feline could recover, Shane was on him. He punched the Feline in the face several times then flipped him around to bang his forehead into the wall. A smear of blood appeared on the pristine subway tiles, then the Feline slumped, unconscious to the floor.

"Sorry," the human guard said softly. "There was only one tranq dart."

"It's fine. Felt good to finally shut that asshole up."

Shane ducked out of the bathroom, gesturing for the guard to precede him to the radio room. The man had helped, but Shane didn't trust him enough to let him bring up the rear.

The radio was on, lights blinking, static softly humming. Shane quietly closed the door to the hallway once they'd entered and sank down to the chair in front of the transceivers.

"Know how to work this thing?" he asked the guard. While he'd talked to Diego's friends about operating ham radios, he'd never done it himself.

The guard immediately began turning dials. "What frequency do you need?"

"Something that will reach about a two-hundred-mile radius, I'd guess. Southern Oregon, northern California."

Ham radio was pretty cool, Shane had always thought. You could talk to someone down the street or on the southern tip of South America with equal ease. Sometimes even the space station. You just needed a good antenna, Diego's friends, mostly retired cops, had told him.

The guard pushed buttons and clicked the computer's mouse. The radio whined a little, then static buzzed and resolved into voices. The guard clicked one more icon on the desktop—turning on the mike—and motioned for Shane to speak.

"Marlo?" Shane asked. "You out there?"

An irritated voice, not Marlo's, answered. "Who the hell is this? What's your call sign?"

"Don't have one," Shane told him. "Emergency here. Looking for Marlo. What airfields are around here?"

Another male voice joined in. "Marlo have a call sign?"

"No idea. What about Diego Escobar? Anyone know him?"

More clicking and static. "You looking for Diego? Who is this?"

"Can you get a message out?" Shane asked. "Tell Diego that Shane's been compromised. Where are we?" Shane asked the last question of the guard.

"About forty miles northeast of Grants Pass across the Rogue River." The guard leaned to the microphone and gave latitude and longitude coordinates.

The radio crackled again and a more familiar voice broke in. "Shane?"

It was Diego. Shane went slack with relief. "You get that?" he asked.

"Yes. What happened?"

"Sorry, dude. I'll tell you later. Gotta go."

"On it," Diego said.

"Oh, hey. Remember after you mate-claimed Cassidy and were all pissed off at me?"

"What? I wasn't—"

"I get it now," Shane said. "Bye, dude."

He nodded at the guard, who shut everything down.

"That what you needed?" the man whispered.

"Yeah. I'll get you out of here, okay?"

"Sure." The guard didn't exude confidence. "What about the Shifters we knocked out?"

Shane grinned at him. "We go wake them up." He gestured for the guard to lead the way. The man, after a baffled look, obeyed.

CHAPTER THIRTY

One of the Shifters had just mentioned to Rolf that Shane and his guards had been gone too long, when they all walked back into the room.

The Feline had bruises all over his face, and the Lupine looked groggy and embarrassed.

"What the hell?" Rolf demanded with a glare.

Freya was grateful that Shane's entrance took Rolf's attention from her. He'd not liked her hesitation when he'd asked her to join him, and he'd been putting forth arguments why letting him make her and Shane go feral was a good idea. They could become part of his army—Rolf needed strong fighters.

He'd start small, but his eventual mission was to put Shifters in charge of the world. Rolf had said all this as though it was the most reasonable idea ever.

His eyes held all the rage he'd accumulated since they'd been abandoned as cubs, and then had to make their way in the world alone as adults. It wasn't altruism, Freya knew, that made him want to give Shifters all the power. This was about revenge against humans, and maybe Graham and his Shifters.

What would most likely happen, was that Shifter Bureau would get wind of Rolf's little army—possibly when he went out to fight his first battle—and send in the military.

Shifters everywhere would be rounded up, and this time, the public wouldn't cry very much when they were all terminated. No more Shiftertowns, no more Collars, because obviously those hadn't been deterrents. The death sentence would most likely include the cubs, so they wouldn't grow up wanting to take vengeance for their parents.

Freya had to stop him.

Somewhere inside, the real Rolf lurked. Freya wanted to reach him, but the feral he'd become kept her out. She sensed him, her fun and warm-hearted brother, begging for her help, but he was buried a long way down, and she had no idea how to reach him.

In response to Rolf's question, Shane pointed at the Feline and the Lupine. "That is what happens when you don't respect my mate or my mate-claim. They're lucky I didn't flush them."

Rolf took in the two Shifters who wouldn't look at him. Shane was being his usual affable self, good-naturedly confessing he'd beat up two Shifters then quietly used the facilities and brought them back with him. Rolf glanced at the human guard for confirmation, and the man nodded. Freya knew Shane had been up to something, but Rolf seemed satisfied with the explanation.

"Clean yourselves up, assholes," Rolf growled at the two Shifters, who slunk out of the room, gazes lowered submissively.

Matt scampered to Shane. *Pick me up, Uncle Shane. He scares me. This isn't right.*

Shane reached one large hand down and scooped up Matt,

who had no fear of Shane's razor-sharp claws. Shane settled Matt on his shoulder and turned to face Rolf.

"I see you disabled the interior cameras," Shane said. "So the humans didn't suss what was coming. Smart."

"Basic tactics," Rolf answered with some contempt.

Shane chuckled. "I can totally tell you were raised by Graham McNeil. You sound just like him."

Rolf flinched at Graham's name but rallied. "He was an asshole but not an idiot."

"A good description for him. His mate probably says the same thing."

"Mate?" Rolf repeated sharply. "Graham doesn't have a mate."

"He *didn't* have a mate," Freya corrected him. "He does now. Surprised me too."

"What female would mate with Graham?" Rolf asked in amazement. "Some pathetic, submissive thing, I'll bet. I can pity her."

Matt quivered with fury. *Don't you say anything bad about Misty.*

"The outside cameras work, though?" Shane asked, drawing attention away from Matt. "You can see people coming?" He gestured at the monitors.

"Yes," Rolf said. "No, I'm not going to let you near them."

"I'm just interested. Never been in a bunker taken over by Shifters. Those cages outside were for you guys, right?"

"When we first started to go feral, yes," Rolf said. "We had to be contained, or we'd have killed everyone, including the other Shifters."

"I'd have torched those, first thing," Shane observed mildly. "Why didn't you?"

"Because they'll be useful." Rolf was clearly growing impatient with his curiosity. "When more Shifters join us."

"In your quest to build a Shifter army?"

Rolf faced Shane squarely. "If you think you're broadcasting this information through the comm Freya has, you're wrong."

When Freya had shifted, she hadn't been able to hide the comm, which had been concealed by her wolf's fur. Knowing Rolf would spot it right away, Freya had unclipped it herself rather than have him rip it from her. He'd not said a word about it, but she ought to have guessed he'd seen her.

"I know." Shane removed his comm from his bear ear. "We're out of range, and this bunker is too shielded. These are useless at the moment."

"Are you thinking of joining us?" Rolf was wary but betrayed a little hope.

"Maybe," Shane said. "How did you plan to recruit more Shifters? Ads in newspapers? Oh, no, that's too old school. Subliminal messages in social media?"

Rolf's face tightened in irritation. "Word of mouth works fine. It's how I found out about Althea's organization. She has Shifters too, but I'll take them from her."

Freya hid a shiver at his conviction.

"I know some guys who might be interested," Shane said.

"I'll not use you for recruiting," Rolf said in a hard voice. "I'd want you as a trainer."

Shane considered this. "Makes sense. I'm a good fighter."

"But first, you need to be more like us."

Before Freya could form a protest, Rolf moved.

Her brother grabbed a shock stick from the nearest Shifter and rushed Shane, the shock stick crackling with electricity.

While his wild state heightened his speed and his reflexes, Freya, who'd been sparring with Rolf since they both were six, knew how to stop him.

She sprang in front of him as the shock stick came down, putting her body between it and Shane. A shock stick would not only hurt Shane but also Matt, who still clung to him.

The shock stick connected with Freya. She screamed as the jolt of electricity went through her, her heart racing with sickening speed. Her nerves tingled, and her limbs jerked.

Just as suddenly, the lightning vanished. Rolf stood over her, holding the stick that he'd yanked away as soon as it had touched her.

"What the hell did you do that for?" Rolf yelled.

Freya collapsed, landing against Shane. Shane gently lowered her to the floor and started for Rolf in fury but fell to one knee when one of the Shifters thunked a tranq dart into his side.

"He's my *mate*." Freya snarled up to Rolf. "You stay the hell away from him."

Rolf jerked back. His nostrils flared, the red mist growing in his eyes.

"No, you're not," Rolf stated. "He's scent-marked you, yes, and I can tell he mate-claimed you, but you haven't answered. Good for you, sis. You're too smart to put yourself into the clutches of a male Shifter. You and I will make a great team. Like we always have."

Sure. He wanted the two of them to be these special Shifters together. To hell with friends, a mate, a home Freya didn't have to run from, any chance at happiness.

"What time is it?" she demanded of him.

Rolf blinked at the non sequitur. "What?"

"I asked you what time it was. It was late afternoon when we found this place, but I've lost track."

A Feline cleared his throat. "Nineteen hundred thirty hours."

Seven thirty in the evening. Good. Freya climbed shakily to her feet. "Moon should be up, then."

"Moonrise at nineteen hundred hours tonight," the Feline continued. He must be the science nerd of the group.

Rolf glared him to silence, but the Feline had given Freya the information she needed.

She turned to face Shane, who still rested on his knee, trying to fight the tranq.

"Shane," she said in a clear voice. "By the light of the Mother Goddess and in front of witnesses, I accept your mate-claim."

The words strengthened as Freya spoke them, and the sentence ended on a shout. A few of the Shifters cheered—a mating was always a celebration.

Matt ran in a circle on Shane's huge shoulder. *I knew it. I knew you were mates.*

Shane gazed up at Freya in triumph and love. *Yes!*

His word clicked inside Freya, a coupling that was *right*. She reached out a hand to Shane, and he gripped it hard as he hauled himself to his feet.

"Too bad for you, future brother-in-law," Shane said to Rolf. "You're going to see that Freya and I together—we *rock*."

Shane released Freya's hand and went for Rolf. Rolf brought around the shock stick, which was still live, but Shane, with his longer reach, grabbed Rolf's shoulder and dislocated it.

As Rolf yelled in pain, the rest of the Shifters attacked.

Shane yanked the dart from his hip and turned to meet the onslaught. He was laughing, striking out with fists and claws at Felines who leapt away and Lupines who struck back with force.

Freya distractedly saw that a few of the Shifters had turned on the others to help Shane defend himself. They were probably tired of existence in a bunker too. One of the human guards joined in—the one who'd followed Shane to the bathroom. He managed to tranq a few Shifters before one felled him with a roundhouse punch.

Freya's first instinct was to get Matt out of here to safety, but he sprang from Shane's shoulder to the head of a Feline, clawing at him while the Feline spun in place, trying to dislodge him. Matt leapt from the Feline and raced through the melee, nipping at ankles, and clawing his way up backs to bite before he ran down again.

A nimbus glowed around the cub. He seemed to grow, becoming a fierce and insubstantial beast striking at the Shifters who couldn't grab him in return.

Freya ripped off the annoying coveralls to shift, not worried about nakedness at the moment. She felt better once on four paws and charged into the fray to help her mate.

Her *mate*. Though she'd waited to voice her decision until now, she realized she'd made it some time ago. Shane was for her, and she for Shane.

Another nimbus glowed in the room, and with a shocked start, Freya realized it came from herself. A wild power filled her as her wolf enlarged to become the size of her between-beast. She howled at the two Felines who'd half shifted to come for her, and they immediately spun away.

As she raced to defend Shane, another glowing wolf

shoved her aside. Not Matt—Rolf. His eyes were eerie red in his Lupine face, his body blurred with light.

Look at us, he boomed at her. *This is what we were meant to be. No one will stop us. Not Graham, not Shifter Bureau, not the humans trying to use us. Join me, Freya!*

Freya's rage increased. *You went after my* mate.

He's not worthy of you. No one is. Stay with me, sis. I'll make you so much better than you were.

And I am not submitting to you. Freya snarled the last before she hurtled herself at Rolf.

They'd sparred and wrestled as cubs, which became a martial arts-like practice when they got older. They were evenly matched, and Freya wasn't going to let Rolf best her.

She felt a crazed strength within her, one that had nothing to do with being feral. She was powerful, ready to vanquish everyone in this bunker, including her obnoxious brother.

No one fucks you up like family, she thought as she hammered at Rolf.

The two of them rolled and tumbled across the floor, knocking Shifters out of the way. One Lupine tried to yank Freya from Rolf, but yelled in pain and danced away when the nimbus touched him.

Shane rose into his full grizzly form, a perfect fighting machine, even half-tranqued. The Felines and Lupines melted out of his way, but they didn't quit. Normal Shifters would flee him, but these adrenaline-pumped fighters would persist until the last blood was drawn.

Freya couldn't help Shane at the moment. Being female didn't make her weaker than Rolf, but Rolf had turned into a well-trained killing machine Freya knew she'd have difficulty defeating.

The strange power inside began to tell her exactly how to

fight him. At the same time, it needled her that she and Rolf turning against each other was wrong. They were supposed to work together to battle a common foe, like the Guards had done in the old times. Like Matt and Kyle did now.

She understood now why Matt was distressed that Freya and Rolf were at odds, why he'd said, *This isn't right.*

Join me, Freya shouted at Rolf. *Let me make you yourself again, and we'll go out for pizza.*

I'm done with normal, Rolf snarled. *Not going back to my humdrum, pretend-to-be-human life, and I'm not going to a Shiftertown.*

Then I gotta trounce you, bro.

Rolf's acerbic laughter rang in her head. *You can try.*

He renewed his attack, and Freya was hard-pressed to beat him off. She started to feel real worry. Freya had won half her matches against Rolf when they were growing up, but she'd lost half of them too.

She feinted right to go left, but Rolf anticipated the move, and they went down in a scrum of fur and claws. Freya couldn't suppress a yelp of pain as his giant paw landed in her spine.

Rolf had always let up when he'd hurt her, but not this time. He pressed his advantage, hurling her hard into the stone floor.

Another wolf, this one glowing and snarling, abruptly landed on top of Rolf. Matt, younger but far more comfortable with his power, pulled Rolf off Freya and lit into him.

Rolf snapped at Matt with his powerful jaws, but Matt was fearless, not worrying about damaging this wolf who had hurt his friends.

Freya leapt back into the fight before Rolf could hurt the cub. She got her teeth into Rolf's throat and squeezed, not to taste blood but to cut off his breath. Rolf scrabbled to throw her off, and Matt beat on him with massive paws.

Rolf fought like the crazy feral he was, but Freya didn't loosen her hold. After a few long moments, he started to gasp for breath.

With a sudden heave, Rolf jerked himself from Freya, spraying blood over her as her teeth scraped open his skin. Rage burned in his glowing eyes. He bowled through Matt and charged at Freya, primed to kill.

Freya met him, but Rolf's momentum sent her down, and she found herself crushed under his weight. She fought and bit, and Matt clawed at him, but Rolf had lost all sanity. Any ties to Freya had been torn away by the feral in him.

Rolf opened his jaws and went for the killing blow.

Abruptly Rolf was torn away from Freya, lifted high into the air by a huge grizzly-man with as much fury in his eyes, but plenty of sanity too. Shane lifted Rolf high into the air and hurled him through two Felines who'd sprung to help him and into the stone wall.

Freya, released, gasped for breath.

Shane crouched down and laid a hand on her side. "You all right, sweetheart?"

Freya drew another breath, this one more solid, and the hurts Rolf had caused started to fade as the mate bond inside her sang.

I will be, she said, her words shaky. *I think.*

Matt was cub-sized again. No nimbus burned around him —he was just a little wolf gazing at Freya with big, scared eyes.

Shane hoisted Freya to her feet, steadying her until she could stand on her own again. Matt climbed to Shane's shoulder and clung to him hard.

"Let's get the hell out of here," Shane advised.

In the corner, Rolf, human again, snatched up a rifle, one that shot bullets, not tranqs. He quickly lifted it and aimed it at Shane and Freya.

There was nothing between them and the gun, nowhere to hide. Rolf's eyes held no mercy.

He never had the chance to fire. The steel door next to him was ripped open and flung aside, hitting Rolf and spinning the gun from his hands.

A huge Tiger-beast strode through the door and turned his great head to stare at a Feline who'd instantly plugged him with a tranq dart. The tiger-man pulled the dart from his striped side, grabbed the tranq rifle, and ripped it in half. Then he picked up the rifle Rolf crawled for and tore it into pieces as well.

One blow from the tiger sent Rolf to the floor, insensible, where he lay still.

Another man with dark hair touched with gray entered behind the tiger, his hard eyes taking in the position of every Shifter in the room. After him came Diego, a tranq rifle at the ready, and Xav with a handgun.

The mercenary woman came next, Althea's cool gaze as assessing as the dark-haired man's. Neal, Sword of the Guardian in hand, brought up the rear.

"About time you guys showed up," Shane said. He unfolded to his feet and pulled Freya to hers. "I had to do all this myself." He gestured to the many fallen Shifters, some of them groaning, some lying motionless. "Well, with a little help from my mate."

Matt yipped in delight, scrambled down from Shane's shoulder, and started running circles around the newcomers.

There was a burst of air, and Reid materialized in the

middle of the small group of Shifters who'd come to Shane's aid. They boiled away from him in shock.

Reid looked around, taking in the Shifters, fallen or standing, Matt howling, Shane grinning, and Freya leaning against him, basking in his strength.

"Huh," Reid said. "What'd I miss?"

CHAPTER THIRTY-ONE

Shane was happy to let Dylan do the cleanup on this one.

He and Freya were taken aside in Marlo's plane during the flight home for what Althea called debriefing and Shane called interrogation. Dylan had them tell him exactly what had happened from the time they were separated from Xav and Reid until Tiger had torn open the door of the bunker.

Dylan also quizzed Shane about the rooms he'd seen in the compound, their setup, the equipment, the surveillance cameras, and the cages for the Shifters. Althea sat in on all this questioning, taking no notes but listening intently.

Shane suspected Dylan was going to turn this into an opportunity for his Shifter defense plans, or whatever the hell he was up to. He'd probably take over the bunker itself. Althea was going to work with him, apparently.

They'd found Mitchell Heaney drugged to the gills in the compound's basement. More of his soldiers, plus his second-in-command and personal bodyguard, were in rooms down there as well.

Diego was all for handing Heaney and his men over to the

cops, to be charged for kidnapping and abusing Shifters, but Dylan forestalled him. Law enforcement would want the Shifters Heaney had taken handed over to Shifter Bureau, where they might be punished for Heaney's doings.

Dylan had decided to take Heaney and company, as well as the feral Shifters, into his own custody. Althea and her team, with Tiger, was helping him with that. No one was going to escape Tiger.

Apparently, the Shifters would be quietly sent back home as soon as they recovered, or welcome to stay with Dylan and work for him. Some who'd turned coat to help Shane had already pledged themselves to Dylan.

The mystery of where Xav and Reid had disappeared to was revealed when Reid made his own report to Dylan. Xav had picked up traces of some of the feral Shifters in the woods. He'd followed them, but they'd doubled back somehow and attacked. Xav and Reid had fought, managing to tranq most of them before Reid had teleported Xav away. They'd returned to where they'd left Shane but been unable to track them.

Dylan sent Shifters to retrieve those ferals as well.

Rolf was on the plane with them, heavily tranqued and sleeping hard. Neal, sword restored to its sheath, watched over him.

Shane was confident Rolf could be cured, as Keira had been, though whether by Zander or Matt, Kyle, and Freya, he wasn't certain. What Rolf would do after that, was another uncertainty.

Then there was the whole part where Freya and Rolf had turned into big, savage wolves surrounded by a bluish light, but Shane didn't want to get into that right now.

Shane cut off Dylan's questions. "My mate's exhausted," he announced, lifting the drooping Freya up with him. "We'll let you finish after we rest. Or better still, we'll tell Eric all about it, and then you and he can confab."

Dylan's eyes widened slightly at his insubordination, but he didn't try to stop Shane as he led Freya down the plane to two empty seats behind the pilot's chair.

Freya was back in her own clothes, having worn the coverall out of the bunker and to the plane, which had landed on a flat plateau beyond the mountain range. She'd changed as soon as she was able, saying the coveralls smelled too much of human and feral Shifter.

Shane had assured her she'd looked hot in them. Freya had rolled her eyes, and Shane had laughed.

Everything about his mate made him smile.

He held Freya close as they sat behind Marlo, the sky dark outside the front window. Clustered lights of towns glittered like jewels on a black velvet background.

"This is why I fly," Marlo said, gesturing at the view. "Nothing like this."

Shane had to agree.

Matt had curled up on a blanket on the floor of the plane and was now fast asleep. Must be nice to relax so easily.

Shane kissed Freya's hair. He'd thought her asleep, but she stirred and looked drowsily up at him.

"Accepting my mate-claim wasn't just a ploy to confuse your brother, was it?" Shane whispered the question he'd been longing to ask. "Because it counted. You said the right words and everything."

Freya shook her head, brushing him with her warm hair. "Not a ploy. I ..." Color rose in her cheeks. "It was time."

"It was a good time." Shane cuddled her close. "It's always a good time to accept a mate-claim. Well, for you to accept mine anyway." He put his lips to her ear. "I'm glad you did."

"I'm glad I did too." Freya slid her hands behind Shane's neck. "A bad time too, though. Kind of stirred up my mate frenzy."

"Yeah?" Shane pretended to be amazed. "Mine as well."

Freya's smile undid him. She pulled him down to her for a thorough kiss, one that told him they were mates in truth. He heard Marlo chuckle as the plane rumbled through the soft blackness of the night.

———

FREYA KISSED SHANE FOR MOST OF THE RIDE HOME. When their lips weren't meeting, she slept, cradled in her mate's arms. It was the most profound and relaxing sleep she'd experienced in a very long time.

When they landed, Brody met them to drive them home. He was ecstatic that Freya had accepted the claim.

"About time," Brody said as Shane's truck rattled away from the airstrip. "I was ready to lock you two in a room and not open up until you figured it out."

"Aw," Shane said as he lounged with Freya in the back seat. "Can we still do the locked in the room thing?"

Matt, a boy once more, laughed from beside Brody. Freya smiled, but holing up with Shane for a while sounded good to her.

When Brody pulled the truck to a halt in Shiftertown, they were quickly surrounded by bear Shifters. Shane stepped out of the pickup first and reached back to help Freya climb out.

Kyle saw Matt and yelled at the top of his lungs. Matt shouted back. The two cubs ran at each other, grabbed hands the second before they'd have crashed into each other, and danced around in a wild jig.

Nell enfolded Freya in a crushing hug the moment she landed on her feet. "Welcome to the family, honey. For real now."

Tears stung Freya's eyes as she hugged Nell. Freya had lost her mom so long ago, and now she had a new one.

Nell finally released her, only to have Cormac grab Freya and swing her off her feet. "This is awesome. Thank you, Freya. You're just what Shane needs."

"What I need too," Freya said when she could breathe again.

A family. She'd always had her brother, through their ups and downs, and Graham had looked after them in his gruff way, but she'd never had a complete family.

Now she did, courtesy of the giant bear Shifter who was grinning widely beside her. Shane hugged his mom and then Cormac before leading Freya up to the porch and inside the house with bear-sized furniture.

"Welcome home, Freya," he boomed, the walls echoing with his words.

"Thank you." Freya's answer was quieter as she rose on tiptoe to kiss him. "But I think we're going to need a bigger bedroom."

———

As much as Shane's mating frenzy pulled at him, he and Freya fell almost instantly asleep as soon as they hit Shane's bed. Shane was unaware of how much time had passed when he woke to see red-orange sunlight slanting through the window.

They'd flown home in the dark and driven through more darkness from the plane to Shiftertown. His window faced west, a beam of sunlight landing on the wall next to his head, so probably it was sunset the next day.

Freya emitted a soft noise when Shane moved to look at the clock next to his bed. Yep, five-fifteen.

When he glanced down at Freya, he saw that she'd opened her beautiful golden eyes to him.

"Sorry," she said, yawning. "Didn't mean to fall asleep so fast."

"Let's see, we climbed down a mountain, swam a river, hiked for miles, and then fought crazed feral Shifters. Plus, you found your brother, but it wasn't the reunion you hoped for." Shane touched her face, softening his summary. "That would make anyone tired."

"What will they do to Rolf?" Freya asked worriedly. "I'm really mad at him, but he is my brother."

Shane wished he could reassure her, but he wasn't certain what Dylan had in mind. Graham would probably insist on Rolf being healed, as Keira had been, but Dylan was like the uber-boss of all the Shifters. Even Eric did what he asked.

"We can find out." Shane forced himself to sit up. He'd managed to slide off his shirt before going to sleep but still wore the jeans he'd donned for the mission. At least he'd gotten rid of his boots before he smeared mud all over the blankets.

Freya had stripped down to her underwear, which she filled out in a nice way. Shane was suddenly less enthusiastic about leaving the bed.

"Remember when Matt and Kyle said they'd fixed Keira?" Freya asked, reaching past him for a clean sweatshirt from her backpack. "And then she was fine, before Zander even touched her?"

"Yep," Shane said, enjoying himself as she shimmied into the sweatshirt.

"Do all Guards have that power? Or just Matt and Kyle?"

"Are you thinking to try it on Rolf?" Shane asked warily. "He might fight you and make you feral with him."

"I want my brother back," Freya said stubbornly. "What would you do if it were Brody?"

"Everything I possibly could to help him," Shane answered at once. "And then kick his ass for scaring me that bad."

"Exactly." Freya folded her arms over her sweatshirt and studied Shane with her gold-gray eyes.

Shane released a breath. "All right. Let's go see what's happening."

Freya waited for Shane to pull on a shirt and his boots, then they left the bedroom together. In the kitchen, Cormac was cooking up a mess of steaks, with potatoes roasting in the oven. The smell was warm and inviting, and Shane's stomach rumbled. He couldn't remember when he'd had his last meal.

"They took your brother to Graham's," Cormac said before they could ask the question. "Nell's there, with Eric. They didn't want you to see him, Freya." Cormac held up a hand to forestall Freya's protest. "He will be all right. Dylan's going to make sure all the Shifters who went feral are healed, even if it takes time to do it. Zander said he'd help. He got back this afternoon, and he's at Graham's now, though really crabby with jetlag."

"Rolf was very lucid for a feral," Shane remarked. "He held the others together pretty well too. I doubt it will be as easy as Dylan thinks."

"Do you think it's because we're these Guard Lupines?" Freya asked. "Stronger than a usual Shifter? And, if Rolf and I are Guards, why didn't we know about this before? We've sparred with each other most of our lives and neither of us started glowing blue."

Cormac shrugged. "Could be him going feral triggered it. The fight-or-flight instinct out of control. Maybe it was also triggered in you when you had to fight him."

"Then maybe I *can* help him." Freya headed for the back door. Cormac, meat fork in hand, didn't stop her.

Shane snitched a morsel of steak from the pan, ignoring the sting of heat on his fingers. He enjoyed the tidbit as he strode behind Freya, who hurried through the gathering dusk to Graham's house.

Shane had no intention of talking her out of going. This was family, and she was right.

Misty let Freya in, giving her a sympathetic squeeze, and greeted Shane with a knowing smile. Everyone must have heard about Freya accepting the mate-claim by now.

Shane made sure he led the way upstairs. If Rolf was still dangerous, Shane needed to enter the room first.

Matt and Kyle were doing handstands in the hall, demonstrating different techniques to each other. At least, they were saying *Look what I can do,* and then shoving feet into the air.

Both came down when they spied Freya and slammed into her, hugging her like they hadn't seen her in years.

"He's okay, Freya," Matt said. "Kyle and I made him not feral anymore."

"Oh." Freya dropped to the floor, relief in her eyes, and gathered Matt and Kyle close. "Are you sure?"

Matt nodded. "We're sure."

Kyle was more somber. "Graham says Rolf's in a bad place, though. Where Shifters go when they're really, really unhappy. I don't know why he says that—Rolf's sitting right there on the bed. But Graham was crying."

Freya unfolded to her feet. "Which room?"

Kyle took her hand and led her there.

Shane knew that "a bad place" meant deep depression. Shifters sometimes sank into it when they grieved—at the breaking of a mate bond, for instance. It could also happen when a Shifter lost himself too fully into his animal. Looking into the dark side of your soul could scare the shit out of you.

Graham's growl sounded as soon as Kyle opened the door. "Freya, do *not* come in here. Shane, what the hell?"

"He's her pack," Shane said. Explanation enough.

Graham let out a very Graham sigh, but he looked exhausted as he gestured for them to come in.

The comfortably furnished bedroom was cozy, Misty's decorative touches everywhere. The last rays of sunshine flooded the room, turning the walls golden.

Rolf sat cross-legged in the middle of the bed, his arms folded as he stared out the window at the sky. He'd dressed in borrowed clean sweatpants and sweatshirt.

He glanced listlessly at Freya when she entered, the red tint gone from his eyes. He wouldn't look at Shane.

Freya sank to the edge of the bed, while Shane remained next to Graham, both watchful. Rolf didn't appear to be a threat now, but one never knew.

"Why are you here?" Rolf asked Freya. His voice was flat, uninflected. Sad.

"Cause you're my bro, that's why." Freya studied him, but he didn't respond. "You okay?"

Rolf let out a weak huff of laughter. "You can ask me that? I went feral, thought I'd take over the world, and I tried to kill you."

"We all have shitty days," Freya said.

The corners of Rolf's lips moved the slightest bit, but his eyes remained listless.

"Does it do me any good to say I'm sorry?" he all but whispered.

"Of course it does," Freya said firmly. "What happened wasn't your fault. It was that man, Heaney, who kidnapped you and wrecked you. His tough luck that he captured someone as badass as you."

"Stop." Rolf sent her the ghost of an annoyed-brother glance. "If I'm so badass, I wouldn't have let him take me. I'm supposed to be a throwback to a powerful Shifter breed, right? But I went down fast and easy."

"Cormac thinks maybe going feral triggered it. That we didn't really understand what we could do until we were in deep shit. Cormac's Shane's stepdad," Freya explained.

Rolf finally turned his head and looked at her, but his eyes held deep shame. "You know all the Shifters around here already."

"Not all of them," Freya said. "But the ones I've met are pretty good."

Her smile at Shane made him want to take her out of here and find the nearest bed not occupied by a healing Shifter. He balled his fists and fought to control himself, but mating frenzy was rising fast and strong.

"Graham didn't even ream me out for running away all those years ago," Rolf said to her. "Means he's really worried about me."

"Oh, I'll ream you out later," Graham said. "Trust me."

"No, he won't." Freya flashed Graham a stern look. "We already had it out—all the whys and wherefores. We're good. Right, Graham?"

"Yeah." Graham's voice was gruff. "We're good."

"See? He's worried." Rolf's half smile made him look more like Freya.

Freya reached for Rolf's hand, and he let her clasp it. "Please stay with me, bro," she said. "I missed you. I'm mated now, but that doesn't mean you and I are done."

Rolf shot a glance at Shane. "You sure? You were pretty adamant when you were accepting that mate-claim. No killing my mate, you said."

"And I meant it." A gleam in her eye made Shane's heart squeeze. "But you're family, my pack. Now, that family has grown."

"Right, because Shane wants a half-insane glowing wolf brother-in-law underfoot."

Shane coughed. "You clearly have never been in my house. My brother, my mom, and her mate … all big-ass bears. Talk about underfoot."

Rolf actually laughed, making him sound almost like his normal self. "Dylan says he wants me to come with him," he said, calming again. "He wants to talk about this Guard thing, and have me help him find out if more still exist."

"Oh." Freya frowned as she tightened her grip. "But I've only just found you again."

"He's not locking me away," Rolf said. "He promised me that. No Collars, no Shiftertowns. I don't know how he'll do it, but whatever. I can visit you whenever I want, he said."

"Make sure it's often."

"I will do my damndest, sis. And I really am happy you found a mate." Rolf squeezed her hand in return, then his voice took on a sad note. "Maybe one day, I'll find one too."

Freya released Rolf to draw him into an embrace. Rolf started, resisting for a moment, then he let out a broken sob and returned the hug, holding Freya tight.

The glow Shane had seen around them as they'd fought touched them now. It flickered with the last light of the sun, and as it did, Shane swore he saw two massive wolves, one with its head on the other's, comforting each other.

The sunset's gleam faded, and with it, the blue nimbus. On the bed sat a brother and sister, holding each other fast.

Graham and Shane exchanged glances—Graham had seen the glow too—but Shane shook his head.

It was another part of the mystery of his mate, one Shane hoped he'd be there to solve for many, many years to come.

CHAPTER THIRTY-TWO

Before Freya went home with Shane, she checked in with Leo. The Lupine was physically almost as good as new, but his arrogance had dimmed a long way.

He shot a fearful glance at Shane when they entered the room he'd been using, but Shane sent him a reassuring nod.

"It's forgotten," Shane said.

Leo didn't look reassured, but he nodded in return.

"I came to make sure you were all right," Freya told him. "You went through a bad time."

"Tell me about it." Leo's voice was as gravelly as ever, but he'd lost his sneer at everything and everyone. "I know you were never going to accept my mate-claim, Freya. I knew it back then, and I knew it this time." He let out a heartfelt sigh. "I was just lonely, you know?"

"I get that." Freya's former anger at him changed to pity. "My advice is to open your mind and broaden your horizons. Your mate is out there, Leo, somewhere. Hey, I found mine with a *bear*." She widened her eyes in feigned amazement.

Leo huffed a laugh. "Hope I'll have better luck."

Freya believed she'd had a shitload of luck, but she only smiled.

She and Shane left him alone after that, saying goodbye to Misty and Graham before leaving to go home. Matt and Kyle both dive-bombed Freya's legs again, and she leaned down to hug them.

Shane bumped fists with the lads, then he and Freya left the house for the cold twilight.

Freya would have to take care of a few things from her old life, like handing in her resignation and ending the lease on her apartment, but these seemed like inconsequential things to resolve. Rolf would have to do the same, and invent an explanation as to where he'd been, but Freya now had confidence they'd figure things out together and begin their new lives.

Keira was in the kitchen with Nell when they arrived home, the Lupine woman setting the table. As Cormac started to dish out what he'd been cooking, Brody burst back inside.

"Right on time for a meal as usual," Shane said, then he and Brody exchanged mock punches.

The kitchen and dining room filled with noise and laugher, and the scent of good food, another comfort. Freya thought of Rolf wrestling with his remorse in Graham's house, and decided she'd make sure he came over here for dinner before Dylan spirited him away. He'd need this.

There were six places at the table, which meant Freya and Shane had been expected back. Shane made sure Freya sat next to him, with Keira across from her, next to Brody.

Cormac had them all stop talking and give thanks to the Goddess for her abundance before they attacked the meal. Plenty of berries had been added to the steaks and potatoes, and Brody made a show of tossing a few high and catching them in his mouth.

Keira laughed at him with everyone else. The Lupine woman looked better, more rested and refreshed. She'd elected to stay in this Shiftertown indefinitely, she told Freya while they ate.

Freya had the feeling that Neal Ingram, who'd returned last night with them all, had something to do with her decision. As Shane had pulled her tiredly inside last night, Freya had glimpsed Keira in Eric's front yard with Iona and Cassidy, waiting for everyone's return. As exhausted as Freya had been, she'd noted how Keira had watched Neal hungrily when he'd piled out of the pickup with Reid, Diego, and Xav.

"Mating ceremony soon, right?" Brody demanded, taking another heaping helping of roasted potatoes. Cormac had seasoned them perfectly.

"Give them a chance to catch their breaths," Nell admonished. "But, yes, the full moon is in three nights. You can have the sun ceremony that morning, then the moon one. Or the sun ceremony tomorrow. That can happen any time. I'll tell Eric."

Freya started to laugh and couldn't stop. This family wanted Shane mated—would rush them into the circle dance to make sure it happened.

"I'll need a dress," Freya said when she could speak again. "How about we go shopping?" she suggested to Nell and Keira. "It's been a while since I did that."

"Tomorrow," Nell promised. "Eat up. We have a lot to do, and you'll need your energy."

Shane didn't say a word. No rebuking his family to stop being pushy or scoffing at his mom for taking over planning the mating ceremony. His eyes sparkled as he listened to them all, a smile hovering around his mouth.

He wanted this mating too.

Freya's heartbeat sped when Shane shoved back his chair at the end of the meal and rose. Freya hopped up beside him.

"Well, we need our rest if we're going to be doing all this shopping and ceremony planning," Shane announced. "Good night."

Freya said a quick good night as well, before Shane towed her at a rapid pace from the table. Instead of heading to Shane's bedroom, he opened the door in the wall that took them down the stairs to the basement.

A quick eye scan from Shane let them into the secret spaces, then Shane flicked on all the lights and locked the door behind him.

"Nice and private," he said, voice going low. "Soundproof, too."

"Keira's sleeping down here, isn't she?" Freya asked.

"She can have my bed for the night. I'm sure Mom has already brought out the clean sheets for her."

They entered another bedroom, one Freya hadn't seen before. It held a large bed, neatly made with a thick bedspread along with a large television and a mini fridge humming away in the corner. A bachelor's room if she ever saw one.

Shane closed the door. "There's clean sheets in here too," he said.

Freya turned to face him, resting her hands on his chest. "Will we ever get to see these clean sheets?"

"Eventually."

Shane skimmed off Freya's shirt as he backed her toward the bed. Her hands worked on his clothes too, and soon they were bare, the room quiet except for sounds of kisses and little growls.

Freya shrieked as Shane tossed her to the bed and landed

next to her. It wasn't long before their groans tore the air, then Freya's cries as the bed moved with their frantic lovemaking.

Freya held Shane as he drove deep into her, erasing all her weariness from their journey and search. She was in love with her big, strong bear, who could sleep in her bed anytime.

"I love you," she cried out, and then her climax enfolded her in dark waves of pleasure. A blue glow flicked around her, gently touching Shane and drawing him closer.

Shane's thrusts became frenzied. "Love *you*, Freya. Mate of my heart. *Love you.*"

"Mate of my heart," Freya whispered in response, and she knew it for truth.

Somewhere outside, the moon rose, cold and clear. Freya felt it, though no windows let it in.

The Mother Goddess smiled down on her Shifters, weaving the mate bond around them like a golden thread, binding their hearts with their love.

Three days later, Freya, dressed in a shimmering gold dress that was the prettiest she'd ever owned, recalled what Misty had said about a mating ceremony.

Shifters dancing around like crazy, many of them naked. Raucous is a good word for it.

Misty had been so right.

Eric had already said the words that blessed Freya and Shane and mated them under the light of the Mother Goddess. The sun blessing had happened earlier that day, and the Shifters had started celebrating then.

By the time of the moon blessing, the party was far along. Shifters danced, ate and drank, shifted, and ran, then dropped, exhausted, to the ground, naked and human once more. Some grabbed their mates or would-be mates and found shadowy corners to continue the merrymaking.

It was cold, the January wind blowing through the desert, but no one seemed to notice. The sky was clear—the sun had shone mightily that afternoon, and now the moon and stars were hard and sparkling against the night.

Shane at the moment was wearing Freya's crown of flowers —specially made for her by Misty, a talented florist—and dancing like the goof he was with his brother. Xav had joined them, his body undulating as he tried to keep up with the bears. Freya noted Lindsay watching him, though she pretended to be absorbed in laughing conversation with Cassidy and Iona.

Keira had ventured out, shyly observing the dancing. Kyle and Matt frolicked near her. It was difficult to tell whether Keira watched over the cubs, or they watched over her. Neal nonchalantly lingered nearby, but neither he nor Keira looked at each other.

Freya had drifted from the Shifters cavorting—there was no other word for it—to stand contentedly and watch her new family.

She knew Rolf was behind her without turning. He'd gained enough confidence to emerge for her mating ceremonies, though she saw he was carefully avoiding any beer thrust at him. He didn't trust himself yet.

"I am so happy for you, sis." Rolf slid his arms around her from behind, and Freya leaned against her strong brother, as she'd done so many times in her life. "Shane is exactly who you need." Rolf's voice quieted. "I'm sorry I deserted you, Freya. I went looking for something I couldn't have, I guess."

Freya turned, breaking his hold. "Do not make it your fault. You couldn't have foreseen what that asshole was going to do to you. We weren't in the best situation. Getting by pretty well, yes, but it couldn't last. We'd have had to find a new way to live sometime."

"I know, but I could have been more careful about it." Rolf let out a sigh, his eyes haunted. "I didn't mean to drag you into all this, make you leave a job you liked."

"Doesn't matter anymore," Freya said. "The work was good, but it wasn't enough. I was pretending it was, but it couldn't last, and I knew that. I don't think either of us could go back to that life now."

Rolf let out a laugh. "After I've gone feral, nearly killing my own sister and her mate while doing it? I don't think I could calmly catch my bus, sit down at my desk with over-brewed coffee, and stare at code ever again. I'm going to take Dylan up on his offer. The guy terrifies me, and he's Feline, but I'm more afraid of what I'd do left on my own. The feral never really leaves us, I think." He shuddered.

Freya laid a hand on his shoulder. They'd been through so much, the two of them. Her heart wrenched at the thought of them going their separate ways, but she also knew this was right. They needed their own lives, as entwined as they would always be.

"Plus this weird thing about us being Guards," Freya said. "I think you're right. Dylan can teach you about that, maybe figure out how to use it without making you crazy. Then you can come back and teach me."

"You were always saner than me," Rolf admitted. "More level-headed."

"Uh-oh." Freya widened her eyes. "If that's true, we're in trouble."

Rolf chuckled, the warm sound Freya had missed. "I mean that you'll probably be all right. You have all these Shifters who love you and want to support you. And you have Shane." Rolf took her hands and squeezed them. "You were meant to be."

Keira, in her feral state, had seen the mate bond between Shane and Freya. Freya hadn't quite believed her at first, but now she realized the mate bond had been there all along, waiting for Freya and Shane to acknowledge it.

The warmth in Freya's heart, the soothing heat that had wrapped around her when she'd first encountered Shane had signaled it like solar flares, but Freya had been too worried about Rolf and her own life to acknowledge it.

Her wolf had known. It gave a smug little growl now as Freya's gaze went to Shane.

At the moment, Shane had one arm around Brody, the other around Xav, as the three of them kicked, Rockettes style, to the thumping music.

She loved him so much.

"Of course, Dylan doesn't scare me nearly as much as *he* does." Rolf's mutter pulled Freya's attention back from Shane.

Rolf's eyes were on the form of the man called Tiger, the huge Shifter with black and orange hair. He'd disappeared after he'd burst into the compound to save them all, but returned with Dylan for the mating ceremony. Tiger had arrived with his pretty human mate, Carly, as well as his beautiful daughter and his daughter's tall mate, who was the nephew of the Austin Shiftertown's leader. Tiger also carried a cub with tiger-striped hair and golden eyes.

That cub was on Tiger's shoulders as he made his way to Freya and Rolf. The little boy, Seth, stared wordlessly down at the two, wisdom in his very young eyes.

"Thank you for coming, Tiger," Freya ventured, uncertain what else to say to him.

Tiger gave her a nod then stared at her the unnerving way he had. Carly had told Freya, as she'd given Freya a hug after the first mating ceremony, that Tiger was a big sweetie, but Freya still didn't know quite how to take him.

The tension was broken by the arrival of Kyle and Matt,

one a wolf cub, the other running as a human boy in a sweatshirt and little jeans.

"Can Seth play with us?" Matt demanded as they neared Tiger. "We'll take care of him. Promise." Kyle yipped in agreement.

Tiger considered the two, then leaned his large bulk down to very gently stroke Kyle' head. Kyle wriggled in delight. "All right," Tiger said.

He lowered Seth with the same gentleness. Seth regarded Kyle and Matt soberly for a moment, then he instantly shifted to the most adorable tiger cub Freya had ever seen. He shook himself out of his clothes, yowled in excitement, and bounded off into the crowd. Kyle and Matt, who also shifted, scampered closely after him.

Tiger watched his son for a moment before returning his intense gaze to Freya.

"Your cubs will come soon," he said, his voice a deep rumble.

Freya dissolved into a smile. "I hope we'll have a cub. Or two. That would be wonderful."

Tiger frowned, as though Freya puzzled him. "They will come soon." He waved blunt fingers vaguely at her abdomen. "They are there now, she and he."

Freya started. Nell had told her a little bit about Tiger when they'd gone shopping—his amazing strength as well as his great compassion, and also his uncanny ability to know things long before others did.

Freya made herself meet Tiger's steady gaze, and the strong tiger within him acknowledged her resilient wolf.

Freya knew in that moment that Tiger spoke the truth. That she and Shane had started twins of their own, perhaps more Guards to come. It was daunting, frightening ... and glorious.

"Oh," was all that emerged from her mouth.

"Seriously?" Rolf demanded. When Freya swallowed and nodded, he let out a laugh that rang with his former high spirits. "Wow. I'm gonna be an uncle. That's awesome, sis." The words ended in a shout as Rolf hugged Freya hard. "Just awesome."

"How did you know?" Freya turned back to ask Tiger, but the big man had vanished. A scan of the crowd showed her Tiger already across the way, sliding an arm around Carly. The two of them leaned into each other as they moved to keep an eye on Seth and the wolf cubs.

"See what I mean?" Rolf said. "Scary."

Freya was too happy to worry about Tiger's unsettling abilities. She kissed Rolf on the cheek then released him to hurry toward her new mate.

"Shane!" she yelled.

Shane broke from his brother and Xav, the flower crown slipping over his left eye. "Freya!" he roared. Shane opened his arms, welcoming her to him.

Freya ran to him, her heart soaring with happiness. She leapt the last few paces, and Shane caught her, spinning her around and around, laughing his great bear laugh.

"We're having twins," she told him breathlessly. "Tiger said."

Shane frowned in confusion at her for a moment, his gaze darting to Tiger and then back to Freya. Then his brown eyes widened, and he let out a yell that rang through the trees.

Shane whirled around with Freya, she secure in her arms, both of them laughing, punctuating their joy with kisses.

"I love you, mate of my heart," Shane declared to the world.

"I love *you*." Freya's response was quieter as she traced his cheek. "My one true mate."

Shane pulled her close, his searing kiss chasing away every last fear in her heart. The mate bond wove around them, and Freya's wolf noted flickers of blue among its golden threads.

The wind caught the circlet of flowers, spinning it upward into the clear sky, petals bursting from it like stars against the night.

Tiger Striped

A Shifter Christmas Carol

Iron Master

The Last Warrior

Tiger's Daughter

Bear Facts

Shifter Made ("Prequel" novella)

Stormwalker Series (w/a Allyson James)

Stormwalker

Firewalker

Shadow Walker

"Double Hexed"

Nightwalker

Dreamwalker

Dragon Bites

ABOUT THE AUTHOR

New York Times bestselling and award-winning author Jennifer Ashley has more than 100 published novels and novellas in mystery, romance, historical fiction, and urban fantasy under the names Jennifer Ashley, Allyson James, and Ashley Gardner. Jennifer's books have been translated into more than a dozen languages and have earned starred reviews in *Publisher's Weekly* and *Booklist*. When she isn't writing, Jennifer enjoys playing music (guitar, piano, flute), reading, hiking, cooking, and building dollhouse miniatures.

More about Jennifer's books can be found at
http://www.jenniferashley.com

To keep up to date on her new releases, join her newsletter here:
http://eepurl.com/47kLL

www.ingramcontent.com/pod-product-compliance
Lightning Source LLC
Chambersburg PA
CBHW022005310726
48972CB00006B/1528